Early Praise for Don't Eat the Pie

"*Don't Eat the Pie* is gothic horror at its most deliciously twisted. It's weird and wild and so deeply unnerving that I couldn't help but devour it and keep going back for more." —Megan Collins, author of *The Family Plot.*

"*Don't Eat the Pie* by Monique Asher is unnerving, panicked, claustrophobic and disorienting. Right when you think you've found your footing, the bottom opens and you're plunged into a pit of disquiet. Deliciously eerie." —Cynthia Pelayo, Bram Stoker Award-winning author of *Forgotten Sisters.*

"*Don't Eat the Pie* is a dark rollercoaster whose twists and turns will leave you breathless, not letting up until the very last page. Asher creates the perfect balance of family drama, occult intrigue, and unrelenting tension in this horror/thriller that is sure to haunt you long after you finish reading. I'm not easily surprised, but this novel had me gasping aloud, as well as squealing with joy, at the delicious twists multiple times. Beside the thrills, Asher's depiction of the central relationship between mother and daughter pulled at my heartstrings. I know I'll be gifting this book to all the readers in my life."—Emma E. Murray, author of *Crushing Snails.*

"Asher's *Don't Eat the Pie* is the unholy offspring of S̶̶̶̶̶ Gilmore Girls, a wickedly entertaining gettable mother-daughter combo at its heart." —Patrick Barb, author of *Pre-Approved for Haunting and Other Stories.*

"*Don't Eat the Pie* is an extremely assured debut about the destructive power of family ties, false community and the prison that familial duty can build around us, presented in a narrative riddled with sinister secrets, morbid visions, odd neighbours, shifty behaviour and, of course ... pie. I loved it."—Gemma Amor, author of *The Folly.*

DON'T EAT THE PIE

MONIQUE ASHER

Cover Illustration © Nat Mack
Distributed by Simon & Schuster

ISBN: 978-1-998076-17-8
Ebook: 978-1-998076-18-5

FIC015000 FICTION / Horror
FIC012000 FICTION / Ghost
FIC024000 FICTION / Occult & Supernatural

#DontEatthePie

Follow Rising Action on our socials!
Twitter: @RAPubCollective
Instagram: @risingactionpublishingco
Tiktok: @risingactionpublishingco

To my daughters Arya and Nora.

DON'T EAT THE PIE

THE WEDDING—EMMA
MAY 31

My fingers are frozen, numb, aching. I keep them beneath the faucet a little longer than necessary and avoid eye contact with the women in the crowded bathroom. The marble walls make everything echo. I wish they would insulate public restrooms.

How does one person even know this many other people, let alone want them to be at their wedding? What has Mom gotten us into?

"She's prettier than the other wife," a woman says under her breath, pulling lipstick from her beaded clutch and fixing her makeup in the mirror. Her lips are bright pink; Barbie chic.

"Don't say that. Krysten was beautiful. So tragic what happened to her. It's nice to see Ben happy, isn't it?" another woman says. She's rail-thin, with wavy, blonde locks draping her over shoulders and onto her blue dress. The women's hips sway in unison as the pair leaves the bathroom.

That's a lovely way to speak of the dead.

Dear God or the universe or whatever, please don't let me be like them. No matter how badly Mom wants us to fit in, I solemnly swear that when I'm an adult I will not become a gossiping waif at a wedding. Amen.

"Hey, you okay, Emma?" Aunt Becca comes out of the stall directly behind me and takes over the sink I'm standing in front of.

"Yeah, just ... how does Ben know all these people? Do *you* know all these people?"

Becca laughs. "I do not."

She dries her hands, and I follow her back into the hall. The ceiling reaches up several floors with giant, arched, glass doors lining an entire wall. They open to the lawn, framed by sheer white drapes that move like waves in the spring breeze.

"I know this is weird for you, suddenly being a part of a different family. It's odd for me, too, but in a whole different way, because I go home with Jax to our little bungalow." Aunt Becca swipes a glass of champagne off a server's tray and takes a sip.

"I'm being indoctrinated into some yuppie cult." I turn toward her and grab her hand and flash my puppy dog eyes. "Can't you just kidnap me so I can live with you?"

"C'mon." She pulls me out of the doorway onto the marble steps that lead down to the party. Tables draped in white chiffon dot the mossy green lawn. It's a perfect scene that suits Ben and his family—us, not so much. Becca extends her arm, pointing at Mom, who is laughing with another guest. "Your mom is so happy. I haven't seen her like this since the moment she saw you for the first time. She's been with some bad apples, but Ben's a golden one."

I seriously doubt that Mom would have been happy to see me. How could she after what she'd been through? Mom loves me, but I know that having me was hard on her. I don't know the whole story between her and Dad, only that he was a really bad guy and that having me almost killed her. *I* almost killed her.

Ben, however, makes her light up like nothing else ever has. I don't blame her, exactly. If I'm going to have any adult man living under the same roof as me, I'm happy it'll be Ben. He doesn't try to be my father. His dad jokes aren't even that bad.

"I know. It's so weird," I say, looking around at the other girls. They look like Instagram models, and even without filters, they still have flawless skin. "I don't know how I'll fit in. I'm not even sure that I want to."

"Your mom feels the exact same way, believe me. We aren't used to this shit." Aunt Becca takes another sip from her champagne glass. "You can do it. You've done everything else together."

"Yeah, yeah." I sigh, crossing my arms over my chest. Sometimes I wish that she was more of a mom than a friend with complete power over my life. I turn and grab a glass of champagne from the server passing by.

"Hah! I don't feel *that* bad for you, kid." Aunt Becca takes the flute from me and starts to drink it herself. "Go find Jax and Hannah. Go be kids. Have fun."

"Alright. Promise you guys will visit?"

"Every chance we get. Ben has kindly offered us the use of his frequent flier miles. We'll probably see each other more than ever." She smiles, but my heart twists. Maybe she's right, but I'm leaving behind Hannah, school, and the place I grew up. *My life.* Aunt Becca's right: Mom is happy. She glows around Ben, and they *get* each other. It's gross. They laugh at everything the other one says. Financially, we won't have to struggle anymore, either. Mom can finally focus on the things that make her happy instead of picking up extra shifts at the restaurant.

Everything will be different now. Sometimes, I wonder if Mom ever stopped to consider what this would be like for me. Jax and I have grown up as siblings more than cousins. It feels strange when we don't see each other for longer than a few days.

"Emma!" A saccharine southern drawl breaks into my thoughts. It's Nadine, Ben's mom. Hannah and Jax are laughing at something across the lawn by the water. *Get me out of here.* "Emma, honey, can you come over here? I gotta introduce you to my girls." A gaggle of geese cackle at the table.

"Sure ..." I march toward them, and the women turn, drinks in hand, to stare at me.

"Girls, this is Samantha's little girl, Emma. Isn't she beautiful?" Nadine rises from her seat. She's older than she looks and is thin and blonde with snow-white skin. Mom says she used to be an actress. She pinches at my cream silk blouse and puts a hand on my waist. I move a little to the right, trying not to shudder.

"Nice to meet you dear; I'm Ginny. I live right across from Nadine on the island. I'm sure we'll get to know each other over the summer." The kind-faced older woman sticks her hand out to shake mine. The skin on her hands is spotted and wrinkly, and her nails are the same bright pink as her lips. She doesn't have a southern accent like Nadine.

"It's nice to meet you," I say. "Gosh, your dress is so cool. I've never seen anything like it." I eye the black lace gown with feathers woven into its fabric jealously. Peacock plume earrings dangle from her sagging lobes.

"Oh! This old thing. I got it traveling years ago. It's a long story for another time, but when you come to visit, I'll let you in on everything," Ginny says, her voice diving to a whisper.

"Even if you're not interested," Nadine says.

"Sorry, doll, you're in the family now." Ginny chuckles. "We're a package deal." They all laugh. I do, too, even though I don't really get the joke, hoping they'll move on to something else—some*one* else. I feel naked with their eyes on me. "It'll be great spending so much time with you all this summer."

"My mom must not have mentioned it." Of course, she didn't; why would she let me in on her grand plan for our summer? I'm an afterthought now. "She said they'd be looking for a new place right after the honeymoon."

"Oh, yes." Nadine waves her hand. "Don't worry, it's only an old woman's hope." She grabs my hand, and her long, polished nails scratch my wrist. "I do hope we get to know each other better, and when you *do* come to visit, you'll entertain some old ladies. We can teach you gin rummy."

The women nod in agreement.

Nadine pulls me in for a hug. She's warm, but all angles, bony and sharp. Over her shoulder, I catch Mom watching us, a smile curving her lips. Ben nuzzles her cheek. *Gag.*

"I would be happy to learn, Nadine, and I can teach you Euchre, as my mom taught me. It's a Michigan thing," I add. "It gets real dicey in our family. You'll like it."

Nadine leans back and claps her hands together, shaking the gold bracelets on her wrists. "I'd be delighted. Now, go enjoy your time with your friends."

I let out a little laugh and curtsy, pushing the charm to the max. I overheard Mom talking earlier to Aunt Becca about how happy she was to finally be a part of a *real* family. A *normal* family. She was angry at Grandma for refusing to come and support her. It feels like she wants to leave us all behind and move on.

"Oh, sweet thing, wait a second. I almost forgot!" Nadine says, walking toward me on the lawn, holding a piece of paper. "This letter came for you at the apartment. I had to run over there for your mom earlier to grab some bobby pins."

The letter *is* addressed to me, with no return address.

"Thanks, Nadine," I say, stashing the letter away in my front pocket to read later.

I take off my heeled sandals and run barefoot across the perfectly mowed, perfectly green, perfectly soft grass. I wonder if it's even real.

"Emma!" Jax shouts from the edge of the water. "Come over here! You gotta see this!" I push myself between Jax and Hannah to look over the railing. The waterline is made up of broken pieces of concrete stacked on each other.

On top of the concrete slab is a pile of slithering, worm-like things.

"Eww, what is that?" I ask, straining to see.

"I don't know," Hannah says. "Jax noticed it a minute ago, and we've been kind of staring at it since, wondering when it's going to stop."

"Maybe it's some kind of sea creature washed up on shore," Jax says, brushing his curly brown hair out of his eyes.

"You mean lake creature," I interject.

"Yeah." He scratches his head and grimaces. "No, that's not a creature; it's a bunch."

"What do you mean?" asks Hannah.

"It's snakes," Jax says. "It's like a hundred baby snakes."

My stomach rolls.

"They're all eating something," Jax says, moving closer with a stick.

"Jax, don't," I say.

"I just want to see." Jax's thin, lanky body curves over the things. The fact that he's a pushy thirteen-year-old isn't hidden behind the second-hand wool suit he wears like a character from a Wes Anderson movie. He takes the stick and moves a few of the snakes away, and they slither in between the rocks, revealing pale, thin bones. "It's a snake. They're eating another snake. Eating all its flesh." Jax's mouth hangs agape.

I grab his shoulder, and he jumps.

"Fucked up little cannibals," I say.

"You think it was alive when they started?" he asks.

I shrug.

Jax and Hannah walk away, but I linger. The clink of forks against champagne flutes starts back up again.

I'd rather watch the cannibal feast.

They are rapidly breaking down every teeny tiny bit of flesh off of each and every bone—polishing them as they go. Their tails wag in unison like the sex ed videos they play in school, millions of sperm racing for an egg, but one snake moves out of sync with the rest. It slithers slowly as if it's trying to sneak away from the rest unseen, no longer willing to be a part of the annihilation of their mother. A baby snake leaving its family. I hope I get out too, baby snake. Just before the little scaled worm makes it into the crevasse between the stones, one of its kin catches it at the tail. It struggles against its brethren, but another one joins the first, pulling the traitor back to the scene of the slaughter. A third snake slithers out in front of the rebel, still trying to get away. The snake at its tail begins consuming it, bringing it inside itself centimeter by centimeter.

I cover my mouth and close my eyes. When I open them, the only thing left is its tiny struggling head before the whole thing is just—

"Uh, Emma, you coming?" Hannah shouts.

"Yeah ... yeah," I say. The tiny rebel vanished inside of the other snake. The surviving snake is puffy and bulging, full with its own sibling. My stomach sours. I shouldn't have watched that.

I run toward Jax and Hannah, away from the scene of the massacre. Across the lawn, I rush past the table where Mom and Ben are kissing. The guests laugh and clap. My heart aches; I can't help but feel like this is the end of my life, the end of things as we knew them.

"C'mon, Emma!" Hannah grabs my hand and pulls me into the dance, the three of us, hand in hand, with no rhythm or care, just like when we were little kids in the backyard with Grandma, Aunt Becca and Mom giggling in a corner.

I smile and pretend I don't want to cry, that I don't already know that nothing will ever be the same.

THE HONEYMOON—SAM
JUNE 3

I cradle my cup and stand sipping, blinking, tempted to pinch myself. I lean against the warm, white railing on the veranda and check my footing, not to ground myself but to admire the yellow and white patterned tile beneath my feet. It's been forty-five days since my last panic attack. I've beaten my record by a whole ten days.

For the first time, I can believe I'm safe. I, Samantha Steward, am in Italy with my husband, who values me, and would never ever hurt me.

The beep from my watch reminds me it's time for my pill. I turn back toward the room. Ben is still asleep, face down, with his Roman-quality ass hanging out of the silk sheets. His golden-tanned body is so like those marble figures in museums that it must have been sculpted by the gods. My cheeks are sore from smiling. I reach into my suitcase, pop a pill from the little clear blister, and swallow it with my coffee.

"What time is it?" Ben groans, lifting his face momentarily from the mattress. "What are you doing out of bed?"

"Oh." I stare down at my watch. "It is 2:55 Sorrento time and 8:55 our time."

"Now, the second part." He turns over and slaps the bed next to him.

"I haven't even brushed my teeth yet—husband."

"Hmmm." He scoots to the end of the bed and grabs my hand. "What if I don't want to kiss your mouth?"

"Mr. Steward, you really shouldn't be so forward." I grin as my cheeks burn.

It's hard to believe that this isn't a dream. It's not, right? He pulls me gently back into bed and begins kissing me up and down my neck and chest; his hands grapple for my robe, which he proceeds to slip off before traveling lower, exploring deeper, and I lean into this bliss.

Afterward, my skin is flush with peach and red blotches, rosy smears of love. Ben struts to the bathroom and starts the shower. I ought to call Emma to check-in. I grab my phone and select her name. She's sixteen, but this will be the longest I've ever been away from her. After several taunting rings, the call rolls to voicemail.

"Hello, it's your mother. You may still be sleeping. I hope you're having fun with Becca and Jax. Call me later; I don't care what time it is. Love you."

I decide to call Becca.

"Who is this?" Becca asks, her voice loaded with snark.

"Your sister," I reply.

"No, that's impossible," Becca says. "My sister wouldn't call me after I told her to relax and enjoy her honeymoon. Nope. My sister would trust that I've got everything under control and take the break she needs."

"Really," I say, my hand naturally gravitating to my waist. "*Your* sister would do that? You sure your sister wouldn't be anxious to make sure nothing is falling apart without her?"

There's a long pause before she answers. "I suppose you're right. *My* sister *would* do that despite knowing she needs to soak in this experience that she's always deserved. How's everything?"

"It's amazing. You'd just love it here. We have to come back one day."

"Sure, when I hit that Mega Millions."

"Ben can take us."

"Samantha, stop thinking about what's next and enjoy what you have right now."

"Alright. Is Emma okay? She didn't answer her phone."

"Emma is fine. Everything is fine. Go have fun. Don't call me until at least tomorrow! I love you."

She hangs up before I even have a chance to reply or retort. I get it. Instead of worrying, I rise from the bed and join Ben in the shower.

A slight smile appears on Ben's face as we take our seats for dinner. He speaks six languages, and thankfully, one of them is Italian, because, frankly, I suck at it. I sound like a cow trying to speak like a human. I shouldn't say that. Dad would say that.

You women, you Stewards, you're evil. You speak in tongues, your heads full of rotten clams. The shells clink together when you walk. You're evil.

I brush my cotton skirt back and forth, using it to dry the sweat on my nervous hands. The other couples and groups of friends in the restaurant fit perfectly with the backdrop of ancient rock and weathered tile and class.

"Where are you?" Ben stares at me with his piercing brown eyes. He's devoted to me, his wife, while I'm lost in other places, wandering through constellations of pain and suffering my father and his father before him created.

"I am ... not here." I laugh to try and lighten the mood, to let go of that tension in my neck. "I'm sorry. I didn't think I'd ever really be here—somewhere I don't know the language, in a fabulous dress, with a drop-dead gorgeous man. Ben, my life feels like a fucking fairytale."

He smiles, always forgiving me. "That is a decent reason to be a little in your head, but, my love, I don't want you to miss it. I know what will bring you back." He leans over toward the server. "Mi scusi. Il mix amanita e io vorremmo uno bottiglia del tuo Pinot Grigio."

"Ah, *vino*. You know me too well." A glass always roots me a little more in place and eases the perpetual tension in my shoulders.

"We will have a glass and come back, right here, right now."

I love how he does that. He doesn't get mad. He doesn't expect me to be different than I am. He goes with me places—even the dark ones.

I'm drinking too fast. An older woman toward the end of the veranda stares at me. Her eyes shine such an intense emerald green that they look like gems encased in the hollows of her skull. As soon as she notices me staring back, she pulls her sunglasses up. My cheeks burn with embarrassment as my gaze falls to my lap. When I look back over, she's still got her shades up, but she's sipping her wine and her head is turned away from me. She sits opposite a man in a suit that is too heavy for the weather. Her bright pink mouth, with the slightest smudge in her lipstick, turns up in a grin.

I swear I recognize her, but where would I know her from?

"You're wearing my mom's charm," Ben says, interrupting my preoccupation with the older woman. "I'm surprised."

I look down at my necklace.

"Yeah, she tucked it in my bag with a little note that said it was good luck to wear it on my honeymoon." The pendant dangles between my breasts, a silver sphere with twists and swirls around it, tiny serpents guarding the herb inside. Well, they were, before I emptied it. The smell was so potent it gave me a headache.

"That's my mom, you'll see. Nadine is quite superstitious."

The next morning, a curious bird call outside our glass balcony doors wakes me. Ben is deep asleep.

I have to make sure that Emma is okay and that all is still well on that front. We talked last night, and she assured me that everything with Jax and Becca was good. Emma and Jax had spent the day at the mall. Oh, to be a teenager again, wandering aimlessly, shopping bags looped at the elbow.

I check my email—nothing but ads. I try my voicemail. Nothing. Not even a text. I message Becca, letting her know I'll be unavailable until tomorrow morning. It's 7:22 a.m.

"Ha!" I say aloud, and Ben doesn't even move. I've beat the jet lag. I brush my teeth and hair, throw on my robe, and head onto the balcony. The smell of the ocean wafts toward me as the sun rises over the horizon, illuminating the city. I sit on the little wire chair beside the edge and look down over the railing.

Today is Monday. People are getting back to the hustle and bustle: vendors push their carts along as a young woman around my age with an apron runs down the stairs after a man. She shouts sweet nothings in Italian, and he whips around to meet her in a kiss. She stops for a beat, watching him walk away before she turns down an alley in the opposite direction. Maybe she's off to work her morning shift at the café.

I will never have to work a shift at a restaurant again. Never have to rush off on a Monday morning again if I choose not to. A sickening twist of guilt grabs hold of me.

You lazy girl, you'll never know what it's like to work as hard as I do. Your mother is a lazy cow. That's all you'll be, a burden to a man.

The tips of my fingers go numb. *He's dead, Sam. He's dead, and he was wrong. You will not let him hijack your life anymore, not him or Jared.*

Every muscle is tight; even the tips of my toes grip the yellow porcelain tile. I take a deep breath and refocus on the world; the woman leaving for work, the tile patio, the ocean, the eroding rock of the cliffs in the distance, and the call of the gulls.

"Hello," a voice croaks from thin air.

My heart nearly leaps from my chest off the balcony to the stairs below. I search for the source of the voice, and on the other edge of the balcony, a large raven sits perched, staring at me. A laugh escapes my mouth. *Lighten up, Sam.*

My heart thuds in my chest, and I reply, "Good morning, raven."

"Hello," he returns.

"Hello, back."

Becca would love this; she's obsessed with birds. She spent a whole summer when we were children trying to befriend the crows and ravens. If you speak with them enough, they repeat like a parrot. They brought her a gift once, a little charm shaped like a saint of protection, a nun had said. We weren't supposed to visit the church, but we often lingered by it on the way home from school. The big, brown-brick building had stained glass windows that were straight from Italy. The nun had said to keep the charm. I wonder if Becca still has it.

"I'm afraid I don't have much for you to eat, Mr. Raven, but I am happy for your company. You see, my husband is still asleep, and I miss my daughter quite a lot."

He looks out toward the sea and then back toward me. "Hello."

"We've cut them off, our families, just for today, to be totally alone. I'm quite excited, but I feel nervous, reluctant, if I'm honest. I feel like I'm missing something, like I've forgotten to turn off the burner on the stove."

"You haven't forgotten a thing, Sam." Ben appears in the doorway, shirtless. "Except that the world is not on your shoulders, and all is well." He walks toward me and puts his hand on my shoulder, then takes a seat opposite me. "Who is this dapper young fellow trying to seduce my lady?" He gestures toward the raven. The raven doesn't answer.

"This is—" As I'm about to name my bird pal, he flies off the rail.

"I feel better with no competition," Ben says.

"He was rather handsome, wasn't he?" I put my feet up on Ben's lap, and he rubs his hand along my legs. The hair has just started to grow back; I'll need to shave again later. "What's the plan for our big adventure?"

"I was thinking Vallone Dei Mulini. We can see the ruins, go shopping, have lunch ... What is that face?"

"Oh, there's no face."

"You were making that face, that face that you want to agree, but you don't. I know you too well for this, Sam."

"Fine," I say, leaning forward. "I was making *that* face. I don't know, I thought if we were going to be away, it would be good to be away, away. Can we get a car and visit Pompeii or hike Vesuvio? I love it here, but also, the history nerd in me *needs* to go there." I flash a smile.

He leans in, closing the gap between us, his lips pressing into my forehead.

"If I'm going to visit a giant graveyard, you are the only person I'd like to visit it with."

Ben flicks on the lights in the room, and his hand grazes my shoulder. My skin, no match for the Italian sun, pulses hot, bright pink and tender from sunburn. Ben's tanned skin seems only enhanced by the day's heat. It's deepened into a warm honey glow.

I want to stop and savor the moment, to allow the heat to spread past the skin, but my bladder is about to burst. I tear myself away from him, rush to the toilet, and sit down with relief. Ben chuckles from the other room, but I ignore it.

When I rise, I look in the mirror. My face is equally as rosy as my arms, and I've developed a tan line from my oversized sunglasses. I can't help but smile looking at myself, in Italy, after another day of adventure.

My case of birth control sits on the counter, staring up at me. Wouldn't a woman in her late thirties on her honeymoon have left this behind, eager to consummate the marriage and create life with her beau?

I'll never experience what it's like to be happy when you see those two pink lines. When it happened to me, I was too young and too stupid to know what to do, and worse, didn't know better than to let Dad find out. I told my family I was pregnant, and I lost everything. Mom wanted me to get an abortion, and Jared wanted me to keep the baby. Dad wanted to kill me. I know it would be different with Ben, but we'd both decided that that was not in the cards for us.

Having Emma nearly killed me, and I've fucked things up with her so badly at times I don't—won't—have another child.

I pop the Thursday pill in my mouth, cup water from the sink in my hands, and swallow it down.

When I open the door, the room is empty, and the lights are off. Ben isn't there. I creep through the darkness and out onto the balcony, where I jump a little at the sound of a champagne bottle being opened. Ben takes a gulp straight from the bottle, then turns toward me and moves his hand along my back but over my clothes, paying close attention to avoid my blistered skin. I grab the bottle from his hand and take a swig myself. The bubbles fill my mouth and spill over the side. Ben takes the bottle back and grabs me a napkin from the room.

"Trying to dull the pain a little bit," I say, taking the cloth and wiping my face. It's not very ladylike. The villas and shops below us turn their lights on, twinkling like fireflies in a Michigan summer. The deep blue sea expands out for what seems like forever, sparkling with the moonlight and the shop's lanterns.

"How was your day, my dear?" he asks, knowing full well how it was. This is a ritual, one that took some getting used to—another person asking *me* how things are.

"Oh, it was okay. Saw some old stuff, kind of interesting," I reply, taking another sip of the champagne with a sly little shoulder shrug. This one, I don't spill.

"Only okay?"

"I'm joking. It was pretty close to perfect, but I know a way we can make it even better." I set down the bottle on the little wrought iron table and pull him back into the room. His skin is dewy with sweat.

His lips press hard against mine, and I pull his body into me. He lets me take control and becomes like a rag doll in my hands. I bring him over to the bed, where I press his shoulders down, and he accepts my lead and falls back on the bed. I pull my top off over my head, and he reaches forward toward me.

"Uh-uh, Mr. Cross ... you are to lie there and watch." My heart lurches in my chest as I watch a smile spread across his face, and his eyes grow hazy. I unlatch my bra, revealing my breasts, the same breasts he's seen a hundred times, but Ben always lights up as if it's the first time.

I lean over him, tracing his chest muscles with my finger, a heat rising in my chest. A tiny moan escapes his lips, and I exercise all the restraint I have to not just melt into him right then.

The room phone rings, causing us both to jump, startled out of our lustful trance.

"Jesus Christ." He huffs, laughing, turning over on the bed to reach the receiver, which he swiftly picks up and then slams back down.

I crawl over him, pushing him back down on the bed. He breathes desire as I straddle him.

The phone starts again, and Ben rolls his eyes and turns over. He grabs the receiver, but this time he puts it to his ear.

"Hello!" he shouts into the phone.

That's right, Ben, let them know this is our time.

His body stiffens. "Alright, yes ..."

Oh God, what if it's Emma? I rush from the bed and over to my bag, my hand fishing for my phone.

Seventeen missed calls. It's as if all the oxygen has left my lungs.

A ringing begins in my ears, and tears run like rivers over the tender skin of my cheeks. Ben's voice is like an echo. I pinch myself. Stinging nails into flesh. Get out of the room. Find air.

My feet carry me numb and floating out to the balcony. My baby is hurt, in trouble. I've let my wanting for a better life carry me away from protecting Emma. My eyes dart around, trying to cling onto something that will settle the spin of the room, anything to distract from the images of blood and broken bones playing in my mind. They won't stop until a new horror snatches them away.

The raven from before lays like a gift at my feet, my bare skin inches away from the body. Its head is backwards, and blood pools beneath it. My desperate scream crests the cries of the birds in the distance.

"Oh, God, okay. I'll call ... call them ... straight away," Ben stutters. I can't move my hands. "Sam? Sam? Sam!"

Ben pulls my stiff form back into the cavernous room, and I push away from him, falling to the ground. Visions of Emma blur in my mind—a tragic teen car accident—bleeding out on the front hood. It can't be true. Get a grip, Sam.

My eyes dart across the room to find Ben. His skin's warm glow has turned gray, his eyes glossy.

"What is it?" I ask, afraid of what his answer might be. Afraid that every image I've sequestered to the back of my mind is true.

"It's my mom, and she's in the hospital. She fell. She's in a coma."

CAMILLIA—EMMA
JUNE 10

This car is a sweatbox, and I'm hoping I pass out and die in it before we get there. A fly slaps across the windshield. Bits of minced guts spread left and right with every windshield swipe.

Becca let me ride in front with her, and Jax is in the back with Hannah. Somehow, she convinced her parents to let her come with us out east. We used the *I'm moving away forever* card and the *my-step-grandma-or-whatever-I-should call-her-is-sick* card for good measure. *Please, please let her come.*

It worked. Hannah's parents love Mom and Becca; they trust them.

"You want some?" Becca asks, tipping a pack of Red Vines toward me, her favorite snack on road trips.

"I'm good."

"Suit yourself," she says and tilts the package toward the back seat. "Hannah? Jax?"

No answer.

I look back at them. They're asleep, lucky them.

"I've always wanted to visit the Outer Banks. There are supposed to be wild horses, you know? We could go horseback riding."

"Yippie," I say half-heartedly. I shouldn't be mean to Becca. She is dropping her whole life to help us adjust to whatever is about to happen to mine.

"C'mon, I'm using up like three years' worth of PTO on this. I know it's not what you imagined, but we gotta have a little fun, okay?"

"Yeah." 'Not what I imagined' is the biggest understatement of my life. When I was little, I imagined that my mom wouldn't stiffen one day when I started to talk about a problem at school. I imagined that she'd tell me the truth one day about *him*, maybe show me a picture or something. When she wasn't there for me, I could always go to Hannah's or Aunt Becca's. I thought they'd always be there—a bike ride away. I lean my head outside the open car window, close my eyes, and let the wind whip at my face. The white noise drowns everything out, and for a moment, I'm alone.

The rank smell of manure smacks me right in the face. I pull my head in fast and open my eyes. We're behind a pig truck.

"Oh, fuck." Becca tries to cover her nose with her arm but fails. There's no escaping the suffocating scent of pig shit.

"Language," I say, pulling my shirt over the top of my nose to block out the smell.

"Wild horses aren't the only thing that North Carolina is known for ..."

"Great," I say. She continues to groan about the livestock, but I can't concentrate.

I pull open my backpack and grab a stick of gum for myself and one for Becca. I pass it to her and shuffle my hand inside to ensure the letters are still in there, the ones Becca would probably yell at me for if she knew that I had them. I couldn't leave them behind and let them go. This is the only contact I've ever had with him. They might be the only pieces of him I ever get.

The spearmint is mixing with the pig smell, creating a sickening wave that makes me want to throw up.

"You wanna talk about how you're actually feeling about this whole thing?" Becca asks.

"What whole thing? Moving fifteen hours away from home to care for a woman I just met?" I zip my backpack up before she can notice what I'm doing.

"Yeah, that's the one."

"I feel fucking terrible about it, honestly."

"Language."

"I have absolutely no say in anything to do with my own life. Everyone else makes all the decisions for me, all of the time, and I'm kind of along for the ride. It's infuriating."

"That's more like it," Becca says, whipping around the pig truck and gunning her little sedan past on the two-lane highway road. The pigs oink and squeal as we pass. "That's honest, and you're not wrong. But that's being a kid."

"I'm pretty close to *not* being a kid, and at this rate, I'm ready to run when I turn seventeen."

"Just like your mom."

"What?"

"I said, just like your mom. She always talked about running away. As you know, Grandpa wasn't the best, and Grandma didn't know what to do or how to leave. It was harder back then. They fought all the time, and it never seemed like anything we said or did changed a thing. Sam got bitter because, of course, she did. She wanted to run away."

My mom wanted to run away. Then Dad happened, and I happened, and she couldn't run away from *me*. A loud yawn sounds off in the back of the car, and Jax sticks his head in between the front seats.

"How are my ladies doing on this fine, balmy afternoon?" His curly hair clings to the side of his face.

"You missed the pig truck," Becca says.

"She says there are supposed to be wild horses," I say to Jax, hoping my voice sounds positive.

"That's awesome," Jax exclaims. "I brought my camera so I can get some footage. We could even make a short film."

"Sounds great," I say. It's hard to focus on the fun we'll have this summer when all I can think about is what's hidden in my backpack and that my senior year won't be Hannah and me getting out early and going to get Slurpees at the 7-Eleven across the street or going out for pizza after Jax's play. My new reality has no late-night Becca visits, no showing up after her shift and crawling in between the gang on the couch. I feel sick.

"Red vines?" Becca tilts the package toward the back seat, and Jax shoves one in his mouth. I take one and put it between my nose and my lip, forming a mustache. The sugary smell of high fructose corn syrup and strawberry flavoring overrides the pig shit for a few seconds.

"Up! We're almost there!" Becca's voice beckons me back to consciousness.

"Ugh," I grumble, peeling my face off the car window. Everything is sticky, even the air. My hand goes to my backpack, making sure it's still zipped up.

There's a drawbridge right ahead of us, forming a wall in front of the car. The sunset is behind us, like my whole life. Every moment we could have snuck out and over to the lake—the moments where I could be a teenager with my friends—have been stolen. Mom's needs always come first.

I can see it now. Summer, totally alone, except for the old ladies picking at my sides if I step foot outside the house. Everyone back home will be doing what normal kids are supposed to do.

"So," Becca says, interrupting my doom daydream. "We go over this drawbridge and there's a nature preserve for the next two miles; the island is tiny. Only a few streets besides Main Street. She's on Branford Street, Sam said."

The drawbridge creaks as it lowers, and it's like nothing I've ever seen except in fantasy movies. It's comprised of curls and ovals of intricate metalwork, not a right angle in sight, and as we pass over to the other side, flowering vines line the sides.

Hannah grabs my shoulder and shakes it a bit. "Seriously, Emma, this is awesome. It's like your own private island. Being Ben's stepdaughter ain't so bad, right?"

Stepdaughter. Ben's stepdaughter. I hadn't really thought about it much.

Maybe it'll be good. I have no idea what it's like to have a dad or a dad's dad or a dad's mom or anything. I kind of remember my grandma on my dad's side, I guess. I remember almond cookies. I remember yelling. I remember Mom taking me by the arm and leaving. I wish she'd tell me exactly what happened with his family, and with him. I'm not a little kid anymore.

The bridge squeals and screams as it lowers back into position.

"Oh, that's comforting," Jax says, pulling his play knife from his pocket. The plastic snap from the blade going in and out of the handle while he stabs the arm of my seat makes me want to snatch it from him.

"They all sound like that, I think," Becca replies. "Windows down! I insist we all get some fresh sea air!"

We oblige.

The fragrance of beachy blooms fills the car, as do the chirps of crickets coming out for their evening performance. Seagulls caw. It's like listening to the sounds of nature on a white noise machine. It's perfect.

"Dude, this place is amazing. I'm so happy I brought my camera." Jax beams. He insisted on packing every piece of film equipment he owns, despite the lack of storage in Becca's sedan.

Vines with vibrant, bright green leaves with spherical buds dotting their lengths grow along the road. Off in the distance sway tall grasses, and a big bird-looking thing takes flight as our car passes by.

A howl breaks through the sound of the wind.

When I look back, Hannah's head is no longer in the car. Jax laughs and sticks his head out as well. Becca grins and smacks my leg as she sticks her head out the window.

The wind is salty, balmy, and fragrant, and there are probably a thousand mosquitos ready to collide with me—but I do it anyway. I close my eyes, stick my head out the window, and howl. The feeling of freedom that the others are experiencing escapes my grasp. The letters in my bag, the things I absolutely shouldn't have, are causing my heart to palpitate and anxiety to vibrate through my body.

We pull past a few houses on the road. There's a new building with brightly painted siding, but most of them are older, with elaborate wood carvings lacing the porches. A large sign, hand-printed and antique-looking, depicts an illustrated cherry pie and boasts:

'Pie to have a better time!'

Leaves, thick and bursting with blooms, surround it.

The road curves at the end, and then we're there. Nadine's house is the largest we've seen on the island, a goliath three-story home with a long, winding driveway. The sunset casts the greenery down the drive in an orange glow. The road takes us to an ornate glass greenhouse to the left of the house, revealing glimpses of the ocean between buttery flowering magnolia trees.

"Shit!" Becca yells, slamming on the brakes. My body whips forward, and the seat belt slaps me back into the seat as the car comes to an abrupt stop. Becca's panting, gripping the steering wheel hard.

The windshield is smeared with blood and black feathers.

"Is everyone okay?" Becca asks.

"All good back here," Hannah says, catching her breath. "What happened?"

"Something hit the window," Becca says, throwing open the passenger side door and looking back at the road. Before getting back into the car. "It was a blackbird, or a raven, or something ... poor thing."

Becca sprays the windshield cleaner, smearing pink fluid and feathers across it until there's enough clear space to keep driving.

The rush of the waves ebbing and flowing grows louder as we get closer to the house.

Becca pulls the sedan to a stop, throws the car in park, and honks the horn three times. The front door opens, and Mom rushes down the wooden slat stairs to our car. Her hair has perfect beachy waves, and she's so tanned.

First, she runs to Becca, pulling open her door and leaning in for a hug. I step out of the car, and she hustles around to my side, engulfing my body in her arms before I even have a chance to say hello.

"Oh my God, I missed you so much." Her cheeks are wet on my shoulder. Happy tears. Her arms are warm, like she's been in the sun all day. Her hair smells like cocoa.

"God, Mom. Calm down. I'm alive. I missed you, too."

She grabs onto my hands for a squeeze. Our sweat mixes, and then she pulls away from me.

"What happened?" she asks, pointing at the crime scene on the windshield.

"Oh, that. We hit a bird," Becca says.

"You guys must be exhausted," Ben calls out, coming down the steps. "You kids go on in and get settled. I'll take care of everything."

"You sure?" Mom asks.

"Yep. I got it." He holds up an arm and kisses his bicep.

"Ben, you don't have to!" Becca yells, but Ben's already going for the hose. "Alright, you have at it, then."

Jax and Hannah are already out of the car and on their way up the stairs.

"C'mon, Emma!" Hannah shouts.

"I'm coming." I grab the strap of my backpack and pull it over my shoulder. Ben runs over to me.

"I can get that."

"I'd prefer you didn't," I say, heart racing.

Ben nods at me with a smooth smile and heads to the trunk. It would have started a fight if I had said that to Mom.

The Greek Revival home is like nothing I've ever seen up close, with pristine white siding and carved Teak trim. Up the stairs, the double doors resemble a Spanish gate. There are sculptures on the grass around

31

the house and throughout the garden, like what I imagine you'd see in an old English castle, based on movies: stone women and children swathed in vines.

Mom and Becca run up the stairs. When they're together, everything lightens, their banter and lifelong corny jokes bringing the familiar to any new situation. Today it doesn't put me at ease at all. Given that we're all together, I should be excited to be here, too, to lay on the beach and swim in the pool—to spend time with them-but my mind is somewhere else. It's going through every possible scenario of what he would say, imagining what his voice will sound like and how it will feel to finally talk to him.

When I get into the house, the entryway leads past a sunken living room to a hall to the back, where the doors are wide open, overlooking a pool and the ocean.

This should be enough. Most people would be grateful for all of this. I walk straight through and out to the back. Palm trees and flowering bushes line the sides of the patio. The torrent of waves coming in and out try to take hold of me for a second, making me forget about what I've got to do. This should be enough, but it isn't. Nothing will put the questions I have to rest until I talk to him. I have to know his side of the story. I turn away from the ocean, and wander into the hallway, opening doors until I find the bathroom.

There, I unzip my backpack and take out the stack of letters from my dad. The hair on my arms stands straight like pins and needles. A small, cold, barely-discernable breath whispers in my ears, *Leave.*

HOMECOMING—SAM

I toss the last bits of pineapple into the blender. I hold the pulse button for thirty seconds before the grinding comes to a halt and I fill our glasses.

Since we've been in this place, I can't help but feel like I'm not really home. Ben said to relax; this place has been in his family forever. I should feel at ease here—a normal woman would. Krysten probably did. She was probably easy and happy living in the house next door on this little island. A baby's cry pulls me from my thoughts.

I stop and look around the house, holding the serving tray as still as I can.

Only silence answers until Becca's laugh pulls me toward the deck. Her laugh is infectious, calming, and inspiring—the exact right thing. Sometimes, it could even pull Dad from a mood.

I carry the tray of drinks through the kitchen into the open concept dining room and living room. That was a child's cry; I know it. It sounded like Emma when she was a newborn as I laid catatonic in bed, wanting to stop the screaming from the other room but completely powerless to do so. I pause for a second and look down the hallway. It's dark despite the ancient gas wall sconces lining the length of it. It's always cold in this hall, even when the rest of the house is muggy. It's far from refreshing.

Every time I try to explore the rooms down there, I catch such a chill it causes stiffening in my bones and I hightail to the embrace of the tepid heat in the main living area.

It's quiet now. The cry was not real.

I continue through the open glass doors and back to Becca and Ben on the patio. This isn't my home; I shouldn't be snooping.

"Here we are," I say, passing drinks to the grown-ups. I sit in the cushioned chair next to Ben and prop my feet up on the propane-powered fire pit in the center.

"Thank you." Becca sips her cocktail and lets out a huge, audible sigh. "Okay, now it feels like vacation."

"Hey, where are ours?" Hannah yells from the hammock. All three kids have squished themselves together on the oversized cloth hanging between two palm trees. Flaming torches surround the porch to keep away mosquitos and palmetto bugs, although they don't do a very good job of it.

"Thank you, my lovely sister!" Becca shouts to rub it in before turning to Ben. "How's your mom?"

Ben grins with excitement. "She comes home from the hospital tomorrow afternoon. She's doing alright. It's kind of miraculous. We didn't think she was going to pull through. It's been a roller coaster." He clenches his jaw and sighs before continuing. "The doctor says there wasn't any brain damage from the fall. They said it could have been a mini stroke, but they aren't seeing anything on the scans. She's talking, walking, doing physical therapy every day."

"Thank God." Becca takes a big gulp of her drink. "Usually, people her age don't come back from stuff like that, not this quick."

The death of Ben's mom, Nadine, was not on the wedding registry.

I'm happy she's alive, but I'd be lying if I said I wasn't worried. The honeymoon phase feels like it's about to be suffocated to death by the weight of Nadine's bony body.

I can't stop thinking of the first day in the hospital when she reached out for me, gripping my arm, and how foreign it felt. Her touch should be comforting, she's accepted me, but it left me uneasy instead. Maybe it's that I can't really trust mothers. My mom always said she didn't want me to have the marriage that she had, but when I got with Jared, she said nothing. She only looked at me with those, *oh Sam, you know better* eyes when I started coming home with bruises on my wrists. Now I'm with a decent man—a good man, and she completely rejects him.

I gulp down a few sips of my piña colada. Ben rubs his rugged hand against the top of my thigh, releasing the tension in my body like tiny hands letting go of the bones within my face.

"You guys have everything ready for her?" Becca asks.

"Pretty much," Ben says, putting down his glass. "I'm gonna head upstairs and double-check the room for her. I'll let you two beautiful women catch up."

"Oh, c'mon, stay a while longer," I protest.

"We have plenty of time to all be together. You two need this." Ben gets up from his chair and kisses the top of my head, sending warm chills down my neck. "Goodnight, kids."

"Night, Ben!" Jax shouts. The girls follow with echoing goodnights.

The house next door catches my gaze more often than I like to admit. Each time, I wonder if Ben and Krysten had laughs that were more joyful than ours within those dark, vacant windows.

"Tell me all about the honeymoon." Becca brings me back to the patio.

"Oh God, amazing is an understatement. Sorrento might be my favorite place on Earth. It's almost too beautiful, too perfect to be real."

It certainly did feel that way, and the call from the hospital was an astute reminder that my life was very much lacking in the perfection area.

"I'm so happy for you." Becca takes another sip of her drink. "What's wrong?"

My leg shakes.

"Nothing. It's nothing. I can't help but worry that this is our life now. Like until Nadine ... dies ..." The last word comes out as a whisper. It always feels so awful to talk about death, like if you say it out loud, it will happen, a spell waiting to be cast on the living.

"No way." Becca waves her arm at me. "Ben is a doting son, but he made promises to you and Emma. He'll keep them."

"Maybe," I say, knowing Becca is right. "I've been having these nightmares ever since we got here. I wake up in a sweat nearly every morning."

"What about?"

"That house." I instinctively look over at it again. It seems so much darker than here; the area itself is lifeless. "I keep dreaming I'm stuck in that house. I wake up, and I think I'm here, and then I get up to use the bathroom or get a glass of water, and I'm in there." A shiver courses down my spine. "In the dark, none of the doors open to where you think they should, and I'm stuck screaming for help. No one comes. There's sand and vines everywhere."

"Shit. That sounds rough. It's only a dream, though."

"I know. Each time, there's this snake. I know it's somewhere, but I can't see it. I think it's going to bite me. I'm done for, and I can't find anyone, then suddenly I'm on the beach."

"Did you look up the meaning or anything?"

"No. I'm sure it's stress or something. Feeling trapped, wanting to escape."

"Are you feeling trapped?" A breeze flows in off the water, and the flames lay on their sides, and the smell of citronella fills the air. The waft is thick and humid, offering no refreshment.

"I don't know. There are worse places and worse people to be stuck with." I raise my glass, and Becca follows suit.

"Did you tell Ben about it?"

"No." I shift in my seat, leaning forward to whisper. "I don't want to bring it up. There's too much pain there. He pretends like the house isn't even there most of the time."

"More reason to talk about it. Seriously, you don't want to start your marriage off with a bunch of lumps under the rug already."

"You're right ..." I sigh, raising my hands in the air. "I'll talk to him. You wanna go with me to the store in the morning? Ben can watch the kids if they wanna stay here and go swimming or whatever. We can pick up some stuff you guys want to eat. Plan some dinners, some more cocktails. I'll show you the fish market. I need to pick up my pills, too."

"Sure."

The dull swishing of the ocean is interrupted by a sudden, loud, painful cry. My body jerks in my seat, and birds take flight over the other house, their alarming caws fading into the sound of the waves.

"What was that?" Emma asks, sitting up in the hammock.

"I'm sure it was nothing," I say. "Being so close to the nature preserve, there are new sounds here all the time—"

Just beyond the leaves of a dwarven palm, a moan ripples through. The sound holds the lot of us tight in its grasp. No one dares move.

"Hello?" Becca breaks the spell, and a rush of panic floods my veins, constricting my muscles in a tight ball. "Is someone there?" she calls again.

Emma and Hannah shrink into the hammock.

A wet, hacking cough rings out. Becca rises from her seat, moving forward slowly like a stalking cat toward the foliage. She looks back at me as if asking me to join her in pursuit of what hides behind the leaves. I don't want to see. A feeble heaving sound pushes through the leaves. Maybe a sick animal? My wobbly legs hit the ground, and I move closer to Becca. Despite my heart screaming to turn away and run, I face the darkness beyond the green petals. Two glowing eyes meet my own, and a tiny gasp escapes my lips.

"What is that?" I whisper.

Becca shoos me back. She parts the green leaves and reveals the hands and face of a person, a woman, trembling and hunched over.

"Oh my God. Are you okay?" Becca asks.

The woman heaves in the bush, her body contorting. When she stands up into the moonlight, her matted, brown bob frames a pale face—inky cobalt paints her parted lips.

Her eyes start to roll in the back of her head, and Becca grabs her by the hand.

"How did I get here?" the woman chokes. "Where am I? Is Lilith here?"

"Who?" Becca asks. "Do you live around here? We're on Camillia Island. I'm Becca, that's Sam."

Her long, black, gauzy dress offers limited cover for her body. Her abdomen is swollen on her thin frame. *She's pregnant.* A silver pendant hangs between her breasts. Instinctively, I reach for the necklace Nadine gifted me on my chest.

"I'm Sam. I'm here with Ben, and this is Nadine's house. Maybe you know Nadine?"

The woman smirks. "I know Nadine." She slurs her speech like she's drunk. "She's supposed to help me with this."

The woman grabs her stomach with one hand and pulls the other away from Becca. She hikes up her dress. That's when it becomes clear there's blood running down her legs. I stiffen, frozen, remembering the blood—my blood and Emma's.

"I can help," Becca assures the woman. "Kids, go get the phone and some towels. Now!"

Emma and Hannah listen right away, but Jax lags behind, entranced by the woman, before Emma's call beckons him inside.

"Come, sit down," Becca says. "We'll get you an ambulance."

"No!" the woman shouts and turns away from Becca. "No. Call Dr. Drear. Call Ginny! It's going to be time soon."

Her eyes roll in her head. They no longer resemble the bright things peering out from the bush, as they're dark and void. Hollow things.

"Call Ginny!" the woman shouts.

Ben rushes out from the back door with towels.

"Annabelle?" Ben asks. "Oh God, what are you doing here?" He rushes over to her and hands her towels.

The woman—Annabelle—takes a towel and pushes it up between her legs.

"Benny!" the woman gushes as she puts her dirty hand on his shoulder. "Take me to Dr. Drear, won't you?"

"Um," he says and turns to me. "Sam, can you grab my phone and call Richard in my contacts? He lives nearby, an excellent doctor. He'll get her taken care of."

"We should call an ambulance," Becca says.

"No!" Annabelle shouts. Blue spittle splatters over the patio. *What the hell was she eating?*

"Call him, Sam!" Ben shouts. "Now. I'm driving her over there."

Ben's never raised his voice like that before. I rush into the house and phone the doctor. Becca follows.

"Hello, Ben!" a man answers with a sing-songy voice.

"This is Sam, his wife."

"Oh yes! I've heard all about you. Hello, Sam!"

"Doctor, there's a bit of a situation—a medical emergency. Ben's bringing a woman over, a patient of yours, I think. Annabelle?"

Someone whispers behind the receiver. Something I can't make out.

"That's good. I'll be ready for her. Thank you, Sam."

The man hangs up the phone. Becca stares at me, waiting for some kind of answer, but I've got nothing. Who was that woman, and why was she wearing that necklace?

THE CAT'S AWAY—EMMA
JUNE 11

After Becca and Mom are safely tucked into bed, and Jax is fast asleep, I peel myself up off the twin lower bunk and grab my backpack. Still in my day clothes, I slip on my sneakers and head into the hall. The strange woman's eyes seem to have burned marks on my brain. Glowing, animalistic, like a lion in the savannah on a nature show. A shudder rushes through my body. She was pregnant, maybe having a complication, and I shouldn't be scared. Still, something about her makes me feel uneasy. I wish I didn't have to go outside to do this, but I can't risk my mom, Becca, or Ben hearing the phone call with my dad.

I take slow, careful steps down the hall. There's a large window at the end of the hall that faces the house next door. The home is empty, and the windows are so dark it gives me the heebie-jeebies. The thick air clings to me, wrapping me too tight. I imagine the woman's face appearing in the window bit by bit until her eyes manifest. I've got to get out of this house and get some air. I shake it off and go downstairs to the front door. Ben's car is still missing from the driveway.

"Hey," Hannah whispers. I nearly jump out of my skin as I turn to face her standing inches from me in the hall.

"Jesus!"

"Where are you going?" she asks.

"Nowhere."

"Don't lie to me."

But that is exactly what I need to do right now: lie and get away from this house. "I can't sleep. I was gonna go for a walk."

I really want to go to a place where I can be alone and, finally, after all these years, have a real conversation with my dad. It wasn't totally a fib that I couldn't sleep. How could I, knowing that he's out there and wants to talk to me? I haven't been able to get any privacy at Becca's or on the road, and now, I have a chance.

"I'm coming with you."

It's no use arguing with Hannah, especially about leaving her alone to wander around in the middle of the night on an island after that bizarre encounter earlier. Maybe she won't be weird about it.

I start a light jog, and Hannah follows. Getting away from the house is top priority. Mom can't find out what I'm up to.

"Are you going to tell me where we're going?" Hannah asks.

"No." In truth, I don't even know exactly where I'm going. Just far away so Mom, Ben, and Becca can't interfere.

Vines and enormous leaves line the gravel road. Every gust of the wind makes shadows dance across the plants and ground.

Hannah slaps a mosquito on her neck. Soon, the gravel path turns to tendril-covered planks that squeak as we walk over them. Grass and reeds have sprung up between each board. After another slapping sound, Hannah lets out a loud sigh.

"Can we go back now? I'm getting eaten alive."

She's following a few feet behind me. I lift my phone high in the air, trying to get a signal. It's 11:56 p.m., and he'd be calling any minute. I need to get signal. C'mon. One bar? Seriously?

"What are you doing?" Hannah asks.

Two bars. *Yes!* I keep walking forward, ignoring Hannah, my heart beating fast. I can't wait to talk to my dad, hear his voice. I know he might end up being a total jerk, but he could also be sorry, and awesome. His voice could sound like mine. We could like the same bands or have the same favorite color.

"Emma!" Hannah yells.

"Ugh, I'm trying to ... Aha, I got it! Three bars, that's good, right?" I ask.

"What are you talking about?" Hannah asks.

"I didn't want to tell you until it happened because I didn't want you to be worried about me. My dad's going to call me."

"Your dad? Like your estranged father that your mom and Becca hate?"

"Listen, he's not that guy anymore. He sent all these letters to me, begging me to hear him out. He's sorry for not being around, says it wasn't his fault that my mom wasn't all innocent—"

"Do you believe him?"

"Why shouldn't I? Mom and Becca won't tell me anything about him." I stomp a few paces ahead of Hannah.

"I don't think this is a good idea. I—"

"This is why I didn't say anything. I knew you'd all try to talk me out of it if it was ever really going to happen. I'm not letting you." Sweat drips down my chest.

Four bars.

"That's total crap. I came across the country to hang out with you this summer. Everyone here loves you. They're not trying to keep you from anything. We all want you to be happy."

"Did you ever think that maybe I don't want your help? I want to make a decision for myself about this," I say, finally turning to face her. "Listen, I don't think he's some saint, okay? He's my dad, and I have a right to know his side, and to see if he's changed."

"Your mom has been there for you, and when she wasn't, your Aunt Becca always was," Hannah says, walking toward me.

"I mean, if he was bad, he could have changed. He wants to be in my life."

"I hate to say this, I really do, but I think you're making a bad choice. This doesn't feel right."

"You're my friend, not my mom!"

Pain washes over her moonlit face, and I feel *it,* the leaking guilt rushing into my gut. I can't let her get to me, to convince me that maybe she's right. I have to know him—he's my father. I check the time.

12:01 a.m.

I stare into the brush. Predator eyes start to appear. Her eyes. My heart pounds. Gooseflesh threatens. Bit by bit, her face–

"Listen." Hannah grabs my shoulder and turns me around. "You're my best friend. I'm sorry I didn't react well, but I'm scared. I'm scared for you to reach out to him. Honestly, that weird lady showing up earlier totally freaked me out. It's just a lot in one night."

I purse my lips. I can't fault her. That woman from earlier, her eyes, they're etched in my brain. The brush is empty and dark. What was she doing in the bushes, and what happened to her? And her baby?

"Wouldn't you be worried about me?"

"Yes," I say. "I would."

12:04 a.m.

"Exactly," Hannah says.

"Are you going to tell?" I ask.

"No, but don't keep stuff from me anymore, okay? I won't tell, but you have to promise to let me know everything."

"Okay."

The crash of the waves washing in and out is taken over by the cries of crows circling overhead. Something moves in the tall grass right off the boardwalk path. Maybe coming out in the middle of the night wasn't the best idea. There could be alligators, snakes, or anything. It seemed worth the risk before.

"Let's go back," I say.

"Are you sure?"

"Yeah, he's not gonna call ... I was an idiot to think one of my parents would give me the decency of the whole fucking truth."

"Emma—"

"Let's just go."

We walk in silence back toward Nadine's. An old, black Chevy Impala arrives from the opposite direction and pulls into a driveway we are about to pass. Hannah and I step off to the side of the road. When the car stops, a man in a light button-down shirt and sunglasses steps out of the car, opening the door for a woman. That's when I notice Ben's car is parked there.

An older lady steps out of the Impala and onto the broken shells and gravel that make up her driveway. It's Ginny, Nadine's friend from Mom's wedding. A girl around my age climbs out of the car behind her, wearing sunglasses, long black gloves, and a form-fitting black dress. Ginny lets out a little sob as they make their way up to the porch.

My stomach twists with guilt. This is private.

"I told you she was weak," the girl says, patting Ginny on the back.

"Harame, grab the cases from the trunk, will you?" Ginny chokes out between sobs. The screen door slaps open, and Ben walks out of Ginny's front door and embraces the woman.

"Thank you for getting her home to me, Ben." Ginny pulls Ben in and kisses his cheek. "That could have been very bad."

"Anything for the family," he says.

I pull Hannah down to a squat as Ben gets into his car.

"What was that about?" Hannah asks after he's driven away. I don't even know how to answer.

We stand back up to find the girl facing us. She must've known we were there the whole time.

She pulls her sunglasses down, and her eyes lock with mine. There's a glow in hers, maybe from the moonlight reflecting in the dark. A little spark ignites in my stomach. She winks and sucks on a vape pen before following the older woman into the house.

Nadine's Back—Sam
June 12

Becca and I sit by the water, and, like the millions of people before us, we search the waves endlessly for answers. They do not hold the answers to questions like: *what do you do when a pregnant lady turns up bleeding on your back patio? How can you be emotionally supportive of your teenage daughter who was forced to grow up too quickly? Why did Dad hit Mom so much? Why didn't she love us enough to leave?*

The questions come with images; tiny movies ready to begin rolling at any second. Dad, screaming, as he yanks Mom into the other room. Jared shouting at me about coming home late. The woman retching in the bushes last night. That damn necklace. The cold metal of my own presses against the skin between my breasts. Had Nadine given one to that poor girl, too?

I force my mind to comfortable places and sensations, like the warm sand between my toes and the ever-present sweet grass, yet the sickly residue of worry stays. It won't be wiped away or forgotten.

Ben snapped last night and expected me to jump at his word. It reminded me of Jared and of my father.

"You think the kids are upset about what they saw last night?" Becca asks, leaning into me as we stare out at the ocean. I don't reply, barely hearing her. "Sam?" Becca says, shaking my arm.

"I don't know," I say. Hannah and Jax squeal from the pool. "They seem ... okay."

"Of course. Don't they always *seem* okay?" She's talking about us. The song and pony show we'd put on at school, in public, trying to do anything we could to avoid our feelings. "Something's up with Emma, I think."

She's right. Emma ran inside as soon as she and Hannah got back early this morning, locked herself in the guest room, and hasn't been down since.

"Maybe I should talk to her." I hesitate because I know myself. I'll screw it up, not say the right thing, and she'll roll her eyes and shut down. "I never know what to do in these situations ..."

"You mean when a bleeding, creepy woman wanders onto the property?"

I snort and shove her shoulder because she's exactly right. No one knows what to do in these situations. I feel like I'm missing that thing, that instinct moms are supposed to have to make it all better.

"What do you think was going on with that girl?" Becca asks. "I hope she didn't miscarry."

"Did you see the blue running out of her mouth? She was puking so much, and she was so thin and frail. She sounded drunk." I shake my head.

"Sounded poisoned," Becca says.

"What?"

"I don't know what I'm talking about. To be honest, I'm a little freaked out by it."

"What do you mean?"

"You know that dream you were telling me about? Last night, I had something—"

A car horn beeps behind us, and I shudder. "Jesus."

"A little jumpy, huh?" Becca says, laughing. She pats my shoulder and starts down the sandy path lined with decaying wooden boards. I follow after her, focusing on the waves as we go, making my feet hit the sand in unison with the cresting of the waves. The flowering plants along the patio are just beginning to bud. Before I can get carried away staring at their beauty, Becca stops and turns to look over at Krysten's house.

"I dreamt of that place." Becca's voice is barely a whisper.

The damn thing's cursed. On the outside, it seems ordinary, but the windows and shutters give it away. The darkness that lurks just beyond the glass tugs at you. You have to look, despite every nerve in your body telling you to turn away.

"It's creepy, right?" I ask.

"Yeah, it's weird. It's new, not like a spooky haunted house. It's just new and empty."

"I don't like to think about Ben's wife dying right next door."

"That's what I dreamt about," Becca says. "I dreamt about being pregnant and being in that house."

A chill grabs my skin and pulls it taut.

Becca is right; it's not an aging haunted estate. Its lines are new and modern, and the shutters look like they've never seen a hurricane season. Beneath the sturdy exterior, the house is hollow, void, and born with a great purpose it will never serve.

Ben and Nadine walk arm and arm through the entry hall. Wrinkles line her face, her skin hangs loosely off the bone, and age spots pepper her arms. A groan escapes her cracking lips.

"Everything okay, Mom?" Ben asks. "I can get the walker."

"I'm fine. I'm happy to be home and see my beautiful daughter."

My cheeks burn rosy. She's talking about me. Her body curls forward ever so slightly as she moves toward me, her bony hands outstretched and waiting to meet mine.

"Oh, honey, I'm so happy to see you here, in my home," Nadine says, her voice projecting, always a stage presence, even in her recovery. "I almost can't believe it's real; I thought I was a goner. I don't know what we'd do without you, Sam. Ben, make us some cocktails; I want to sit by the water with my daughter."

Her spindly fingers grasp my arm, and her perfectly manicured nails scratch my skin. I breathe deep and ignore the itch, leading her to the back patio.

"Hello, children," Nadine says, addressing Hannah and Jax. The two look up from the pool with bright smiles, wide eyes, and a friendly wave. "We're missin' one."

"Emma's upstairs," I say. "They went on a hike at the nature reserve earlier, and the southern sun's tired her out."

"Oh, that's alright. We have plenty a' time to get to know each other better." Nadine shuffles over to the lounge chair, and I cradle her lower back as her frail body lowers to the young chair. She pats the one next to her, and I take my seat.

"I do mean what I said," Nadine continues. "I appreciate you, Samantha, holding my home together. Ben loves you so dearly, and I do, too. Just like my own daughter, like how I love Krysten."

Krysten.

The clink of glasses on the table between us breaks the silence—Ben has brought us Manhattans, an older lady's drink.

"Enjoy, ladies," Ben says, kissing his mother's head before running back into the house.

"I hope it doesn't bother you that I talk about her," Nadine says, eyes piercing into mine. "I can't talk about her with Ben too much—too painful for him. But I miss her. What life would have been like having them visit in the summers with their children?"

Children. The kids they would have had, the lives they would have lived—a life where I never came along.

The whiskey dulls the sting in my chest.

INTO TOWN—EMMA
JUNE 13

The cards slide back and forth, waxy in my palm. I'm two-suited, hearts and diamonds; this is good. My eyes meet Nadine's across the table; she's my partner against Hannah and Jax. We've been teaching her Euchre the last few days since she's been home. I'd like to bring up that lady we saw in the backyard the other day to see if Nadine knows her or what was happening to her.

The ten of diamonds stares up from the pile next to Nadine.

"Pass," Hannah says.

I purse my lips and examine my cards, pretending I'm not sure what to do next. Mom taught me to bluff, much to her disadvantage, cause now I can tell when her hand sucks.

"Pick it up," I say.

Jax lets out a puff of air. Nadine keeps a good poker face. The room returns to silence as Jax and Hannah look over their cards. Hannah is the first to lay. The crash of waves from the ocean mixes with the big band music Nadine has playing on the record player in the other room. They lay their cards, and I take the hand.

"Dammit, Emma!" Jax shouts, sounding totally unnatural.

"Jax!" I say, scolding him and trying to hide my laugh.

"Don't worry," Nadine says with the lightest wink. "I'm an old woman, and I've heard it all. You go ahead and 'dammit,' Jax. We're about to bury you two."

Nadine nods to me, and I smile back. As the rounds go on, it plays out just as we had wanted.

"Hey Nadine, a lady was in the backyard the other day. I think she was pregnant. Do you know her? Is she okay?"

"Oh." Nadine waves her wrinkled hand. "Annabelle. She's fine. We've got one of the best doctors in the country right here on the island. He fixed her up."

She doesn't elaborate, so I don't press. Nadine takes the last round with an off-suit ace.

"This is beyond beginner's luck. We suck," Jax says, burying his face in his hands.

"Yeah, I need a break from the beating," Hannah says, resigned.

Nadine starts to get up from the table, but sits back down. She raises a hand to her forehead, her skin pale, like clay.

"You okay?" I ask, putting a hand on her shoulder, the bone apparent beneath her sheer, button-down top.

"I'm fine, dear," Nadine pants. "Just a little dizzy still when I get up too fast."

"I'll get you some water," Hannah says, running to the kitchen. She returns a moment later with water and Ben.

"Mom, you okay?" he asks, rushing to her side.

"I'm fine. Don't fuss about me. I got up a little too fast. Happens to everyone." She rises from her folded-over position on the wooden card table. "I'm going out to the greenhouse to help Sam. She's out there, right?"

"Yes ... but can you please use the cane in case it happens again," Ben pleads, already on his way to fetch it from the corner where it's been collecting dust since the day she came back.

"Whatever makes you feel better." She sighs, grabs the wooden cane from Ben, and hurries out the back door.

His brows gather to the center of his forehead.

"She was fine the whole game," I say to Ben.

"I'm sure she's fine, but she was in a coma. I don't trust it's not going to happen again."

I shrink a little.

Ben stops me with a hand on my shoulder. "Hey, you're doing a great job, kid. Teaching her Euchre, playing with her every day. I know it's not what a teenager wants to be doing."

It takes me a moment to realize that Ben actually does respect me. His eyes meet mine, and I know he means it. My muscles relax. Is this what a dad is like?

"What? It's not?" I say with a sly smile. "What should a teenager want to be doing? Nadine is cool—she's got all kinds of weird stories, and we smoked Hannah and Jax. I'm having a good time. What are you up to in the kitchen, anyway?"

"Pie recipe for the big party," he says.

"Are we really all going to that?" A pie contest? Boring.

"Oh yeah. It's *the* event on the island." Ben laughs. "Anyway, Ginny and Nadine would punish you forever if you didn't go."

"Alright," I say. "Should I be preparing something?"

"No. Absolutely not."

"Things are complicated here, huh?"

"Tradition is tradition on Camillia."

My phone buzzes in my pocket. I pull it out and find a text from a number I don't recognize.

> *I'm sorry I didn't call. I'll make it up to you. I have a plan.*

My heart about pops out of my mouth, its panicked beats slapping at my chest cavity.

It's been two days since he was supposed to call, and nothing. Now this? *A plan? What the hell does that mean?* I can't help but feel like I'm betraying Ben, who's trying so hard to be there for me and for Mom.

Mom walks into the kitchen. I shove my phone into the pocket of my jean shorts as fast as I possibly can. Her sweaty arms are flicked with dirt.

"Hey, kiddo," she says, eyeing me while she walks toward Ben, standing at the farmhouse sink. He intercepts her, grabbing her by the waist, and kisses her. I turn away.

"Sorry," Ben says. "Can't help myself."

Lovely.

"It's fine," I snap.

Mom grabs a glass of water, and oniony earthy notes hang around her as she walks right past me, heading back out into the blazing heat. She has always had the ability to make me feel completely inconsequential. It's either we're best friends, or I'm hardly there. I bet she thinks of Dad sometimes when she looks at me—but Ben doesn't.

I follow Mom, my pulse rising. The bricks on the patio are damp from the heavy morning rain. Huge waves rise and crash against the sandy shore as a blackbird, big as a Pomeranian, pushes into the sky over the house next door.

"Did you ever go over there and check it out, the electrical thing?" I

55

ask, following quickly in her footsteps.

"Oh, that? I haven't," she says, not breaking her stride to the greenhouse. Nadine waits on a bench just inside the entrance. "I'll do it, though. I forgot, honestly."

Forgot. Of course, she did. She'd rather pretend nothing is happening like when I was little and I'd wake up screaming that something was in my room, that someone was calling my name.

You're okay.

Go back to sleep.

It's not real.

Nothing's there.

Go to sleep, Emma. I can't handle this right now!

Inside, the air instantly makes me sticky, moist. The glass windowpanes reach high above us. Cuttings from different plants lay in heaps on a woodworking bench, and above it, shelves of glass bottles are waiting to be filled.

"Forgot about what?" Nadine pipes in. As old as she is, she's got the ears of a dog.

"Oh, nothing," Mom says, pulling on her work gloves.

"It wasn't nothing," I say.

"Here, hold this for me." Nadine places a flower in my hand. "What are you two talking about?"

Mom lets out a sigh and turns toward Nadine.

"The other night, I got up to use the bathroom," Mom says. "I saw a light on in the other house. The upstairs bedroom. I was going to go check it out, but I guess it slipped my mind."

"Maybe a flashlight? Like kids had broken in or something?" Nadine asks, standing and leaning an elbow on the wooden table.

"No, the whole room was lit up," Mom says.

"Oh honey, there's no electricity in that house. Hasn't been in a few years. Sometimes we use the generator to make sure things are still working, but it's empty."

"That's ... I must have been still dreaming," Mom says, shaking it off and continuing to prune leaves from the stems of a deep purple flower.

"Don't go saying anything to Ben," Nadine says, waving me to lean in closer to her. "I see things over there sometimes, too. I don't think Krysten is fully at rest, or maybe it's Ben's father."

Mom's vibrant face suddenly drains of color and her brow furrows. She grabs more stems to prune.

"I don't know if I believe in all that," Mom says, shaking her head. "Isn't it much more likely the kids around here broke in? Or the reflection of the moon? No offence, but I don't believe in ghosts."

"You oughta," Nadine says with a tone in her voice like Grandma gets when she's afraid. "There are things out there that can't be explained. When I lived in Hollywood for all those years with Ben's father, well, there's a lot of tragedy out there. A lot of ghosts, a lot of things you can't explain. What happened to Krysten was a tragedy. Sometimes people get stuck." Nadine turns to face me, her eyes hidden behind her big black sunglasses. "What do you think?"

"I dunno," I reply. "I like to think that ghosts exist, like we don't go away, you know, when we're gone."

"Smart girl." Nadine pats me on the shoulder and turns back to Mom. "Samantha, you have done such a lovely job with these herbs. Will you grab the twine? We'll cut 'em and hang 'em up to dry in the garden house. Emma, why don't you, Hannah, and Jax run down to the market for us and grab a few things? There's a list on the fridge in the kitchen. Go explore a little, too, alright?"

Mom smiles, but her cheeks burn red—it's her tell when she's angry.

###

Hannah's curls whip behind her as our bikes speed past another Victorian home, brown shingles reaching high into the sky. Plants drip from the gutters.

Hannah always leads the way, an unspoken rule of every adventure we've gone on. She always knows where we're going. Even if we get lost, she somehow finds the way home.

We round the corner of Elm Street. Sycamores tower on either side of us and Spanish Moss lolls in the breeze, draping off the trees' gnarled branches. The lilacs are in full bloom, and they sweeten the gentle breeze, making the heat a little more bearable.

Colonial-style structures appear on the horizon. It's Main Street. They're set close to one another and lousy with climbing roses and vines that marry the varying stone and brick patterns. Large black butterflies with delicate silken wings and buzzing bees dance amongst the bursting fuchsia florals. That girl from outside Ginny's house the day we got here scurries into the apothecary shop through a wooden doorway. Ever since that night, I think about her and the woman with the blue lips. The blue vomit stained the stone on the patio. People leave stains, like watermarks on a photograph.

Like Grandpa.

We haven't talked about it since the day it happened, and I wonder if Aunt Becca thinks I can't remember, but I do remember the feeling of Becca's hand in mine, the blood on the floor, and the smell his body emitted. I wasn't supposed to be there. I was never allowed at their house without Mom, but Becca needed something. So, we went in, and there he was at the bottom of the stairs, bloodied and dead. I knew right away that he was as dead as a squirrel at the side of the road, flattened by traffic.

I slow my pace, and Jax pulls ahead of me with Hannah, heading straight to a specific store. A sign juts from the top of the building of a smiling Pip Boy with an ice cream cone.

"Miss!" a man shouts with a southern accent. My wheels slow to a stop, and I plant my feet on the ground. "Miss!"

He approaches me, panting, his light pink button-down translucent with sweat. He's wearing dress slacks, and his dark hair is slicked back like he's going to a fancy event.

"Me?" I ask, a little worried about this random dude chasing me down on the street. His eyes dart back and forth like he's looking out for someone.

"You dropped this," he says, nodding and handing me something I'm almost entirely sure I didn't drop.

"Hey, wait!" I shout, but he's already sprinting around the other corner. The object is heavy and cold. I turn it over in my hand, examining it. It's a charm with a man bent over, a staff in his hand. The metal is tarnished.

Something slithers over my foot.

I jump, pulling my foot back. A little black snake disappears between the vine-covered brick.

I stash away the charm in my pocket and catch up with Hannah and Jax.

"Who was that?" Hannah asks.

"I don't know," I reply, looking back over my shoulder and down the road. "He gave me this." I reach into my pocket and take out the charm. "He thought I dropped it."

Hannah looks at it. "That's St. Christopher."

"Who?"

"Us Catholics believe he's the saint of protection. He said *you* dropped it?"

"Yeah," I say, looking back.

"Weird," she replies.

"Can we get some ice cream now? I'm *dying*!" Jax moans, folding his body in half.

The Pip Boy hovers over us as we pass under the awning.

The doorbell dings. Behind the Formica counter, the boy puts batter into a waffle press, and steaming burnt sugar billows our way. He flashes us a nod. Blonde hair peeks out from beneath his soda-jerk hat.

"Hey! New faces." He smiles, revealing a perfect set of white teeth. His pale blue eyes lock with mine. He looks like he fell out of a 1950s movie.

"Hi," Hannah says.

"I'm Daniel. You're Nadine's, er, step-grandkids, right?"

"I guess so," I say. "I'm Emma. It's nice to see someone else under the age of thirty."

He laughs nervously, beaming.

I share his enthusiasm. Jax and Hannah aren't staying the whole summer. I'll be left with only Mom, Ben, and some little old ladies.

"Cool! You're not the only ones, you know. Some of us kids come to stay with the grandparents or great aunts here in the summer. Most just don't stay the whole time. Emma, are you staying for a while?"

"I am. I don't think we're leaving until the fall," I reply.

"Awesome! Oh, jeez. Y'all probably didn't come here to talk to me all day," Daniel says, his tan skin growing flush on his cheekbones.

"No, it's alright; you have to be seriously bored out of your mind, right? There are like, what, fifty people on the whole island?" Hannah asks.

"Maybe even less than that. It's weird, right? Like a tiny little society. The ladies tip well, at least. I'm hoping to save enough for a few semesters of college," Daniel says, leaning against the counter. "I'm so sorry to hear what happened at Nadine's property."

"Oh," I say, blushing a little. How do I reply to that? It's not my house, and I never met the woman. "Uh, thanks? We just got here, so we hadn't really met her or anything. It's horrible what happened, though."

"Yeah. You guys going to the pie festival?" Daniel asks, throwing a wet towel over his shoulder. "My grandma won't stop talking about it."

"Yeah, but can I ask what the heck it's all about?"

"Oh, uh... It's just an excuse for everyone to get together, I think. Some of them take their recipes very seriously, though, and everyone gets really wasted."

"Really?" Hannah says. "Most the people here are ... you know, older."

"I know, it's like totally bizarre. Anywho, what can I get y'all?"

It's unclear if I actually find him attractive or if my limited selection of human interaction for the summer is causing my stomach to flutter.

"Mint chocolate chip." Hannah's fave.

"I'll have a banana split, my good sir," Jax says.

"Me, oh, uh, strawberry with sprinkles," I say.

"You got it. I'll be right back."

Hannah and I walk back toward the bikes.

"He's cute," Hannah whispers.

"I know, right?"

"He thinks you're cute, I can tell."

"What are you guys talking about?" Jax interjects.

"Nothing," we answer in unison.

When our ice cream is up, I grab my cone last. It's already starting to melt in the heat. Cream runs down the edge of my hand, and I lick the sweet strawberry off. Out of the corner of my eye, I spot Daniel watching me, and a hint of desire blooms in my chest.

Another man in a pink shirt is putting up an enormous sign in front of the grocery store. A crooked smirk forms on his face as he works. He's missing a tooth.

The sign is canvas with a mid-century-style illustration of a woman with iridescent green eyes holding a cocktail next to a tower of pies. A little caption sprouts from her mouth.

'Pie can hardly wait!'

A bell rings from across the street as the girl from the driveway the other night emerges from the herbal remedy shop. Emerald eyes surrounded by smokey eye shadow meet mine. She nods toward me before hurrying around the corner with a little brown bag.

FREEDOM—SAM

A breath escapes my lips, the only disturbance in the home outside of the micro-movements of the leaves outside, the creak of the wood floors as the air cools, and the drip of the tap from down the hall.

I grab my phone, finding it's nearly ten a.m.

Sam, you actually slept in.

There's a missed call from Mom, like yesterday and the day before that. Does she expect me to relay the tragic end of my honeymoon to her? I bet she'd love that, bask in it. Say, *I told you not to marry him. It's too soon and you don't know him. You don't know his family.* She knew what she was doing when she said those things. She called me naïve and ignorant of the workings of the world and said I was making a worse mistake than she had. There's no coming back from that. Not with our history.

I stretch, leave the empty bed, and make my way over to the window. It's cracked enough to let the scent of sweet grass and salt inside. I think back to last night's horrific escapade.

I'm in the other house, in the shower, naked and warm, letting the spout flow onto my face. The vanity lights above the sink give the room a rosy tint. The smell of that herb Nadine put into the pendant necklace burns my lungs, clinging to the walls of my throat and nostrils. The air is suffocating me.

The water suddenly stops flowing. I turn to get out, but the glass door won't open. I'm panicking, frantic, smashing my fists against the glass—screaming in silence, desperate that someone will hear me and come to the rescue. Suddenly, through the fogging glass, I see an outline of someone in the room. When I turn back to the tile wall, it's become a doorway leading out to the beach. I want to go, but my body won't move forward. The glass door opens behind me, and the figure's hand grabs my stomach, and then I wake up.

I pull my robe closer into myself and stare over at the nightstand, at the charm necklace. Nadine isn't here. I won't wear it today. No matter what I do, I can't get that damned scent out. Maybe it's stuck permanently to the tiny cilia in my respiratory system that captured its molecules.

Nadine and Ben left hours ago for her check-up. One week home and healing splendidly, they said last time.

The creak of footsteps creeping down the hall breaks the silence. Panic catches in my chest. I turn toward the door, expecting Becca to burst through, since she's the only other person who could be home. The next logical step would be the turning of the doorknob. Instead, there's silence, emptiness, not even the slightest jiggle of the handle.

I let out a deep sigh. *Silly, Sam. You don't believe in those things.*

You oughta, Nadine's voice, with her thick southern drawl, repeats in my head. The dullest sensation of fear pulses in my stomach. I don't believe in these things, and I won't let my issues ruin this marriage.

The only real monsters are people, and I've seen them.

I stride to the door and yank it open, stepping into the hallway. To the left is the end of the hallway, with the built-ins, where Nadine keeps the linens. To the right are doors and doorways. Nadine's door is across from ours, always closed. The kids left theirs ajar, and they must've left the light on in the bathroom.

Steam billows out into the hallway, creating a thick haze that obscures the window to the other house. I hate that window, but blocking it feels dangerous, like there could be something beyond the fog.

I put one foot after the other on the carpet runner lining the hall, my thudding heartbeat growing louder with each step. The misty, wet heat invades my nostrils, my throat, my lungs.

"Sam?" Becca calls from the stairway behind me. I scream and whip my head around to Becca. "Woah, are you okay?"

Relief floods my body.

"Yes ... Oh my God," I say, grabbing my chest—the cold silver charm. I don't remember putting this on. I swear it was on the table in our room. "You scared the shit out of me! That's all." I must have left it on when I went to bed. It wasn't on the table. Right?

My fingertips trace the edges of the charm.

"Hey, not my fault you're easy to scare. I made coffee. Want me to make breakfast?"

"No," I say, catching my breath. "How about we get away from the house for a little while? There's a beach across the island I want to visit."

The two other houses on Nadine's short street belong to her friends. The one on the far end is Ginny's, about a five-minute walk from Nadine's toward the nature reserve. It's smaller and older. Her landscaping is what you'd expect in a beachy town: canna Lillies and banana trees between rocks and crumbled shells. A beach cruiser leans against the covered porch.

A wooden sign that appears to be from the 1950's is staked into the ground. A smiling housewife in an apron holds a pie. Her stomach is bulbous, near-bursting with life.

"How far's the beach from here?" Becca asks, dabbing her forehead.

"It's the other way. I thought a walk would be nice; check out the neighborhood. That was before the heat settled in," I reply, adjusting the beach bag over my shoulder. The metal charm sticks to the skin between my breasts.

We turn around and walk down the little side street. Hollyhocks line the road on either end. Fat, furry honeybees suck nectar from them. I remember those only blooming in September back home.

Here, the plants don't seem to care what season it is.

"What's that?" Becca asks, pointing at a fenced-in garden at the corner, just past Main Street.

"I'm not sure." I'm working hard to ignore the sweat on my feet and the thong between my toes rubbing hard against my skin, no doubt bubbling to a blister. It's fine. We're almost there—I think.

Becca's phone rings.

"Hello, Mom," she says, shooting me a dirty look, her stride coming to a halt on the cobblestone sidewalk.

I don't stop until I reach the corner of the fence surrounding a large Victorian home, twice as big as Nadine's. Willow trees and flowering bushes cover the yard. My hand lingers over each hump on the wrought iron fence, the metal cold beneath my hands despite the weather. I reach a gate and take a closer look. The gate is designed to resemble snakes woven together like a Nordic braid. They meet in an intricate circle and surround a cursive 'D.'

"Don't worry, she'll call you. She's been adjusting to life with Ben and Nadine," Becca says. I continue down the line of the property, hoping to get far enough away that I don't have to hear their conversation.

A covered breezeway connects the main home to a carriage house. Three men in pink shirts are huddled together, smoking cigarettes. One sports a tiny mustache like the kind men wore in the 1920s. His glance catches mine, and he waves.

My stomach warms like a fire inside, embarrassed to have been caught staring. It's like when Becca and I would sit at the top of the stairs trying to listen to Mom and Dad fighting. Was it going to be a bad night? Or was he going to pass out early on the couch?

I wave back, cheeks burning. I divert my gaze, trying not to look, but it gets caught in one of the home's upper windows. The woman, the pregnant one from the yard the night Becca and the kids arrived. Her face is in the window—her mouth open in a wide howl. Her gums are exposed, pink beyond the glass, pink and bloody. She's missing all her teeth. Her hand is pressed against the glass. I scream and point toward the window.

Becca's hand pulls at my shoulder, her phone pressed to her chest. "What is it?"

"There!" I point up toward the window, but it's empty. "I saw ..."

Becca puts the phone back up to her ear. "We're all doing fine. I love you. I'll tell Sam to call when I see her later today."

Becca ends the call and places it back in her bag.

"What the hell was that?" she asks.

"I swore I saw that woman we saw the other night. I—"

"Hey!" A woman with the brown bob runs past the men in pink and toward me. What the hell is happening? Was she fucking with me? "Sam, right?"

"Yeah."

She, Annabelle, smiles big, and all her teeth are there. Her skin is flush and pink. Healthy, unlike when we saw her the other night.

"Were you just up there?" I say, pointing up toward the house.

Annabelle's eyes grow wide. "No, I was in the library. I saw you through the window and wanted to thank you both for helping get me to the doctor the other night."

"Of course," Becca says. Annabelle takes her hand. "I wanted to make sure you were alright. You looked hurt."

"Oh, no." Her smile grows even wider. Bigger. Exposing her sharp canines. "I'm even better than before. See! Baby's growing healthy!" She pulls Becca's hand to her stomach. Where there was a bump before is only hollow flesh. My heart sinks. She must've lost the baby and is having some mental breakdown.

"That's so great," I say. "We were just headed to the beach. Do you want to join?"

Immediately, my stomach lurches. Why would I invite her? I don't know her.

"No, I need to rest. That's what Ginny says. Rest, drink my smoothies, and take my vitamins. Make the baby healthy, and then, soon, I'll be able to meet her."

Her makes my heart skip a beat. *Her. Meet Lilith.* That's what she'd said the other night. This woman is clearly having a rough time grieving.

"I'm sorry, her?" Becca asks.

"The baby! Silly. You girls go have fun. I'll be here."

The woman skips off back toward the house. The pink-shirted men look back at us, gazes tense, and I shrink. They're looking at me as if they knew what I was thinking. I did probably look a little crazy screaming and pointing at the place.

"That was strange." Becca pulls my hand.

I nod. Not listening to Becca's follow-up conversation. *What the hell is happening?*

"I'm not lying for you again. You need to call Mom and let her know how you're doing." Becca's voice rings through my ears, bringing me back to the present.

"Why should I?" I reply, walking a few paces ahead of her toward the dead end of the street.

"Because she cares about you, and she's our mom."

"Uh-huh."

Becca runs up next to me, grabbing my hand, stopping me in the middle of the road.

"Are you ever going to forgive her? You know what it's like, you know, to end up in a situation like that," she says. I pull away from her and run ahead. Gravel grinds beneath my feet. The skin between the thong of my flip-flops rips away.

She's talking about Jared. How can she say I'm like Mom? I got out. I protected Emma and ensured she never had to see anything like Becca and I did. Becca wants me to forgive her?

Becca's footsteps echo mine. Tall striped grass lines on either side of the narrow sand path. I sneak past the brush and immediately regret it, as I step right in front of a bright green snake.

I shriek. Cold terror spreads up my legs, rendering them stiff. I falter off balance. Becca runs behind me and catches me, making us fall back together in the sand. I stare, holding my breath as the snake makes its way past us and into the tall grass that frames the sandy path, leaving sweeping traces on the ground.

"Holy shit," I whisper, waiting to make sure it's really gone before standing up and brushing off the sand. Becca takes my hand, and I pull her out of the sand.

We walk closely, carefully, to the edge of the water. Waves lull back and forth, pulling small shells back out into the ocean with them.

"Can we talk for real now?" Becca asks, throwing a towel down on the sand.

I take a seat next to her and surrender. "Fine."

"I'm sorry I compared you to Mom. I know you hate that."

"Thank you."

The hot sand cradles my feet, easing the tension and grounding me in place. I shouldn't have gotten mad at Becca; she only wants us all to be okay.

"What we went through as kids, it wasn't fair at all, and we didn't have a choice. I get it. I was mad at Mom for a long time, too, but we experienced it together, and I had to forgive her, or I couldn't go on. You were so young, but I've been thinking about Nanna."

"Nanna?" What is she talking about? I remember seeing my maternal grandmother maybe once or twice. My father hated her, and as far as I knew, Mom did, too. Mom ran away from her young, to be with my dad to be away from her.

"Yeah, visiting her in the hospital. She was so mean to Mom at the end, despised her, and blamed her for all her pain. She blamed her for dying, if you can believe that."

"You visited her at the hospital?"

"You probably don't remember; I think I was nine or ten, so you were like seven, maybe?" She opens her purse and pulls out two cans of White

Claw, handing me one. "Mom would take me out of school to go with her because she didn't want to go alone; she told me I could never tell Dad where we were going. He didn't want her seeing Grandma."

"That's where you were?" Anger plucks at my muscles.

"You remember?"

"I mean, a little bit. I remember ... I just remember you left me with him."

"Grandma was awful," she says, taking a long swig of her drink. "I could see why she had to get away. Grandma hadn't spoken to her much since Mom left real young, before us, except to ask her to come home. When Mom wouldn't agree, she'd call her a heretic and always used to say our family would be cursed forever unless she did her duty, whatever the hell that meant."

"Jesus."

"Yeah. Listen, Mom wasn't great, and your relationship, that's between you two, but she did protect us from her even though she didn't protect us from Dad. I don't think she knew how to do that. But she protected us from her."

"I mean, you're right," I say. "I guess it could have been worse."

"I don't say this enough, but you and I got out. We got out of that house, and we made different lives. You should be proud of that. The odds were totally stacked against us."

"I didn't totally succeed at that," I say.

"Jared? You were so young, and that was all we ever knew of love. I'm sorry I brought that up. We had no good examples—none."

I lean into Becca. There's still a secret I wish I could tell her—but that's for another day.

"Sam!" a shout comes from down the beach. I put my hand on my brow and strain my eyes to see. It's Annabelle, at the top of a dune. "I won't let them take her from me!"

A man with a pink shirt bursts through the brush behind her.

"Stop!" he shouts.

My chest tightens. She raises a glistening knife—a pie knife—into the air, then plunges it into her neck. Her body crumples, and blood rains down over the sand. She falls like a rag doll to the beach below. Her body makes a dull thud as it collides with the earth.

The Funeral—Emma
June 15

They haven't woken us up to get ready for the funeral yet, but I've been lying in bed for ages, and I can't get myself to fall back asleep. The heaviness of my bladder is getting quite uncomfortable, so I betray my tired muscles and rise like a zombie from the bed and crack the door to leave the bedroom.

"Ben, you don't think it's weird that there wasn't an investigation about Annabelle?" Mom says in a low voice, probably trying not to wake us.

"I mean, the cause of death seemed pretty obvious to me," Ben says.

"That's not the point." Becca enters the hall with curlers in her hair. "The point is that she lost her baby under strange circumstances; clearly, she was dealing with mental illness, and no one got her help. There should at least be an inquiry or an autopsy or something."

How had she died? Mom and Becca were vague about it; they only really mentioned she passed away, not how it happened.

"The girl really didn't have any family," Ben says. "Maybe that's why there's no one to look further into it."

"Were police even called?" Becca asks. "Maybe we should be the ones to raise a flag here."

"Don't you think it's painful enough that the whole community is dealing with her suicide?" Ben says. "I don't think my mother could handle an investigation in her condition."

"What condition?" Becca's voice is stern, and her arms are crossed.

I accidentally lean a little too hard against the door, and it creaks. They all turn toward the doorway.

"Emma." Mom rushes over to me. "I was about to wake you guys up to get ready."

"Mom." I bring her in close and whisper in her ear. "Annabelle killed herself? Why didn't you tell me?"

Mom pulls me in for a hug. "I didn't want to tell you kids, especially Jax. I'm sorry. I didn't know how to explain it."

"It's okay," I say. "I won't say anything to Jax about it. I get it."

She squeezes me tighter. The scent of that necklace thing she was wearing burns my nostrils. Maybe she's got it on for Nadine's sake today. Despite the smell, I don't let go of her.

She pushes away gently and summons a fake smile, a mask she often wears on the island.

"You go hop in the shower," she says. "I'll wake Jax."

Ginny's house is stuffy, though less from humidity and more from layers of dust that fly off various items around us. Each of the lace doilies under every lamp and every vase carries a dinginess. There are an obscene number of rugs, and more than one Afghan rests on the back of every ornate chair.

Nothing matches at all. It's both delightful and upsetting.

The dining room is windowless, hidden in shadow. We make our way to it, past the front room, a labyrinth of couches, tiny tables, and wingback chairs. Men, servers or something, dressed in pastel pink shirts, whip past us with cocktails on trays. Ben sets our contribution on the table next to three other potato dishes, which all look basically the same. Funeral potatoes, Ben called them. Apparently, it's a thing. Ben says everything we notice that's a little off is *a thing* in the south.

"Oh darling, I'm so sorry for your loss." Nadine embraces Ginny and wipes a tear from her face with a lace handkerchief.

"Thank you. I can't believe it's real. It's still such a shock. I thought she was happy and doing better, you know?" The older woman blubbers for a minute, her mouth wide before she reins it all back in.

"You can never predict these things," Nadine says, comforting her friend. "You did all you could for that girl."

"Sam, Ben, I'm so happy you made it," Ginny says, moving from Nadine with open arms to embrace Mom and Ben.

"Of course," Mom says, giving Ginny a peculiar look. "We are so sorry about Annabelle."

"She was a lovely young girl; the world will miss her terribly. The house doesn't feel the same without her." Ginny wipes a tear from her face. Her face turns to mine. "They dragged you to a funeral, huh?" Ginny shuffles toward us, her warm, wrinkled paws at my arms. "You should be out living your lives."

I can't help but agree with her—even though she doesn't really mean it. Nadine and Ben made it sound like not attending a funeral was the same as leaving a bag of flaming poop on someone's porch.

"We're happy to be here. I wish it was under better circumstances," I say. I think I've heard someone say that at a funeral in a movie.

"Who is this handsome young man?" Ginny says, moving on from me and stopping directly in front of Jax, shoving right past Hannah.

"Uh, hi, I'm Jax," he says, holding out his hand.

"You are simply magnificent. What a polite young man. Oh, you're all just so wonderful."

Jax's face turns bright red.

"Daniel's in the backyard with my niece if you kids want to go join them," Ginny says, moving back to Nadine. Nadine links arms with her, carrying her off to the kitchen.

Mom gives a gentle nod. We're free to go.

Jax and Hannah follow me as I make my way through the group of mourners, older women holding tiny plates of food. Pitchers of lemonade, sweet tea, and cocktails are distributed throughout the house. There's someone in the corner decked head to toe in black velvet, a shawl over her head, so I can't see her face. Her hands surround a crystal ball. I crash right into one of those men in the pink shirts.

"Oh, sorry," I say.

"No worries, Miss. Have a drink—you look stressed," the guy says. His smile is so big and bright and unmoving. It sends a chill through my body, but I grab the drink to be polite.

"Cheers," a woman slurs. She looks like one of the people at Nadine's table from the wedding. I can't remember her name.

The stiff older ladies are loose, flushed, and cackling.

Is this what funerals are like in the South? A bunch of older people getting really drunk and playing parlor games? It feels so off to be playing games at a funeral for a woman who died by suicide. I turn to look at Mom and Becca as we get closer to the back of the house. Mom smiles at me and waves for me to go on, so, I do.

Ginny's backroom is a glass-walled conservatory which smells predominately like jasmine. The air is even thicker back here, and instantly I'm sticky. Birds of paradise reach the ceiling, and tendrils of white fragrant flowers hang from the rafters.

"How do we get out of here?" Jax asks behind me.

"We have to reach the end eventually," I say, moving leaves and Spanish moss out of the way. The deeper we get, the sounds of what I assume are the niece and Daniel grow louder, until we're finally out of the dense foliage.

"Emma!" Daniel says, sitting up from a metal lounge chair. Despite the heat, he's dressed in white linen pants, a black polo, and a black sports coat.

"Hey," I say, turning to make sure the other two made it through. Hannah picks little twigs from her hair.

"This is Juniper," Daniel says. "Basically, my adoptive big sister. She's . Ginny's ..."

"Grand-niece," she says. Her eyes sear into mine. She's the girl from the other day in the driveway. She's tall and blonde with a nose ring. Her perfectly beachy hair defies the humidity, and I'm suddenly aware that my frizz must look like crap next to hers.

"This is Hannah and my cousin, Jax," I say, introducing everyone.

"Hey ..." Hannah says reluctantly.

"You're Nadine's new adoptive grandkids. I like it." Juniper approaches me and runs her fingers down my arm, sending a heat wave through my body that makes me want to curl inside myself.

Her green eyes pierce mine. My eyes dart from hers, the intimacy of the moment getting to me. It's almost as if those eyes see right through me.

"You guys wanna take a little stroll?" Juniper asks, and, because there's nothing better to do, we follow her.

The brick wall behind Ginny's house opens to a garden that connects to the other yard on the street. We pass ornamental flamingos and an entire gnome army before we hit the road that leads to Nadine's place. Juniper struts in and takes us on the path past the greenhouse, into the yard, and down to the beach. She stops not in front of Nadine's house but the house next door.

"Have you guys gone in there?" Juniper asks, pulling a vape out of her pocket and sucking in hard. She offers me the pen, inviting me to use it. Jax is here, so there's no way.

"What?" Jax shouts from the back of the line.

"No," Hannah says. "Why would we?"

"Uh, because it's like super haunted. That's where you know, Ben's wife ..." Juniper makes a hand gesture like a knife slitting her throat and sticks her tongue out. The fact someone died there is the reason I avoid looking at it.

"So, again. Why would we?" Hannah asks.

I love that Hannah doesn't give one shit about what other people think.

"What's it like living with the infamous Nadine?" Daniel asks, changing the subject. His hand grazes mine as we walk through the sand.

"Infamous, eh?" I reply.

"She's like the leader of the pack with these women. She organizes everything they do," Daniel says. "Did you see the signs for that pie thing? She started it all, even though the Drears host it now."

"Huh, I was wondering about those," I say. "What's it all about?"

"Do you have the keys?" Juniper steps directly in between Daniel and

I so she's facing me. Her breath smells like bubblegum; it's gotta be the vape.

My phone vibrates in my pocket. It's an unknown number; it could only be one person.

I glance at Hannah. She clearly knows something's up.

"Um, I don't know. I'm sure they're somewhere in the house," I reply, wishing I hadn't said that at all.

"Can you get them?" Juniper asks.

"No. I mean, not right now. Maybe like ... another day?" Why the hell did I say that? I don't want to break into the house. I don't want to go in there, ever.

My phone vibrates again. It's a text. My heart skips a beat, and my blood pumps harder ... what if it really is him?

I glance at my phone. It's not my dad; it's my mom.

> *Where did you guys go? Are you okay?*

"It's my mom. We gotta go back."

"Friday night then, midnight?" Juniper runs her hand up my arm to my cheek. I freeze. No one's ever touched me like that before.

Daniel smiles at me.

"I don't think she wants to do that," Daniel says.

"No, it's cool. We can do that," I reply, acting nonchalant. If it means I get to see Daniel again, I'm okay with it. "Jax, you can bring your camera—maybe we'll catch something."

Jax blushes. "Sure, awesome."

Hannah's already walking back to the funeral, many paces ahead of us. I'm guessing she thinks this is a terrible idea. She's not wrong.

Another buzz on my phone vibrates on my thigh.

I let them all get ahead of me and check it; it was a voicemail from the unknown number.

Hey kid, it's your dad. I'm so sorry I didn't call the other day. Give me a call. I want to talk to you. I'll answer all your questions. I'll let you know what really happened. Your mom isn't innocent. I won't let her keep us apart.

My legs tremble. I can't believe I'm actually going to get to talk to him.

"Emma!" Jax yells from ahead of me. "C'mon."

"I'm coming!" I shout, putting my phone back in my pocket.

After the funeral, I wait until everyone in the house is asleep and sneak down the hall. I try to avoid even looking out the window toward that house, but a chill grips me like frozen little fingertips scratching at my spine. The sky must be clear, because the moon shines so brightly that I don't need a light.

I tiptoe down the stairs, trying my hardest to keep quiet and not wake anyone. This is something I have to do alone. I know Hannah would want to be here, but I need to hear him out and form my own opinion without anyone else. When I reach the back glass door, a whistle comes through the open kitchen window, raising goosebumps on my arms. I push through the fear and choose to focus on the excitement, this moment only, as I open the door and turn to press it ever so lightly shut. No one is behind the door, so I'm in the clear.

The beach seems like the perfect place to call him. I take a seat in the sand and pull out my phone. My eyes are watering, and I suck in a huge breath, trying to pull myself together.

The waves whoosh back and forth, a rhythmic beckoning to step further into the unknown, and I listen. I press the callback button on the voicemail and wait.

It's ringing, it's actually ringing. My body trembles, shaking and sweaty with anticipation. It doesn't even get to the second ring.

"Hello? Kiddo, is that you?"

I gasp, trying to hold back tears. "Dad, it's me."

"Oh my God. I never thought I'd hear those words. I'm so happy to hear your voice."

"Me too." I'm giggling and crying at the same time. I can't believe this is happening. He sounds nice; he sounds *normal*. Maybe this is going to be the start of a real relationship.

"Tell me everything."

So, I do. I relay what it was like in elementary school. I tell him my favorite food— cheeseburgers, same as his. I tell him about Hannah and about what art schools I'm going to apply to next year. We talk for so long that the sky starts to change, and the gulls begin to caw.

"You are such an amazing kid." His voice sounds like he's getting choked up. My face is raw from the tears. I've never cried from being happy before. "I can't believe even with you living without me that we're so alike. It's like you got the very best parts of me. I can't wait to see you."

My stomach clenches like it does before an art show, nervous but excited. Meeting each other is the next step, so it makes sense he would say that, right?

"I do want to meet you, but I don't know how that could happen right now. Mom doesn't know about this."

"Of course, she doesn't. Your mother would never want us to meet, or for you to be away from her; then you might realize how toxic she is."

"What do you mean?"

He sighs over the receiver. Mom has her problems for sure, but, I don't know what happened between them. This whole time, we've just been talking about me. "Mom never told me exactly what happened between you two. I want someone to finally be honest with me about it."

"Listen, you're almost eighteen, and I know there's a record of what your mom said when she called the police that night."

"What night?"

"Before your mother, I had never done anything like that. I swear I haven't done anything like that since." His voice changes—it's bitter humor. "That family, those women, there's something not right about them. Your grandmother, her mom, your mom. She used to tell me when we were first dating about how her dad, your grandfather, would smack around your grandma. I hated him until I saw how your grandma was with him, and then how your mom was with me. My mom told me that when she met Samantha. She said, 'That girl isn't right, something's off about her. That family's cursed; you can smell it on 'em.'"

What the hell is he talking about? I stare into the ocean. The gulls caw noisily, and he's getting louder, engaged.

"I didn't believe her until it was too late, and she had me in her grasp. We got into a fight, and she pushed every button. Something about Sam made my blood boil, and I hit her. I didn't know how to stop."

My insides turn. It feels like my heart has swollen like a balloon and blown up into a thousand pieces, splattering all over my ribs and lungs—weighing them down so I can't breathe. My fingers are numb, and the sound of the gulls is so loud.

"Oh my God," I choke. "You're a monster."

"No, no, no. You don't realize what she is, but soon, Emma, you'll be away from her, and you'll see. Your life will be so much better with me, and like I said, I've *never*, you hear me—*never*—hurt another living soul except her, not ever."

"I don't give a shit. You can't even take accountability for what you've done."

"She's poisoned your mind. I'm not the enemy."

"I wish I'd never talked to you." How could I have been stupid enough to believe that he could really be good, or that I'd have some kind of happy ending with him?

"I'll come and get you. Meet me on the beach. I'll take you away from there, and you'll see, it'll all be better when you're away from her."

"No ... wait. The beach?"

"You're on that Island, aren't you? I saw you and your friend Hannah's post. You didn't think I wouldn't keep an eye on you, did you?"

Oh, God.

"Leave us alone!" I scream and hang up the phone.

I go right into my settings and turn off the GPS. Sobs escape me, and I still can't catch my breath. On shaky legs, I try to make it back to the house. The caws are so loud, and my vision is blurry from the tears. I run to the side toward the greenhouse and scream again.

A figure stands in the glass house.

I back away, quick as my feet will let me, and run through the path of roses, thorns tearing at my bare legs. I run toward the pool and grapple with the handle of the back glass door. I latch it the instant I'm inside.

The house is still, and I cower on the floor in the living room, crying, until the sun comes up.

To the Market—Sam

June 17

The decaying older man at the makeshift pharmacy inside the grocery store wipes a tendril of snot dripping from his nostril with the sleeve of his wool cardigan.

"What do you mean you don't have my prescription?" I ask.

"I'm sorry. After it sat for a few days," the man says, the corner of his lips curling upward, "we filled it for someone else."

"Who else on this island is on the birth control pill?" I retort, cheeks burning.

Becca puts her hand on my shoulder. An older lady in a shawl giggles behind us in line.

"When can it be here?" I sigh.

"We have to order more," he croaks, and his skin hangs like tented leather over his bony cheeks.

I close my eyes, and red flashes across the inside of my lids.

"Don't bother. I'll go off the island!" I turn around to leave.

"Miss, don't get so emotional. You're newly married. Maybe it's a sign."

White-hot anger floods my mind. I imagine reaching over the corner and hooking my nail into his cheek like I would a fucking fish, splitting

84

DON'T EAT THE PIE

his leather skin in half, blood flying across the counter.

Becca takes my arm and hurries me out of the store before I get a chance to make it a reality.

"The fucking Cryptkeeper is telling me to go get pregnant," I say. I don't ever want to be pregnant again.

"Don't worry. We'll have it called into some place off the island. In the meantime, do you have something else?"

"Well, they don't sell condoms here, either. So, I guess it's abstinence." I rip the pungent necklace off my neck and stash it in my pocket. *It's good luck, helps women bear fruit.* Ben needs to tell his mom that we are never having kids.

"I can't believe the nerve of that guy," Becca says. "What an asshole. Hey, are you okay?"

"It's fine. I'm fine." Tears form in my eyes before they spill down my cheek. "It's what happened the other day with Annabelle and back then with Emma. I don't even want to think about the possibility of becoming pregnant."

I catch Ginny staring at me from across the street, and then she's walking over.

"Oh, Samantha, are you okay?" she calls, shuffling over to us.

"Can't do much around here without everyone knowing, huh?" Becca whispers in my ear before Ginny gets too close. "Ginny, hi, it's so nice to see you."

"Oh, you're too sweet, Rebecca. I couldn't help but notice you were upset, Sam. What's going on?"

"I'm fine."

"No, you're not. You ladies got anything else to do right now?" Her bright pink lipstick appears neon next to her pale, crêpe-like skin. It's hard to know what she's looking at. Her face is mostly covered in a floppy black hat and sunglasses.

A pair of crows lands on the roof of the doctor's office across the street. My heart pounds, and I close my eyes. I concentrate on my breathing, but it's all too much, and the tears come out again, harder this time.

Everything running through my mind is selfish. I want *my* space with *my* people and not to care for Ben's mom, who won't shut up about babies and children or how happy I make her son.

"Alright, alright, let it out, dear," the older woman says. "You two follow me."

Ginny leads us back to her house and ushers us past the counters still full of cookie plates and a stack of casserole dishes from the funeral. "You two sit," she orders.

We sit in the front room, and the teak couch squeaks as I rest my body weight on it. Becca rubs her hand on my knee, and I push it off.

Ice and glass clink together on the tray in Ginny's arms. She fills our glasses with gin and takes a seat next to me. Her perfume, jasmine and lemon, clings to the humid air, almost overpowering the scent of the damn necklace.

I take the glass reluctantly, careful not to chug its contents despite my desire to down a whole bottle. She's Nadine's friend, not mine. My fingers catch on the raised pink elephants dancing across the glass.

"Take a couple of gulps and tell me what that asshole at the pharmacy said to you."

I nearly spit my drink out.

"That old limp dick is always saying things to women here, oh yeah. He thinks he can get his jollies off with you young things coming to the island 'cause he knows not to fuck with us old gals." Ginny downs her beverage in a few swallows like it's water.

"He told her she shouldn't be on the pill," Becca answers for me.

"That imbecile. What's it his business what a woman does with her body? These people are always trying to say what a woman should or shouldn't do. Devote yourself to your man? Garbage. It's why I never married one," Ginny says, filling her glass to the brim.

Her eyes are an emerald green. They look almost unreal—so vibrant for a woman her age.

"Ginny, can I use your bathroom? I want to clean up my face," I ask.

"Go on up the stairs, and it's the first door on the left." Ginny sips on her second glass.

"Thank you."

Across the room, photos line the mantel. In one, Annabelle stands in black and white with a wide grin. I set my drink down, hands shaking all the way to the table. Wobbly legs, buzzing with alcohol, float me to the stairs.

"You play cards, kid?" I overhear Ginny from the other room.

"You betcha," Becca says, before I disappear out of earshot upstairs.

The floor at the top of the stairs is carpeted, old, an ugly turquoise color, faded from the sun shining through the window at the end of the hall.

First door on the left.

A sliver of darkness from the door on the right pulls me from my original path.

It doesn't even creak as I push it open, practically an invitation to snoop. I've given in to more than one emotional urge today; why stop now? I used to do this as a little girl. Back then, I never knew what I was looking for, but I searched drawers in people's houses. I'd been caught several times, but it never stopped me. There was always that feeling, the urge to find their secret. My family had so many that maybe it made sense to my little brain that everyone else had to have a bunch of secrets, too.

I step carefully, trying not to make a sound. The thick black velvet drapes cover the window; practically everything in the room is black. The turquoise carpet stops at the end of the doorway, giving way to a black and white tiled floor of mosaic swirls, like something out of a Moroccan palace. Goosebumps rush over my arms as I pass into the room.

An old bookshelf with wooden carvings of winding flowering vines stands in the corner like a towering apartment building of antiquities. It's a built-in, shiny and black, tall with gables at the top, and features glass doors, keeping the trinkets behind them safe and secure. Dried herbs hang from the deep green walls beside the shelf.

The room feels soundproof and insulated, and the slightest shift in the air forces me to whip around quickly. A silk sheet slides off the little pedestal table in the center of the room. A pewter pie tin lays in the middle of the wooden table.

How odd.

I trace my finger along the shelf on the wall. Not a speck of dust lingers on the surface that holds a taxidermied toad, a mouse, and the skull of some type of sea creature.

A book suddenly drops from the shelf above it, landing at my feet. I gasp, listening below to see if they noticed the thud. No one comes up the stairs. I need to get to the bathroom. I've lingered in here too long, but the book stares up at me. The words on the front cover are familiar.

Modor Aeon

Just like the book in Nadine's bag that I saw in the hallway when I was searching for a credit card. Had Nadine meant for me to see it? Before I replace it on the shelf, I open it just to take a glimpse. The first thing I see is a sketch of twelve women standing in front of a table holding pies. Laughter makes its way up the stairs, reminding me that I'm snooping.

I close the book quickly and put it back on the shelf, crossing the hallway over to the bathroom.

When we finally get back to Nadine's, it's dark. Ginny kept us all afternoon and invited her friend Norah over to join us for pinochle, and the time melted right alongside the ice in our drinks. A twinge of guilt grips my stomach, the buzz leaving my body.

"We're home!" Becca announces as we enter the darkened doorway.

"We're in here!" Emma calls. We follow the noises of family and laughter.

The kids are nestled on the couch in the living room with Ben, giggling. There's an old home movie playing on the television.

"Mom, you've got to see this! Ben was a total dork in high school," Emma says.

The room is dark except for the flashing light of the television with visions of Ben and a young, vibrant Nadine dancing across it. Despite Emma's smile and chuckles, her face is swollen and the tip of her nose red, a sure-fire giveaway she'd been crying earlier.

I hop over the back of the couch between Jax and Emma.

"How was your day, my loves?" I say, swinging my arms around them.

"Better now that you're here," Emma says. She leans her head onto my shoulder, melting into me. I can't remember the last time she did that. "I love you."

I kiss the top of her head.

"Me? Oh, you know, the usual sand, sun and water," Jax answers. "I got some footage of a weird bird formation, though. It's so cool, I have to show you later. I've never seen anything like it; they all formed in this weird triangle, these crows, the prints they left in the sand was insa—"

"Jax, shut up about the birds. Look at Ben going to prom!" Hannah shouts.

"I was a late bloomer!" Ben says, defending himself, throwing popcorn at the kids, who—completely unbothered, pick it up and eat it. The boy on the screen looks about twelve years old, scrawny, with a mouth full of braces. His hair is four times as big as his head.

I let out a warm sigh of surrender, wishing that I could capture and bottle this feeling. *Happy family*. My girl laughing and my amazing husband smiling ear to ear. It's everything I've ever wanted. Nadine is curled up in the chair on the opposite us, and even she looks in good spirits. She tips her tea at me and takes a sip. Maybe I've been too critical of Nadine—too worried about what she thinks of me.

I turn back toward the TV, and there she is.

Krysten. They are in their early twenties, and she is dancing with Ben. They're arm in arm underneath the willow tree at the big house we passed the other day.

My heart sinks, and Ben stops laughing.

Nadine grins in her chair behind her tea, seemingly mesmerized by their dance.

My eyes are glued to the screen, but not for the reason Nadine's are. In the back, there's a flash of something black. Was it a snake? A person?

"Did you see—?" I begin.

"What?" Emma looks up at me.

I shake my head. The drinks are getting to me. "Never mind."
The pit in my stomach tells me that something isn't right.

I Made a Mistake—Emma
June 20

A scream echoes through the room. I wake in wet sheets, drenched in sweat, and my body trembles. The room is silent, and I gasp as Hannah's gargantuan snore breaks in. I kick at her, my toes nudging against her leg. She rolls over. *Exhale.* Maybe I should wake her up and make her check out whatever that was. Was it a dream?

Light spills in from the crack beneath the bedroom door, then the light goes out immediately.

I sneak to the door. It moans as I press it open, the sound sharp in the quiet hallway. Perfume burns my nose. My skin shrivels against itself in my cropped tank top. I'm drastically underdressed for the cold that permeates the hall. I step out, drawn to the window at the end of the hall—the one I catch Mom staring at most nights. The upstairs room in the other house is alight. I move closer to the window to get a better view despite the fear surging through my veins.

A black figure passes right in front of the window next-door.

Jesus Christ. I jump back, falling over, ass skidding across the carpet, desperate to be far away. Blinking will make it go away, or at least it's supposed to, but when I open my eyes, the horrible static figure is still there. This can't be happening. A woman's sob echoes up the staircase from the first floor. Mom?

I gasp, filling my lungs with air.

I crawl toward the staircase, trying to remember how I breathed without effort most of my life up until now. The sobs continue. It must be Mom. As my foot grazes the first wooden step, the sound stops. There are no sobs.

No crying.

No screaming.

Only silence.

I strain to hear anything besides my heartbeat and the creaking of the staircase as I descend it. With every step, my fear of some invisible force out there grows, something hiding in the dark, just beyond where I can see. I persist into the windowless hall at the end of the steps, dark except for the dull light pouring from the kitchen. I'm a few feet from the doorway when the light goes off.

I suck in a breath. Darkness envelops everything. Trying to move my feet is useless as they're heavy laden with fear.

I have to get out of here.

I reach the bottom step and grip the banister when the light flicks on in my peripheral vision. Someone is in Nadine's office. Maybe she's awake. Maybe she's working on something and doesn't even know I'm wandering the house.

Tiny gasps escape my mouth between tremors with every forward step I take. I reach out for the chair rail molding on the side of the wall to guide me to the room that's lit up in the middle of the fucking night.

I reach the doorway, the scent of that herb that Nadine gave Mom smacking me right in the face. It grows stronger and sharper as I turn to look inside.

No one's there. The muscles in my legs liquify, and I grab the doorway to stay upright.

A desk stands in the middle of the room. Its heavily lacquered ebony is commanding. It looks centuries old, but there's not a speck of dust on it. An antique typewriter sits on the desk. I breathe out. The keys clack, loud ticks echoing off the walls of the room, but there's no one there. The machine is just clicking and clanking on its own, the typebars bouncing up and down.

My eyes grow wide enough that they threaten to pop from my skull. I can't blink, can't move. I am stuck until the keys suddenly stop moving. I step toward the desk, just a foot or two, and wait, expecting them to start again. Nothing happens, so I turn the corner of the desk and approach the typewriter. The paper loaded behind the cylinder begs me to look at it, to read it.

Save her. Save her. Save her. Don't eat --

The chair is flung to the side as if by some unseen force. I sprint out of the office, away from the room, and up the stairs toward Becca's room, where my body collides with someone else.

"What the!" Becca shouts. "Oh my God, Emma, are you okay?"

I struggle for air, panting, grabbing onto Becca for dear life.

"I saw something. Someone was here," I cry.

"Someone broke in?"

"I don't know. Yeah," I say, panting. "Downstairs in the kitchen, in the office."

Becca pulls me into her, wrapping her arms around me.

"Ben!" Becca yells.

"Everything okay out here?" Ben asks, stepping into the hall and wiping sleep from his eyes.

"Emma saw something or someone. What happened?"

"I ... I don't know. I ... I heard a scream, and I got up and went into the hallway and then ... I ... I saw someone in the house next door." I point out the window. "The light was on. Then I heard a noise downstairs."

"It's okay," Ben says, opening a hall closet and grabbing a wooden bat. "Hey, it's okay. I'll go check it out. You two stay up here. Grab Hannah and Jax and go into my room and lock the door."

"Sorry, I woke everyone up," I say once we've gathered everyone. I plop myself into the chair across from the bed. I didn't actually see anyone. There probably wasn't anyone in the house. They'll never believe me about the typewriter going on its own.

"No apologies; Ben will take care of it. He'll make sure everything's okay." Mom's trying to reassure me, but I'm sure she's frustrated, too. I'm making her life harder, waking everyone up in the middle of the night. "Come here." Mom pats the spot beside her on the bed, and I resign myself to the comfort.

The five of us squish in together, my body still trembling. Those crying sounds, were they Krysten? Or the woman who stabbed herself? A ghost? The typewriter said, "Save her." How can I save someone who's already dead?

Creaking footsteps sound down the hall. I hold my breath.

"All clear," Ben says on the other side of the door.

Mom hurries over and opens it.

"What about the other house?" I ask.

"I called the police; they'll be here in a while. I figure if there is someone over there, we should let *them* handle it, not this old girl," Ben says, slapping the bat.

"What did you see?" Hannah asks, turning to face me.

"I saw someone over in the other house, then there was someone in the kitchen, and then Nadine's office."

"Mom's office?" Ben asks. "It was locked when I went down there."

"That's impossible!" I say.

"I'll go ask my mom for the key. It's five a.m., so she'll be up anyway." He runs across the hall to Nadine's and returns with the key. "Let's go see about this, huh?"

"Let's all go together. It's safest," Becca says.

When we get downstairs, the rising sun spills in through the kitchen window, making everything appear a little less threatening and ominous.

Ben fiddles with the ornate key and opens the office for us. Ben flicks on the light, and the typewriter is empty. There's no paper. No sign of anything. Not even the chair is out of place.

When Friday night comes, the incident is all but forgotten. The police never found anything in the house next door, and Nadine still says it's a spirit.

I'm starting to believe her.

My phone buzzes in my pocket. Unknown number. I send it to voice-mail. I thought I was ready and that it was time to talk to him.

"Is it him?" Hannah asks.

"Yep," I say, turning to hide the fact that tears have welled up in my eyes.

"I'm sorry," Hannah says.

"You told me so." She did tell me so. Maybe Mom was right to leave it alone. I hate that she was right.

I turn the key to Krysten's house over in my hand, my fingers tracing each groove. We're supposed to sneak in tonight with Juniper and Daniel finally.

Hannah wrinkles her nose.

"Okay, so yeah, I told you so," she says, kicking the sand up and into the waves before us. The ocean is a little stirred up today, matching my mood. "But I was hoping it wouldn't turn out exactly how I thought it would."

I lay back on the hot sand, staring at the clouds through my shades. Everything is pink and orange, distorting the world.

"I thought I'd feel something—like closure, I don't know. It was like this big hole in my life, in my story, that I didn't know anything about, and now I do. Somehow, it's worse. It's not a hole. It's like a mucky, tarry pit," I say as disgust ripples through me for never being happy with the family that I had.

The waves are picking up, crashing harder against the shore. The tar pit my Dad left bubbles and boils inside of me. The worst part is that I can't even talk to Mom about it. She'd feel so betrayed, and she's already going through enough.

Hannah sits up and takes a sip from her water bottle.

"Are we really going to do it?" she asks.

"What?"

"Break into the other house."

I sigh and turn over to look at her, my stomach pressing into the cotton towel beneath my exposed belly.

"I think so. I don't know. Maybe I shouldn't do it. It's mean to Ben, isn't it?" I ask, but I already know the answer.

"Oh, thank God, you agree." Hannah lets out a breath of relief. "I really didn't want to."

"I'll cancel right now," I say, grabbing my cell phone. "Should I say you have diarrhea or—?"

"I don't care. Whatever it takes to get out of it and keep whatever you've got going on with Daniel." She nudges me.

I sit up, smiling, and pull up our text stream to let Daniel know it's off. There's a family thing we can't get out of; it's going to be late, maybe another time.

A huge gust of wind whips sand at our faces, and a chair flips off the deck. I turn to the house as the back door slides open, and Becca runs out.

"Emma! Hannah! Get in the house, now!" Becca screams from the back patio.

I put my hand over my brow to block the sun and get a better look at her rosy, orange body shaking.

"Now!" she shouts.

There's yelling—a man is screaming. Then Ben is also yelling. He doesn't sound like himself. Something is wrong. I get up, finding my balance on the sand.

A huge man emerges around the side of the house. Ben's right behind him, grabbing his arm, trying to pull him back.

He's scruffy, bearded, red-haired, and his face is contorted in anger. His eyes bore into mine.

"Emma! Let me see her, dammit, she's my daughter, too! Let me see her! You can't keep her from me! That bitch didn't even want her!" the man says.

The stranger is my father.

I stumble back toward the ocean, nearly taking Hannah down with me. He's pulling away from Ben, then my dad turns and throws a punch—hitting him in the eye. Ben barely flinches, but blood erupts from his nose.

"Run, Emma!" Becca screams.

Hannah pulls me through the sand, but each step feels like we're wading through molasses as we run toward the other house. I hear Mom off in the distance.

"Come back here!" my father yells.

"The key!" Hannah says.

I pull it from my pocket as Hannah yanks me toward Krysten's house. My legs are heavy, my muscles stiff.

Craning my neck back to look at my father; he appears different from the pictures. He looks a little like me—my father. No, I don't have a father. That man is dangerous, and I led him here. Spit flings from his face. Ben's nose is bleeding. His baby blue shirt is stained with blood.

I've done this. This is all my fault.

Hannah pulls me up to the glass doors that lead inside the house where people die. My hand shakes, and I drop the key. Hannah grabs it. My legs are jelly.

She opens the door and pulls me inside.

WHAT DID YOU DO? — SAM

Where is Emma?

Where the fuck is Emma?

Hot blood drips down the front of my face. He hit me again. Sixteen years later, and he's found me. He knocked me right back to the floor of his apartment, bloody and helpless.

I force my eyes down to my hands, my feet, ignoring the metallic taste in my mouth.

When you feel like going back, remember your feet on the ground, see the floor, notice the sounds; Elaine's voice echoes in my mind. I see my bare feet on the tile floor. The tile floor of Nadine's house. My head swings back and forth, searching for something. I hear the ocean and his screams. *Concentrate on all five senses.*

I need to find Emma.

"Oh, dear Lord," Nadine says, trembling. "What happened?"

I don't have time to explain. I need to get to the back door to find Emma.

"Call the police!" I yell back to Nadine. My vision is a little blurred, but it is coming back to normal. The blast of heat from the sun outside worsens the thumping in my face.

"Becca, where's Emma?" I shout.

"Oh my God, Sam," Becca says, running toward me with her arms out. I push her aside.

"Where is she?"

She points in the direction of the other house. *Krysten's house.* "They ran to the other house ... Emma and Hannah," she stutters.

I have to get over there to protect her from *him.*

Shouts and grunts echo off the houses. Ben's on top of him.

Bright red blood spatters Ben's shirt and skin like confetti. Jared is on the ground, his face turns toward me, and time slows—every millisecond, micro movement.

"Go inside and lock the doors!" I shout at Becca.

The wind off the ocean wicks away the blood still gushing from my mouth as I run toward Krysten's house. I'm praying that Ben's fists barrel into Jared's eye socket—that they crack through the skull.

Take his smile from him.

I have to get inside to protect Emma.

I cup my fingers around my face, trying to see inside the house. The dark figure of a woman drenched in shadow stands in the doorway on the far side of the kitchen. She turns and walks away.

That can't be real. My mind must be breaking. Emma peeks out from behind the kitchen counter and rushes to the door.

She lets me in, her eyes wide. Her pouty lips tremble and are slick with snot.

"Mom." She sobs. "I'm sorry. Oh, God."

She wipes the blood from my mouth. I push her inside as quickly as I can and shut the door behind us, locking it and grabbing a dining room chair to wedge up against the door.

Emma shakes like a frail leaf in the wind. I wrap my arms around her and bring her back behind the kitchen counter. Hannah's crumpled in the corner, hand covering her mouth, hiding her tears. I slouch to the ground, pulling her and Emma into a hug.

"It's okay. Ben will protect us," I say, hoping he will but knowing that nothing is guaranteed. How did Jared find us on a remote fucking island in North Carolina? I pull the kitchen drawer closest to us, searching for a weapon. It's filled with dish towels.

Emma clutches me closer when I pull away.

"I have to get a knife, just in case," I assure her.

I move to the next drawer, and the next one is stocked with knives. The hallway looms in my periphery. Someone was there. My mind floods with horrifying things in trying to deal with this one actual threat. It was a figment of my imagination.

"Did Jared contact you before this?" I ask her.

"Mom," she says, a whimper in her voice.

"Did you contact him, Emma? Tell me now." *You stupid, naïve kid.*

"I'm so sorry."

This isn't her fault. It's mine. I should have answered more questions. She never would have done this if she had known it all.

"*What did you do?*" I did this, but the venom escapes my lips anyway.

Emma lets out a cry. Beyond the walls of the house, a car pulls up, and doors slam.

"He's back here!" Becca's muffled voice yells from outside.

"I'm sorry, Emma." I bend down and grab her face, forcing it up to mine. "It's not your fault. I should have told you about him. I should have told you everything. I'm so sorry."

Emma cries harder. "Is Ben going to be okay?"

"Down on the ground!" someone shouts from outside.

"Stay down, you two, stay down."

I raise my head to look through the kitchen window. A female officer has her gun drawn and pointed at the scuffling men.

"It's me! Beth, it's me! Ben!" Ben shouts.

"Oh, shit. Ben, get up," the woman says. My breath finally releases.

Ben stands, his hands raised in the air. Even more blood stains the front of his shirt. The officer approaches Jared, who is lying on the ground, hands on the back of his head.

"Don't try anything!" she shouts at him. As she cuffs him, Jared turns to the side. His face is red. I duck down on instinct. Shame floods my body. My eyes narrow. Fuck this, I'm not hiding from him anymore.

"Stay here!" I command Emma and Hannah, handing them the butcher knife. "Stay here, and don't come out until I tell you."

This house feels haunted by the woman who used to live here—Krysten. Was she the figure from earlier? The rooms are all closed, but to the right is a single door and a bureau, and to the left is a hall of doors with light spilling in at the end. That must be the way to the front. My breath quickens, heavy, echoing off the walls. When I reach the front door, my legs are numb, and my hand trembles gripping the knob.

I can do this. He's just a weak, angry man. I turn the handle, step out, and immediately descend the porch stairs. If I stop, I might freeze and never move again.

Two more officers struggle with him, trying to get him to the car. He's not so young, thin, and muscular anymore. He's chubby, swollen, and puffed up.

I don't say a word as I walk closer to the scene.

"You fucking bitch. You kept her away from me. She wants me. She needs me! She doesn't need you."

I'm quiet, ignoring the terror in my bones. I want to say that she doesn't need him, but I won't waste another second. Instead, I let a smile form on my face.

"Emma!" he screams. They're reading him his Miranda rights. "Emma! I'm here to save you from this fucking whore! She didn't want you! She wanted to abort you!"

I press my fingernails into my palm so that I don't cry. I won't let him see me cry or shake or scream, not ever again.

"You will never see Emma again," Ben says, taking his place next to me. His palm grips mine, and his bloodied knuckles don't flinch. Copper and sweat waft off him, and I never want to let him go. We must both look insane, covered in blood and holding hands.

They push Jared into the police cruiser, still red-faced and yelling. "I need an ambulance! I'm going to sue the hell out of you!"

"We'll escort you to the hospital, sir." The older police officer gets in the front seat, the younger man in the passenger seat, and they pull away leaving Beth, the one Ben knows, behind.

"Are you okay? I called an ambulance. I wanted to get him out of here." She touches my arm and my whole body jerks. Nadine comes around to the side of the house.

"Sam, are you alright?" she asks, nearly sprinting to me. She keeps talking, but I can't make out what she's saying.

"I'm alright," I say, but my words come out funny. My mouth is swollen from the blow, but I am alright—for now.

I look back at the house where the girls are safe. Krysten's house. My gaze goes up the siding, following a large clematis plant to the second floor. The shape of a woman stares down at me, then turns away from the window.

LIKE NORMAL KIDS—EMMA
JUNE 27

It's been a week since Jared showed up at our doorstep. I have the answers to all my questions: he's a monster.

Mom's been weird since then. I know she blames me even though she says she doesn't.

"Emma, can you grab the butter from the fridge?" Mom asks. Everyone is trying to act like things are totally normal.

"Mhmm," I say, turning to do my task. At least it's over, and I never have to see or think about that guy again.

Despite everyone returning to their routine, things are still off—maybe worse than before. The house next door pulls me toward it, my eyes drawn to it like steel to a magnet.

I put the cold bowl of chopped butter on the granite countertop. Becca and Mom are practicing making pies for the annual contest. Honestly, they've made so many I'm getting sick of the smell of freshly baked pies. I didn't even realize that was possible.

"Can you open the kitchen window? It's so cold in here," Mom says, pouring the butter over the bowl of flour and using a weird tool to smash it all up.

I open the window, revealing woven vines that block most of the sunlight—the heat from outside filters through, creating steam in the cool kitchen.

"Blueberry pie?" Becca asks. "That's the winner?"

"Yep, that's what we're going with. I guess Ginny always bakes an apple pie. Nadine does peach. Most of the other pies are taken so ... Emma, can you turn off the water?" Mom asks.

I don't remember turning the faucet on, but my hands are all wet. I can't stop thinking about the other house, Krysten, and hiding there with Hannah while Jared screamed for me.

Officer Beth called the day after the incident and let us know Jared was escorted to the hospital. Apparently, during the scuffle or sometime before, he'd been bitten by what they think was a snake and fell into a coma. There haven't been any updates since, so he can't be dead.

I miss Hannah.

Her parents took the funeral for Annabelle pretty well, but after Jared, it was too much for them to handle. They booked her a flight that night, and we cried all the way to the airport.

"Shit!" Mom screams. "Emma, move!"

She bumps me out of the way and runs her hand under the faucet I didn't bother to turn off. The blood swirls around the drain.

"What ruckus is happening now?" Nadine walks into the room. She looks older today, saggier in the face, with hollowed eyes. Maybe she's not getting good sleep either.

"Oh, don't worry, I just sliced my finger a little; it's not a big deal," Mom says.

"Let me see it ..." Nadine examines the cut. "Put pressure on it. Becca, grab a bandage. I've got something for this to help it heal. Emma, you and Jax go into the garden and get that purple herb nearest to the door."

I trek across the living room, where Jax sits playing on his Switch.

"C'mon," I say, tugging at his T-shirt and rushing out the door.

The overcast sky and moist heat are a relief from the cold, dry house. The path to the greenhouse is so overrun with plants it's hard to get through without tripping.

"How you doing?" Jax asks, running up behind me.

"I'm okay."

"No, you aren't. I know you," he says.

I open the doors to the greenhouse and grab the pair of snipping scissors from the garden table in the middle.

"Ugh. I hate that, you know?"

"It's our superpower," Jax says, referring to the sixth sense we all have in the family to know how the other is feeling.

I ignore him and start snipping at the purple herb. "Nadine doesn't have anything labeled and there are like a thousand plants in here. I don't know how she keeps track of them all."

"Emma," Jax nags.

I head back out of the greenhouse with Jax trailing close.

"So, you're not doing okay, but that's alright. Let me help. Do you miss Hannah?"

"Of course, I miss Hannah, and I miss home. I miss our shitty little apartment. But our old life was never enough for Mom."

"I thought you liked Ben," Jax says.

"I do!" I shout. I take a deep breath. "I do—I miss ... normal."

Jax puts his hand on my shoulder. "I know," he says. "Listen. I know this whole thing sucks, but what doesn't suck is that it's summer, and we can do whatever we want."

"Uh-huh. Whatever we want."

"Seriously! Why don't we go hang out with Daniel and that girl tonight? It's Friday night, and that pie thing isn't until tomorrow. We'll just meet up like we were supposed to before. Say, you know, eff this shit and have fun."

I laugh. He's right. It's better than another card night with Nadine or another moment of Mom and Ben giggling together. I want to be a teenager for once—a kid like I should be.

"Okay," I say.

"Okay?" Jax asks, almost in disbelief that he got through to me.

"Yeah. I'll text Daniel."

"Cool. Now let's go fix Aunt Sam."

It's dusk when we meet up. Mom and Ben are out to dinner off the island with Becca and Nadine. They left us the house. I make little ripples in the pool water with my toes. I know that with Juniper around, we likely won't be spending the entire evening here, but she's not here yet. Jax, Daniel, and I have bellies full of pepperoni pizza and cherry Coke.

The water around my feet is calm and cool, and Daniel and Jax are shooting the basketball into the floating hoop. Daniel looks back at me every so often and flashes this toothy, adorable smile that makes my stomach feel all bubbly. I like that feeling.

My phone dings on the lounge chair behind me. So, I get up and check. It's Hannah.

> *How are you and Jax and paradise? This sux!*

> *Nothing too interesting, just swimming… miss you :'(*

> *I miss you too. How are you feeling about your dad?*

I go to type a reply, but I can't come up with one. What should I say: better now that he's in a coma or worse because everyone was right about him, and I know now I'll never have a real dad.

I stand up and throw the phone down on the chair. Daniel and Jax splash me.

"Hey!" I shout, laughing. "Not funny, guys!"

Something shoves me from behind, and I fall face-first into the pool. Under the surface, the saltwater burns my eyes, but in a blink, a glimpse of a shadow lurks behind the guys' legs—a swirl of darkness before I kick the bottom of the pool and emerge through the surface. When I look from above, whatever it was is gone.

"What's up, bitches?" Juniper stands above us, taking a hit from her vape pen and blowing it out toward the sky. "We gonna do this thing or not?"

Jax is smiling. Daniel audibly gulps.

"Oh, come on, don't tell me you're all scared," she says.

"I'm not scared," Jax says. He rushes out of the pool to grab a towel, then stands next to Juniper with his arms at his sides. "You all don't mind if I film it, do you?"

"Of course not. I am in full support of your famous film career," I say, trying to act relaxed. It's hard not to be curious about the shadows that lurk in that house.

"You sure you want to do this?" Daniel asks, turning toward me.

"Yeah, it's cool." I give a blasé shrug for effect. "I don't even believe in that stuff." Really, I do—a little bit, anyway. I mean, I'd never seen anything before we moved here. I'm not even sure what I have seen. What happened in Nadine's house the other night is all foggy now.

Grandma always claimed her childhood home was haunted and warned me about this stuff. When she caught Mom and Becca with a Ouija board as teenagers, she grounded them and threw it in the garbage.

"Well, you should," Juniper says. "That house has bad vibes, and I've seen these things before. Ginny says it's bullshit, but I know she believes it, too. She's got this room upstairs full of books on the occult and shit—black candles, herbs, crystals, the whole nine yards. I took these to help us tonight." She pulls six black candles and a Ouija board out of her backpack.

"I gotta get dressed and grab my camera!" Jax runs into the house.

"I like him!" Juniper says.

I let my mouth bob below the surface of the water and stare over at the other house, drenched in darkness. Maybe we can help Krysten rest at last.

The sliding glass door opens smoothly. It's pitch-black inside, but Jax uses his cell phone flashlight to illuminate the room.

"What time are Ben and your mom supposed to be back?" Daniel asks.

"They said not to expect them until at least midnight." I rub my hands together nervously.

"Good," Juniper says.

She leads the way like Hannah would if she were here. The bottoms of her butt cheeks stick out of her daisy dukes, and I catch Jax staring at her—infatuated, like she's some nymph.

"Do you know, like, where she died? Or, like, have you guys seen her anywhere?" Juniper asks. The bracelets on her wrists jingle as she struts, the only sound in the house besides our breaths and light footsteps.

"Woah, when did all this sand get in here?" Jax asks. There's sand piled in the corners of the room, like dust or cobwebs would be. We all follow Juniper toward the hall.

"I don't know," I reply.

"Was it in here when Jare—ow!" Jax wails as I punch him square in the shoulder.

"Shut up," I whisper into his ear. "I don't want them to know anything."

"Alright. Jeez ... the sand thing is weird, huh?"

"Yeah," I say, turning my head back to the kitchen counters we cowered behind. "Weird."

Juniper opens a door in the hallway, and, like worker bees, we follow.

"Ew!" Juniper shouts. "Look, all the furniture is draped in cloth. This is seriously sick."

"Isn't that what you wanted, Juniper?" Daniel locks eyes with me and smiles.

Just as I return the gesture, a door slams somewhere down the hall, clapping so loudly that it shakes the wall. I jump, gripping Daniel's arm.

"I think the spirits know we're here," Juniper says.

"Holy crap. I gotta get my camera rolling." Jax pulls the video camera close to his face, his hands shaking as he turns it on. The little red recording light glares at me. "Emma." His voice cracks. "Describe what happened."

"Umm, a door slammed in this creepy ass house, and I'm thinking this was a terrible idea."

A wave of heat moves through the room from the hallway, thick and humid.

"She's ready to communicate," Juniper says. She leads us back to the open area of the house, and walks around looking at the floor until she settles on one particular spot between the dining room and the kitchen area.

"I think this is where she died. That's what Ginny said back then. She bled out here," Juniper says.

My stomach sours thinking of someone dying here. Krysten, bleeding out on the floor alone, listening to the same sounds we are right now, the waves coming in and out repeatedly while she faded away, unable to get help.

"Daniel, grab the cloth from my bag," Juniper orders, taking a big breath in and stretching like she's about to start a yoga class.

Daniel does as she asks and grabs a black muslin fabric with symbols printed all over it. He lays it down directly in front of her.

My eyes scan the room as I listen hard for any more sounds. Everything seems to be back to normal, except for the air growing hotter by the minute. As Juniper finishes her last stretch, she bends down toward her bag. Her movements are smooth, like a dancer's. She sits down legs crossed and places the Ouija board directly in the front of her.

The board is different from any I've seen before, as it's made of solid wood with letters etched into it, flooded with crisp black paint. Juniper reaches back into her bag and pulls out a triangular white planchette.

"What's that?" Jax asks.

"This is how we're going to communicate with the dead. This planchette has been in the family for years, Ginny says. It's made of real bone." She's beaming with excitement.

My chest is heavy as dread pulses through my body. Daniel sits next to Juniper as she lays out six black candles around the board. Jax sits down on the other side of her, and they all stare at me.

"Are you scared, Emma?" Juniper asks. "Don't be. Ginny showed me how to do this so that no evil spirits can come in. We have to say goodbye at the end. That's very important, or we'll leave a gateway open for them."

Sweat rolls down my neck; the heat has reached a smothering level.

"Them?" Daniel asks.

"The spirits, silly," Juniper says.

"Oh, of course," Daniel says sarcastically. "The spirits ... Emma, if you don't want to do this, we don't have to."

"No. I mean ..." I know full well that I don't want to do this, but I don't know what else to do. I feel like I've completely fucked things up with my family. I don't want to screw everything up with these new friends, too. "I don't care. It's fine. It's just a game anyway, right? Anyone else hot? I'm going to crack a window first." I go to the closest window and shove it open.

What we're doing is pretending that nothing will happen. This isn't real.

"Emma," Juniper calls.

"Yeah, sorry." I take my seat next to Daniel at the board. Juniper lights the candles one by one. She sits cross-legged and settles herself a deep breath before opening her eyes.

"Spirits, we are here to communicate with the women who died too soon. Krysten, who died right here, and poor cousin Annabelle, who slit her own throat. We only want to talk to you. We are friends and want to learn what you have to teach us. Everyone go ahead and put two fingers lightly on the planchette, and do not remove your hands until it is all over and we say goodbye."

My fingers graze the planchette. I expected it to be cold, but it's warm.

"Do the spirits have anything to say to us tonight?"

We wait in silence for a few moments.

"Emma, you ask. You're the closest to the spirits," Juniper says.

"I don't know her at all."

"You're living with Ben, so maybe—" Daniel says, but immediately gets quiet.

A vibration erupts beneath my fingers, and our eyes are fixed on the planchette as it glides shakily to the top left side of the board and stops over the word yes.

"You guys are moving it, aren't you?" I say because this shit doesn't work. Right?

"I swear to God, I didn't move it," Jax says.

I don't think Daniel would move it, but I don't trust Juniper.

"Thank you, spirit, for answering us. Who is moving the planchette?" Juniper asks.

My fingers are barely touching it. It slides easily across the board, stopping at each letter.

K

R

Y

S

T

E

N

"Krysten. We know you died here, and it must be hard to be stuck in this house. Is there anything you need to tell us about how you died?" Juniper asks.

A breeze moves through the room. The planchette is still hot beneath my fingertips, but I can see my breath for a second, and the sweat that's drenched my shirt is freezing.

Is it really Krysten talking to us?

The candle flames bend to the side.

B

A

B

Y

My stomach turns, and the sweat cools over me, drenching me in musk.

"The baby?" Daniel asks.

"Mom said she died on the floor during childbirth," I say.

The planchette moves quickly to the top right of the board—tugging at my fingers.

This can't be happening.

NO

"What do you mean, Krysten? What are you trying to tell us?" Juniper asks. Jax gulps, and even in the dim light, I can see he's gone pale. The planchette begins to move again, quicker than before, jerking back and forth between the letters.

A

L

I

V

E

2

2

2

2

A candle blows out, and my stomach drops—my mouth is a desert. My heart is about to erupt from my chest.

Then, the planchette stops moving.

"What does that mean?" I ask.

"I don't know. Sometimes the spirits get confused," Juniper says.

As if in response to Juniper, the planchette moves again.

B

A

B

I

E

S

"There were two babies? I didn't think there were twins," I say, trying to make sense of the revelation. The planchette moves again quickly, and a draft cools the room.

S

My breath quickens.

A

My heart drops.

M

Mom.

"What about my mom? What is it?!" I shout.

Jax holds his breath, and Juniper turns green. The room is so still, so quiet, I can't even hear the waves outside. I try really hard, but it's like my head is in a bubble.

Suddenly, the planchette tugs my fingers. I try to pull away, but I can't. I turn to Jax, his eyes growing wide like full moons, and then back down at the board.

D

I

E

D

I

E

P

I

E

P

I

E

I want to scream—the doors in the hall to my back slam.

P

I

E

D

I

E

I try to pull my hands away, but they won't move.

The planchette just keeps going in this loop. The doors down the hallway slam. It shakes the whole house.

D

O

N

T

"Make it stop!" Jax shouts.

"I can't," I cry.

D

O

N

T

E

A

T

I try to move my legs, but they're dead weight.

S

A

M

S

A

M

D

I

E

Tears stream down his face, and I realize they're falling down mine, too. They're so cold; I'm crying ice.

P

I

E

D

I

E

"We have to get it to goodbye," Daniel says.

The planchette is like a hot pan out of the stove, the skin of my fingers blisters.

D

I

E

S

A

M

The lights turn on in the room. They glow bright. There's no electricity to the house. The lights shouldn't be on, and they're glowing red like blood.

"Push it to goodbye!" I shout.

The back door flings open. The planchette flies from the board across the room, and the scream that was dying to get out finally escapes my grasp.

Don't Eat The Pie—Sam

July 1

*D*ON'T EAT THE PIE.

    I can't get those silly little words out of my head. That and the image of Annabelle with the pie knife. Her stabbing at the skin. The eruption of blood like tart strawberry sauce from her neck.

I need to perfect this recipe; it's stupid, but I feel like if I can impress Nadine, maybe she and everyone else in town can forget about all the trouble I brought with me. Flour, butter, and egg are caked beneath my nails. The sensation is something that I can hold onto, a feeling that I don't despise, unlike the one dancing in my stomach, left over from facing Ben on Friday night when we found Emma and her friends.

He thinks I don't notice the look on his face or, rather, that fades from his face when he sees that house. It's an unabashed expression of disappointment and grief. Our histories, the ones that we have both tried to move on from, have come back to bite us in the ass.

I can't stop reliving the moment I saw Emma's face. The look of pure terror—not from us finding her at Krysten's house and not from being caught—but from the damn Ouija board.

The words won't go away.

Don't eat the pie.

"How much time is left on the pie?" Ben asks from across the kitchen, flashing a smile. "Um ..." I check my watch and wipe the hair from my face. "Twenty minutes, give or take. What?"

"Oh, nothing." He chuckles, approaches me, licks his thumb, and wipes flour from my cheek. "You are perfectly adorable."

"I am, huh?"

"You are." He leans down and kisses me. His lips melt into mine like he means it. Maybe all is not lost.

"Love birds, you about ready to go?" Nadine asks as she walks into the kitchen with her cane. She's been having to use it more the last few days. The stress of Jared's presence must've set her back.

"Just about," I reply, straightening my apron.

"You have to try Ginny's apple custard pie. It's the best there is, but don't you dare tell her so. I want to win the damn ribbon this year." Nadine winks at me. "We take great pride in our pies here, Sam."

"Oh, I get it. I love stuff like this. We attended the county fair most years growing up. My parents loved it. We had a neighbor who used to enter the pie contest every year—"

"I say this," Nadine interrupts me, almost like she hadn't heard me speaking at all. "Because there will be a few pies there that you may not recognize, and they might not look all that appetizing, but you must try a bite anyway. Ben tried to get out of it one year, and how'd that go?"

"It went like Mrs. Rosie not speaking to me for two years," Ben says, starting on the pile of bowls in the sink.

"Alright. So, eat the pie. Got it," I say, nodding. The energy in the room shifts as Becca walks in, radiant. She's wearing one of those faux-1950s dresses, green and sleeveless, with a Peter Pan collar. She can

121

pull off anything. Looking down at my apron, I realize I'm still in my yoga pants and tank, not dressed for the occasion. "Shoot, I gotta get dressed."

"Yeah, you do," Becca says, pushing me out of the kitchen. "I'll take the pie out when it's done. You go get made up pretty."

I run upstairs and glance down the hall toward the kids' room. Emma and Jax are grounded. They won't be attending the soirée. I hate to do any of it, but a fucking séance? They pushed it too far. Although, since they did it, I've stopped waking up so much in the night, and nothing's happened at the other house. I just have constant guilt and those damn words on repeat.

I should talk to them before we go. I push my head through the door.

"Hey guys, we're getting ready to leave," I say to my teenage prisoners.

"I'm really sorry again, Aunt Sam," Jax says, looking up from his book. Their devices were officially confiscated, including Jax's camcorder, on Becca's insistence, though I found that a little over the top.

"I know. I forgive you guys, but you have to have consequences."

"When we did the Ouija board—I think it was trying to warn you." Emma turns to me, almost pleading. "I don't think you should go."

"I don't want to talk about what the *board* said." My face flushes with heat, and my nerves instantly jag.

"What if something bad happens?"

"Something bad did happen. Lots of bad things happen. I don't believe in Ouija boards. It was probably Juniper and Daniel trying to freak you guys out," I say, dismissing her.

"It wasn't," Jax says. "Seriously, Aunt Sam."

"Okay, then you're saying there's the ghost of a dead woman trying to communicate with you? Even if that were so, the dead don't get to dictate the lives of the living. I'm not going to change my life based on a game that a bunch of drunk teenagers—"

"We weren't drinking!" Emma says.

"So, there are killer pies at the contest, huh?"

"I'm not joking. I don't care if you're mad at me or never forgive me. I don't think you should go. It was real. It said your name." The colored pencil is shaking in her hand, she's trembling, looking up at me like a scared sliver of a girl whose mom is going to leave and never come home.

I kneel beside her on the floor, my Emma who's been so badly hurt, who is so mixed up because of the choices I made. She turns to me, and I throw my arm around her shoulder and squeeze her in tight.

"I am not scared of going to this pie contest, but I believe *you* are really scared. What you did the other night was—"

"But—" Emma tries to interrupt.

"No. Listen. You did something scary and upsetting. You shouldn't mess with that stuff. If you believe it happened like you say you do, I want you to talk to Grandma about Ouija boards, because she thinks they speak to demons and they trick you. So, this is just a big trick then, right?"

"I don't think it's a trick."

"I'm going. I can take care of myself. I love you guys. We'll be back soon."

I kiss Emma on the top of her head and smell her hair, like when she was really young.

I don't believe in ghosts, and yet, when I go back into the hallway, I can't help but glance at the house next door—into the darkness of the windows—searching for a sign that someone is actually there.

123

The pie-eating competition is held annually at the doctor's house. His home, the oldest on the island by at least a hundred years, is also the largest. It's the home with the winding gardens that Becca, and I saw on the way to the beach the other day. Inside, the architecture is that of something you'd see at a debutante ball in Savannah, Georgia.

The entryway is two stories tall with a winding staircase made of shiny walnut wood, leading to a balcony overlooking the room below. The wallpaper is illustrated with scenes of women lunching on a blanket in a park, varying shades of blue set against a cream-colored background. Wisps of smoke linger in the air.

"Oh, my word, is this Samantha?" A slender older man with a graceful stride makes his way over to us. His gray eyes are dull, doll-like, the complete opposite of his eccentric suit and patterned bowtie. "My boy, you've done well for yourself, haven't you?" he says, slapping Ben's shoulder with a high-pitched chuckle.

"You don't know the half of it," Ben says, winking at him and pulling me to his side.

"Yes, I'm Sam," I say, holding my hand out for a shake, but he turns my palm to the ground and brings my hand to his lips. They're moist and wrinkly on my skin like fingers submerged in water for too long.

"I'm Dr. Drear, but you call me Richard. No formalities with family." *Family.*

Am I really a part of this strange family? Ben is my family. These people accept me, are more happy to see me than Jared's family had ever been.

"Alright, Richard," a woman says, approaching. She's blonde with curls so large they frame her face, ornate and round. She's dressed in a deep yellow, A-line dress with a floral print and red pumps to match her bright lipstick. "Don't overwhelm our new girl." She speaks with that transatlantic accent old Hollywood actress used to have. "I'm Richard's wife, Eloise. It's great to meet you, love. Come on in; we've got gin fizzies at the bar if you'd like to partake."

"Oh, thank you," I say.

Her skin is impossibly flawless, and she can't be a day over forty. Richard is old and southern, overbearing, and Eloise is so poised and warm. They don't fit together at all. Becca walks over to my side, holding the pie out in front of her. "This is Becca, my sister. She and her son are here for a summer vacation."

"Welcome, Becca. How are you two liking the island so far?"

"It's beautiful. I haven't had a vacation in so long. I'd forgotten what it's like to be anywhere but Michigan," Becca says, flashing a smile. "We are so fortunate that Nadine opened her home to us so we can enjoy everything you all have here."

"It's my pleasure. Becca and her son are just delightful," Nadine interjects, approaching from behind. "I feel so blessed to have them all here with the grandchildren."

"I'm sure there are more to come." Eloise winks at me, and my breath catches in my chest.

My fingers close harder on the pie pan I'm holding. "Where do we set the pie?" I ask, changing the subject.

"Follow me!" Eloise turns with grace, gliding across the floor in three-inch heels.

Richard stays behind with Nadine and Ben while Becca and I follow Eloise through the entry and into the great room. A fireplace dominates the center of the outer wall, with huge windows surrounding it.

Deep burgundy velvet drapes frame the windows, like blood against the creamy walls. Pie crust, nutmeg, and citrus mix in the air with the distinct smells of cigar smoke and cologne.

As we enter the room, everyone turns to look at us. It's full of elderly men I've never seen before and, Daniel, Emma's friend. He smiles and nods from the corner, drink in hand, then looks away. All the conversations die out at once, and the room grows silent aside from the background music, old-timey jazz, as they gawk at me like I'm a show pony.

Sweat breaks out on my forehead. The men's fervent stares continue unabated. Ginny grabs one man's hand, breaking his gaze, and suddenly, they're all talking to each other like normal. The noise of the party is back on track.

"Right in here," Eloise says, taking us back to the formal dining room. I've never seen one so big in my life. The table goes on and on. It appears to seat twenty-four people, fit for a royal banquet, and it's lined on both sides with pies of all shapes and sizes, some with crumble tops, some with burnt sugary syrup leaking out the sides. Every pattern and variation of lattice adorns them. One pie in particular catches my eye. *Ginny's pie*. The label suggests as much, and it's full of fruity custard with a golden-brown lattice around the rim that resembles braided serpents.

Becca and I set our pies down next to each other like the last two pieces of a puzzle. Our perfectly penned names stare up at us. A pie knife lays beside every pie. They look identical to the one Annabelle shoved into her throat at the beach.

"Now, go grab yourselves a drink and mingle," Eloise says. I try to forget the image of Annabelle's suicide and just be in the moment. She takes my hand and one of Becca's, pulling us closer to her. She smells like cherries and chocolate. "You two are new to this. I'll give you a hint: cocktails help the pie go down. One before and one after. Start with a gin and end the night with bourbon, and you'll be floating home, alright?"

"Thanks, Eloise," I say as she releases her gentle grasp.

"I'm so happy you're here. You're going to make everyone's lives better for being here, for being with Ben," she says. A little tear forms in her eye. She must be thinking of Krysten. I wonder if they were friends.

When she's left the room, Becca turns to me.

"She's nice, but what was with all those men?" she says under her breath. "The way they stared—strange."

"I thought I was crazy. That was weird, right?"

I'm standing opposite the longest conga line of pies in the universe.

"We're supposed to try every single one?" Becca asks.

"It's tradition." I sigh, patting my stomach and readying myself for an awkward night.

Eloise said there were drinks—that wouldn't hurt my appetite or my anxiety. I unclench my jaw.

"You coming?" Becca looks back from the doorway on the other side of the room. "Are you alright?"

"Yeah, fine," I say, stepping back toward the room crowded with men and cigar smoke.

We're Breaking Out—Emma

J ax is lying back on the bed, playing with his plastic knife, stabbing himself in the hand repeatedly. "What are we supposed to do, Emma? We're grounded."

He's not wrong, but I also can't help but imagine the toy falling directly on his face and getting him to wake up to the fact that being grounded doesn't matter right now.

"Grounded is just a word," I say.

"So is pie," he says.

"Seriously? You saw it. You saw the whole thing happen."

"I don't know what I saw."

"The videotape. We should watch it. We need to see it again; maybe it will make more sense."

"Did you ever think we were just having one of those weird mass hallucinations? Or that Juniper was doing the whole thing?"

"I thought she was at first, too, but how could she have been? How could she have made the doors slam and stuff?"

Jax drops the plastic blade and sits up. "My mom took the camera."

"We'll take it back then! We're already grounded, and you're leaving next week. Something happened in that room, and what it said about my mom ... we have to figure it out. I can't let her get hurt again."

Jax sits for a few moments, silent, mulling things over in his head.

"Fine. Let's do it. Let's watch the video. Maybe we'll see it was all rigged or something and then you can chill out about it."

"Thank you."

I walk out to the hallway, purposefully avoiding looking back at the window behind me, facing that house, and walk straight into Becca's room. Jax is a good kid; Becca knows he won't just take his stuff back. She hasn't even tried to hide the video camera. I grab it off her dresser and take it back into our room, flopping down beside him on the bed.

He grabs the camera and presses a few buttons.

"What are you doing?" I ask, fidgeting with the hem of my shirt.

"Replaying it, hold your horses," he says.

Finally, he starts the playback. I lean in, our cheeks pressed against one another's, the room dark aside from the light from the little monitor. We watch in silence. I listen to myself describing what just happened: the door slammed. Then we're back in the main room. I watch myself, the last to sit down in the circle. I'm waiting, anticipating, hoping that some clear string or an unseen friend of Juniper's hiding in the background gets picked up on the camera. There's nothing, then the Ouija board starts to move, and the candles flicker around. We watch—

"Pause it. Jax, pause it!"

"Okay, you don't have to yell."

"Go back!"

"To when?" He rewinds too far.

"Right there, press play and watch, something moves."

"All kinds of stuff moved."

On the little video screen, right in the corner, there's a view of the room where the door slammed shut to. That door opens, and then a figure with long dark hair walks through the door and closes it again.

"Did you see?"

Jax's mouth is wide open. "What was that?"

"Rewind it, watch it again. Can you zoom in?"

Jax is frozen.

"Jax, c'mon!" I say, shaking him a bit.

"I'm going to put it on the TV." He shakes as he gets up and rummages through his duffle bag, pulling out a few cords and running down to the living room. I follow right behind him.

When it's booted up on the large flatscreen, he presses play, and we watch the whole video again. Juniper was weird as hell, and then things began to happen. We're both inches from the huge screen like children when we see it. I gasp and press my finger to the television.

"There."

"Uh-huh," Jax says, nodding.

"She's ... rewind a little and play again."

He does, and right there on the screen is a woman with dark brown hair, going into the room but first turning back. Her spindly finger motions for all of us at the séance to follow. She has no eyes, no face. There is no doubt inside my quaking body that it's Krysten, that she's looking right at me, and that she needs me to see what's inside that room.

"This is crazy. We're going to be in so much trouble," Jax says as we round the brick path toward the house next door. We nearly trip on the overgrown vines in our hurry.

"That window should be open," I say, heading to the kitchen. After everything that's gone down, I don't care what happens to me. I can be grounded for life. I need to know what she's trying to tell us about how to protect mom."

I scratch my stomach as I pull myself through the window. I lower myself face first in the room, then turn to Jax.

"You don't have to come in," I say. "If we get caught, I'll tell them it was all my fault and I forced you."

"I'll stay outside so that I can keep watch."

I know he was lying, and really, he is scared as hell, not about us getting in trouble, but about being back in the house where Krysten died. I mean, I am too, but that's not going to stop me.

"Thank you."

"Be careful."

"I will." I give a false nod of reassurance. Everything in me feels like it's on fire being back in here. I pull the flashlight I snagged from the closet at Nadine's out of my pocket and head to the doorway I don't want to go into—the one that I saw Krysten in on the video.

The closer I inch, the colder it gets. My hot breath hangs in the air.

The left end of the hallway leads to a bathroom, an office, and the front door. At the very end of the hall is a mahogany cabinet, a commanding piece of furniture. Sweat forms on my palms despite the cold.

I've got to get into that room. The door is shut, its shiny metal knob mocking me.

Just turn the damn doorknob. Protect Mom.

I turn it. My saliva is thick as I attempt to swallow. White cloth drapes over shapes in the room, like in a freaky horror movie. I swear one just moved.

It could be a chair. It could be a person. It could be a demon. The room smells like a cold January afternoon. One of those days where there is no hope of heat from the sun, only frost that makes you wonder if eyes can actually freeze, then crack and shatter.

"Everything okay?" Jax yells from outside. I jump out of my skin, bumping into one of the monsters—*chairs*.

I force myself to return to my body, taking heaping glacial breaths and leaning my head out the doorway.

"Fine!" I shout to Jax.

The chest of drawers at the end of the hall is still staring at me, so I duck my head back into the room. The chair across the room is now naked of its sheet. I gasp, the air frigid and sharp as it hits my lungs.

The chair squeals across the floor, hurling at me, coming to a stop a foot in front of me.

What.

The.

Fuck.

What the hell do I do? Sit on it? What does she want?

I shine the flashlight on the chair, casting long, fingerlike shadows over the room. The upholstery is floral velvet, beautiful aside from a tear in the seat cushion. As I move closer, something in the air shifts like someone just walked right next to me. An orange scent wafts over me.

Something deep in my stomach stirs, a sick ache to find out what's inside the dark tear in the fabric. My finger presses through the smooth velvet to the stuffing inside. I search in every direction, but I don't feel anything. I tear the cushion more, and the ripping breaks the silence of the room. I tug and split it down toward the wood base of the chair. Despite my fear, my instincts, I stick my whole hand in, this time feeling around the stuffing for something, anything.

I saw her motion us in here on the video and saw the planchette move that night. I know I did. There has to be something, or I'm just crazy and ruining everything like I did with Jared.

The tip of my pointer finger brushes something cold and metal. I'm not crazy. I grasp at it, digging my hand deeper when it nearly slips away. I pull it out. A silver key.

I turn to head straight to the chest of drawers that wouldn't stop staring at me. When I reach the hall, it's gone. There's just a paneled wall now. *What the hell?*

I am going insane, aren't I? I'm going nuts. Mom said when you're under too much stress, anything can happen.

I run my hands over the cool wall. I spin around and slam my back into it, letting out a breath of frustration. I slide down until I'm seated on the floor. Then, the faintest sound of music drifts through the wall behind me. I press my ear to listen.

"Emma!" Jax yells.

This kid is going to kill me.

"What the hell is it?" I shout from the hallway.

"Are you in the kitchen?"

"No!"

"Someone's in the kitchen."

Shit.

Moving back up the wall, I shove the key into my pocket. I tiptoe back toward the kitchen. Please let the room be empty.

No one's there, but the faucet is running. A steady drip begins beneath the sink. I open the cabinet and flash the light inside. As I'm about to close the door, something catches in my peripheral vision. There's writing on the right side of the old cabinet, behind the cleaners and washcloths.

SOMETHING IN THE PIE. THEY WANT THE BABY. WITCHES.

DINNER AND A SHOW—SAM

S he wasn't lying; the drinks do help.

I empty the last drips of a fizzy gin sour onto my tongue, and they trickle down my throat. Tonight, I'm Fun Sam, not Worried, Traumatized, Broken Sam.

The wrinkled women swoon over their aging male counterparts, laughing at every joke. Their heeled shoes scraped against the polished wooden floor.

It'd feel reminiscent of being at a club on Friday night if the tunes they were playing weren't so dated.

We're shouting at each other over the music. A man in a pink suit jacket puts another drink in my hand, and I take a huge gulp, liquid respite from the worry and responsibility.

"Oh, and then Sam actually said," Becca is laugh-yelling over the loud trombone solo of a musician who likely died half a century ago, "she goes ... that's umm, my friend grows catnip. It's for Mittens."

A roar of laughter erupts around me, and like a contagion, it takes hold of my cells and cackles billow from my mouth. Becca's crying as she's telling the story, her makeup running down her face. She nearly drops the slice of boysenberry pie she's holding.

"So, our mom," she continues between laughing bursts, "pretends to believe her, and we both ... think we've gotten away with it, but when we wake up in the morning, she's let the cat have what we think is the weed, and we both start freaking out that the cats are going to get sick. Oh, but Mom knew. She was waiting for us to say something."

Ben grabs at my shoulder for support; he's in hysterics. Nadine and Ginny are howling like wolves by the fireplace while shoveling bites of custard pie in their faces.

"You never told me that one, Sam," Ben says. "Why ... why not?"

"Oh, hush! Shhhhhhh!" The muscles of my abdomen spasm from this forever laughing. My plate is empty, and someone brings me another.

"Apple and custard, madam," the man says. He bends and bows like an emperor penguin and holds it up.

Spit flies from Richard's wrinkled mouth as he laughs at something Ben's said. The bright chandeliers slowly dim to darkness, and the wall sconces every few feet around the room glow, making the room reddish-orange. It's like we're inside a giant peach.

"Drinks!" Nadine shouts. Ginny grabs her around the waist, and a man swiftly appears to take the empty dish from her hand. Another man, in a pink tuxedo, flies past a crowd of old folks toasting.

Ginny grabs him to join her in a hug before he can move away. His eyes meet mine, and they're deep and black, like looking into the bottom of a well. As he breaks his gaze with me, relief floods my chest and cheeks. His eyes are so deep I nearly got stuck in them.

"Come back, Juan! Don't be shy!" Ginny hollers.

He ignores her and goes through a panel in the wall that retracts on itself and disappears. Ginny takes a drink from the table. There's a whole new round of cocktails and rows and rows of purple fizzy drinks with little flowers resting on the edge. Ben grabs one, too.

"Sam?" he asks.

"No, thanks," I say, taking a bite of the custard apple pie. The crust on this isn't like the others. There's an inscription pressed into it. *Tudorfaest Cennestre life death.* That's odd. My mouth is filled with rich cream. At first, it's like a flan, flavors mixing on my palate like a group of dancers. The tartness of the apple hits next, overpowering the cream. I swallow it down, and once I do, there's a lingering aftertaste. I can't place it. The longer it sits on my tongue, the worse it is.

Eloise is telling Becca a story and sipping the purple cocktail when Richard sneaks up behind her and kisses her neck, staring me directly in the eyes as he does it. A shiver runs through my body.

I move my tongue around my mouth, distracted by the lingering flavor. The taste has a texture, like if you ate ground beef fat by the spoonful. It's on my teeth, down my throat. I set the plate down and grab for a cocktail, but there are hands all around taking them. I need to get one before they're all gone. Ben snatches my other hand and twirls me before I can take one, so I take a sip of his.

"I thought you said you didn't want one."

"I want to share with you."

"Look at you two lovers," Ginny says, staring at us like a cat would a mouse, her pink lipstick smeared on the bottom of her face, giving her a distorted look. The waiter in the pink suit walks by again, and he carries a tray filled with impossibly stacked pie plates. A swarm of black flies follows the stack as he whisks it away. I cough uncontrollably. There's something caught in my throat. I try to swallow, but the thick, greasy feeling won't go away.

The table of drinks is empty, and the penguin man hands me another plate of pie. It's dark raspberry with a crumbly top, the berries and butter trying to distract me from the oily, fatty taste. Cigar smoke hangs heavy in the air.

"A toast!" someone shouts from the middle of the room. I turn to look, and a young woman I've never seen before hangs off a stranger's arm. Her black strapless dress is slipping off one of her breasts, and the top of her nipple shows. I'm embarrassed for her, and the lump in my throat grows fatty and full.

I unwrap myself from Ben and shovel another piece of pie in my mouth as fast as I can to get this taste out. I take another bite and swallow it down, and before I know it, the whole pie is gone. Becca looks over at me.

"Dang Sam, I don't know how you're so hungry after all that." Her drink is empty, but a waiter quickly replaces it with a glass of champagne. Another waiter sneaks behind me and grabs my plate. I look him in the eyes, and the orange glow of the room makes his blue eyes look like they've caught ablaze. Two molten eyes turn to four.

Another waiter hands me a drink: a glass of champagne. The bubbles rush over the top of it. The last bits of the oily, greasy flavor are washed down my throat. The alcohol wraps itself around my muscles. I want Ben. I want his warmth on me. I grab his jaw and bring him in for a kiss, and his wet lips press into mine. The room empties from a bustling party to a warm, hollow peach where Ben and I can live and be happy.

His hand grazes my hip, and an electric wave moves up my body. A fire lights inside of me.

"Ben! Join us for a cigar!" Richard yells from the boys' club that's begun in the corner.

"To be continued?" Ben says. I burn inside, knowing I'll have to wait.

What's come over you? Do you want to be like that girl with her breast hanging out, on display for all to see?

No, I can't be like that. That's not me. Maybe I don't want to be me right now. My hand pulls Ben in closer, moving down his body ...

Stop it. You're drunk.

"Yeah." I nod, pulling away. "I need to use the ladies' room, anyway. Where is it, Eloise?"

Becca and Eloise turn to me, their hair disheveled like they've been dancing and sweating all night. They start to blur together, like the parts where one of them starts, and one ends don't really exist in concrete reality anymore.

"Are you alright?" Becca asks.

"I'm fine, I just—Eloise, the bathroom?" I manage to get out.

"Off the entrance, there's a hall; it's the second door on the left."

"Thanks."

Leaving the back room behind is like stepping out of a dream. *Go to the entryway with the staircase, down the hall, second door on the left she said.* I'm all alone, and I can't help but stop and admire the tile floor beneath my feet. It's hundreds, perhaps thousands, of little triangle pieces of all different colors, like a kaleidoscope. It takes my breath away, and, for some reason, the blur in my mind goes away.

A giggle comes from down the hall.

Annabelle, but it can't be. It must be someone else.

I'm going to be with her, Sam!

"Hello!" I shout.

I finish my glass of champagne and set it on a table as I make my way to the bathroom on wobbly feet. Annabelle, wearing a smocked, sheer, black dress, disappears into the second doorway on the left. *What am I doing? Chasing ghosts?*

I have to see her. The door bursts open at my push, the momentum making me stumble inside. The bathroom is empty. There are stalls made of marble, like in a great public theatre, and each of them is empty.

I can't help but laugh at my reflection in the mirror. It's not only Becca and Eloise that look like they've been dancing all night. My hair's all out of place. It needs to be tucked back in, but first, *pee*.

As my urine is leaving me at an alarmingly loud and fast pace, I hear the door swing open. I look beneath the marble patrician and see men's shoes. Black crocodile skin and a pastel pink pant leg. *Juan.*

I wipe and flush. When I open the stall door and walk back out, he's standing there, like he's been waiting for me.

"Miss. You have to listen to me."

I look to my left and my right. The champagne, drinks and pie have made my brain fuzzy. I know I should be panicking about the man following me, but my body isn't. It remains lax and warm. I force myself over to the sink to wash my hands, ignoring him.

"You have to get out of here."

I look in the mirror to see he's sweating profusely, and my body goes numb.

"I can't do this again." His voice is raspy, and tears begin to fall from his eyes. "I can't let this happen to you. Leave, and take your daughter—"

"What are you talking about?"

"Listen to me. Take your family and run. Get out of here. They aren't who you think they are."

I leave the sink running and turn to him. His eyes are huge, popping from their sockets.

"What are you talking about? Ben?" The effects of the alcohol are seeping deeper into my bones.

He grabs hold of my hands like he's pleading with me. Emma said I needed to be worried. That's impossible and, besides, I'm having so much fun here. Nadine and Eloise love me. They love Becca.

"You have to leave. Leave here now, don't go back in—"

Men bust through the door: the one that looks like a penguin, the other one with the eyes, a man with silver hair, and, at the very back of them, Richard. They grab Juan as his hands grip me harder, but I shake them off, and he's dragged out of the bathroom.

"No! You can't do this!" He screams down the hall.

Richard is the only one left standing in the doorway of the bathroom. "I'm so sorry, Samantha. He has a drug problem. We've tried to get him help and keep hiring him so he can make ends meet. I don't know what that was all about."

"What? Where did they take him?"

"Dear." Richard waltzes over to me, his elegant cadence lapsed into a drunken swerve. He throws his arm around me. His musky scent hits me in the face as he chauffeurs me out into the hall. I glance back down toward where they took Juan, and the armoire is gone. There's a dark doorway where it stood before. There's no sight of anyone. Before I know it, we're back in the main hall, where Ben stands waiting for me.

"What happened?" Ben asks.

"Someone, one of the waiters—"

"One of our staff has been having issues. I don't think he hurt Samantha, but he may have said strange things. Drugs, truly awful what they do to young people," Richard says.

"Yeah, he didn't hurt me or anything, he was trying to tell me something. Richard's right, he was probably—"

141

"You don't want to miss this entertainment. Don't let this ruin the evening, alright?" Richard insists with a hint of desperation.

He pats my back, and Ben takes my hand to lead me back into the grand room. It's different again. The lights are even dimmer, and the colors have changed. The room is tinged crimson and the tables around have been cleared away.

Velvet sofas encircle little tables which hold more drinks. Ben leads me to our own next to where Becca sits with Nadine and Ginny.

I grab a drink from the table and sit on the crushed red velvet. Ben wraps an arm around me, and I sip. The drink's color is elusive, since everything is drenched in red. The first sip makes my lips pucker; it's as sour as an underripe apple. A pair of women enter the room from the service door on the right, cloaked in black. The music changes into something ethereal—the sound so guttural it shakes my insides.

The oily taste returns, stronger. My tongue feels shriveled and old. I gulp the drink, swishing it around in my mouth before swallowing. Smoke billows from the stage area, and the air is hazy. I lean my head over on Ben's shoulder and look toward Becca; her eyes are closed.

The women move close to each other. Ben grabs my hand; I see him do this, but I can't feel it. My limb is dead weight. Tingly. Numb.

One of the women disrobes the other.

She has large pendulous breasts. Little discs cover her nipples, and her curves bounce as she carries a big silver ornament, smoke swirling around it. That must be where the haze is coming from. It smells sweet. She's beautiful.

The other woman lights a fire in a spherical metal flail. She's completely nude except for a choker. Music that you'd imagine would play at a circus or sideshow starts. My cheeks heat up, and I look slowly up toward Ben. Despite the entertainment, Ben's eyes are on me.

"You sure you're okay?" he whispers in my ear, his breath warming the side of my face. The heat from the fire in front of us sends a comforting rush through my body. I hadn't realized I was trembling, shivering a bit after what happened in the bathroom, or maybe from when Richard touched me.

I nod to Ben.

My hands and arms feel foreign to my body. Becca is out like a light, her head lolled back on the sofa.

Have they drugged us?

"They aren't who you think they are," Juan had said.

There's no way he was talking about Ben. He's out of his mind. My body relaxes deeper into the couch. The woman in front of us twirls her spherical flail. The fire makes swirling designs through the air. Ginny laughs and claps on the other end of Becca's couch.

The sweet smell has faded but leaves an lingering scent like the herb in my necklace.

My other arm still works. I grab my drink, slowly aiming it at my mouth.

Take your daughter and run.

I drink, and the taste, the smell, and the bad feelings all dissipate.

DON'T EAT THE PIE.

Ginny laughs loudly. When I turn to her, her lipstick isn't even on her lips anymore. It's like she's got two mouths.

Where did Nadine go? She's in the corner, near the service door, talking to a man.

Is that my father? No, he's dead. The man looks straight at me, but his eyes aren't there. Only black holes stare back at me, dark and smokey and frightening. I can't hear him, but his mouth's moving. He's yelling at me again, isn't he?

No.

I shake my head, shake him away. Nadine's been on the couch the whole time. There she is next to Ginny, with Ginny's hand on her knee, moving up her skirt. I'm imagining things.

Watch the show.

The fire whirls and whirls. I fall deeper and deeper into the sofa as my eyes close, and the red room turns black.

Take Me to My Mother—Emma

The sounds from inside the building echo through the night. Its height towers in

the darkness and the glowing lights from the windows make it look like a living, breathing monster, and Mom's in there, ready to be eaten. I have to stop this.

The silence of the rest of the town licks at our backs as we head up the cobbled path, past the overgrown plants and toward the growling, howling beast. I have to get to Mom and Aunt Becca. These people aren't who she thinks they are. Krysten is trying to help us, and whatever happened to her from happening to Mom and anyone else who comes to this island. Does Ben know? I go straight for the door and wiggle the handle, but it's locked.

"There has to be another way in," Jax whispers, tugging at my shorts. As we sneak

around the house, it becomes clear that all the first-floor windows are closed up tight, but the smell of cigarette smoke and incense pulse from the second-floor openings.

We reach the corner of the house, and a man's muffled voice carries over the insect orchestra outside. I put my arm out to hold Jax back and peer carefully around the corner. A man. *The* man who handed me that saint's charm has his hands held behind his back by another two guys in pink shirts with some version of a scarf around his mouth. My heart races. He's in trouble, and he helped me. Maybe I should do

something, but if we get caught, we won't be able to save Mom and Becca.

I pull back behind the wall and crouch below the windows, making my way back to the other side of the house. Jax follows until we find a trellis.

"I don't know if this is safe," Jax says, wringing his hands together.

"We have to try something. We have to give them the message. Krysten said the pie had something to do with it, right?"

"I'm scared."

"I am, too, but I'm even more afraid of what will happen if we don't try to stop this."

Jax nods.

I grip the metal trellis and thick vegetation that runs up to the second floor. My skin crawls at the idea of ants or spiders getting on me as I ascend. Ignoring the tickles, the scrapes, and the cringe factor, I finally reach the top and pull myself through the window into what appears to be a guest room. Caroline sconces illuminate a four-poster bed with black velvet bedding. Stacks of old luggage lay in the corner near a closet.

"Hey!" a loud voice calls from outside.

Shit.

"Emma," Jax says. "Help."

I pull him up quickly and lock eyes with the pink shirt below. He pulls a walkie-talkie up to his face. It is likely he's telling someone we've broken into the house.

Double shit.

"C'mon!" I say to Jax, grabbing his hand and pulling him out the guest room door. We emerge into a long hallway, and already the clicks of footsteps coming up the stairs and the distant humming of circus music make my skin crawl.

We run down the hall toward the nearest door. It's locked.

We get to the next door, and I look back as a pink shirt emerges from the staircase. My heart is pounding out of my chest. Jax opens the door, and we stumble inside. Our arms and hands struggle like quarreling snakes, trying to lock it behind us.

What the hell are we going to do now?

It locks, and we slide down and sit with our backs against the door. I raise my finger to my mouth to shush Jax, but it's so dark he probably can't even see it. The footsteps move closer to us. Did that guy see me looking at him? The thud of each step comes right to the door before they move away.

My fingers search the wall for a light switch. Flames light the room. This isn't a guest room. Chairs and couches fill the space, and an antique record player sits in the corner. Three tapestries dominate the walls.

"What now?" Jax whispers.

"I don't know," I whisper back, moving closer to the left tapestry. It depicts a group of people in the forest. Five men and women look up at a figure hovering over them. Around the kneeling figures are bodies of dead children, their bodies gaunt and starved. The hovering figure has horns on her head to crown her curved body. She holds out a pie to the kneeling people.

The next tapestry looks like a map of Camillia Island with a few houses, a garden in the middle, and a big Magnolia tree in the center.

Intricate vines line the border.

The third tapestry is the same figure as the first, the woman with the horns on her head. She's surrounded by children, all with blackened eyes. She's holding a baby to her breast.

"Emma." Jax pulls my attention toward a door. He's got his ear to it, and I do the same. Strange, ethereal music seeps in from the other side. Someone's talking, and then—loud footsteps.

Someone pulls the door open. "Emma? Jax? What are you doing here?" Daniel stares at us. Two men in pink shirts stand behind him.

"I, uh ..." I have no words, just burning cheeks and a pounding heart. "I was worried about Mom and Becca."

"We need to see them," Jax says.

"They're watching some ... adult entertainment at the moment. I can assure you they're totally fine. I was just down there with them. They were drinking, dancing, and laughing. Are you okay?"

Daniel reaches his hand out to me. I take it. "How about I take you two home?"

"I'd feel a lot better if I could see my mom," I say, trying to hold back tears of worry and embarrassment.

"Sure." Daniel looks back at the pink shirts. "We can peek in for a second, right?"

They exchange glances before bringing us downstairs. Daniel holds my hand the whole way. When we reach the doorway, the man pulls back a velvet curtain and reveals Mom sitting on a couch, snuggled up to Ben. I sigh in relief.

"See," Daniel says, "Everything is fine." He turns to the men. "Mind if I walk them back home?"

The men nod, and Daniel escorts us home. He makes small talk the whole way, and tells us about the party. Everything seems normal. I can't believe the messages were for nothing. It felt so real.

At the house, Jax goes inside, but I linger at the door with Daniel.

"Daniel?"

His warm, soft hand brushes the hair from my face. His pearly smile shines, his face aglow from the light of the moon. My heart pounds with a mix of worry over what occurred tonight and the excitement of his flesh against mine.

"Yes, Emma?"

"I saw some guy getting carted off. Did something bad happen?"

"Not that I know of. Maybe the guy got in a fight with someone... "

"Well, what was the whole thing like?"

"Weird. Everyone there besides your mom, aunt, and a handful of people were well over fifty, and there was smoke everywhere. They were all drinking. It was ... awkward, to say the least."

The breeze off the ocean cools the sweat on my skin. Daniel wraps an arm around me and pulls me closer.

We giggle. The other house catches my eye, and it's seemingly dead, when it felt so sentient just an hour earlier. So full of secrets, signs, and warnings.

"What do you think it meant? The Ouija board."

"I think Juniper might've been messing with us."

"But how?"

"You believe in witches?"

My heart skips a beat. *All of them witches.* "Do you?"

"I don't know. The women on this island are strange. Juniper is possibly the strangest person I've ever met. Sometimes, she does things, or things happen around here, that I can't explain. I've been coming here my whole life. I guess it doesn't really faze me. Does it scare you?"

Yes, it scares me, but it piques my curiosity. The moment we crossed over the bridge, something felt off about the town. Something lurks in the background, as persistent as the crashing of the waves. It's so certain and so constant, but it's almost undetectable if you don't stop and try to feel it.

"Yes," I say.

"Don't be too afraid, Emma," Daniel says. "This might be kind of odd to you, but I've been here long enough to know it's their normal."

I nod. Maybe he's right; different cultures celebrate in different ways.

"Okay?"

"Yeah," I say.

Daniel pecks my cheek and gives me the sweetest smile as he walks away.

"Be careful."

He salutes silently and saunters off into the night. I make my way, defeated, toward the back door of the house. I have to stop every few feet because I swear I can hear a heartbeat and shuffling. Something curls around my ankle, and I gasp and pull away. It's a vine. It tried to coil around me, grasp onto me like an animal. My eyes follow its tendril to a mossy, leafy, snake-like creature pulsing into the brush.

A pale face.

Glowing eyes.

I stumble back, my flesh ice cold.

Then I see what it is: a newly bloomed set of white flowers with giant yellow pistils. My mind is playing tricks on me. I need to get some sleep. I dash into the house. Instead of comfort, I'm met with the creaks and groans of the old house. Each makes me jump until I'm tucked under my sheets upstairs in bed.

Fertility—Sam

I must be asleep.

The room is quiet and red. All the people are smiling at me--Eloise, Ginny, Richard, and Nadine. Where am I? Oh, I'm on a bed or ... something. I'm lying down. A chill hits me, and my nipples become erect. I'm naked. I look around frantically for my clothes and realize Ben isn't here, but all these people are. Even the waiters are here, the penguin man and Dr ... Dr. I can't remember from the drug store.

He puts a carved wooden mask on his face. It's sculpted to look like the face of a woman, her mouth wide open in pleasure. I don't want him to see me without my clothes on. I can't move. The tiny fibers of velvet beneath me press into my skin.

Where was I before this? On the couch with Ben in the great ballroom, and there was a whole circus—with lions, elephants, and little clowns in cars.

Ginny and Nadine are staring at my body like they want to eat me. Richard comes closer, and my heart beats faster. I don't trust him. Maybe that was what the man in the Ricky Ricardo suit was talking about. Richard's holding a goblet in his hand over the top of my stomach.

A sound erupts from behind all the people, a swell of organ music. It's deep and loud and makes the room shake. He's pouring the contents of the goblet over my stomach. It warms my skin, and it's thick and viscous, like syrup. The people are all sinking down. No, I'm rising up. My body is weightless, and it feels good. I'm so close to the ceiling that I fear I'm going to hit it, be smashed into it, the shape of my body perverted and bloody like the crow on the balcony in Italy.

Oh no, I'm definitely dreaming. The ceiling is gone, and I'm floating naked above the island.

Don't worry, Sam, it's just a dream; lovely, and horrible.

The light of the moon shines on my breasts, and so many stars surround me. I've never seen them so bright before. A warmth suddenly bursts within my abdomen and spreads down my legs and up to my head.

Ecstasy.

My body lays still in the air, then the stars begin to go out one by one, and suddenly, darkness returns.

Ouch—Krysten

June, Sixteen Years Earlier

"They're so beautiful," I say to no one in particular, as no one is around—no one I can see, anyway. It's funny here, on the island—a person never really feels alone.

The petals of the rose are so intensely crimson it's like they radiate, unlike anything I've ever seen before. That's how all the flowers are here—bigger and brighter than anything I ever imagined was possible. I raise my hand and wipe the sweat from my brow. Ben should be home any minute from the market.

I rub my swollen abdomen beneath my dress—Benjamin Junior. *Only a few more months now, little Benjamin, and you'll be here right here in my arms, your sweet little face pressed to mine. I won't let anything happen to you. No, I won't, not ever.* My heart swells with love. I never thought that I could love something so much.

"*Caw.*"

"Ouch!" I gasp, my finger torn by a large thorn. Blood wells and drips down my thumb to the crease in my wrist. "Dammit."

I take my finger into my mouth, the coppery taste running over my tongue. When I take it out, it begins weeping blood again. The wound is deep.

"*Caw.*"

Is there a crow on the gutter? It's a raven—*son of bitch*. I should have worn gloves. Why didn't I? I hold my hand up, hoping to slow the bleeding. It's fast, running down my elbow and dripping, leaving little red spatters down my dress.

I'm barefooted and didn't wear gloves. Stupid girl.

I need to get to Nadine's, and quickly. We aren't well equipped over at our place yet. I don't want to go to Nadine's alone, but she's got to have something to help over there. I walk past the pool to her backdoor. This is going to be embarrassing, as she has guests over, and she invited me to join her for tea. Ginny and her niece Jen or something—

"My God, Krysten! What happened?" Nadine meets me at the back door. I look down, and she's right; I'm a mess. My thumb pulses, the pain stretching further up my arm each beat.

"I cut my thumb pruning," I say, my voice small like a mouse.

"Get in here."

"The blood ... I don't want to mess up the floors," I say.

"Oh, nonsense. I'm a mother; I know how to get a bloodstain out. Get inside."

The room is empty, so the guests must be in the other sitting room. "Thank you, Nadine."

"You sit tight, darling. Juniper!" She yells for one of the guests as she runs to the kitchen and grabs a towel. "Were you wearing the gloves I bought you?"

"No ..."

"Juniper!" she yells again. A little blonde girl with freckles walks right up to me with a smile.

"You have a lot of blood on you," she says. There's no emotion in her voice, no look of surprise or terror, more like fascination. Nadine walks back through the door with a wet kitchen cloth and a sewing kit.

"Juniper, I need you to go into the greenhouse. You remember the purple plant I showed you? The one with the pointed leaves?" Nadine asks.

"Mhmm." She nods.

"I want you to grab Mrs. Nadine five leaves and bring them to your Aunt Ginny. She'll show you what to do with them, okay?"

"Yes, Mrs. Nadine." She grins ear to ear and skips out the door toward the greenhouse.

"This needs stitches," Nadine says with a sigh.

"Oh no, I'm sure it's fine," I say, grabbing the kitchen towel from her and putting pressure on my thumb. Nadine playing nurse for me is not what I want.

"Look at how much blood you're losing. Keep the pressure on it. We'll clean it with alcohol and sew it up, then apply that salve; it'll be good as new," Nadine says, smiling. I don't remember her teeth being so yellow.

Good as new.

That's what she says to me every single day. I couldn't get out of bed the last two months, so if I hear her say it again, I'll cut her in half with the garden shears.

Jesus, Krysten, get a hold of yourself; she's only trying to help. She probably thought that herb mixture would make you good as new. Why would she try to hurt you? She wants this baby. Her baby, *or so she thinks.*

We'll leave when the baby turns three months, Ben said. He said she just needs to be around for the newborn stage, since she missed it with him. She was sick after childbirth, nearly died, and never got to experience it. Never got to nurse him. She looks like she's going to cry every time she says it.

My hand instinctively retracts to my abdomen at the thought. Maybe Ben wants to be away from her just as badly as I do. He says it's the pregnancy making me dislike her.

"Let me see it now." She pulls off the kitchen cloth, and the bleeding's slowing a little. She lays it across my lap and pours alcohol onto the wound.

"Ouch!" I shout. It stings like someone's stuck a fire poker inside of it.

"You're alright. We have to clean it, you know. Can't have you getting an infection, not with the baby."

Not with the baby—it's all she cares about. She used to be so good at pretending to care about me, but not so much anymore. She brings me smoothies every day that are so healthy it tastes like I'm drinking the lawn, and tea each night—I can't stand it.

I want to be alone with my husband; is that too much to ask? I keep telling Ben that I worry that she watches us and listens at night. I don't think it's a coincidence she didn't install a single drape or curtain in the whole damn house. We're never alone, always being watched.

"*Caw.*"

I jump, and Nadine slaps my wrist and then pulls it close to her.

"Be still."

Ensuring I keep my arm still, I crane my head. Outside of the window sits the damn raven or crow or whatever that caused this situation in the first place.

"Here you go, Mrs. Nadine," Ginny says, walking back into the room with Juniper. She holds a gray stone bowl.

"Oh, Krysten, I'm so sorry you've been hurt. Is the baby alright?"

Ginny asks. Her bright pink lipstick has the slightest smear in the same corner she always turns up when she's giving her half smiles. I've only seen her whole smile at the pie dinner. Ugh, I'm sick just thinking about it.

"The baby is fine. I've just cut my thumb."

"Didn't Nadine give you gardening gloves for your roses?" Ginny asks.

"She did. I didn't use them. I know, silly me."

Nadine rubs the ointment or remedy into the wound. Surprisingly, it tingles a bit, then numbs. "Oh no, dear, just pregnancy brain. Juniper's mother had it, too. Why, she grabbed a hot pan of cookies out of the oven with her bare hands when she was pregnant with her. Did you know that, Juniper?"

"Mommy did?" She looks up at her aunt in surprise and then giggles.

Strange thing to laugh about.

"Nadine, that made it feel a load better. Thank you."

"No worries, dear. I know I don't do things the conventional way, but these ways have been around for centuries. They work."

She's right. I only feel the slightest tug as she pushes the needle and thread into my skin. The sharp end slices through the calloused part of my thumb. It's fighting the good fight against its point, but inevitably, the skin gives way to the power of Nadine. I can't feel the pain, but a shiver runs through my body, then a wave of nausea.

"Juniper, grab her a bowl from the kitchen!" Ginny yells.

A tingling starts at the top of my head, moving down toward my eyes as Ginny comes to sit next to me. She puts an arm around me to hold me up. The stench of that terrible herb, the one in the necklace, hits me in the face. Juniper returns just in time with the bowl to catch my vomit.

"Oh dear. Did you drink all your smoothie today?" Nadine's tone is accusatory. "You know it's supposed to help with the morning sickness."

This morning, I'd taken a sip in front of her like I'm supposed to do every day, and then I put the rest down the toilet. Ben fought me about it in the beginning, saying that it was good for the baby, better than prenatal vitamins. When I stopped drinking it, Ben relented that I did look better. My pale face has shown color again, and the stomach pains that left me in the fetal position have vanished.

I retch again, and Juniper laughs, taking the bucket away.

"There," Nadine says. I look up to find I'm stitched like the Frankenstein monster. "No pruning anymore. Not until this baby is delivered. It's too much stress, do you hear me?"

"Yes."

"Now, let's get you to the guest room to lie down, and I'll bring you some of your tea."

Do That Again—Emma
July 2

The ocean laps against my legs, and I block the setting sun with my hand to see the grownups finally emerging from the house with their hangovers.

I woke up in a panic this morning, but it was quickly dispelled when I heard Ben and Becca snoring so loudly that I thought a bear had broken into Nadine's house.

"They have risen," I say, splashing Jax.

"Mom!" Jax calls out, splashing saltwater even harder at me, soaking my face.

They stumble across the beach like zombies. I almost expect the plants along the patio to trap them and wrap them up, but they saunter on. That was one heck of a party, but it's over now, and they're alive.

"My children!" Becca shouts, sounding excited, but the pace of her walk says her body can't match her energy.

I give Jax a look and stifle a giggle. He follows me up to shore.

"Some party last night, huh?" I ask.

Becca rubs her bloodshot eyes and pulls off her swimsuit cover-up.

"Yep. Can I offer you some advice, kid?" she asks. "Don't ever drink as much as we did last night."

"She's right," Ben says, approaching from behind in swim trunks.

"You sure you're up for swimming?" I ask.

Mom grabs Ben by the waist and leans into him.

"Nadine suggested it," Becca says. "Said the water here is like some kind of hangover cure. I think she's full of it." Another Nadine miracle cure. Another special thing about this island. Maybe Nadine already knows that the vines pulse in the night. Becca walks past me and straight into the water. Jax follows her.

Ben and Mom lag behind.

"You alright, Mom?"

She nods.

"How was the party?"

"Fun and a little weird," she says, "From what I can remember ..."

"But no evil pie," Ben interjects.

"Good," I say.

"Honestly," Mom goes on. "The last thing I remember was this man, clearly on some drugs, yelling at me about something in the bathroom. I remember a sparkly drink that was very tasty and then ... fire."

"Fire?" I ask.

"There were fire dancers," Ben says. "Mom and Ginny really blew it out of the water with the entertainment this year, but we should have come home." Ben places his hand on the top of my head. "Learn from our mistakes, little one. Three drink limit."

Mom laughs and then grabs my hand.

"Take me to the hangover cure, Emma."

"Alright," I say. Her hand feels soft in mine. Warm and sweaty. Like home. Mom and I float on the waves for a little while as Ben watches from the shore. Becca and Jax jump the bigger ones. Mom and I join them, laughing and lapping up the sun and the salt water. The cool ocean waves are breathing life into me, numbing the aches from the failed rescue mission last night. I let my body float with the greater buoyancy of the salt water. I relax. Mom's safe, and everything is going to be okay. My muscles melt into it, and I think back to last night, to the feeling of Daniel's hand on my face. I imagine kissing him, passionately, more than a peck. Heat rises in my chest.

Something slimy brushes against my leg. I stand in the water, searching for the fish or seaweed that could have been the cause. The cerulean water is distorted by the waves. I feel it again. Something hard and slimy brushes against my leg. Something wraps around my ankle and tugs. My stomach drops, and I scream.

"Mom! Something's in the water." I've floated away from the rest of the group. They haven't even heard me. It tugs again, making my other leg flail, and I lose my fragile grip on the ocean floor. "Help!"

My hands and arms grab desperately at the top of the water. It tugs again.

"He—"

My face plunges beneath the surface. The bubbles from my scream tickle the skin on my face as I swim as hard as I can, kicking and straining to get back to the surface. Whatever is wrapped around my ankle grips harder, so tight that it burns my skin. I open my eyes beneath the water, the salt stinging them, as I strain to make out what's at the end of my foot.

Beyond the length of my leg is swirling darkness with yellow glowing eyes. Two of the tiny moons float closer into view. Cat eye marbles set into a rotting human head. Bloated purples and grays have replaced Annabelle's pale, gentle face. Her rotten flesh has torn away. The bones of her skull are visible; barnacles grow along the alabaster bone.

Bubbles obscure the scene as a scream escapes me beneath the water. My air supply is gone. My lungs ache. Annabelle's rotten arm grips my leg harder as I kick away from her and the rest of the glowing eyes. I'm going to drown. Her nails perforate my flesh, and red drops float in the water like pollen in the spring breeze.

I kick away from her, not daring to let my gaze escape the thing trying to kill me. Her mouth cracks open like a clamshell, wider than a human mouth should ever open. Her lips split, and purple globs of flesh spurt off into the water. Her glowing eyes are fixed upon me; her repulsive hand tears my flesh and pulls my foot toward her gaping mouth, her foul teeth inches away from my flesh. Strong hands wrap under my shoulders, pulling me away from her. She's not letting up; her wide mouth is ready to consume my flesh, her eyes hungry to consume me whole. My body is being pulled in two, and I can't breathe.

The hands pull my torso above the surface. I gasp. Air fills my lungs, and I erupt in sputtering coughs, inhaling too much air too quickly.

"Emma!" Mom's voice calls from behind me. The vice grip on my ankle lets up. I scream.

"Get it away!" I gasp. "Get away!" I kick my legs as what I realize is Ben pulls me toward the shore. His grip loosens. My whole body is trembling as I try to stand. Ben keeps an arm around me as I run to the shore. When we're just past the surf zone, I collapse on the sand, still gasping for air.

"Emma, what happened?" Ben asks, panic dripping from his voice like the salt water from his skin.

"There was someone out there. I saw…" I start to cry despite myself. "I saw a woman in the water. She grabbed my ankle."

Mom, Becca, and Jax catch up and stand around me. The end of my leg and around my ankle, where I expect to see torn-up flesh and gushing blood, is perfectly intact skin. A thick, mossy green vine from the garden is wrapped around my ankle. I kick it off. Ben presses his hand to my shin.

"I'll get it off." He pulls apart the tendrils until my ankle is free. There are no marks at all. "Is this was pulled you under Emma?"

"I ..."

"Jesus, Emma," Mom says. "Are you okay?"

"These vines are crazy around here sometimes." Ben tosses the limp thing in the sand.

"Look," Becca says, pointing toward the other house. Green vines have settled into the entire deck area there. Ten times thicker than yesterday. The greenery is so dense it blocks parts of the house. "Let me check you out." Becca kneels in the sand and listens to my breathing, checks my eyes, and presses my hand to see the color. "You look okay. Did you get any water in your lungs?"

I shake my head.

"Maybe we should be careful not to swim where the vines are growing. Scout the area before we go in," Mom says. "It's clearly not safe."

"You're right," Ben says. "I'll see if I can cut some of this stuff back, away from the beach."

"You're okay now, Emma. You don't have to be afraid anymore," Mom says, patting my shoulder.

"I thought I saw someone out there," I say.

"What do you mean?" Mom asks. "Someone under the water?"

I nod.

"Sometimes those vines can really trick the eye," Ben says. "The water, too, especially when you're panicked."

"Were they in scuba gear or something?" Mom asks. "Otherwise, they'd be drowned for sure by now."

I stare into the ocean.

Mom gets down into the sand on her knees and takes my hand. "Sometimes, when we're under a lot of stress, we can see things or trick ourselves. Maybe in the panic and with all the sleep deprivation and stress ..."

"Not that we don't believe you," Becca says. "Your mom's right. It could be stress. Ben, let's go check it out just in case."

"No!" I reach toward Becca. "Don't. It's okay. I'm sure it was just my eyes playing tricks on me. I was scared."

The ocean behind them is calm. In the shimmery, sparkly blue, there is still a dark patch lurking. I don't know how to tell them about what I saw. They haven't believed anything I've said so far. Who would ever believe that a dead body had turned into an evil sea creature and tried to drown me?

If what I saw was real, I can't let any of them go near it.

Don't Touch Me—Sam
July 7 and 8

F ood poisoning. This must be food poisoning because no one else is sick. *Oh, God.*

Cool feedback from my breath on the toilet bowl hits me in the face with each heave. There is nothing left inside to come up. The smell of old, acidic waste and bleach burns my nostrils. My esophagus and stomach contort, the muscles exhausted from days perched over the toilet.

I fall back against the pedestal sink next to the toilet. The cold porcelain makes the room feel more solid. The room doesn't tilt and turn as much anymore.

"Sam, can I come in?" Becca's voice beckons me from beyond the door.

I don't say anything because, frankly, I don't have the energy. The door opens nonetheless, and my sister is on the ground with me. She checks my pulse and lifts my head to look me in the eyes. It makes the whole world go off-kilter. I lean toward the toilet and heave again.

"Okay, I'm calling it. We have to go to the doctor. Your pulse is off. You look like fucking Regan from *The Exorcist*. We have to go now. I made an appointment."

"You did what? I'm not going to that doctor!" I say.

"Nope, I found someone off the island. I'm taking you now."

"It's food poisoning," I say, but even I know my argument is getting less convincing. Every ounce of vomit that's come up has had that fucking aftertaste, the one from the pie that night, before I'd gotten dizzy and gone to the bathroom.

He warned me. That guy warned me that they'd poison me. One of those people did—probably that fucking doctor, so I'd have to go see him. I saw how he looked at me, how he touched me.

"You might be right, but it can still kill you," Becca says. "Emma's worried sick. I'm not going to let you basically die of dysentery when there's plenty of treatment for this."

Ben's muscular, hairy legs come into view. I want to reach out for his help, a bit of comfort, but I won't let myself. Something stops me. Ever since the party, I've been sick and irrationally angry at myself, Ben, and Becca, all the time. Little bursts of hateful fury pop up constantly.

"Don't touch me," I say, moving back to the toilet and steadying myself.

"Ben's going to help you get to the car, and then we're going to the doctor."

I should have known I could never trust Nadine or any of them. Ben let me get so drunk that night.

I press my eyes shut, and the world slips away again. It's all dark, but I'm on the beach; the water laps in and out—Nadine's calling me from far away.

When I open my eyes again, we're in the car. I'm lying on Becca's lap in the back, and she is stroking my hair. Ben must be driving. Emma's in the passenger seat. She's looking back at me; her eyes are puffy and red.

"Mom? Mom, are you awake? We're going to the hospital. You're going to be okay."

My lips are cracked and broken. My mouth is so dry, but the taste still lingers, that beef fat, custard pie, despite the blood from my broken skin. My eyes close.

I'm in the hospital, on a stretcher. There's blood between my legs, and my stomach is swollen, huge, with my little girl inside me. Blood is pooling around her, where Jared hit me over and over and over again. The radiating pain from my jaw where he kicked me thumps like a toxic pulse throughout my body.

"Sam."

Someone's holding my hand.

Annabelle.

Blue ooze and clotted blood rings her mouth.

"Don't touch me!"

"It's me—it's Ben. You're okay."

I blink and it is Ben. I must be hallucinating. I'm too sick. I'm going to die.

My eyes sting from the fluorescent light. The big pregnant belly is gone. They must have taken Emma out again.

"You're going to be alright," Ben says.

My lids are weighted blankets over my eyes. Emma squirms inside of me.

The whooshing noise from an ultrasound machine wakes me. I wipe my eyes. The tubes from an IV tether my arm.

"Ben? Becca?" I manage to say.

"Sam ... you're back with us," a familiar voice says.

I rub the sleep away. Dark purple marbling runs over my hands; my skin is so pale it's translucent.

"Can you hear me?" the man's voice repeats again. My vision clears. It's Richard from the pie contest. No, Dr. Richard—Dr. Richard Drear.

"Am I dreaming?" I ask, blinking away the blurriness.

Ben's next to me. Becca and Emma are in chairs at the foot of my bed.

"You're not dreaming," Ben says, lifting my hand to his mouth and pressing his lips against my frigid skin. I want to pull away, but I don't.

"You're okay?" Emma asks.

"I'm fine." My voice is so hoarse it's foreign.

"I need to ask you two to leave the room for a few minutes," Dr. Drear says, looking back at Becca and Emma.

"Why? Is something wrong?" Becca wipes tears from her face and holds Emma's hand tight.

"She's stable, but dehydrated. There's something I need to discuss with her and Ben." His soft tone wraps me like a blanket in security and warmth. What if I have cancer in my stomach, tumors growing like snakes around my intestines, constricting blood flow until I die?

Becca nods. Dr. Drear turns to us, and the warm, gooey wand presses hard into my stomach.

"I'm not going anywhere." Emma glares at Dr. Drear.

Dr. Drear laughs. "Oh, don't worry, little thing—"

"I'm not some little thing. She got sick after your stupid pie contest—the one you wouldn't let me into, remember?"

"Emma, it's okay. We'll be right outside," Becca says, taking her arm.

"Young girls and their mood swings, am I right?" Dr. Drear laughs.

The tiniest bit of anger tries to light inside of me; what right does he have to—

"Sam ... what have you been experiencing?"

I clear my throat. "I've been throwing up everything, haven't been able to keep anything down. I've been dizzy, fatigued, but restless. I'm really cold all the time. What is it? Am I dying?"

His eyes are dark, black and hollow, like holes, and the skin around them creases in smile lines as he moves the wand. Richard turns the ultrasound screen toward us, where Ben and I can see a tiny gummy bear with a flicking pulse on the screen.

"You're pregnant."

My breath comes in so quick it chokes me, catching in my throat. I hack and cough, my eyes watering. I can't be pregnant. Not again.

"She's pregnant?" Ben asks, and his grip loosens on my hand until it's gone.

Come back, Ben.

"Yes, by the size the fetus is measuring, I'd say she's pretty early on."

"How?" I say, staring at Richard, stunned. I can't look at Ben.

"I assume the old-fashioned way. Congratulations." He puts his warm hand on my arm. I don't move, but suddenly, the room's moving, wonky.

"This is a dream," I mumble to myself. Every time we've managed to be alone together on the island, we used a condom.

How could this happen?

"It's a dream come true," Richard says. A tear forms in his eye. "A true miracle for you two."

"Can we have a minute?" Ben asks as I'm trying to catch my breath.

"Of course," Richard says. "Hyperemesis gravidarum—I've got some supplements for it. Nadine should as well in her garden."

"What?" I ask.

"Hyperemesis gravidarum, it's why you've been so sick. Some women get it, but we'll get you right as rain now that we know what's going on. Did you have it with Emma?"

"Uh. No, I didn't. I didn't even have morning sickness with her. I'm sorry. I'm pregnant?"

"Yes. Oh!" He sits back down and presses a few buttons on the ultrasound machine. "Pictures. I almost forgot. I'll print these and get them right back to you."

Pictures? This early? I guess it's been a long time since Emma. While it's early, there's an odd feeling of how swollen I am.

Ben clears his throat as Richard starts toward the door.

"You are a blessing to Nadine's family, to our family. Everyone will be so overjoyed," he says, opening the door to leave.

"Richard," I say.

"Yes?"

"Don't tell Nadine," I say. "Don't tell anyone yet."

His face is stunned, and he's staring at me like I've grown a third eye.

"My dear, I'm her friend, but I'm your doctor. I took an oath to keep your secrets."

"I just ..." I choke out, trying to sound happy. "I want to tell everyone when the time is right. We ... weren't expecting this."

"Oh, yes. It's *your* good news. Don't worry about me spoiling the fun." He presses his finger to his lips and leaves the room, gently closing the door behind him. When I hear the door latch, I let out a huge breath.

"Sam." Ben's voice catches in his throat.

Tears pour from my eyes, down the sides of my cheeks. I don't want to look at Ben. I don't want to be the source of his pain. How could I let this happen?

"Look at me."

I turn my face to the side.

He tugs gently at my arm. "Look at me," he says.

I turn to face him, blinking the tears from my eyes. His are full of tears, too. The edge of his mouth turns into a smile.

"I'm okay," he says. "I'm happy."

"You're happy?"

"Yeah." He nods. What escapes him now is a tiny laugh of disbelief and relief all at once. "I didn't know. I thought it'd be different; I thought I'd feel differently after what happened, but you're not her. You're my Sam, and we made this." He moves his other hand to my abdomen.

I squirm a little and then settle. "You're not mad at me?"

He laughs and wipes at his eyes.

"Mad at you? How could I be mad at you? I'm so relieved nothing's wrong. You're my family, you and Emma and ..."

"Really?" I ask, a stinging pain rising in my chest.

"Really." He embraces me. I cradle him in my arms, my breath quick and heavy. I try to settle it, to push away my own feelings about this.

Becca and Emma come through the door.

"Mom, is everything okay? I can take it if you're not. I want to be here with you. I'm so sorry for everything." She rushes over to the bed and lays herself at my feet. My sweet little girl, the one who almost killed me—twice. Her fiery hair slithers against the white sheets of the hospital bed. Becca stands with her arms crossed in the corner.

"I think she's alright," Becca says. "Right?"

"I'm fine ..." I can't believe I'm saying this. "I'm pregnant."

"What?" Becca's face turns from concern to shock and surprise. Emma raises her head, her brow furrowed as if trying to process what she's just heard. She's not going to be an only child anymore.

Emma smiles, her eyes wide. "That's great, Mom. Ben. I'm so happy for you."

Ben rubs my stomach and nuzzles his head into my chest. I float out of my body, because I don't feel what they all feel. I'm not relieved or hopeful or happy. I don't want this—at all.

THINGS HAVE GOTTEN WORSE—EMMA
JULY 18

The plastic flamingo floaty squeaks against my skin as I reposition myself on top of it so that my stomach is pressed against it and my head hangs down. Daniel's hands rest on my shoulders. He pulls me on the floaty closer to him. Our lips meet, and electric waves course through me. My lips part, and his tongue penetrates deeper into my mouth.

Suddenly, we're covered in a wave of water. I clear my eyes to find Jax has cannonballed feet away from us in the pool. Excellent.

"That's my cue," Daniel says. "I need to get out of here anyway."

"No," I moan. Jax emerges from the depths of the pool.

"Unfortunately, yes, but I'll call you later?"

"You better."

Water drips from Daniel's lean body. He wraps himself in a towel and disappears into the house.

"Thanks for that," I say, splashing Jax.

"What? Did I miss something?" He says with a grin on his face.

My phone vibrates at the side of the pool. I paddle to the edge.

"You're going to drop it in there eventually," Jax says as he jumps into the pool, mimicking Becca.

"It's waterproof. Besides, it's Hannah. I need her. I'm dying without her."

I scrape the phone across the brick and pull it into my hand.

"I dunno. Daniel giving you mouth-to-mouth seems to be helping keep you alive," he teases, splashing water at me.

"Jax!"

"Hey, you said it's waterproof," he replies, swimming to the edge of the pool. "I'm going to check on the moms, see if they need anything."

The greenhouse behind him is back to normal, overgrown plants and all. The phone dings and vibrates in my hands.

Hannah:

> So how's it goin there? I just got back from the city pool. What are you up to?

> Oh you know, I'm making it work. Who am I kidding? I'm dying without you.

> You're probably floating around in a private pool. It's not that bad. How's your mom?

> She's worse. Well, I don't know how much worse you can get. Like she's fine, but she's got this hyper pregnancy thing where you puke constantly. The doctor says she'll be fine.

> Is she taking meds or anything?

> I don't know. They have her drinking this weird smoothie every day that Nadine makes, they say it's better for her than prenatal or something.

> Well, I'm glad she's okay now. How you doin?

> I'm fine.

> So … Do you think things there are like … okay?
> Are you safe? Also, how are things with Daniel? ;)

A whole row of crows caws from the roof of Krysten's house. More show up every day. Nadine can't stand them.

"Emma! I told you to get your phone out of the pool," Becca says.

"It's waterproof!" I shout.

"Not that kind of waterproof. Come on, dinner's ready," she says, waving me toward the house.

"I'm not hungry."

"Kid," Becca says in her best strict mom voice. "Your mom actually came down from her room today. Can you just pause the angsty teenager thing for a few hours for me, please?"

An audible sigh rushes past my lips as I make my way back to the edge of the pool. Becca throws a towel at my face.

"Dry off," she says. "I need to know you'll take care of her when I go home. I need to know you'll look out for her here, with all these people."

"Ben's here, too, you know," I reply, trying to ease her mind.

"I know," she says, lowering her voice. "He's going through his own stuff with that other house, and his last wife and well … I don't think your mom is totally off base about that pie being weird. I mean, I felt funny after that night, too."

The words itch in my mind. *They take their babies, witches.* The message from Krysten, or whoever, under the sink. I'm reminded of the key I found that day and have hidden in my suitcase upstairs.

"Okay," I say.

"Okay?" she replies, putting her hands on her hips. Her eyes are puffy and red.

"Yeah, I'm gonna step up. I'm going to help out."

She grabs my arm and pulls me closer to her. "Listen, I gave your mom the first dose of a new med today. This is what I wanted to talk to you about. I had a doctor from back home call in her prescription the other day and went to pick it up. Don't tell Ben, and don't let Nadine see it. When I leave, I need you to give it to her. They're super weird about medication here because of what happened the last time with Krysten, I guess, but it's the first time your mom actually wants to eat at the table, so I think it's working."

I nod, then go inside and upstairs to change. After getting into some clothes, I head downstairs and wait at the table.

"I'm so excited to have all my kids in the same place," Nadine says from her place at the head of the long, black dining table. She grabs Ben's hand. "Emma? Why don't you come sit next to me on the other side—here."

I take a seat just as she asks. There's a glass of wine staring up at me from the table as well as an abundance of silverware. A stranger dressed like a butler is standing in the corner.

"Hello," Mom says from her seat. Her once-bright eyes are dull and surrounded by sunken purple trenches. Her lips are cracked and pale.

She's been between the bed and the bathroom for the last two weeks, her bulbous stomach sticking out. It sits unnaturally beneath her floral ruffled dress. She's bony and bruised, as if that thing inside her is leeching out every bit of *alive* she has. I press my nail into my hand and take a deep breath to keep from crying. How can Becca and Jax leave me with this? Leave *us* like this?

"Oh, my beautiful daughter-in-law. How are you today, my dear?"

Nadine asks.

"Better," Mom says, taking a seat next to Ben across from me. Nadine's smile is the only genuine one at the table.

How can she be happy to see my mom like this?

"I am so thankful for the bounty of plants that have grown back in the ruin, despite those damn crows," Nadine says. "They'll help heal our beautiful Samantha and bring this blessing into the world," she says.

Mom smiles and nods. The butler brings plates out two by two, placing them in front of us.

"I had a special meal prepared for tonight," Nadine declares. "With Becca leaving soon and Sam finally feeling better, I know I won't have everyone here again for a while. I wanted to make it memorable."

The guy lifts a silver dome off the plate. The smell is something I'm not familiar with. It's metallic but sweet, like a spoiled fruit.

A large gray fish lays on the plate—roasted full. There's a frothy green thing to the side and a big lump of tiny black balls next to that.

I look across to Ben. His brows are raised, then he glares at Nadine for a few moments.

"Shall we say a prayer? This meal is so special because it's supposed to bring health to the baby growing inside Sam. Health and abundance to all of us."

"What are the weird black things?" Jax asks Becca under his breath, trying to be discreet.

"Those are caviar," she says.

"Caviar?" he asks.

Nadine chuckles.

"Fish eggs. They were in these fish, which is why this meal is so special, Jax," Nadine replies.

My stomach turns.

"I don't want to be rude, but we don't usually let the kids drink," Becca says, looking at the glass of wine in front of Jax.

"Oh, I'm sorry. He doesn't have to. It's tradition. It's been in my family, on this island, for ages. I don't mean to offend."

"Oh ..." Becca says. "Well ... we want to honor tradition. Jax, you can have a sip if you'd like."

"I think I might." He takes a gulp from his glass, and I do the same. We share a moment of eye contact, commiserating over the screwed-up meal we're about to eat. I press my fork through the ashen skin of the fish, separating the flesh from the bone, and take a piece into my mouth. To my surprise, it's actually delicious, so I take another bite.

"It's great, Nadine. You didn't have to go through all this trouble for me," Mom says, but her voice is unsteady. Something besides the pregnancy has to be wrong with her, right?

"Oh, honey, it's for you and for the baby. You're doing an amazing thing for all of us, carrying the next generation."

I take another bite and swallow it with another gulp of wine. Ben won't look up. Mom's smiling and taking small bites. The butler, from his corner, can't seem to keep his eyes off her.

"Try the caviar with it, Emma," Nadine says. "It's divine."

"Oh no, it's so good without it and I—"

"It makes you uncomfortable that the eggs came from the fish?"

I nod and put my fork down.

"Oh, dear, I know you're not accustomed to it. It's a delicacy. It's just so common for us to eat like this that I never think twice about it. All around, people no longer eat meat, leaving behind their traditions. I get it, you know. When I was around your age, I got it in my head that I should leave this island, live a modern life, go to Hollywood and become an actress and have a beautiful family. You know what? That didn't give me what I wanted, and the island and all the ancient things that have been around forever brought me home, back here, where I belong. When Ben's father passed, I realized that I had made a huge mistake. I could have been fruitful here, but instead, I went out there. I had my Ben, but I lost a lot, too." She scoops a huge pile of caviar onto a piece of fish and swallows it. Sweat forms on Ben's brow, and he looks like he's practically steaming. What the heck is up with him?

"When you think about it, don't you believe it's better for them anyway?"

"What do you mean?" I ask.

"Humans need to eat animals, living things, for our nutrition, to live long and healthy, with vitality. Don't you think if one or the other has to go, the parents or the children, don't you think it better that they both go together? To be together always?"

"I don't ... I guess I never thought of it that way," I say, because I hadn't. Who thinks about that?

Ben's chair squeals back from his seat, his eyes fixed toward the ground.

"I'm sorry, excuse me," he says and leaves the room.

"Of course, dear." Nadine wipes a glob of food from the side of her mouth. "Jax, would you pass the salt?"

Jax passes it to Mom, and she reaches her skeletal hand across to Nadine. No one talks again until dessert is finally served. Mom takes one look at it and barfs all over the table.

Amongst the ruins of her food is a cracked molar.

Sorry, Ginny—Sam
July 19

G inny invited us over to play cards, and I couldn't say no again. I
didn't *want* to say no again. I want out of the damn house for a
few hours.

The orange, hazy sky peeks over her back fence. The fan on her back
patio offers little respite from the stagnant, sticky air surrounding us all.
Ginny was kind enough to offer me lemon water, a welcome change from
Nadine's constant teas, tinctures, and smoothies.

"She's seeing Dr. Drear," Nadine says.

Ginny's smeared lipstick catches my attention, as it's the slightest bit
off-kilter, swimming in the wrinkle that's carved down to her chin.

"Look at the girl, Nadine. She doesn't look herself," Ginny says, a tiny
bit of spit hanging on her lower lip. "I'm sorry, Sam." She does look sorry.
Ginny was the one who said I shouldn't trust the men here, and anyway,
she's right. Excluding the bulbous profusion beneath my shirt, I look like
a fucking walking skeleton, which I can't quite wrap my head around; it
all seems to be happening so fast. Am I completely losing track of time?

The fetus moves inside me like it knows I'm thinking about it.

"I want her to see someone in the city," Becca says, sipping her gin
cocktail.

"Wasn't Richard at that fancy hospital you took her to, anyway?" Nadine doesn't let Becca answer. "He was, because he's the best."

"I'm just saying that a second opinion wouldn't hurt. You don't know what she went through the first time."

I suck water up through the straw, and the cold liquid hits my stomach but won't go any further. It never feels like it goes any further. I'm always too full or too empty in there. Does the baby stop it and use it for itself—never letting me have any of it?

"Wasn't he the doctor to that poor girl who ended up miscarrying? Who ended up—"

"That's enough!" Nadine shouts, rage flaring in her eyes.

"Becca is her sister," Ginny interrupts. "Something isn't right. Look at her. You can see her insides."

They're talking about me like I'm some sick dog. It's like they're a struggling couple debating whether it's acceptable to take it to yet another vet and rack up the bills when they only live so long, anyway. Maybe they shouldn't take me to another doctor. Maybe whatever's wrong with me isn't curable. Maybe it will take *the thing growing inside me* before it takes me and let me get back to my life.

"I'm only saying—he's won awards, and he's in all the medical journals, ask anyone! He is the best in the state—in the country!" Nadine boasts.

Ginny rolls her eyes.

I wish I had a big glass of wine, like the ones Ben ordered me in Italy, to take the edge off, and make things a little more tolerable. I keep smiling when he rubs my stomach, but I bet he can tell that I don't want it.

"That might be true, but even the best don't always see everything," Becca says. "I'm a nurse. I know what I'm talking about. Something is wrong with her."

"I don't see the harm in Becca taking her for a second opinion," Ginny presses. She gets up from her seat and stacks the plates from the cookies she served earlier.

"Let me help you with that." Nadine gets up and grabs the empty glasses. She moves like a swan these days, perfectly recovered as if nothing happened to her at all. What was the use of us coming here in the first place?

When they're in the house, Becca turns to me.

"I already set up an appointment for tomorrow. With a real doctor. I don't trust this guy," she whispers to me.

I nod.

"Do you even care?"

"I don't even know what to say to that," I whisper back. Then a tiny laugh escapes me because I don't know if I care. It feels like the post-partum depression I had after Emma. Does it even matter if I wake up tomorrow? Everyone would be better off without me.

"Sam?"

"Of course, I care. I care what happens to me, but I mean, my fate is sealed, isn't it? I don't know what's wrong. The pills you got are helping. Why do we need to find something else? You and Mom were always fine with ignoring the issues back then; why do you care now? Why does it matter if Nadine is confident in Dr. Drear?"

Becca looks at me, her brows gathering in the saddest little bunch above eyes ripe with pity. I want to slap her. "Are *you* confident in Dr. Drear?"

"I don't know. What's the difference between him and anyone else?"

"Something is wrong here. Why can't you see that?"

"Because I don't know, and maybe I *don't* care," I hiss. It's like I'm watching myself say all these things, but I'm not actually in charge of any of it. "This is my fate and my burden. Who cares if this kid kills me as long as everyone else is happy? What does my happiness matter anyway? Emma would be better off with you or Ben."

Becca takes my hand in hers, warm and soft against my scaly, dry fingers.

"Look at me." She's staring at me with tears in her eyes. "Emma would not be better off without you, no matter what. If this baby is killing you, it might be best to terminate the pregnancy. No one's said it, but maybe that's what needs to happen. There could be something wrong with the fetus, and it's hurting you. That doesn't make you a bad person. Okay?"

She's looking at me with such desperation, the same way she looked at me when we were little, and I was panicked that this would be the time Daddy hurt Mom so bad she wouldn't wake up. Becca would tell me, "Everything is going to be fine," and we'd sit up in bed and play little games. She'd smile, and all the while, I'd be listening so hard for Mom's cries to know she was still alive.

"I want you to live through this. I'm scared." She pulls my scrawny hand to her face and presses her lips against the taut skin. "Mom is, too."

"You told her?"

"Yes, I told her. Wouldn't you want to know if it was Emma?"

I shrug. "I don't want to worry her. Mom and I are different than Emma and me. Mom can't even take care of herself."

"She can. She needs to be worried—we all do. In fact, the only person who isn't is Nadine. She recovered so quickly that she must not fear death at all. Ben's worried, but he won't say anything to you about it."

I know he's worried about me, but I worry about him, too. He leaves the bed at night when he thinks I'm asleep.

"Mom thinks you should go home," Becca says.

"My home is where Ben and Emma are!" I snap.

"Fine, but I'm taking you for a second opinion before I leave. Nadine is better. You don't have to stay *here*. You and Ben can go anywhere. He has the money."

It's so like Becca to make this all about me and not the fact that she really won't know what to do without me back home.

"We have an appointment tomorrow morning with a woman named Dr. Morgan. It's only about an hour's drive. We'll leave before Nadine even wakes up," she says.

"Absolutely not. I'm not leaving Ben." I cross my arms like a pissed-off toddler.

"We have to do this. You don't realize how bad you look."

She's wrong. I do realize how bad I look, but what am I supposed to do? Go against the family I *chose* and that chose me?

"Will you look at me?"

"What?" I demand. A fire wells up in me, and I want to burn her.

"We'll leave in the morning to check things out. Don't say anything to anyone. If they catch us, I'll tell them that I'm going to an appointment for myself. A bikini wax or something."

I bite my lower lip to keep from screaming *I hate you*. She needs to leave me alone. I don't know what the hell is going on with me. My stomach churns like hot oil is rolling around inside of me, igniting and burning. It's like every bit of resentment I've ever had toward anyone is suddenly pointed toward Becca, even though I love her.

She should have protected me back then. She left with Mom, but she was a kid. Now, she's trying to protect me, even if it's an overreaction.

"Fine." There's a part of me that wants to tell her how I'm feeling, but I can't. Everything I say and do right now is moving through some filter of rage. "But I'm not taking Emma. She's staying home with Ben."

Our conversation ends with the approaching footsteps of the older women.

"Let's get you girls home. It's late, and Sam needs to rest," Nadine says. I don't meet her eyes, but I *feel* her looking at me.

###

It's dark when Becca sneaks into my room and shakes my shoulder. Ben's not in bed. He's gone again to wherever he's been in the middle of the night. Hopefully, he doesn't worry when he gets back to an empty bed.

We don't make a sound as we go out the front door and get into the car. We drive in silence over the bridge out of town until Becca breaks it.

"Do you want anything to eat? I packed granola bars," Becca says, opening the compartment in the middle of our two seats.

I don't answer.

"Sam."

"I'm fine."

"You act like I'm some terrible person for doing this. You're my sister. What am I supposed to do?"

The sunrise peeks over the horizon. I press my lips tight and move them around in a circle before I answer. I'm thinking through what I'm going to say and letting anger come out anyway. "I'm a grown-up. I don't need you or anyone to take care of me."

"Is that right? Then why aren't *you* taking care of *you*?"

"I'm doing what I'm supposed to for Ben and his family."

I wish we were in Italy and this tiny thing hadn't wormed its way into our lives, but I have to have this baby and play happy pregnant wife.

"What about *your* family? Emma, Jax, me, Mom? Do we even matter to you? I know you've been trying to escape us since the moment you could walk."

"Can you blame me?" As the words drift through my lips, I instantly wish I could shove them back into my mouth and down my throat.

"You are acting the same way you did when you were pregnant with Emma. You didn't want my help then either, remember? How did that turn out?"

My nails claw into the armrest, bending back against the pressure. The pain is there, but I can barely feel it—like I'm not even in my body. I'm tingling.

"I get it. Dad was a jerk. He was the worst example of a man I've known besides Jared, but when are you going to see that we aren't him? Mom and I were there, too. We're not the enemy!"

Dad was awful, not only to Mom, but to me. There are things I hid to spare her—it's the things that my mom pretended not to notice.

"We want to help you! Mom wants to help you. I thought she was nuts too, at first, for not approving of this family, and not wanting you to marry Ben, but something isn't right. Clearly, you need our help!" Becca shouts. "I won't let you end up like that poor woman. I won't attend your funeral."

I smash my wrist against my knee, hard.

"You're so stubborn," Becca goes on.

"You weren't there," I mumble under my breath.

"What are you talking about? I was."

"You weren't there, Becca! You and Mom abandoned me to go see the grandmother that Mom supposedly hated and was evil. You two left me alone."

Becca's driving too fast.

They weren't there then, and they weren't there when I nearly lost Emma. Regret and confusion flood her face. My hands graze my stomach, and there's the strangest feeling. Though it's too early for a kick or a nudge, there's sharp movement inside.

"This is about Grandma and Mom? God, Samantha, that's no reason to treat yourself this way."

"I want to be Ben's family! I don't want to let them down."

"You can have both. What the hell has gotten into you?"

"I don't want to be in *our* family anymore." The silence in the car is deafening. Becca's pain permeates in the air. "What do you think happened when Mom wasn't there for Dad to beat up? What do you think happened?"

"What are you talking about?"

"He took every bit of anger out he had toward her on me, and I hid it from you both. Mom never even asked. She didn't want to know. I don't want her as my mom, but you're always encouraging me to reach out to her. Nadine loves me. She actually cares about me!"

"I'm sorry for what happened but abandoning us for Ben and his fucked-up family isn't the right answer!

The first time it happened was a Thursday evening. Dad walked in from work. I was scared and disappointed that it was him, and he saw it on my face. His mouth turned up in a crooked smile under the stubble of his beard. He puffed up his shoulders and wrung his hands together. I saw stars, like they say in the cartoons. Then it all went dark. The world went away, and I wasn't sad or scared anymore. I was okay with it. It would have saved me and everyone else a lot of heartache if I hadn't woken up after that.

"Sam, I found out things about this island, and about Ben's family, that don't seem right."

I thought I was going to die with Emma, too. I didn't fight against it. Not when I was on the stretcher in the hospital, feeling the pain slip away to numbness and nothing. Not when the blood was running down between my—

"Becca?" I choke out.

I pull my hand up from between my legs, and my fingers are coated in bright red.

"Oh, God. It's okay."

The tears are coming out so fast that I am having trouble breathing between sobs. My hand is dripping with blood; it's pooling beneath me. My other hand grips my stomach.

"It's going to be o—"

My head slams against the glass on the right and whips back toward Becca. Everything is shaking, like someone's come and picked our car up in the way of a little kid playing with a toy car. I clutch my stomach with one hand and push my other out in front of me, although I can't tell what's in front of me anymore.

Glass is flying and raining down on top of me, on top of us, like a million diamonds for the Steward girls, a glittering show.

Thud.

The most unnatural sound surrounds us: the screech of metal on cement. Sparks from the friction raise welts on my skin. Something new is added to the chorus, a wailing so loud it overshadows the squeal of the metal. It's Becca, and it's also the sound a person makes when their arm is being ripped from their body beneath a silver sedan.

TAKE ME AWAY—EMMA

When I wake, the house is silent and vacant, like something is missing. This house never feels empty, even when no one's home.

My fingers trace the space along my neck that Daniel pressed his mouth to yesterday. I want to disappear into him. I want to leave this mess behind--the baby, Mom's illness, all of it. Hannah reminds me what it's like to be stuck in the shitty mid-west town we'd dreamed of leaving. We fantasized about getting out together. It was never a part of the plan for me to be flung across the country with Mom's husband.

Daniel makes it tolerable and makes me forget about the rest of the stuff, but soon he'll go, too. They kept saying that we'd be moving, but that was before the baby and before Mom got so sick.

It was before the stupid pie contest.

Krysten warned us. Sometimes, I feel like I hear her more than anyone listens to me. There's something wrong, and I need to tell Mom before anyone else wakes up.

I get up and put on fresh clothes. I pull my hair up into a ponytail, grab my phone, and take the key I found in Krysten's house from yesterday's shorts. I don't know why, but I need it with me. It's almost like Krysten needs me to have it, that it's something to keep me safe, like that ...

I stop and remember the little saint charm that man gave me in the street a few weeks ago. Maybe he knew something was wrong, too. Was he trying to protect us?

I had put it in the nightstand. The brass knob beckons me, so I pull it open and look for it underneath the notebooks and colored pencils strewn about. It's not there. It's not in the next drawer full of swimming suits either. It's gone.

I'll have to ask Jax when he wakes up if he took it. I wish we could leave the island with him and Becca.

I step catlike down the hall to Mom and Ben's door. I turn the handle, careful not to make a sound. When I open it, no one's inside. The bed is empty. Before I can leave, I see something through the window. My chest tightens—someone is walking around in the house next door.

My movements are sneaky as I head out the back door to Krysten's. I cup my hands around my face and press them to the glass. It's dark inside. The sun has just begun to light up the beach. Inside, there's no flashlight or anything at all. My heartbeat steadily rises in my chest as my eyes move left to right, scanning for any sign of Mom, Ben, or even Krysten.

The hair on the back of my neck stands in warning. What if it's someone else in there? What if someone did break in this time? What if it's Jared?

I should turn around to go wake up Jax. Instead, I reach for the key—the metal is warm, heavy, *real*. Whatever is going on here, Krysten wants me to know. Fear won't hold me back.

I push the glass door open and step inside. It smells good in here, like potpourri and pine.

"Hello?" I ask to the empty room. No one answers, not even the armoire from the hallway. A cold settles into my bones; my legs move like sticks, as if the muscles are trying to seize up and hide.

My feet carry me past the spot on the floor where Krysten lay alone, bleeding to death. It's where we set up the Ouija board.

I pause when I reach the door leading to the hallway where the armoire lives. Where the armoire *lived,* I correct myself, before it disappeared into a wall. I gasp as a noise, unmistakable footsteps, sound from upstairs.

I crane my head toward the ceiling and train my ears to listen. My eyes follow along the paneled cream ceiling as creaking footsteps make their way along a clear path; someone or something is walking up there.

Krysten.

She might have something that could help my mom. I let out the breath that's been stuck in my lungs and hold tight to the key in my hand like a rosary. Something to protect me and connect me to *her.*

I move away from the hallway, back to the main room, and make my way to the steps. My hands grip the oak railing for dear life as I ascend the staircase to the top floor. It's dark, but the light pouring in from the windows illuminates a rattan chandelier hanging from the ceiling. There's a bookshelf and a reading nook with two large pastel pink wing-backed chairs. This looks like Krysten, not Nadine—not like the study downstairs. A black leather-bound book lies on the little marble topped table between the velvet chairs.

I pull the key from my pocket. The symbol on the top matches the golden symbol on the book. The footsteps start again. They're louder, more pronounced. The wood moans with every step.

I pick the book up and open it, flipping quickly through the pages. Something inside me says to stop. A quarter of the way through the book is an illustration, like the one in the mansion where they had the Pie Party. The next page has a passage on it.

Every year, she takes one.

For the special, for the chosen.

When the island awakens, when Eden overgrows.

She is ready to—

Something crashes down the hall.

My body jumps as I gasp and drop the book. The squeak of a door opening in the hall beyond this little loft makes me freeze. *Holy shit.*

A cool chill makes me shudder. A few more footsteps, careful and creeping, come down the hall. My stomach is in my throat. After a loud disembodied sigh, the scent of baby powder wafts toward me. I need to be brave, need to see Krysten, despite wanting to sprint in the opposite direction. She must need to say something. She wants to protect us. She cares about me and Mom.

There's movement in the next room. I let go of the fear and push myself forward toward Krysten. I gulp. "I'm here, Krysten," I whisper, trembling. "I'm not afraid of you."

"Emma?" Ben emerges from the closet inside the room. I scream. He's holding a stuffed blue rabbit in his hands. His eyes look tired, defeated. The air releases from my lungs.

We're in a nursery. Cardboard boxes are stacked on one side of the room. A rocker sits in the corner with a floral silk robe draped over the back of it.

"Sorry I scared you," he says.

"Are you okay?" I ask.

Ben bites his upper lip. His eyes are glossy with tears just begging to break the surface. He swallows hard and puts the rabbit down in the white wooden crib.

"I'm fine. I think. It's time to clear this stuff out," Ben says. "I was trying to do it when no one would notice. I don't want to worry your mom."

"Are you sure?"

"I can't be attached to this anymore. This loss." He wipes his eyes. "After it happened, I left, and I never wanted to come back, but I'm here again. We came here to help my mom ... but I think I had to come back here to be able to let go. I wanted to pretend it didn't happen, that being a dad wasn't something I could do or be, that it wasn't even something I wanted." He turns and looks at the crib. "But it was, and when I met your mom, and I met you ... you were going to my kid. I know you're grown, and you've got your own life, your own family. But I—"

"You're more of a dad than I've ever known."

His cheeks puff up with air, and he pushes it out. He's trying to stifle a cry. "I have to clear this out so I can mourn Krysten and the son I didn't have. Then I can embrace this life with you guys and the baby."

Ben lets out a sob and then pulls it back in. "I'm sorry. I don't want to put this on you. You've had to grow up so quickly. I hate that, but it's also made you into the coolest fucking kid, man. Your mom is so proud of you, every day. Do you know that?"

My eyes are watering, and I sniff hard. "Yeah, I know."

"I wanna sell this place. I don't want to keep it as some mausoleum next door. I want to make a home with you and Sam—a home away from all of this."

"Really?" I ask.

"I haven't wanted anything more in my life."

"Good." I laugh and wipe the tears from my eyes. "I was starting to think we'd be stuck here forever."

"No way, I wouldn't let that happen," he says. His phone rings, and he pulls it out of his pocket. "It's Lee."

How do I know that name?

"Hey, Lee. What's going on?"

The air stirs behind me, like someone passed by in the hall. I turn to see if it's Krysten or Mom coming to investigate. There's nothing there.

If Mom isn't here with Ben, where is she? I turn back to Ben, and he's leaning against the crib with one hand, mouth agape, eyes dull.

I hear through the receiver. "Ben? Ben, are you there?"

"I'm here; where are they going? What do I do now? Okay. Okay." The chill passes by me again, and I hear a door creak somewhere down the hall. "Oh, God." Ben cries out. "Alright, yeah, we're on our way. Thank you, Lee." Ben turns toward me. His eyes meet mine, but something in them that was there before is lost. "They're at Patrick Grace. Dr. Richard is on his way."

"What? Who's at Patrick Grace?"

"Your mom and Becca. Go get Jax. We need to go now."

Ben parks the car, his body shaking as we get out and start toward the hospital. Jax is crying, his hand gripping hard on mine, cutting off the circulation. He has to be as worried as I am, and I need to stay strong for him. We walk inside together, being strong, present, even though I want to leave, run back into the car, and scream.

The wallpaper is a sickly yellow with pink and green swoops. Who designs this shit? This is a hospital where people die or nearly die. Why not just paint it all black?

The woman behind the plexiglass doesn't seem to notice that we're here.

"Excuse me," Ben says. His voice is hoarse from crying.

She puts a finger up in the air and the phone rings.

"Hello," I say, waving my hand in front of the woman. "I need to see my mother, now."

"Hold on," the woman says to whoever is on the end of the line. "I'm sorry, but you're going to have to wait like everyone else."

"Ma'am, we are here to see my wife. She was rushed to the hospital after an accident. Can you please tell us where she is?"

Her brow furrows. Her eye makeup is smeared. She is probably overworked, overwhelmed, and underpaid, but this is our family.

"What'd you say her name was?"

"We're here for Rebecca and Samantha Steward," he says.

"Hmm ..." She scrolls down the list of names on her computer. "They're still in triage and haven't been assigned rooms yet."

"Are they okay?" I ask.

"I'm sorry. I can't tell you that." Her eyes widen like she knows something and she won't say.

"You can't tell us if they're alive or not?" I spit at the woman. Ben looks at me, but I don't turn to meet his gaze.

"I am not at liberty to divulge medical information, and I can't tell you how they're doing. I can only tell you they're here, and they're with very good doctors. It looks like Dr. Sedeski is working with Rebecca, and Dr. Drear has been assigned to take care of Samantha."

"Richard is a family friend. He would want us to know what's going on," Ben says. "Where is the waiting room closest to them? We'll go there, and I'll see what's going on myself."

"You go down this hall straight back, where it splits, go to the right, follow the signs for ER/Triage."

The woman picks the phone back up and starts talking.

"Thank you. C'mon." Ben puts his arm around Jax, and we set off down the hallway. Ben's demeanor changes from a wounded sheep to a wolf ready to fight.

When we get to the waiting room, Ben rushes to the receptionist, but it seems like another dead end, another gatekeeper unable to tell us what's going on. The same yellow wallpaper surrounds us, and the occasional flicker of the halogen lights make shadows dart across it every so often.

"They don't know anything yet. I'm going to text my mom and have her make some calls," he says, after taking Jax to get coffee and snacks from the vending machine.

Screw waiting around; I need to figure out what's going on right now.

"I'll be right back," I say, and Ben nods. I make my way over to the nurse's desk.

"Excuse me?" I say to the young woman working behind the plexi-glass. She greets me with a small smile. She's got fancy scrubs with Disney princesses all over them, and a gold cross dangles off her protruding collarbones. She seems sweet, and she must know what's going on with Mom and Becca.

"Oh, hi, sweetheart, aren't you just the prettiest little thang. I know this is tough ..."

"Thank you. I'm just so worried about my mom. I think I need to be alone for a few moments. Where is the ladies' room?" I fake a sniffle, as I can't let the real feeling out yet. I'm fucking terrified.

She looks left and right, then presses her hand against her face like she's going to tell me a secret. Her tone is muffled. "The public one is over there, but it's disgusting. You can come back and use this one us nurses use. Just don't tell anyone, okay?"

"Oh my, thank you so much," I say with a smile.

Her blond hair bounces in her ponytail as she slides her chair back and presses a button buzzing me in. Ben turns around to see me as I go beyond the doors.

"Oh, it's nothing, darling. I'm praying for you and your momma. It's right down there." She points to the end of the hall. There's a sign with a big arrow that says:

TRIAGE ROOM 1

"Thank you." I wipe my dry eye. I head down the hall and duck into the bathroom. I peek back out, wait for a nurse to pass, and head straight toward the triage room. Over the intercom, a woman's raspy voice calls out: *Code Blue Triage unit. Code Blue.*

We're Not in the Midwest Anymore—Emma

I keep my back pressed against the wall as I go, the ugly yellow wallpaper rubbing my shirt as I sneak from one doorway to the next. I'm trying my damnedest not to be seen but also to get there as soon as possible. I know code blue can't mean anything good. The smell of antiseptic lingers in the air. A nurse jogs down the hall but doesn't see me.

When she passes, I move back int o the open. My sneakers squeak on the laminate floor. I gasp, then look around, checking to make sure no one heard.

I might have actually pulled this off.

"You incompetent imbecile!"

A man in a white coat streaked with blood stomps into the hall from the connecting hall right below the triage sign. My breath catches in my throat. *Ugh.* I know that voice. I push myself into the nearest doorway and press my body as flush as I can to the door, hoping not to be spotted.

"You didn't think to look and see if anyone else was in the car?" Dr. Drear shouts into his phone.

I pop my head out—then quickly retract it. He's coming right toward me but, thankfully, seems too distracted to notice me. I hold my breath and pull my ribs together in my chest, trying to make myself as small and unnoticeable as humanly possible.

The footsteps stop at the doorway before the one I'm hiding in. A wave of relief floods my body.

"Nadine is going to have you exiled. You realize this, don't you?" His voice is raised, yelling at whoever is on the other end of the receiver.

He slams the door shut behind him. My heart beats heavily in my chest, and my palms are sweaty and tingly.

I tiptoe, moving closer to the door so that I can hear. He's pacing the office. A loud bang sounds off in the room like he slammed his fist on something.

"I can't help you, friend. I know you've been dedicated. I know you want this baby born just as much as any of us do, but you fucked up. You fucked up big time, and I can't save you. Besides the accident, your guy almost ruined everything that night, Harame. How could you not vet your people better? Now you pull this? I'm sorry; I can't protect you."

What the hell is going on? Isn't Harame that guy who helped Ginny? What does this have to do with Mom?

"It's not baseball; we don't have a three-strike rule. This is it: you crossed her. You jeopardized everything." I hear a loud sniff, like someone clearing their nose, and jump back for a moment. I look left and right down the hall; it's empty. "Oh, for Christ's sake, don't cry, Harame. You know who should be crying? Nadine, Ben, those poor women. No one living or dead can help you now, buddy. You'll have to face *her*."

Panic grips my chest. My mom's dead. Becca is dead. A heavy wave of nausea hits me, and my legs quiver like Jell-O.

"If I were you, I would pack all the shit from your room and never show your face here again. You know what we're capable of and what *she's* capable of."

Shit.

My body freezes momentarily, overcome by what he's saying and that he's coming out. I quickly duck back into the other doorway. My back slams into the wall. I try to slow my quickened breath. His quick footsteps fade down the hall.

The A/C fan kicks on above me, and the sweat and tears on my face turn cold. I'm going to be sick. I can't actually have heard what I heard, right? What the hell do I do? What will he do to me if he finds out I heard that?

I can't chicken out. I need to know what's going on, what happened to them. I owe her this.

I quicken my pace, heading in the direction I think he went. I wish Hannah was here. I wish we'd never moved, and I'd never tried to find my dad. A bloody footprint lies a few feet ahead of me, a red smear on the dirty vinyl floor. It's almost like it's a part of the decor, like the yellow wallpaper.

Voices resound inside the triage room, and not just nurses or doctors. I duck down below the window and check around me—there's no one behind me. Inside, I can hear them—older women singing some kind of hymn. I poke my head up enough to see inside the window. They're standing over Mom. She's got a tube down her throat.

I know them. I know their voices. I know those eyes, the ones that stood out back at Mom's wedding.

Something tugs my arm, and I scream, ducking. A woman's babylike face stares at me with understanding. It's the woman from the front desk.

"Oh dear, I thought you fell in," she says.

She gives me a small smile with a look I've gotten my whole life: sympathy.

"I ... uh," I say.

"I know you're curious about your momma. This is so hard for you, dear, but you can't go back there. There are things back there you can't ever unsee, and I tell you, you don't want that. You don't want that at all." She holds out her hand, her nails pastel pink, and I grab hold. She pulls me up. She's stronger than she looks, and we walk down the hall back to the waiting room.

Jax sits, staring down into a Styrofoam coffee cup. Ben paces back and forth.

"I'll be right with you folks." The woman gives me a wink. "Dr. Drear will be giving an update soon, okay?"

Ben and I nod, then she returns to her desk behind the glass. I run my hand over the small book still in my back pocket—the one Krysten wanted me to find. Could it have something in it to save Mom?

Ben pulls me off to the side, near the vending machine, before I can take it out to investigate further.

"Did you see anything?" he asks.

"Yeah," I say, swallowing hard. "She has like a tube down her throat."

Ben winces, stifles a sob, then composes himself.

"Okay, she's on a ventilator," he says. "Did you see anything else?"

"It was weird. There were a lot of people in there. Do your mom's friends work here?"

"What? No." Ben's eyes go back and forth as if he's missed something. "None of those women work anymore. Why?"

"They were in there with Mom. All standing around her and—"

"Benjamin?" Dr. Drear has snuck up on us. He wears a fresh, crisp white coat—no more blood. "Would you come back to my office?"

Ben nods, then looks back toward me.

"I'll be right back. I'll let you know what I find out, okay?" he says.

I stare as Dr. Drear throws his arm around Ben like they're family and walks him back to his office. Ben will tell me what's going on.

"I talked to grandma again," Jax says, approaching me. "She's on her way. Her plane leaves at two." He scratches the matted curls on the top of his head. I sit down next to him.

"You did a good job. Grandma needs to know what's going on. Maybe she'll be able to help."

"Did you see anything?" Jax asks. "Is my mom okay?"

"I ..." I don't know what to say. He's so sad and distraught. I want to tell him everything I saw, but I can't do that to him. None of that stuff matters if Becca is ... if she's ...

"Emma, did you see her?" he asks again.

His eyes have never been so desperate yet so vacant at the same time. It's like some big part of him has left and gone a million miles away, but he's sitting right here next to me. I don't know how to bring him back. Tears stream down my face.

"I didn't see her. I don't know."

His little gasps for air pull my heart into pieces, and I wrap my arms around him. The frizz of his hair presses into my wet face. I don't know what our family will look like after this.

TAKE ME WITH YOU—SAM
JULY 25

This was a very painful labor. Worse than with Emma, but at the end of it, there he is. He's the most beautiful boy I've ever seen. He looks like Ben and me, except for the eyes.

The salty air whips at my face. Emma waves at me from the end of the beach before she and Hannah dive into the ocean. I look down at his sweet little face—his cheeks are round and fat with tiny dimples on each side. This baby makes me feel whole, finally, after all this time. There's something to love me and someone who won't hurt me. Wait, no. Emma loves me.

The wind blows the reeds next to us, and the little cat tails bend sideways and tickle my shoulder. He's suckling at my breast. We've been here in this little meadow for—

No, we're on the beach. Yes, there's the ocean and sand beneath my feet, a great dune behind us. How long have we been here?

It feels like forever; we've always been here. He looks up at me and giggles. His dirty blonde curls frame his face—a beautiful cherub. The tide is low now, leaving stretches of wet sandy beach. A decorated crab scurries up toward us. It has a partner ... or ... it had a partner. It did. I know it did.

I saw them earlier together, running along, but where is it now? It's moving back and forth along the sand, leaving little scrape marks as it goes. Poor crab wandering forever in search of its partner. Oh, there it is. It died. The waves are creeping up—the tide poking at its body.

The other one is pinching it over and over, trying to wake it up. I want it to stop doing that. I put the baby down on the creamy linen blanket and go over to it.

The damn thing won't stop. I reach out to pick it up, and it finally moves away. My hand looks wrinkly. It looks like my mother's hand, the skin thin and spotted with bulging veins.

"Momma. We have to go to Daddy now."

The little boy grabs my hand and begins to pull me away from the beach. I look back at the blanket, and it's empty. There's only darkness, dark, dust-like black mold on the blanket where the baby was. Where *my* baby was.

Oh my God, where's the baby?

"I'm the baby, silly." The boy laughs, and I look at him. He's right, the same bouncy blonde curls frame his older face. Yes, of course. My son. I must have been daydreaming of the old times, the times before, but then, where's Emma?

I try to shout for her, but my voice isn't working.

"Don't worry, Momma," the little boy says.

My eyes dart to the ocean, searching for her head, her silhouette, anything.

"Don't worry! She's just fine. She's right where she's supposed to be!" Nadine yells from the distance. She's up on a dune, wearing a billowing black dress and surrounded by sweet grass. Annabelle stands next to her with an infant on her hip. A flying roach lands on my arm. I shake it and shriek.

The boy laughs. "It's just a palmetto bug, Sam."

When I look back toward the ocean, the tide is high. It wets my feet, and the boy is tugging harder at my hand. He's grown more—he looks to be eleven now.

Thunder cracks in the distance.

Deep black, sooty storm clouds roll in from the horizon toward the shore.

"Sam! Bring the baby and come up here!" Nadine calls out. Ben's next to her now. The boy's fingernails dig into my hand.

"C'mon, Momma."

I want to say I that have to find your sister, let go. I want to call for Ben, but I can't. I yank my hand away from the boy. His eyes, the ones I don't recognize, turn stony and harsh, and then he hisses at me and runs toward Nadine.

I need to find Emma. I run into the water, soaking my dress; the white crepe fabric clings to my thighs. The waves are all pushing in, toward me, and the water is rising so quickly. The sea foam is thick, and something brushes against my leg, maybe a fish, maybe seaweed. It's red.

Emma's hair.

"She's awake!"

It's Ben's voice. His soothing voice. I know it. Am I dreaming still?

"Dr. Drear! Get Dr. Drear right now!"

I press my eyes hard together. They burn like someone's poured sand from the beach at Nadine's into them while I was sleeping. I'm not in my bed. I'm not at Nadine's, and I'm not in my apartment. There's something on my face. I try to grab at it. My left arm won't move. A surge of pain slithers down my arm from my shoulder to my fingertips.

The fiery grip is like a boa strangling a man to death.

"Samantha. Oh, God. Samantha."

Mom?

I peel my eyes open to see her. I think of Emma's hair floating in the sea and want to speak. Why can't I speak?

There's a fucking tube in my mouth. I'm gagging. I squeeze my eyes shut to yell, but only a grunt comes out.

"Stay still, Sam. Someone's coming."

A nurse approaches and pulls the tube from my throat. It bruises the flesh as it's yanked from inside of me. I hack and cough. Mom's hand clasps my shoulder like an animal protecting its young. I shrug her off.

And hack and hack.

"I know, this hurts," the nurse says. "You're okay, though."

The plastic tube slaps down on something outside of my vision. Little gasps for air turn into bigger ones. Oh God, I was on an intubator. We were in an accident.

Where's Becca?

"Mom!" Emma bursts through the door. Maybe I wasn't in an accident. Maybe I dreamed it like I did about Emma and that little boy. The tubes of the IV run down my purple hand. I've been holding my stomach tightly. Something moves beneath its touch. This can't be right. I must be imagining it—it's too early.

Emma runs to the bed and lays her head down on my stomach.

"Be careful!" Nadine shouts. "Don't hurt the baby—or your mom."

I want to scream in Nadine's face to shut up. Don't tell my daughter, my child, not to run to me. The baby is alive, clearly.

I pull my hand up. I'm weak, and my arm trembles when I lift it to rest on Emma's head, in her crimson hair, her *dry* crimson hair. *She hasn't drowned. She's alive and right here.*

Becca.

"Oh, honey, your lips," Nadine says. My mouth is as dry as the Sahara fucking desert. I don't care about my lips, Nadine. "Ben, get her some water, get her some Vaseline for her lips."

Ben hops up and grabs a glass of water.

"We should wait for the doctor to examine her," the nurse says. "Excuse me, sweetie." She's asking Emma to move, but she doesn't. The nurse moves around her, pulling out a little flashlight from her pocket.

"Sam, I need you to stare straight as best you can," the nurse says.

I look straight despite how much my eyes sting.

"Good," she says. "We'll need some blood, but—"

"Samantha," Richard says as he enters the room. He's excited to see me, but what about my sister? "I'm so happy to see you're awake. Do you know what happened? Nod yes if you can, or shake your head no."

I nod despite the stiffness of my neck. Is that actually true? Do I really know what happened? We were driving ... Why were we driving? Wait, Becca wanted me to see a doctor. And then I ... we were driving. Then, I was so awful to her. She was trying to help me.

The beeps on the monitor chime in.

"Her blood pressure is rising," the nurse says. "She's hypertensive."

"Try to remain calm," Richard says.

"Is it safe to tell her?" Ben asks.

My eyes bulge, staring at Ben. He's not looking at me, but his chest is moving up and down in a way I know that something terrible happened.

I look at my stomach. They said I need to protect the baby, so it's alive, it's alive but—

"We should wait," Nadine says. "Just until we know for sure she and that baby are out of the woods."

I grab for Ben's hand, and Nadine puts her hand on my arm. I use the little strength I have to try and pull it away—to try and pull it away from *her* ...

"Don't touch her," Mom says to Nadine.

I glare at my mother. I don't want Nadine touching me, but Mom is the last person in the whole world who I want defending me.

My arm trembles, reaching for Ben. Where's Becca? What happened in the car?

That scream, the squeal of the metal against the pavement, the moment before everything went black. I was dreaming. It's not real. I was on the beach.

Ben finally sees me reaching for him and puts his hand in mine. He sits back in his seat and leans toward me. His eyes are puffy and red. I know what he's going to tell me before he does. I felt it when I woke up when I was at the beach. I felt that my sister wasn't there anymore. I want him to make it not real. I'm begging him to make it not real; if I look sad enough or if I try hard enough, it won't be real. Right? He won't annihilate me.

"Sam." He takes a deep breath. "I'm so sorry ... Becca didn't ..."

The sounds that escape me are incomprehensible, a moan so deep it seems to come from the bottom of the ocean. A burning begins in my stomach and rises to my face. The machine next to me is beeping, and Richard shrinks as Nadine presses her hand against my arm.

"Calm down, it's okay," she whispers, her voice crackling because she knows I can't. I could never. Her words mean nothing.

Mom starts crying.

I contort my body in the bed because the molten despair inside me is rolling itself and growing bigger by the moment. It's the kind that swallows people up and never lets them out again. I scream, writhe, and Emma lays on the bed with me. She holds on for dear life, trying to stop the convulsions of my misery.

I gasp for air in a world that exists without Becca, and there isn't any. Every fight, every bruise, every ounce of blood I shed that she bore witness to doesn't exist anymore.

I don't exist.

I scream.

"It's alright," Nadine says, raising her voice. "We'll get through this like we did with Krysten."

I turn to meet her gaze directly, commanding her to see me now. She's trembling. Her mascara is running down her cheeks, and her perfectly blow-dried hair is falling flat with sweat. She's looking at me like I'm a fucking creature from the depths of hell. I'm every bad choice, every bad thing, morphed into a person. I scream as my lungs heave and my throat splits. Nadine gets up from her seat and runs into the hallway. Emma holds me down. Ben wraps his arms around my shoulders.

"Careful of her bandages!" Dr. Drear shouts.

The beeps on the machines are growing louder, going off in unison, a chorus of alarms and emergency signals. Send help! The thing inside me writhes around like it wants out. I want it out.

I want out!

"Nurse, she needs to be sedated, now!" Dr. Drear orders.

"I'm sorry," Ben pleads. "I love you, Sam."

The screams don't stop. I can't let them. I need Becca to hear me, wherever she's gone.

Don't leave me!

Let me come with you!

I never knew a person could feel like this.
I need to go!
The child kicks at my sides.
I'd rather be dead.

Goodbye—Emma

"What do you mean I can't see my daughter's body?!" Grandma shouts, pointing her finger at Dr. Drear in the hospital hallway.

I've got my back to the wall, and I peek around the corner to see what's happening. A tiny gasp escapes my lips, tremors lingering from crying.

"Vera, listen, we do things a little differently here," Dr. Drear replies. "In this climate, we have to move quickly, or the body starts to ..."

"I don't care. Why don't you explain why here, in America, I can't see my own daughter's body? I don't think climate changes that."

My whole body hurts. I'm crying all the time.

"No one is saying that you can't see her," Nadine interjects. She steps between the doctor and Grandma. "She's on the island—like your mother would have wanted."

"Who the hell do you think you are!" Grandma shouts, stepping to Nadine. Her gray hair is disheveled and hangs in her face.

"I'm your daughter's mother-in-law, and I love her. I loved Becca, too. I understand that you're devastated by this loss," she says. "We were just doing our best. You weren't here for them."

A crack rings through the hall as Grandma's palm collides with Nadine's cheek. She falls into Dr. Drear.

"Hey, now!" Dr. Drear catches Nadine, steadies her on her feet, and steps in front of her.

"No, it's fine," Nadine says, smiling again. "She has a right to be upset." Nadine brushes down her dress and stands tall but a bit distant from Grandma. "Becca is on the island. She's at Richard's. His home is equipped to host a funeral. Her body was in a condition that a mother should never see."

"Was?" Grandma asks.

"She was cremated. When we couldn't get ahold of you, and Sam was unconscious, we did what we saw fit. We went according to what her grandmother would have wanted. A traditional funeral."

My great-grandmother? What would she have to do with this?

"Traditional for who?"

"You might not share our beliefs, but it was important to her."

Grandma cries out as if in agony.

"I'm sorry for you, Vera. I wish things had gone differently, back then and now," says Nadine.

Back then? What does that mean?

"I don't know exactly what happened back then, but I know your alliance with my mother and how insane the two of you acted that summer. I never wanted my daughter on your island, in your home. You've taken enough from me—I won't allow you to take any more," Grandma cries. "I'm taking my daughters home—both of them—and *my* grandchildren. You may have convinced my mother to be a part of your weird cult, but you will not take my family from me."

"You will do no such thing." Dr. Drear shakes his head. "Samantha is in no condition to go anywhere. She needs to get back to Nadine's and stay on the island until the child is born."

"No." Grandma pushes past Dr. Drear to the door to Mom's hospital room. "Becca knew something was going wrong here. Something bad. I won't dishonor her by letting you have the rest of them."

"There is no room for argument about this. She will be transferred to Nadine's home, and she will only be permitted to leave the house for an hour or two a day, or they may both die, Vera."

Grandma ignores him and goes back into Mom's room.

I duck back around the corner and head to the waiting room to meet Jax, my hands sweaty and muscles tight. If Grandma had been here before, why had she left? What had her mom and Nadine tried to do? Cult stuff?

Jax clears his throat, taking me away from the swirling thoughts running through my mind.

"Are you okay?" I ask.

"Yeah." He sighs. His face has been permanently swollen and raw since Aunt Becca died. "I just wonder what they were doing, driving out so early, anyway."

"I do, too." I collapse into the vinyl seat next to him. I'll be happy if I never have to sit in these chairs again.

Jax nods and pulls his trick knife out of his pocket. He presses it against his palm over and over again.

"Wait," I say, sitting up.

"What?"

"Listen, I heard Dr. Drear say something on the phone before Mom woke up, about how he should've checked to see about more than one person being in the car. What if they did this? I got the feeling that Becca was worried about Mom. It sounds like she might've even said something to Grandma. Grandma hates Nadine, for some reason. She said they tried to do 'cult stuff' with her a long time ago. I don't know what any of it means."

"Should we ask Grandma?"

The nurse from the hall stops and stares at us.

I press my finger to my lips and grab Jax by the arm. We head outside. A cool breeze has dissipated the thick humidity slightly. The clouds above us are gray, and palm leaves swish together in the wind.

I look around to make sure no one is there before I continue.

"I heard Grandma say that Becca was onto something, like something on the island wasn't right."

Jax shrugs his shoulders. "I mean, we've suspected that since the séance, right?"

"Exactly. My Mom keeps acting like everything is completely normal, but maybe Becca was trying to get Mom off the island. We need to see her phone."

"It got wrecked in the crash," Jax says.

"That is what they said, but what if they're lying, Jax? What if something is going on?"

"Well, we don't have the phone so ..."

"I have a plan. They're taking Mom back to the island tonight. Dr. Drear and Nadine told me earlier that Mom is going to be seen on the Island, at Nadine's or at Dr. Drear's house, so she can rest. That means we'll both be back at Nadine's tonight."

"What about Grandma?"

"I don't know, but listen. Meet me out by the beach tonight after everyone's asleep. Okay?"

Jax nods.

Nadine approaches, with Grandma at her side.

"Kids," Nadine says with wide open arms. "Your grandmother will be staying with us for a while. Isn't that great?"

Grandma stands next to Nadine, practically oozing disgust. She has to know something about Camillia Island that we don't.

Surreal—Sam
July 26

I t's three a.m. and I'm awake again, like most nights in this house that's not my home. Maybe it's because here, Nadine sleeps across the hall. The baby is sleeping; it's not moving. I know it has to be too early to feel it, but somehow, I do. Maybe it's psychosomatic.

My mom keeps trying to get me alone to talk about Nadine and their family. You'd think that for once in her life, she'd let a relationship issue go and pay attention to what's actually important. Becca is gone, and outside of Ben, Emma, and Jax, as far as I'm concerned, I have no family.

A cry escapes my mouth, and I shove my face into the pillow. I'm going insane. Sometimes, I think Becca will be down the hall. When I woke up in the hospital that morning, I could have sworn I was in *my* bed, in *my* apartment with Becca only a few blocks away, probably trying to sleep after a long shift.

She's ashes now.

Every day, for a brief second in the morning, I forget that she's gone, until I realize where I am, and what's in my stomach, alive—the thing that wasn't supposed to be here.

The light of the moon shines in through the sheer drapes covering the window. The house is silent. There are no creaks, no footsteps, and no noises from the house next door. When it's quiet like this, when it's so still, the sounds of what's happened whisper to me. They're not too loud, sometimes I can drown them out, but they creep.

Thud.

Waves.

Smash.

Shriek.

Moan.

Stop.

I rock Ben by the shoulder, my hands desperate to find some relief from the sounds, from the pain writhing inside me.

"You okay?" he asks with creaky breaths. He's exhausted, and I don't blame him. I do this more nights than not. I press my lips to his shoulder, warm against my mouth. "You sure?"

I have to feel alive again if I want to get through this. If I want to feel anything except the suffocating cloud of death.

Becca would want me to live, and so I live.

Thud.

I am the reason she's dead.

Waves.

She was driving me to a doctor.

Smash.

We were arguing.

Shriek.

Moan.

My hand traces a path down Ben's chest, wet with sweat from the muggy night, to his stomach before it takes a grip on his erect penis—and the sounds of tragedy, the sounds of this island fade away.

Ben leans into me and kisses my neck.

I'll do anything to make the sounds go away.

I cradle my stomach as I descend the staircase. My mother's eyes catch my own at the bottom, and I realize that my attempts to ignore her are quashed for the time being. Her eyes are bloodshot, her face blotchy and swollen. Today, I'll hold my tongue. I won't tell her how much I despise her or how my worst fear in this world was becoming her. A sickening twist at the base of my lungs makes me want to throw up.

I never used to want to hurt my mother, the poor battered woman. She was the woman who stood by when her husband threw a vase at her daughter's head when Emma began to grow so big that I couldn't hide the bulge.

The fight never would have happened, and everything would have been different if she would have—

"Samantha, we need to talk," she says, trying to take my hand. I swat it away and head to the gardens. She follows, but I don't object. After this, after the funeral and this talk, I will never speak to her again.

The salty air makes me gag. We come to the darkest place in the garden, the vines crowning over my head. I stop and turn toward her.

"What do you need to talk to me about, Mother?" I sigh with the little energy I have left in my chest.

Her eyes meet mine, and she cries out, a panting sort of sob.

"God, I miss her," she says, clutching her chest. I want to say that I miss her too and let her hug me and make it all better, but the mother that could make it all better is a fantasy, a different version that never bothered to show up. "I should have tried harder to keep you away, but I couldn't remember everything. Hell, I could hardly remember anything except Nadine and bits and pieces of a party."

"To keep me away from what?" My cheeks flush fire, and heat surges in my stomach.

"This island, these people, your husband. Don't you see that if you'd never come here, none of this would have happened?"

An angry laugh takes up the empty space around us. "What are you talking about? You're really worried about me having a bad life? That's rich. Where was this concern when I was a child and I actually needed you?"

She slouches like a whipped dog. "They did that to you. Your Grandmother, whatever they did on this island. That's—"

"What the fuck are you talking about?"

"I know this is going to sound crazy. I couldn't remember everything before I came back here. Even on the ride to the hospital, bits started coming back. It's like my mind only showed me so much, and coming here was the key to unlocking it all. It's still foggy, but my instincts about them never went away."

I cross my arms across my chest and stare at her.

"We were supposed to visit just for the summer." She stares off into the distance like she's seeing someone she recognizes. "This house was here. I know it, because it's where we stayed. We were only here for a few nights before I saw something that I wasn't supposed to. I saw a man in a pink shirt killed in the moonlight, in a garden." Her hands paw the air like she's trying to grab something. "I wanted to save him, but I couldn't ... I was too afraid they'd see me. Nadine, she was there. She witnessed it and did nothing. Then they started preparing for this big dinner, pies and all. They tried to let me drink alcohol."

My lips purse. Maybe she *was* on the island. The man in the pink shirt. Those are details she couldn't make up.

"What happened then?"

"I wouldn't drink, and I wouldn't eat. It just didn't feel right—all these old men staring at me." The uncomfortable feeling of being prey creeps back up my spine. "I snuck out, and I ran. My mother and Nadine tried to bring me back, but I wouldn't go. I hit my mom. I hit her so hard. I still feel guilty about it, you know? I had to get away." The fear in her eyes is real, and it scares me. "She was evil. She cursed us. I don't know how, but I know it has something to do with this island." The morning light shifts in the vines, casting shadows across her wrinkled face. "She doomed us to have a hard life, but it was better than staying here."

"You're right."

"What?"

"I don't think you're crazy. I think you're right. Grandma was probably awful to you. I know she had to have abused you emotionally, she uprooted you as a teenager, and she always put herself first." Mom softens, her wrinkled face filled with hope more than fear. "That created you, the broken woman who stood by and let her husband beat her and her kids so that she could avoid her own mother and whatever she made up in her head about this island. You made up excuses about why it was justified—getting knocked up and staying with a monster. You had to make up a curse, an evil, a big bad boogeyman so scary and so awful that you had to stay, and we had to stay."

"No. You're not listening."

"I don't need to listen to any more of this. I know my own life story, and I know yours, too. We were beat up and spineless and more scared of made-up monsters than the ones in our own beds. I know that story, Mom. It's called intergenerational trauma, and it stops with me. Becca wanted me to be Jax's guardian. The lawyers already called. No grand-children to corrupt. Ben and I will take care of the kids the way that grown-ups should and finally end this madness."

I turn away from her and start down the path.

"You can say whatever you need to me, but I love you, and I won't let you stay on this island. You need to take your own advice. Stop making me out to be the monster and take a look in your own bed. You need to come home with me."

I whip myself around to face her and stride back until I'm inches away from her face.

"I'd rather be dead than spend another moment of my lifetime under your guidance and care."

Her face trembles. Guilt swells like a beast in my stomach.

"Then you'll die here." Her hands reach for her mouth, her eyes desperate to put what she said back into her mouth, but she can't.

There's no ghosts in the window, no evil islands. There are only broken people.

CALL ME BACK—EMMA

The mansion still smells of fire and herbs. Mom and Grandma both carry boxes with Becca's ashes. Daniel's hand squeezes mine as we sit, staring at the two of them blowing out a candle for Becca. Nadine can't be all that bad. She had the decency to host Grandma after she slapped her in the face.

Jax rests his head against my shoulder, and I lean into it. An organ tune plays for Becca, but all I can think of is the buzzing in my pocket. Based on the text Hannah sent earlier, she must've found something.

I need to know what Becca was doing, what she was thinking, before she died. It's all happened so fast, everything with my dad, the body, and the car accident.

I think of the wedding. Becca in the bathroom, smiling at me. Watching Mom kiss Ben.

Mom takes a seat in the row right in front of us. Her sniffles behind a black veil make my heart ache. Pieces of it have been dying little by little since the day that I found out Becca was gone. She was the only constant in our lives, and now she's gone forever. I try to hold it in, but trying to stop the tears creates a burning ache in my face, and they spill out. My chest heaves up and down. Jax starts to cry, too. I hug him hard.

A hand rests on my shoulder from behind, making me jump. I turn to see Nadine; she gives a knowing smile, and I turn away. Something isn't right. My aunt shouldn't be dead. Jax shouldn't be motherless. I kiss him on the cheek and get up. The elders stare at me in rows, their heads moving in unison. Their smiles are all alike—full of fake sympathy. I walk as fast as I can to the doors. Pink shirts stand at either side and open them for me. I have to get out of here.

Daniel walked me down these stairs not too long ago, escorting us from the party. My hands stiffen on the chilly railing as I move my way to the upper level to try to find an unoccupied room. The faint sounds of muffled talking echo from a room down the hall. I creep toward it, making sure my Mary Janes don't create any noise on the black and white tiled floor. I reach the door and press my ear close to it. It's hard to hear over the blood rushing through my temples.

"She was the one all the way from Roanoke, a descendant," a muffled woman's voice comes through.

"But her ..." I can't make out the word, but I hear the next line, "... was a traitor."

Traitor? Who's a traitor?

"It doesn't matter, Eloise. There aren't that many of us that can do it. We can't just think of this cycle. We need to consider the next."

"This is the most important one ... this is the one," the words disappear again, "... thought it was Nadine, but remember how that went?"

What are they talking about? I'm missing key information.

"How?" another woman asks with a thick Scottish accent.

"She was barren. They need a partner." Their voices are growing quieter, and my heart is thumping louder.

"Yes. If Lilith doesn't get it—you know what that means?"

I lean harder against the door.

It creaks.

"What was that?"

Shit.

Black doors line the hall.

Someone moves inside the room.

I've gotta go.

I dash across the hall, reckless with my footsteps, but I need to be quick. I select the nearest door and turn the doorknob, but it doesn't give.

There's a potted palm tree in the corner.

I dart behind it and use my hands to try and steady the leaves. It's dark; maybe I'll actually get away with this.

A woman opens the door and steps out. She looks left down the other side of the hall and then right toward me. Her eyes light like they're bioluminescent. They glide over me, and she ducks her head back in and closes the door.

A breath fans from my lips, and I wait a moment before venturing down the hall until I find an open and quiet room. Once inside, I carefully close the door and pull out my phone.

Hannah called three times. She must have something. Her brother is a hacking wizard. I don't even want to think about her coming up empty.

An open door in the room leads to a small bathroom. I duck inside and close and latch the door before calling her back. She picks up right away.

"Emma, I'm so sorry. How are you doing?"

Hannah knows me too well. Her question makes me stop and actually feel for a second. A weight bears down my shoulders.

"The funeral is super weird and sad and awful."

"I'm sorry." She pauses. "I think I found something."

"What is it?"

"Are you on any Wi-Fi or anything?"

I check my phone, and I'm not. Just two bars of cell phone service.

"Why?"

"I'm going to send some stuff to your email, but here's what I've got so far. You know that woman that they held a funeral for, the one we attended?"

"Yeah," I whisper, pacing the green tile bathroom.

"Her death was never reported anywhere. I searched her name a ton and found out there was no report of her death, only a missing person's report filed by an ex-boyfriend. That's not normal. Becca didn't see that. She was researching something else, about the island itself. Stuff about the plant life and memory loss. Stuff with the Steward family name. Do you know that your great-grandmother lived there?"

I cover my mouth, trying to muffle my audible gasp. I silently celebrate. "Maybe that's what Grandma was talking about!"

"She did. You want to know something really weird?"

"Weirder than everything that's already happened?"

"Fair enough. Anyway, I can't find any census record of your great-grandma's birth, who her parents were, or where she came from, at all. No other family listed; in fact, not even a residence address outside the ten years before she passed when she was in the hospital."

"What the hell?"

"The island itself has almost no history, nothing in the news, nothing at all. No deaths reported or anything. That seems like, impossible, right?"

"Yeah."

"I'm not saying what happened to Becca wasn't an accident, but there was an email she got two days before she drove off with your mom. It was deleted. Never opened. I recovered it."

"What does it say?"

"I'm going to forward you the full thing. There are pictures in the email that don't make sense. Nadine and Ginny looking very old even before Ben was born and then looking young again, holding him as a toddler. If the dates are right, that seems impossible."

"She looks so young now compared to when we first got here, doesn't she? Or even at the wedding? Hannah, remember that weird ass cult room with the horned lady pictures I told you about? What if they're sacrificial freaks who drink the blood of the dead or something to stay alive? Like vampires?"

"I'm sending the email. You can see the pictures for yourself. The guy who sent it said he worked for them. He was sending it and then leaving the island. It could all be nothing, though, Emma. I don't know what to think. I mean it's not like Becca even read it."

"But someone must've seen it, right? Hacked her account and then deleted it before she had a chance to see it? I heard people here just now talking about Roanoke— descendants or something. Do you know what that is?"

"Yeah, of course. You don't?" Hannah forgets that I'm not as obsessed with history as she is. "It's the lost colony."

I hear voices in the hallway. I have to hurry. "What do you mean?"

"The that was first established in America, way back when. They were low on supplies, so some people took a ship back to Europe. When they came back, the settlers were all gone. They think they starved or died or something, but they don't really know. They never found bodies. You know, it's really close to where the island is. Maybe you should get away for a bit, check it out and see if there's anything there."

The floors creak in the room next door.

"I gotta go. I'll call you back when I can. Thanks, Hannah."

The door handle creaks back and forth.

"Love you, girl."

"Love you, too."

Shit. Roanoke, a lost colony. Descendants? Missing people?

Maybe they are some kind of crazy cult ... but how am I going to get Mom to see that? What if I'm wrong, and I ruin Mom's life even more?

I take a deep breath and open the door. Daniel stands on the other side of it.

"I had to pee," I say, pushing my phone in my pocket.

"You needed some privacy," Daniel says, taking my hand in his and pulling me close. "I get it. I'm so sorry, Emma." He kisses me on the forehead and then takes me back downstairs. Ben is waiting at the bottom of the staircase.

"Your Mom left with Jax for home a few minutes ago," Ben says. "I tried to get your grandma to come back with us, but she ignored me and ran off."

"Sorry about that," I say.

"Hey, no worries. What matters right now is that you, Jax, and your mom have space and time. That, and that we remember Becca. Anything you'd like to do when we get back?"

I examine Ben, search his face for something sinister—something off or wrong or evil, but I come up short. He loves my mom. I wish Becca was here. She'd know what to do.

"Let's watch a movie, something spooky. She would've liked that."

"You got it."

Daniel pulls me in closer and holds me the whole way back to Nadine's.

I'm Stuck—Sam

Shadows play on the cabinets, counters, and tile floor. Despite it being nearly nine a.m, a haze hangs over the kitchen. Twisting vines have taken over the side of the house, smothering any light that may try to wriggle its way inside.

My morning drink sits on the counter half-finished because it tastes like a front lawn thrown into a blender and smells like that disgusting herb. The baby is awake. It seems to enjoy the drink, so I finish the rest of it and resist the urge to spit it down the drain.

Just the two of us. This pregnancy feels so different. Everything about it, from the illness, to the movement, and the growth rate, is off.

Dr. Drear says my abdomen may just be swollen from the crash, that I need to take it easy, and that things will get back to normal. Not bedrest per se, just more rest than movement.

I run my hands along my stomach. It hurts. The skin just beneath the fabric of my clothing is marbled with black, blue, and purple from the accident. Why do I feel it move in there? It scares me. It's too early.

With Emma, I felt I needed to protect her from everything and everyone, the helpless little thing. This child feels like it's aware and cognizant of every event that takes place, like it's in charge of itself already. It doesn't really need me at all.

Ben turns the light on in the kitchen and interrupts my thoughts. He grabs a glass of orange juice from the refrigerator.

"Ready for our morning walk?" Ben asks, greeting me with his beautiful face that carries a few more lines around his eyes than before. We decided together how I'll be spending my allotted one-to-two hours out of bed for the next however many months.

"Why yes, I am," I say, crossing over to him.

It's been almost a week since the funeral. Since then, I've been ravenous, shoving food in my face like I'll never see a morsel again. My mother has either stopped caring or has given up; she left after the funeral, and that was that.

Ben holds my hand as we make our way toward Main Street. Tentacle-like tendrils, green and lush, whip through the air from the willow trees. Camillia flowers encroach on the cobblestone street, seeming to have grown overnight. My shoulders relax, and I feel like I can breathe, but then a pinch in my stomach takes my breath away. I use my empty hand to cradle the thing growing inside of me.

"You alright?" Ben asks.

"I'm fine."

"Yes, dear," Ginny approaches from across the street with an older woman. "That didn't look normal. Are you okay?"

"Oh no," the other woman says in a thick Irish accent. "I'll fetch Dr. Drear."

"No—" I say, but the woman's already run off toward the doctor's house. *This is ridiculous.* "I'm sure that's not necessary. It's just round ligament pain."

"What?" Ginny guffaws. "You don't know that." She takes my shoulders in her claw-like grip and leads me over to a wrought iron bench.

"I'm fine," I say.

"You were just in an accident, and you don't know what's normal," Ginny says, waving her finger like a teacher scolding me.

My cheeks flush. "I've been pregnant before. This is normal."

"You don't get to judge that." Her tone is harsh. "You think you're so smart. So did your—"

"*Stop it*," Ben says, putting his hand up between the woman's pointy finger and my face. "We'll get it checked out, but it's our child, and you can't talk to Sam like that."

Ginny puts her hands on her waist and lets out a puff of air in the opposite direction.

"Sometimes people can be so selfish," the older woman mumbles. "You really need the walk? Selfish girl."

Ben and I share a wide-eyed exchange. I fight back both anger and the urge to laugh at the woman. This is my child and my pregnancy. Everyone here seems to think the bruising is normal *healing from the accident*. That the rapid growth is normal *swelling from the accident,* and the incessant craving for raw meat is *low iron, dearie.*

Becca's face and the car flipping flood my mind. I choke back a sob.

I breathe in and out, trying to catch my breath as my heart threatens to burst through my chest and splatter blood all over Ben's face.

A racket of pebbles and heavy shoe falls pull my attention.

"I came as soon as Marie here told me. Is everything alright?" Dr. Drear asks. He's wearing street clothes, a checkered button down and shorts with tall socks and gator loafers.

"I'm fine," I say. "Really. I'm just anxious."

"Not good for the baby," Ginny chimes in with a judgmental stare.

"Now, now, Ginny." Dr. Drear pats the woman's shoulder.

Ben sits on the bench beside me, putting an arm around me, protecting me.

"I'd like to check you out," Drear says.

"No, really, I—"

"No buts. You were just in an accident, and you went through a lot." He pats Ben on the knee. "Let's have a look, just in case." Men in pink jackets trail in from behind with a wheelchair. "We'll use this wheelchair to get you home, and we'll check you out."

Emma and Jax are out front when we get back home.

"Mom, are you okay?" she asks.

"I'm totally fine." I give her a tight smile.

"Your mother had some belly pain. We're just going to check everything out to make sure she's okay," Dr. Drear says.

Emma's eyebrows meet. Hasn't this kid been through enough?

"I'm good," I say, authoritative this time. It's no use. They wheel me around back and into the house. Ben and Dr. Drear, who's rather able-bodied for his age, lift me up the stairs and roll me to the bedroom. I lie on the bed. Ginny and that random lady follow them in. The women smell like wet dog. Vomit threatens to come up my throat.

"You're right," I say. "I'm not feeling well. I don't want guests. Ben?"

"Ladies, I think you'll need to go," Ben says. The women huff and puff. Their eyes practically glow red. "Emma, wait right outside, okay?"

Ben closes the door, and Dr. Drear lifts my shirt, the fabric tickling my stomach. I can't help but laugh.

"Feeling terrible, huh?" Ben asks, laughing and pressing his warm lips to my forehead.

Dr. Drear takes out a measuring tape and presses it on my pelvic area; it makes my insides hurt. He pulls the measuring tape up between my breasts. His hot breath presses on my face.

"You are measuring quite big. I'd say our calculation initially was off."

"How off?" I ask. It can't be. I've been on birth control until we got to the island.

"I'd say, oh, about four, maybe five months."

"What?" I gasp in shock. "That's not possible. I was on the pill."

"You know things have a way of working out if they're supposed to," Dr. Drear says.

"That explains the kicks you've been feeling," Ben says, seemingly accepting this as true.

"That can't be right," I protest. "Five months? I would have known."

"All pregnancies are different," Dr. Drear says, patting my hand. His mouth smells like a vat of mothballs. "Good news is you're almost out of the second trimester, so morning sickness will be gone soon. Right?" His smile is huge and white and glistening and makes disgust roil inside. The morning sickness should have been gone two months ago if it were a typical pregnancy. Something isn't right. I turn my face away from him and toward Ben, who's smiling like a fucking dope.

"So that's it?" I ask. "I'm five months pregnant, just like that, no ultrasound?"

"Not needed," Dr. Drear says. "You don't want to expose the baby to more than it needs to be." He stands and goes to the door. I almost wish my mother was here to ream him out and slap someone, like at the hospital. "No more trips off the island for you, Samantha. You or your family. Stay close to home. I think you're right that this pregnancy is different, and that might mean an earlier labor than with Emma." My hands go numb at the thought.

"I need to rest, I think, Dr. Drear. Thank you so much," I say with a smile and malice in my throat.

Emma rushes in after he's out the door.

"You okay? Like for real?" Emma asks. I pull her toward me and kiss her cheek. "Ben, can I talk to my mom alone for a few minutes?"

"Sure, kid," Ben says and leaves the room.

"What's going on, Mom?"

"They said the baby is a little older than we thought. I don't know what to think, but it has been kicking ... so I don't know." I sigh. "I guess it could make sense."

"You didn't get sick until after that party," Emma says, concern growing in her eyes.

That's true. I didn't feel anything before the party. Not a thing. Normal energy, normal appetite, all of it normal.

"I see what you mean, and I agree, it's really weird–"

"Then you might actually believe me when I say this ... what if they're not who they say they are?"

"What? Who?" I pull her hand to rest on my stomach and pat it, trying to soothe her. "What if who isn't who they say they are? What are you talking about?"

Emma takes a big breath in and continues. "What if they're like .... not good people? Nadine, Dr. Drear, Ginny?" She pauses before continuing. "Ben ..."

"Where is this coming from?"

"I had Hannah hack into Becca's email."

The blood drains from my face. "You did what?"

"I had to know if she thought something was weird here. She did."

"Stop it."

"She did. You know the girl who died next door?"

My heart is racing again. A flash of Becca's face just before the crash. My breathing is rapid. Her face again. Her face. Her face. Before she—

"It's being reported as a missing person—no one ever reported her death."

"I can't deal with this right now." The wetness of my palms and the incessant thumping of my heart make me want to crawl out of my skin. It's like every sense in my body is overwhelmed, every prick of my skin is painful, every sound in my mind drives me to the edge.

Thud.

Crash.

Thud.

Her face.

"Get out!" I regret it immediately; why can't I put the words back into my mouth?

"Mom ..." She looks as if I've whipped her.

"I'm sorry. I'm stressed, and the baby isn't well."

Emma stares, wounded, utterly betrayed by me.

"Mom, I'm so worried about you." Emma sobs.

"I know sweetheart." I reach a hand toward her; I want to pull her into me and make her feel better.

"I don't trust Dr. Drear."

"Truth is, I don't either, but I feel like I have no choice, Emma."

Pain runs through me like molten lava. My abdomen twists like some external force is trying to juice me, the pain so blinding I lose my thoughts.

"I'm going to find out what's happening, Mom."

Roanoke—Emma
August 7

The mating calls of toads in the nature reserve create a white noise that hides our whispers and footsteps.

"You really think we won't get caught?" I ask Jax behind my shoulder. The bridge that we came to the island on is guarded by two men in pink coats.

"Shit," Juniper hisses, sneaking back behind a giant banana leaf. Daniel, Juniper, Jax and I, are sneaking around like the gang from *Scooby-Doo*, trying to figure out a way off this island and over to Roanoke. To be honest, I'm surprised that Juniper is helping us, but we'd be lost without her right now.

Juniper stares into Jax's eyes, pulling his face close to hers. "You wanna get off the island for a while, don't you?"

Jax nods his head in her hands.

"I need you to go out there," Juniper says. Jax stares into her eyes as she speaks, as though mesmerized by them. "You need to run up, act like you're panicked. Act like something is terribly wrong with Sam and Nadine. Say ... you can't find them anywhere, and you saw blood in the house, and they have to go try to find them, okay?"

I grab Jax by the arm and pull him away from Juniper.

"You don't have to do that," I say.

"I want to," he says. "Roanoke might give us what we need to know, Emma. I know I'm younger than you—but I can do this."

Maybe I am babying him too much, but he's my cousin, and he just lost his mom—he's my responsibility now. He's right, though. We won't know what is really going on unless we investigate all leads. The people at Becca's funeral were talking about a sacrifice. I need to know what the hell this place is about.

Jax emerges from the jungle of leaves.

"Help!" he cries, his voice broken by sobs. He's really crying. Where did he learn to do that? He does have a lot to pull from. "My aunt, my aunt Sam ... she..."

The guys in pink jackets pause.

"What, kid?"

Jax cries out. "They ... umm ... Nadine went after her. There was blood. They ran into the nature preserve. You have to help!"

The men look at each other and back at Jax.

"Please, she's gonna die!" he shouts, crying like a freaking baby. "That way!" He points in the opposite direction of us.

The men run off into the bush, and Jax bounces back to us with satisfied laughter.

"Don't be too impressed with yourself," Juniper says. "The pink shirts will do anything to make sure Sam's okay."

Jax ignores her, and we all head to the car Juniper lifted from one of the neighbors on the island.

Stevie Nicks' "Edge of Seventeen" is blaring on the radio, and the windows are down. Jax is in the backseat with Juniper, and Daniel is in the passenger seat next to me. The island is far behind us, and we're headed up Highway 12. I can't help but feel a little relief to be away. We're going to finish what Becca started.

"Are we there yet?" Juniper calls from the back. Her bare feet with red painted toenails snake their way between Daniel and me.

"Not yet." I roll my eyes. In the rearview mirror, Juniper's glowing eyes stare into mine. She winks, and my cheeks flush. My focus needs to stay on the road.

This part of the Outer Banks is desolate. Unlike Nadine's house, there are sparse beach wildflowers, but most of the view is sand and ocean. There are areas we pass with forests of oak and cedar trees, but nothing like the island at this time of year, crowded with bushes, flowers, and vines that slither over every empty surface.

We arrive thirty minutes later. Jax yawns himself awake from the backseat. I turn left onto a concrete bridge leading to the island, passing signs for Cape Hatteras National Seashore.

"Is this it?" Jax asks from the back seat.

"No, that's Pond Island. Roanoke is a lot bigger than that." Daniel points out as we pass through a small plot of land before the last stretch of concrete bridge carries us toward a land mass.

There's a dense forest ahead. The trees, branches, and leaves grow one on top of the other, like a fortress. Goose pimples rise on my arms despite the tepid heat of the day.

The trees are quite beautiful, but knowing what happened here makes it ominous, scary. It has *get out while you still can* vibes. But I can't. We can't. Even if this has nothing to do with anything, I need to see it and make sure. I have to protect Mom like we should have protected Becca. She was onto something.

The trees on either side make whooshing noises as we pass through them, and the canopy above us blocks out all the sun, insulating the road. It's quite cool inside, and I hold my breath.

"You alright, Emma?" Daniel asks.

"Yeah." I nod. "Just kind of creepy, knowing what happened here."

"You're that freaked out?" Juniper laughs from the backseat. "There's nothing to be scared of, Emma."

"You go up here, and then you make a right," Daniel says, ignoring Juniper. "The island consists of two towns. We want to go to the very north end."

"Okay," I say. My stomach swells with the feeling that you get when an amazing beat drops on your favorite song. It's as though I've been here before. The knots on the trees look familiar, as do the salt box buildings and the cobblestone streets.

"I feel like I've been here before."

"Déjà vu, right?" Juniper says from the back of the car. "It's like you almost know what's going to be around every turn before you actually get there."

The car takes a left and then a right; it's like I learned to drive here. I know each turn is coming before we pass them. I think Juniper feels it, too.

"Roll down your window," Juniper says from the back and shakes my seat a little. "Roll it down, Emma."

I don't really like Juniper, but right now, she's the only one who gets what's happening. When I do roll down the window, it smells like home—a home I never really knew but had always dreamed about, like a mix of a Renaissance festival and an oceanside cottage. The scent of hot roasted, sweet almonds fills the car, alongside fresh grass and the incessant sound of the waves.

Juniper pulls her body into the front seat, her face meeting mine. Her nose grazes my cheek, and my body lights up like hot coals on a campfire, the kind you want to press your hands into on a cold night on Lake Huron. "Thank you for bringing me here," Juniper whispers, her breath moving something within me, deep down in my lower abdomen. I want to turn to her and away from the road, confident that the car would drive itself wherever we needed to end up, then pull her close to me, and touch the coals.

"Emma!" Jax shouts from behind. His eyes are wide, panic-stricken. I slam on the brakes, and a white Porsche blares the horn from directly in front of me before it pulls off. "Are you okay?"

Holy shit, that was stupid. Spiky nerves prick my skin. I blink, trying to get a grip on what I'm doing to calm down and concentrate. Juniper leans back in her seat. Jax gasps for air, tears in his eyes.

"Don't worry, Jax, she's okay," Juniper says, giggling. "We're all going to be just fine."

We park and hit the trail. I wish I'd brought bug spray. The forest trail is rife with mosquitos that stop to bite me and suck my blood every five seconds. I whack the one on my shoulder, leaving behind a splatter; it serves them right. Pines and oak make the scent of the air earthy, homey, and comfortable, despite the rising temperature.

Sweat forms on my brow and the foamy saliva in my mouth makes my lips pucker—I'm parched and clinging to the last sip of stale cola from the car.

"The mosquitoes are nuts here," I complain, continuing down the trail where a stone statue emerges from behind the dense foliage.

"Funny, they don't like me," Juniper replies, taking a hit of her vape pen. The beads from her purse clink together with each step, interrupting the symphony of grasshoppers.

Daniel's been silent since we left the car. He keeps rubbing his arms as he walks and looking behind his shoulder every so often. Jax is quiet too, but that's what I'd expect given our recent situation and how he's been coping with things. He's along for the ride, ready to be my partner, focusing on anything other than reality.

Ahead of us stands the stone statue of a woman, the skirt of her dress creating a perimeter around her, shielding and protecting her royal highness from the peasants.

Juniper takes another pull of her vape pen before running directly up to the statue of the queen. She crosses her legs to curtsey, holding an imaginary skirt and rising with her middle fingers pointed at the grey woman.

"C'mon, Juniper," Daniel protests.

"God save the queen!" She cackles and passes me the vape pen. I turn to make sure Jax isn't looking and take a hit myself. My face goes fuzzy, and I cough, then hide the pen behind my back until Juniper snatches it. Jax doesn't appear to notice, and my cheeks flush. I didn't even want to; why did I do that?

The thought is fleeting because Juniper grabs my hand. A warm wave travels up my arm to my already-flushed face. I don't pull away as she takes me deeper into the forest.

The wind whips at my frizzy hair as I watch Juniper's body bounce in front of us, pulling me along. Wait, is it us?

I turn back, and the boys are gone.

"Wait!" I call out to Juniper, but she just laughs and keeps going. I don't want to stop either. I want to be here surrounded by the hum of insects and the smell of sycamore trees and feel the dirt beneath my shoes. She jerks my arm to the right, leading us onto a smaller, thinner path.

A branch from the pine rips a bit of skin from my arm.

I'm okay with a part of me living here. A tiny voice creeps up inside of me. *You need to make sure that Jax is safe.*

I shake the thought away. Jax will be fine; he has his phone and can call me.

Still, I reach into my front pocket to double-check for the car key and that my phone is still there, too.

The dirt path gives way to soft, red pine needles, and suddenly the sounds are gone.

No cicadas, no crickets, no buzz of mosquitoes.

The soundtrack of waves crashing in and out has gone silent. The pines surround us so fully that I feel like Snow White running through the woods from the evil queen. If I'm Snow White, who is Juniper?

"We're almost there," she says.

Yes, I *know* we are. I don't know what's there, but I can feel she's right. We are almost to the reason why I had to come here to this familiar distant place left abandoned and soulless hundreds of years ago.

She slows her pace and takes another left, taking us further into the pines. They're denser, blocking out any bit of sunlight. Mushrooms litter the forest floor, bulbous pillows. The light is dim, and the breeze is blocked, so the smell of rotting worms and pine needles, earthy and sweet, lingers. It's sickeningly sweet, like maple syrup and the dead body the morning after the girl threw herself from the house next door.

Juniper stops and turns to face me. "We're here."

I don't want to drop her gaze. I imagine her eyes moving like water all day long as they sit inside her head.

"Where?" I reply.

"You *know*." She takes her hand and presses it gently against my stomach beneath my navel. I choke. "You felt it; you feel it. You know exactly where you are."

I move past her and lower myself to the ground. On my hands and knees, I crawl. My heart skips a beat, I breathe in, and I don't move. A snake with glistening black and gold scales approaches from the underbrush.

"It won't hurt you. Just stay still," Juniper assures me, and I believe her.

I let out a sigh as its body slithers over my sneakers, only thin bits of fabric and rubber separating us. Its tail flicks at the skin of my ankle, and I don't flinch. I'm elated, like a burst of energy was whipped into my body, dancing up my legs.

Butterflies swirl wildly in my stomach. I bend down and brush away piles of pine needles. My fingers press into the ground; I have to dig, my nails tearing at the soil and pines. Bits of stone are revealed as I do. I keep going even as pine needles, mud, and caked wood sting my fingers.

"I told you," Juniper says, coming to meet me where I kneel on the ground. My fingertips begin to weaken, torn and scraped from the earth and stone. I pull them away and look down at what's beneath us. With the piece of stone unearthed, the winged creatures inside me grow bigger, more desperate, and work faster. It's not butterflies, but crows that circle within me. I want to burst and let them free. The stone is carved, the soil caked into its grooves.

picce næ fær deað

I don't understand the words, but I recognize the symbols from the key in my pocket that's pressing into my thigh.

"Picce næ fær deað," Juniper recites as if she's read these words a thousand times.

"What does it mean?" I ask, but Juniper doesn't answer. She pulls my face to hers, and my lips move to hers like magnets. Her mouth is soft like rose petals. She smells of honey and spice. She tastes too sweet. I kiss her harder, and her softness turns solid. She prods past my teeth, and our tongues dance like serpents in the sand before she pulls away and stands up like nothing's even happened.

"Let's go find the boys," she says, turning back down the path we came in on. I brush the pine needles back over the stone. I don't know why I do this, I don't know why I know this place, and I don't know why I kissed Juniper. It just *is*. Then I rise on stiff legs, ignoring my burning and bloody fingers, and follow Juniper back out of the pines.

"What the heck is this stuff?" Jax asks, pulling a vine from his ankle. It's like the ones back on the island but fuzzier. "You okay, Emma?"

I blush and stick my bloody hands in my pockets.

"That's what I call a special ingredient." Juniper rips the vine from around his feet. It's furry and dotted with cobalt flowers. I avoid eye contact with her while she explains, gathering more and more vines. "This stuff is absolutely delectable, though it does leave a strange aftertaste." She plucks handfuls bent over on the ground. "Aren't you gonna help me carry some?" She reaches her full hand out toward mine, and I pull my bloodied fingers out to grasp it. Soft, with a delicate floral smell. "They say if you take enough of it, you can see God. Do you want to see God, Emma?"

Coming and Going—Sam
August 8

D aniel spots me from the ice cream stand; his wide white smile nearly glimmers in the sunlight. He raises his arm in a wave, and I reciprocate.

He seems kind. I've always worried that Emma would be attracted to dangerous men—that she'd be like I was when I was her age. Maybe my being with Ben has shown her that they're not all so bad.

I hope she's talking to him or someone else about what she's going through. Since I pushed her away the other day, she has barely wanted to speak to me. I can't blame her. She was trying to help, and make sense of her aunt's death. She must feel like I've got no space for her, with the baby and with my own loss.

"Look, Sam, it's a hummingbird." Ben points toward the archway to a little garden I haven't yet explored. I've spent so much time trying to impress Nadine, to care for her and Ben, and then I got so sick. I haven't had the opportunity to get into this place's nooks and crannies.

The hummingbird's wings beat at immeasurable speeds as it sticks its sharp beak into a trumpet vine. Its red blooms are like clusters of fruit grown especially for them. I squeeze Ben's hand, and he squeezes back. I manage a smile. Emma will get through this, and so will I. We're both doing our best.

I have to live. I have to let myself be happy.

Camillia is truly a beautiful place, special, unlike anywhere I've ever even imagined being. I guess I can see why the women of the island wanted to retire here. It makes sense why Nadine would leave Hollywood after Ben's father's death, away from all her friends, and return to this place. Anytime I've ever asked her why, she's just said *people who leave here always come back; one way or another, they have to. It's like a safe haven for our families. You and Emma are our family.*

I suppose her heart will break when she realizes we aren't staying to raise our child here. The beauty of the island, the sweet grass, the charming closeness of it all; it's easy to get swept up in it. It makes it hard to imagine any other place in the world could be more beautiful. There's also the feeling that it must be unnatural somehow, too perfect, strange. That you're never truly alone.

"Do you want to go in?" Ben asks, stopping at the gated archway. A yellow butterfly dances through the air around his head.

"Why not? I'm sick of the nature reserve paths."

Ben pulls his keys out from his pocket and rifles through them until he finds an ornate brass one.

"It's locked?" I ask. "It's such a small island—why do they keep it locked? Don't they know everyone here?"

Ben chuckles. "My thoughts exactly, but Nadine, Ginny, and Helena keep this place up. It's been here since I was a kid. There are things inside, I guess, worth quite a bit of money. Or so they tell me. They don't trust all the ladies."

"Gossip and suspicion even on a private island."

"Maybe more than other places." Ben winks.

He turns the key, and the weathered wooden doors swing open with a creak. A beautiful white marble fountain with dark purple clematis snaking up and down its base stands in the center of my view. Wisteria branches weave up and around the walls of the place, leaving small gaps that reveal pieces of brick and stone that look hundreds of years old.

"Oh my gosh, this is beautiful! How have we been here all this time, and you haven't shown me? Nadine's never mentioned it either." A swallowtail butterfly bobs over bright orange blooms. The garden is layered with creeping thyme at the bottom, and vines growing up walls behind bushes and stemmed flowers. There's so many blossoms and different plants that you can't see soil beneath them. They're not competing for space, but it's like they're all working together. There's not a neglected blossom in the bunch.

"I don't know. I guess I didn't really think about it."

"I'm glad you did today. Honestly, I've never noticed the gates before. I must have passed by it at least ten times going to the market or the pharmacy." Emma, Jax, and Hannah came down here quite a bit as well, but not one kid ever mentioned the locked wooden gates. The island isn't very big. Surely, they came across it.

"It's meant to be that way."

"What way?"

"Mom says you can set intentions for things. That's what they did anyway. The three of them wanted to protect the things inside of the garden and keep them away from prying eyes. They set intentions that it would be protected, that it should go unnoticed, that no one unwelcome would step foot inside."

My mind whirls, thinking of the little black books in the women's houses, of the strange room at Ginny's place.

"Like a spell?" I tease. The baby kicks at the left side of my stomach.

Ben smiles and takes my hand. We walk around to the other side of the fountain where there's a pergola with wooden slats that leads to another pathway. The cobblestones beneath my feet change to old oyster shells and dirt. This path was made a long time ago. Had Nadine and Ginny found it?

I didn't think the island had been established that long ago when it was common to use shells in roads.

"When was Camillia Island founded? Did Ginny and Nadine find this place like it is?"

"Honestly, I have no idea. Maybe they found it and worked with what was already here."

A small green garter snake slithers next to me and into a small hole in the wall between colonies of moss. Ben pulls me further down the path, where it's shaded. The top of the tunnel is made of slats of wood with flowering ivy like plants hanging down, that brush the top of my hair.

I run my fingers across the rough walls. Like the ground beneath us, it's encrusted with oyster shells and other bits from the sea. I catch my nail on a shiny silver shell that's been perfectly preserved within the wall. Ben lets go of my hand and disappears into the next room. I stay. Twisted little things surrounded the bits of ocean debris in the wall, spiraled like a snail shell.

I use my fingernail to scrape at one, and a tiny bit falls to the ground. Ignoring the discarded piece, I continue to pluck at the thin, paper-like swirl stuck in the cement. I can't get anything out, but the texture is that of old parchment or newspaper. There's dozens of them in the wall.

"C'mon," Ben calls from the other side of the tunnel. There are dozens of these spirals sticking out.

"They're little paper spells ... intentions," I say, shocked when they escape my mouth. *Magic.* Spells and magic are something older women like Nadine and Ginny like to believe in, remnants of the Protestant pilgrim fear of all the things they didn't understand.

I still don't understand what happened the night of the party. Everything feels like a blur, or like a spell, but there are explanations for everything. Sometimes, we don't see doors that we aren't looking for. We pass by them every day for years on our commutes, never once stopping to investigate them. They still exist, and it's not magic or enchantment or curses that cause that. It's just that people are busy, and they see what they know and what they want to see.

"You good?" Ben asks.

I emerge into the other room, leaving behind the spirals in the ancient wall.

"I am better than that—I am enchanted," I say.

Ben pulls me in close and kisses the dip in my neck. This room is somehow more alive than the last. The winding vines and bursting blooms are larger, the sweet smell of honeysuckle inescapable. Bees and butterflies swirl back and forth between the plants, feasting. A magnolia tree with buttery yellow blooms sits at the center of the path. "I wish Becca could see this."

The sound of rushing water gets louder with each step we take toward the tree.

"She would have loved it," Ben adds.

"She would have wanted to come back at sunset with a cocktail." I laugh. Ben pulls away from me, but the child moves, so I grab his hand and press it to my abdomen. The baby kicks steadily toward Ben's hand.

"Holy shit," he says, his eyes lighting up with excitement. "That's a strong kid, like her mom."

"Her?" The image of that little boy on the blanket, running off to embrace Nadine, takes hold in my mind.

"Oh," Ben says, releasing my stomach. "I don't know. It's a feeling, I guess. Come here. I want you to see this."

Ben makes his way around the full magnolia tree, its fallen petals scattered along the stone path leading to the other side. I follow him. On the back wall, I find the source of the rushing water: a little person-made waterfall. It's pouring down next to a towering statue. A marble woman stands before me, with a swollen stomach mirroring my own. Stone fabric drapes over her full breasts, and her skirt hangs to the floor, becoming one with the rock path at her feet.

"I thought it'd be nice to see her," Ben says, staring up.

"Who?"

"My mom says this is a symbol. This garden is supposed to bring health and fertility to everyone who comes here."

I go forward. My hand moves as if on a string attached to some force I can't see. I'm drawn to press my hand against the stomach of the woman standing frozen.

I hold it there, waiting for something I don't even realize: a shudder, movement inside of her womb. I pull my hand back quickly with a gasp.

"Are you okay?" Ben asks.

I stare up at the woman. I must have imagined it. Nothing happened. I'm being silly and freaking myself out with this occult mystic nonsense.

"I'm fine ..." I say, stepping back a few feet away from the statue. "She's looking at something, isn't she?"

The wind picks up overhead, and the sun is snuffed out by a passing grey cloud.

"Huh, I never noticed that. It does seem like she is, doesn't it?"

I follow the statue's gaze across the garden, back toward the entrance.

"Stay there," I say, walking across the stone steps until I'm nearly at the opposite wall, directly where she would be staring. A rose bush bursting with pale lilac blooms is waiting for me there. "Hmm, it's just roses."

I push my nose, nearly touching a bloom, and inhale the scent, closing my eyes to take the moment in.

"Roses were her favorite," Ben says, his steps creeping closer to me. I know he means Krysten.

I turn to him as he walks toward me. "Do you miss her?"

"I do. I never brought her here."

"You didn't?"

"No," he says, shaking his head. "Nadine wanted me to. She said it would be good for her, but I didn't want to."

"Why not?"

"My mother ... the women here. I hated their infatuation with herbs and old wives' tales and ghosts; my dad did, too. I didn't want anything to do with it."

"And now?"

Ben pulls me in close to him, my stomach making it impossible to get too close, but we're as embraced as we can be.

"Now ... I think I understand why people cling to superstition. It's easier to believe that there are ghosts or that if you mix this herb with that oil, you have some semblance of control in a world that feels totally out of control. I don't hate it. I don't believe it, but I understand it. I understand wanting there to be more than what we can see and feel and touch."

"I get that, but I also quite enjoy what I can see and feel and touch."

I push myself up on my tiptoes, bring Ben's face to mine, and kiss him. He's warm and sweet and kind. "Let's head back. I could use a little more of what I can see and feel and touch."

"The door is locked," Ben says, raising an eyebrow.

"Benjamin Cross!"

"Hey, my honeymoon ended early."

I push myself up again to a kiss. My stomach stretches like it's growing larger every minute. I press my hand between Ben's legs, and he's not bluffing; he's entirely ready for me. My breath quickens. Ben's lips move to my ear, making little bursts of warmth flutter down my body and deep between my legs.

I open my eyes. The statue stares at me, at us, at what we're doing in *her* garden, at what he's doing to me in front of Krysten's favorite flowers. I press my eyes shut and let Ben's lips, supple and warm, move back up to my own. He reaches his arm down under my abdomen, his hands grasping at my skirt, pulling it up to reach beneath my underwear. I gasp, letting out the smallest moan in ecstasy, and hear a whisper next to my ear.

"Do it."

I open my eyes and turn my head back and forth. My body stiffens, and Ben meets my gaze.

"Is everything alright?"

"Yeah," I say, nodding.

Ben unzips his pants. I look around, but there are only insects buzzing back and forth, butterflies resting on magnolia blooms, and that stone statue, still and staring. Her cold, dead eyes peer over at me. He pushes himself inside of me and I groan.

I wish she wasn't here, but she is, and the feeling of her stare is forming a sick sourness in my stomach. I close my eyes again to retreat from her gaze.

A windy whistle starts as the breeze becomes stronger against my body, contrasting with the warmth growing inside as Ben moves his body with mine. I let out another moan, ignoring the feeling like someone's here, because no one is. It's a statue, a bunch of stone.

Oh God, that feels good. Then there's a breath in my ear, it's not Ben's.

"You're going to die."

Startled, I open my eyes, unable to ignore the whisper, and the sensation of a breath in my ear. I pull away from Ben.

"What's going on?" he asks.

I look left and right. There's nothing, no one, except the statue.

"Does it seem closer?" I get myself together and walk back over to it. The courtyard seems smaller somehow, like it's closing in on me. My fingers start to get all tingly again. I look at my feet.

Remember to look down and realize where you are.

A snake slithers close to me, and I jump backward.

"It's just a garter snake," Ben says. A huge gust of wind blows through the courtyard, through the tunnel from the other space.

"I want to go back."

"For sure." Ben nods. The insects are gone. I can't see a single butterfly or bee anywhere, and they were everywhere just a few moments ago. The statue feels bigger, and the whole place looks smaller.

I'm ahead of Ben, walking quickly to the tunnel, trying to get out of here as fast as I can. I feel like the statue is ready to pursue me, to lurch at me. I'm in *her* place, and I don't belong here.

"Wait," Ben says.

I turn quickly. "What?"

"There's something here—something that she was staring at. You were right."

Ben pulls back the baby's breath to the left of the rose bush, and beneath it, there's a stone with words that I don't recognize carved into it.

piċċe næ fre deað

"Huh," I say. "I wonder what that means."

"I don't know. I should ask Nadine."

"Don't," I say. "Don't tell Nadine we came here. I want this to be our secret, okay?"

"Yeah," Ben says, letting the baby's breath fall back to its place, hiding the stone. I can't help but feel like the statue is going to tell Nadine we've been here, and we've been watched the whole time, but that's crazy. I'm hormonal. I'm having a hard time because Becca died, and nothing is safe.

There's no such thing as magic or witches. Still, I don't look when we pass by the scrolls embedded in the walls.

A Cigarette—Emma

August 9

Ginny's house reeks of booze and florals. The bamboo chairs around the table squeak beneath us with each movement we make. "You two are just such beauties. Be careful with these boys," Ginny says. I stare at Juniper, sitting opposite me across Nadine's dining room table. Ginny and Nadine insisted on a girls' afternoon. Nadine complained that she hadn't spent any time at all lately with her *grand-daughter* and wanted to reconnect.

"Nothing to worry about, Auntie. Emma and I know what we're doing. Boys couldn't handle me, anyway. Besides, Emma's already betrothed to Daniel, right?" Juniper winks, taking a sip of her iced tea: sweet, Southern, and adorned with a mint leaf.

"That is a handsome boy," Nadine says. "Comes from good stock, and he treats you right?"

I kick Juniper under the table. She giggles into her drink, bubbling the mixture in the glass.

"He is handsome," I say. "He's always a gentleman. He's level-headed and kind, predictable. I like him a lot."

Juniper lowers her glass, placing it down hard on the table and rolls her eyes.

"Use a coaster, Juniper," Ginny says, and plays her card. The Jack of Spades, the left bower. "Emma, I don't know what I would have done without you. Euchre is quite superior to most games Nadine chooses to play with me. I'm glad you finally convinced her to learn. No one else has ever been able to."

"You know other Michiganders?" I ask. "Are there other people here who used to live in the Midwest?"

"Oh, no," Nadine says. "Not for a long time now, but there was one who I thought would be here with us forever. She was a lifer like Ginny and me, but she passed away, and we never heard from her family again."

"It was quite upsetting," Ginny says. "Very nice woman, but her children, they didn't appreciate her, or this place."

"I love it here," Juniper declares. "I hope I always spend my summers here, especially now that Emma lives here." Juniper's eyes meet mine, and that deep, fuzzy fire sparks for just a second before I push it away.

"I promise I'll visit." I smile and wink at Ginny.

"Oh dear, I almost forget sometimes that you all are planning to leave me," Nadine says with a slight slur to her words. She and Ginny are having a boozy gin drink. They've been teetering toward being drunk since the finger sandwiches were eaten.

"You can come visit with us, too, Nadine," I say.

"Ginny will have to drive me up the coast."

"Oh, I will? Up where? To Massachusetts? What a nightmare. I never understood what people see in that place. They were vile to people. They try to erase their history up there because there's so much shame. They should be ashamed of themselves for what went on." Ginny throws an off-suit ace. "Shit."

"I had 'em all, Ginny." Nadine throws her last card, takes the hand,

and cackles.

"Not Massachusetts. I guess Mom and Ben have found a place in New Hampshire that looks promising. You should have gone alone," I say, referring to the cards. "We woulda got 'em all."

"That might be but let me tell you something. Even if your partner lets you down, it's always better to have one, to have people, than to go out completely alone," Nadine says.

"That's right," Ginny says. "That's why I tolerate her." She nods to Nadine and takes a long sip of her drink.

"Even when we were both married and making our families, we never really left each other. Never plan to either," Nadine says.

"You don't know what I have planned," Ginny responds.

"I suppose that's true, but I don't think I would have known what to do after Ben's father died if I didn't have you all to come back to."

"I wish I had that," Juniper interjects. "I wish I had closeness like you and Ginny, and Emma and Hannah." She pulls together the deck before slapping it down on the table. Her seat slides back with a squeal as she turns and stomps out the back door.

"Wonder what's wrong with her," Ginny says.

I rise and leave the two older women to their drinks. "I'll get her," I say.

When I walk outside, Juniper's lighting a cigarette and standing against the brick wall, tears streaming down her face.

"You smoke now?"

"Ginny said I can't vape, that the original is better anyway." She shrugs. She crosses her arms over her chest as she leans against the wall with one bare leg over the other, like she's twisting up inside herself. "I know you don't like me."

"What?"

"I know you don't like me. You think I'm obnoxious, annoying, a pain in the ass, just like everyone else does."

"Juniper—"

"No one takes me seriously—no one on this island, no one at home. No one believes I can do anything, but I can." She takes a drag of her cigarette and ashes it on the ground. "I know the only reason we spend any time together is because of Daniel."

I blush a little because she's exactly right. I would never have spent a day with Juniper had it not been for Daniel. I can't even say that I truly like her, but there's this closeness, this freedom, that I feel when I'm with her that I'm not sure I've ever felt with anyone else.

"Listen, no, people probably don't take you seriously, and, yes, you can be a little much."

"What the fuck—" she cry-laughs, turning away from me and walking toward the back gate.

"Wait!" I call. I catch up to her, grab her shoulder and turn her back to me. That radiating electric pulse moves through me again.

"What?" she yells.

"I ... like you. I like being around you. You're strong, Juniper. You're a huge pain in the ass, but I'd be lying if I said I didn't admire that about you, your ability to just do whatever you want all the time and to not give a shit. You come off as so confident, so sure of yourself. I want that."

She sniffs and takes another puff of her cigarette, blowing the smoke out of the side of her mouth. "You really mean that?"

"Yes."

"Do you trust me?"

Every thought in my head is fuck no—she's strange. She's the exact opposite of everything Hannah would say it is okay to be, but a deep signal, bleeping out from my heart and a yearning in my gut, tells me that I should go wherever she takes me. "Yeah, I trust you."

Juniper hands me the cigarette, and I take a pull, trying to look like the girls in old high school movies. My lungs protest, and I cough uncontrollably until Juniper takes the cigarette, throws it on the ground, and grabs my hand. "C'mon, you've got a lot to learn."

I follow Juniper from Ginny's house into town, closer to the main drag, where only a few huge houses stand tall. We stop in front of Richard's.

Gargoyles sit atop the building. Out front, two old sycamore trees create an awning or tunnel up to the stairs. It's an enormous mansion. Its gardens rival Nadine's, not in their tenacity, but in their exactness. Tidy plants grow in precise rows with perfect blooms on each stem.

"What are we doing here?"

"Don't worry, Richard isn't home on Fridays. It's just Eloise and the staff. Sometimes out-of-towners crash here, too. It's the party house."

Juniper fusses with the clasp on the wrought iron gate before it opens with a creak. "You said you trust me, right?"

I stare up at the place. It's different in the daylight. That night of that fucked-up party, it seemed bigger, darker, scarier. It's just a beautiful old house. I step through the gate and onto the property. Juniper takes my hand in hers; it's warm and the slightest bit sweaty.

"What's that smell?"

"The rot?" Juniper asks.

I nod.

"It's the Carrion flowers." She pulls me over to the side of the house, past the towering hollyhocks that smell like the desert. They seem to be strategically placed by the Carrion flowers, because the odor gets worse as we pass. "See?"

The plants are growing in pots around a fountain. The blooms are huge, nearly half the size of my body, towering over us as we stand. I pull the neck of my shirt up over my face to block out the smell. The red and peach petals mimic what I'd imagine the flesh torn from a body would look like. A long, sharp staff rises through the center of the plant. It feels grotesque, perverse, like something I shouldn't be looking at.

"They're not even pretty, so why have them?"

"Why not?" Juniper asks. I guess I really have no answer or argument in return. She jerks my arm down a garden path that winds past a weeping willow tree. Its branches tickle my arms as we run underneath it. Suddenly, she stops and presses her finger to her lips.

A pink shirt exits the back door. Juniper watches closely to make sure he's gone before rushing toward open door and pulling me in before it closes.

"Juniper, I don't think I'm allowed here."

She guides me deeper as we pass through a black-paneled hallway with ivory and charcoal tiles on the floor. Little lamps with tiny flames that cast the slightest glow stand at attention like guards along the windowless pathway.

"Why wouldn't you be allowed here?"

Juniper's nearly dragging me down the hallway. Something just doesn't feel right in here, like we're walking into a private scene. This place is a place I shouldn't see, like a bedroom with a naked relative inside. I just know it.

"If I'm allowed, why are we sneaking around?"

"Trust me." She stops and turns my face to meet hers. "I know you know something's going on here. I do, too. I know Krysten knew that something wasn't right. That rock in Roanoke, you felt it, didn't you? Like *really* felt it?"

That place in Roanoke, the snake, our kiss … they almost feel dream-like, like something that didn't really happen. In my mind, that day is like a glowing lantern hidden by a thick fog. I nod because I did feel it and because Krysten is trying to tell me something. No one else has said it aloud like that. No one has spoken it except Becca, but she's gone, she's dead, and I have to find out what she wanted me to know.

I follow Juniper. My hands long to touch the paneled walls, but I don't let them. I pull them in tight. Something about this place just feels *alive*.

Juniper yanks me into a doorway and shoves me up against the wall. Her heaving chest is pressed to mine. She smells like apple butter. A woman's high-heeled shoes click against the tile floor. Our hearts are beating so hard and so close to each other that I can't tell where hers begins, and mine ends.

"Finn! Oh shit, he didn't leave already, did he?" She's practically at a run when she passes in front of the doorway where we're hiding. A young man—Daniel—trails right behind the woman. When they pass our doorway, Juniper pushes us through the swinging door behind us and into a room. I try to get my bearings in the darkness. She catches the door, being careful to make sure it doesn't simply slam closed and give us away.

She takes my hand and draws me around a wall, hand in hand, our backs to it. Breathing quietly, we wait in the dark until we hear the woman and Daniel walking back in the direction that they came from. The woman is still huffing about Finn. I hold my breath, staying absolutely still. When the hall is silent again, Juniper grabs a match from her pocket and lights it.

"Whew, that was a close call."

"I thought we could be here," I whisper back at her.

"Oh, we can, but there's something I want to show you that I'm not supposed to, that almost no one sees unless you live here. I'm not supposed to have seen it, but they underestimate me; they always—"

I gently grab her shoulder. "Juniper, was that Daniel?"

"Uh, yes, it was."

"What is he doing here?" The match goes out.

"Emma, you just got here. You can't expect to know everything. What do you think Daniel's doing here?" Juniper strikes another match and walks around the room.

"What? I don't know. What are you doing?"

"I'm looking for a lantern; there's usually one just about ... ah, here." She lifts the glass of the old-fashioned lantern, turns the key, and ignites the kerosene inside. The faint orange light brightens the faces that were all around us but completely undetectable in the dark.

The walls are lined with ornately decorated frames that hold moments from over the last few hundred years frozen in time. The black and white, ghostly images are of people stuck in eternal delight. There are hundreds of people in the photos. I take the lamp from Juniper's hand; she smiles and lets me do it. She knows something.

I move the lantern up to the wall to look closer at each photograph before moving on to the next. Juniper follows closely behind me, and I can feel her watching me as I take in each scene: a dinner party on the beach captured in peeling and bleeding sepia; the next one is the oldest I've ever seen, of two women, both wild-looking and weathered, standing by a fire. Their skin clings to their bones, like mom's looked a few weeks earlier. Their stomachs are stretched with children buried inside, their bodies visible beneath sheer and tattered clothing.

A large photograph in the center of the room is where I stop. "Is that *this* house?" Juniper grins. I don't need her to answer. The blooms surrounding it and the gargoyles are exactly the same. The photograph looks at least a hundred years old. I suck in a breath and look over at Juniper, who doesn't break her stare.

Standing in front of the house are Ginny, Dr. Drear, and Eloise, and the date at the bottom says something impossible. The picture was taken over a hundred years ago. One hundred years ago, and they've hardly aged a day.

"That's impossible."

"Nothing's impossible." Juniper runs the length of her hand down my back. The heat from the lamp pales in contrast to the warmth she's summoned inside of me. "That's not all I wanted to show you. Follow me. I'm taking you to the secret garden." She heads back toward the hallway in the darkness. While Juniper's back is turned, I snatch my phone out of my pocket and capture a picture before I follow her.

Lost Hope—Sam

August 10

D r. Drear breathes out a mixture of mothballs and cigarettes. He coughs, and I look around the white-paneled room that I've called my own for the last few months.

He brought a cool white cloth with him to the house. It feels medical, and though this room is not a hospital, I can still smell the faint whiff of antiseptic. It reminds me of the hospital that Becca and I both went into, but from which only I left.

Dr. Drear's hand grazes my thigh with sticky, rubber fingers. His head is beneath the sheet, and his face is close to the parts of me that I want to only be for me and Ben, not for this baby, and not for Richard.

My eyes focus on the ceiling. The sun coming through the window makes it easy to see the dust caked up there. In the night, when I'm usually staring up at the ceiling, the shadow covers the neglect. I wonder if there are little bits of Becca up there.

Ben kneels next to the bed. The window behind him is open, and the breeze wicks away the sweat on my forehead. It's the cold, pale sweat that came with a wave of nausea and a few drops of blood and slimy, clear fluid. I replay the conversation I had with Mom back at Becca's apartment before I left on my honeymoon. She begged me to stay and told me that

I couldn't trust Ben. Something bad was going to happen—she seemed certain. She pleaded with me to move back into my apartment or in with Becca or with her, and the memory plays on a loop in my mind.

I knew she never approved of me marrying into this family, but I could never figure out why. I assumed that it was just because they were so unlike her. Laying here, staring at the ceiling of Nadine's home, it feels eerily similar to the afternoons when I stared at the cracked paint back home, listening to Mom and Dad spit their venom back and forth.

Before I called for Ben from the bathroom, I sat there for a few minutes, watching the blood and fluid drip on the white tile next to the claw foot tub, watching the surface tensions of the drops expand and melt one into another until they broke free and began to travel down the grooves in the tile grout. I felt the thing move, kick at me from inside, kicking to get help, to save it.

I sat motionless like some sort of monster, imagining it dying. It kicked me straight in the stomach, and I retched loudly, alerting Nadine from the hallway. She didn't even so much as knock before she came in and saw what was happening. She phoned Richard immediately. While he examines me, she sits on the chair in the corner, per my and Ben's insistence. She was hovering over me, and it made me want to throw up again, so I asked her to move to the chair. Begrudgingly, she obliged.

As I stare at her from the bed, I see anger in her eyes. It's fury at me for keeping her from the side of her grandchild or whatever *thing* lives inside of me. Its kicks aren't sweet reminders of the life inside me—they feel vile and personal.

"How is the baby? Is everything okay?" Nadine asks.

"Be patient, Nadine." Dr. Drear sounds irritated. At least he's on my side, wanting to be left alone, maybe noticing for himself that things inside of me aren't quite right. When Nadine called him, she wouldn't tell him any of my other symptoms. The flashes of red anger, the constant craving for meat, how certain foods are continuing to make me sick, the strange movements and rapid growth. Nadine chalked it all up to normal pregnancy stuff.

"Samantha, what does it feel like when I do this?" He presses down hard on the bottom right side of my abdomen, the pressure causing a strange sensation like warm fluid being flushed into the womb and a distinct and urgent need to pee.

"It doesn't feel right. I can feel fluid moving around inside," I say.

Ben pats my hand.

"It's as I suspected," Drear says, rising from beneath the cloth and patting my knee. His gloves have bits of blood clinging to them, and the air is saturated with the smell of it.

Nadine gets up from the chair and takes a peek beneath the sheet. I want to rip her hair out. She pulls back and clutches her chest like a God-fearing woman viewing pornography for the first time.

"What is it? Is she gone?"

"Mom!" Ben shouts.

If the baby is gone, would that be so bad?

"No, no, no. Don't worry, Nadine, your grandchild is alive and well. Sam is a strong mother; there's no better place for the child to be."

The doctor throws his gloves, coated in my blood, onto his traveling tray.

"The baby is fine, but your placenta has grown much too close to your cervix. Do you understand what I'm saying?"

I'm hoping that it's the unwavering look of calm on my face that's made him say this and not that I'm a woman who could have no clue about the parts of my body. "Yes, I understand. I'll need bed rest?"

"Such a bright young lady. That is exactly right. I don't want you up and walking for at least a week, except to use the bathroom assisted by Nadine, your daughter, or Ben. After that, I'd say standing for under ten minutes and the rest in bed, I'm afraid."

"I understand," I say. The baby is resting, happy, slumbering. It knows it's here to stay and that I'm to stay put for the next however many weeks. I turn my gaze back to the ceiling. It figures that I'd end up right back on restriction—nothing about this pregnancy is normal.

"Oh, this is just fine. This is great news, isn't it, Sam?" Nadine says, spritely and full of hope.

I nod and smile as I am supposed to do.

"Now, Nadine, I need to discuss something in private with these two, and I need you to leave the room."

"There's nothing they don't want me to know. I'll stay," she says.

I turn to look at Nadine's face. I want to see her sorrow at being left out. Ben throws his arm around his mother's shoulders, and escorts her out of the room. When the door is shut, Ben joins me once again. Crouching next to the bed, he pulls my hand up to his mouth and lays a soft kiss on it. I try to remind myself that this thing growing inside of me is part of this man right here who loves me, and that I must learn to love it.

"Alright. Now that we're alone. I have to advise you that if you've been having intercourse to stop for the time being. Anything that could cause an orgasm will result in a contraction and be detrimental to the baby."

My heart twists upon itself, and I feel myself recoil. It's as if what the man has said is the most vile, disturbing thing I can imagine—because it is. Sex is the only thing that stops the noise.

Ben clears his throat uncomfortably, then turns to giggle at me. "Perhaps slowing down for a bit won't be so bad."

"There are other ways to be intimate, you know," Dr. Drear says, raising a brow and turning to his medical equipment. "I'm going to have Nadine clean these things and keep them here. I'll be coming or sending a nurse by three times a week, and if anything changes, the slightest thing, you let me know, alright?"

"Alright."

He's addressing me this whole time, not looking at Ben. I must admit that I had my doubts about Richard's feelings toward women and toward me having ownership of my body.

He peers over at the door before saying anything else, but then he leans in closer. "If you believe that the drink she's giving you is making you sick, I will do anything I can to make sure you never have to drink that thing again. Is that something you'd like?"

"You think it's the drink?" Ben asks, confused, like he's hearing some secret for the first time.

"I told you, Ben," I say.

"You didn't."

"Well, I guess I ..." I suppose I hadn't told him. It's been only in my head that I thought the drink had something to do with everything.

"Why didn't you tell me?" Ben asks.

"I didn't want to make Nadine upset. I didn't want you to be upset with me either. I'm living here in your mother's house. In a place, far from home, in a place I never thought I'd be for so long, and it's uncomfortable sometimes."

"You have to admit, Ben," Dr. Drear says. "When Nadine has decided something, you'd better not get in her way. I understand why Samantha hasn't spoken up. She's a quite convincing and concerned woman, your mother."

Ben looks back and forth between Dr. Drear and me, almost in awe.

"I had no idea, but you won't have that drink again going forward. I'm sorry you didn't think you could come to me," Ben says, like a wounded boy on the playground.

"No, we shall not have you take that drink anymore. I can write you a prescription for prenatal vitamins," the doctor says, pulling a white pad from his suit pocket, the pages crinkled and dog-eared.

"Can I take these?" I reach across Ben into the drawer of the nightstand and pull out a bottle—the one Becca gave me. I hold them out to him, and he takes them from my hand and examines them for a moment before returning them to my hand.

"These are just what you need. No worries about Nadine. We will take care of it, won't we, Ben?"

"Of course," he says. "I'll meet you downstairs."

Dr. Drear walks across the room and opens the door.

Ben stands, staring at the doorway, in unison with me. Has Nadine been standing there the whole time, waiting? Her gaze is razor sharp and aimed at me, at my failure to carry the child the way she wants me to.

Her glare stirs a guilt I can't ignore. The child turns in my stomach. The door latches, leaving Nadine to the wrath of Dr. Drear.

Ben walks the length of the room and opens the other window. "It stinks in here."

Embarrassment spreads like fire through my body. He's talking about me, about the blood and fluid leaking. He's talking about the baby. His baby. *My baby.*

"I know Emma is going to be disappointed," I say. He lays down on the bed next to me, making sure not to disturb my body too much. He lays atop the pillowy, down blanket and rests his palm on top of my swollen hand. I hadn't even thought of Emma until now. What day is it? When does school begin? How long exactly has it been since my sister was spread across a highway not four miles away from here? "We're going to have to stay; we can send her in the fall. Ahead of us, but I don't know. It doesn't feel right. Honestly, Ben, nothing feels right anymore."

"Her school offers an online program by the semester."

I don't want Emma to have to make yet another sacrifice for me. How could Ben even consider it? Had he been preparing for this talk?

"How do you know that?" I ask.

"I looked it up when I found out that you were pregnant," Ben says.

"Why didn't you tell me?"

"I didn't want to say it out loud. I didn't want to jinx it, and I didn't want to pressure you in case it wasn't what you wanted."

"You just didn't say anything, Ben."

"Sam."

Tears pool and spill from my eyes. I move my hand from beneath Ben's grasp to wipe them away. "I saw your face when you found out, and we never talked about it, not really. And now ... Now it might kill me, and you've been researching what to do about it behind my back?"

The mattress rises as he leaves the bed. Anger flashes across his face, but he catches himself and stops. He comes back toward me, laying a hand on my shoulder.

"That's not fair. This isn't about the baby. I want to keep you safe and—"

"Alive."

"Yes!" he shouts. "Is that so terrible?"

"There are worse things than death," I say, no emotion evident in my tone.

"Would Becca say that?" he snarls.

My teeth sink into my lip. Focus on the dust. The particles of her skin and mine—

of Nadine's and Krysten's—stuck forever in the creases of the paneled white ceiling, ashen bits never to live again, only to float together and apart in the crevasses of a wall.

"I'm sorry," he says.

I hold my breath as I turn to him. His eyes well up with tears.

"I'm moving us into the other house," he says.

"What? Are you sure?"

"I can't watch you live like a guest here, struggling to stay alive, to care for yourself in someone else's home. I don't want to be here, either."

"You don't?"

"No." He laughs. "We won't stay a minute more than we have to. Emma will have a place to study. The baby will have a nursery. Jax will have his own space, too. We can be together there comfortably without my mom staring at us at every turn."

"You feel it, too? I'm not crazy?" I wasn't alone. He *did* feel the shift in her. When we first arrived, I thought that she'd be my friend and that she'd look out for me. I don't know anymore. She's so obsessed with the baby.

"Why do you think I rarely come back here? Why do you think I wanted to move hours away as soon as I possibly could to start a new life with you? I love my mother, but she's too much. I won't let anything happen to you or Emma, and I won't let you live under another woman's roof any longer."

The fear that gripped my heart so tightly loosens a little. A flood of warmth fills my chest. It's like the first time I saw him—eating alone in the diner—and how, when he looked at me, it was as if he'd been waiting for me to arrive the whole time.

"Are you sure?"

"I am a thousand percent sure. I'm so sorry for what Emma is going through, for what you're all going through. What I ..."

"I know you loved her, Ben. Are you ready to go back there? Where Krysten died?"

"I am going to make it up for us. It's just a house. It's my house. I'm going to make it ours, and then, when the baby's out and you're healthy and ready, we will go to our new place, far away from here."

"Really?"

"Yes." His lips meet my forehead. "You spend your bedrest time looking at our future home. We still haven't found the one. When you find one you like, I'll set up meetings. Emma and I can look at them. Or just me and Jax. Whatever. We'll find a place."

I thrust myself toward him, pressing my lips to his. I let the tears pour out. I don't need to hold them back, not with Ben. I am not a bad mother. I deserve to feel happy and *safe*.

"Okay," I say, smiling and sniffling.

"Okay?"

"Yeah."

"I'm going to meet the doctor downstairs. Are you alright?"

"I'm fine." I lift my cell phone and wave it at him as he walks over to the door. "I love you, Ben Cross. Can you hand me my bag from the chair?"

Ben retrieves it and sets it next to me on the bed. "I love you, Sam."

I smile.

When he's outside of the room, I let out the rest of my breath. I am going to have to tell Emma that everything we had planned is gone, but if I know Emma, she probably already knows.

I stare back at the ceiling, the paneled landscape that I won't have to view for much longer. The waves crash outside the window.

A crow greets me hello.

There's a thud outside.

Don't eat the pie.

The squeal of metal on concrete.

My sister's scream.

I reach into the slouchy leather bag, my fingers brushing past a tube of lipstick, a tampon, my wallet, until they reach the very bottom, to the book I shouldn't have.

The book with the gold lettering.

Moving Day—Emma

August 11

In light of the less-than-fortunate news, Ben has enlisted our help. I wish I could say that I was angry, upset, surprised. I knew we wouldn't be leaving Camillia anytime soon. I don't think the island wants us to.

"Good morning, Emma," Nadine chirps from the tiny table in front of the greenhouse. The breeze off the ocean carries with it the scent of salt and fish. You'd never be able to tell that anything had happened in the greenhouse. The windows are back to normal. Nadine's herbs are growing somehow taller than before the incident with the crow. She has a way with plants, she says. She sings to them sometimes—or maybe she's casting spells.

"Good morning," I reply.

"Daniel's already over at the house with Ben. Are you two an item?" She peeks her head up from her knitting. It looks like a blanket for the baby. She's more excited about it than Ben and Mom are.

"Just friends—for now," I say, but there's a tiny dig at my heart. We definitely like each other, but I can't shake that moment with Juniper, the kiss in the forest. The feeling that I had with her was unlike anything I'd ever experienced or even heard about before. When we are together, it feels like we are one, like we are an entity ourselves that has always been and will always be.

Nadine's lips open to a great white smile, a true Hollywood one, impossibly clean and white.

"Dear, I want you to know that even though you're moving to the other house, you can come over anytime, and I wonder if you might do an old lady the favor of giving me some peace of mind in return."

"Sure, what is it?"

"You know that Ben's father died when he was very young, and it was hard on him. I hardly think he has a memory of him at all or memories of most of his childhood, really. I must admit, I could hardly take care of him. Ginny came out to live with us for a couple of years. Helped me attend all the red carpets, but was never in any of the pictures. She loves Ben like her own son. Then Krysten, when she passed ... it hit me hard, but I tried to be there for him. He pushed me away and ran off. Who can blame him? I checked out emotionally when his father died. Well, now we're all here, and I have him back again. I have all of you. With the news of your mother's bedrest ..."

"What do you need from me?"

"You know this place is special, don't you? You feel it deep in your bones? Juniper thinks you do."

She's right: I do feel it, but I keep that to myself.

"You can't leave here. Ben must stay, no matter how rough things get. If they plan to leave before the baby's born, I need you to tell me. I can't let my son run off in his feelings. It wouldn't be good for anyone." Her body tightens, and her voice becomes more urgent. "I need him to know that I'm here this time. I need the courtesy of being able to talk to him, to be there for him this time around. You'll tell me, won't you? If they feel like they need to leave before—"

"The baby gets here," I finish her sentence. "I think it's all going to be okay. I think my mom will be happier in the new place, and I think we will be too."

Nadine's shoulders relax. She nods and picks up a glass and copper floral mister then starts her little songs for the plants again.

I'm dismissed.

The path outside the garden is hard to follow, as the steps are totally swamped in plant life, mosses, and leaves.

Vines grow up the side of Krysten's house closest to Nadine's where they hadn't before—closing the gap and connecting the two homeslike an umbilical cord.

A home of death and dying tied to one of curiosities and mystery. I still don't understand what happened that night in the first few weeks. When I woke, I was drawn to Nadine's office. The message there, the paper—it had to be Krysten.

I wish I could communicate with her. Since the accident, things have been relatively silent. I wish she'd give us a sign if moving in is a bad idea.

I wouldn't blame her if she gave up, as absolutely no one besides me and Jax believes the messages she's sent. Juniper does too, but she's not disturbed by them—she's excited.

This house is quite the thing during the day—not nearly as scary as when it gets dark, and Krysten must feel free to roam around to wake us.

When Ben broached the subject of taking over this house and moving out of Nadine's, I was okay with it. I don't fear Krysten anymore. Mom seems okay with it, too—happy even.

It already has a nursery.

I push the sliding glass door open.

"The sliding door needs oiling!" I shout, coming into the house that reeks of paint and plaster. The kitchen has turned into a flop spot for all the supplies and equipment.

"Anyone home?" I call out.

"Huh, that's strange," Ben says from down the hallway.

Daniel, Jax, and I have been slowly working on the rooms off the main living area downstairs for the past couple of days. Ben could only line up a painter for three days and wanted to make sure the primary bedroom and nursery were completely different than before. They lined the nursery walls with wallpaper featuring cute little scenes of rabbits and children playing in fields and meadows, contrasting with the bone-white wainscoting on the lower half.

"Emma, come here," Ben calls.

I move through the room, careful not to touch the newly-painted, emerald green walls. The living room furniture, couches and wingback chairs are bunched into the center of the room.

The floor creaks beneath my paint-spackled Converse—Ben's at the end of the hall where the bureau used to reside.

"See this here?" Ben points to the corner where there's a visible seam. "There's a draft or something coming in from here—I'm not sure how. We need to make sure this place is secure, safe, and no nasty insects or anything can come in. The last thing we need is palmetto bugs invading the house. I need to get someone out to examine the structure since it's been without a host for so long, but I can't get anyone to call me back about it. Can you have Daniel caulk over this, and we'll just paint it for now?"

He is right; there is a tiny gap between the two walls. Ben gets up to walk away, scratching his head. His eyes have bags beneath them. He's sweaty, dirty, and tired. It's a version of him that I haven't seen before, but it's comforting. Nadine seems to be aging backward, but Ben at least still looks like a real person.

"Why do you think they built it like this?" I ask.

He tosses his hands in the air. "Probably an oversight; Nadine had it built so quickly. You know how she is; when she wants something, she gets it. She probably rushed them, and they did what they could as quickly as possible. We didn't live here that long before..." Ben pauses. "I'll make sure it's right this time." Ben turns to Jax. "Hey, bud. Why don't you and Emma start on your room today? We've got the rest of this stuff. Your furniture is being delivered tomorrow."

Ben scruffs the top of Jax's head, and he sighs.

I nod to Jax as he follows Ben down the hall toward the stairs. I run my finger down the tiny little gap. There is a draft coming in, a cold one, but it's 105 degrees and muggy. It must not be coming from outside.

"Daniel," I call out.

"What's up?" he asks, approaching me and wrapping his arms around my waist, pulling me into him. He's warm and sweaty. He has a musky smell. I try my best to make a smooth turnout—pretending to be playful and not rejecting him.

Which I'm not.

There are more urgent matters at hand. "Do any of these houses have basements?"

He shrugs. I was less effective than I thought I was. He seems annoyed at me, not wanting to just drop everything and make out. "Huh, maybe? I'm not sure. Juniper or Nadine would probably know the answer to that."

"There's not supposed to be a basement in this house," I say. "I don't want Nadine to know. I know that something is going on."

"What do you mean, *something's going on?*"

I bite my lip and turn.

"You're hiding something, what is it?" Daniel asks, seeming more curious than angry. "Why did we go out to Roanoke? Why have you been spending so much time with Juniper? You need to tell me what's happening."

"I *need* to?" I reply, turning to meet his gaze and letting out a pronounced *ha*.

"You know what I mean. Listen, you don't have to tell me anything, but I know you're up to something and ..." He lets out a breath before reaching out to me. His hands are dirty with dried paint but as gentle as they've ever been. Warm and safe. "I know that your life hasn't been easy, but you can trust me. I wouldn't be here if I didn't care about you."

I twist my mouth and avoid eye contact. He's right; why else would he be helping with all this? Why else would he come over and paint all day, and listen to me go on about literally nothing for hours, if he didn't care about me?

"It all started with what we saw that night, here, when Krysten was trying to talk to us. Will you keep a secret? Don't even tell Juniper, promise?"

"Of course, yeah."

"I came back here after the night with that fucked-up pie party. Jax and I broke in. I swear Krysten was trying to tell me something. It's why I went over to Dr. Drear's mansion that night. She was trying to tell me that something bad was going to happen that night."

"Jesus, Emma. I don't know. You really believe in this stuff now, huh?"

"You were there that night with the Ouija board. You saw it, too. I know this sounds insane, but I'm not crazy. I'm a lot of things, but I never believed in this stuff either, before. You believe me, right?"

"I do." He twists his lips. "I don't want to, but yeah ... I do. I've been trying not to think about it."

"We can't not think about it anymore. Something is happening to my mom. There's something strange about this island, and something is not right about Nadine. Becca knew something was going on, too."

"What? Becca?"

I pull Daniel in closer to me. I don't want Ben to hear. "She thought something was going on with this island. Something, like devil worship or sacrifice."

"A bunch of grannies worshiping the devil? That seems a little—"

"You were there that night. You saw what happened." I stiffen. "Don't you remember this?" I slap my hand against the wall.

"What?"

"Think back to that night—what used to be here? What was here the night we did the séance with Juniper and Jax but isn't here anymore?"

Daniel's hand meets mine against the wall, and the collision of our pinky fingers sends gooseflesh up my arm. Then he runs his hand along the wall, up and down.

"Wait ... wasn't there an armoire or something here?"

I nod. "Yep, and now there's a wall."

"Ben must have moved it, right? To get things ready?"

"No. That night, Jax and I came back, and it was here, then, just suddenly gone. Like turn my head, and it's gone."

"That doesn't make sense. Where would it go?"

"I don't know, but you know that armoire? I have a key to it. Krysten led me to it, and I'm going to find out what's behind this wall."

Mommy Dearest—Sam

August 12

I'm at the beach again, the sugary white sand pressed between my toes. The storm is closer than I remember. Happiness radiates through my body at the sight of my boy up on the hill with Nadine and Ben—I feel safe.

Suddenly, I'm knee-deep in the water, and it's warm and soothing. The tide at my knees is being sucked back toward the house. It's the house where Ben and I live now, where Krysten died, and the water is all the way up to it. I watch as enormous dark waves crash against it.

I'm in a shallow spot. All the water decided to leave me and take its place over at the door. Maybe it will wash the house away, wash away everything that came before, all the death. Maybe it will make it all clean again, a fresh start.

"Samantha!"

I turn toward Nadine's voice. She's yelling from the patio of her home. The water seems to be ignoring it like some kind of impenetrable, invisible barrier protects it. Ben and our son wave at me. I wave back.

"You should wake up now." Her voice carries so well over the distance. It's like Nadine is right next to me. My feet trudge through the water and sand, trying to make my way to them.

Oh, God, Emma.

I forgot about Emma—her red hair floating in the water. I look down frantically, splashing through the water, trying desperately to find her. There's hair, so I tug at it, pulling it closer—the weight of a body behind it. Her stringy hair slips out of my fingers, but I claw it back into my grasp, pulling with all my might as the strength of the ocean tries to take her out to sea. I turn her over, and her face is pale. Her eyes are open and milky and rotten. Bits of her flesh have been eaten away by creatures of the sea.

My beautiful daughter.

I stumble in the water, trying to regain my bearings and pull her to me, falling back into the sea. When I finally stand again, she's gone.

"Samantha, wake up! Join us!" Nadine calls from high up on the sand dune. Ben's holding our son up on his shoulders. They're waving to me.

I wake with a start.

"Samantha, you need to wake up. It's nearly twelve in the afternoon." Nadine barges through the door with a cup of tea and some cookies. "Good to get rest, though, darling."

Nadine's dressed to the nines today. She's wearing a pencil skirt and a ruffled grey top with a fitted, short-sleeved jacket over it. Her make-up is done. She looks striking and young—much younger than I've ever seen her look before.

I struggle to catch my breath. The metallic taste in my mouth, likely from brushing my teeth in bed on and off for the last few days, never quite seems to go away. She places the tray on Ben's side of the bed and brings the cup of tea over to me.

My body trembles from the abrupt waking. The smell of spiced tea gives me something to focus on.

I take the cup from her hand and gulp it down. I'm thirsty and famished. Nadine presses the back of her hand to my forehead.

"You're all wet," she says.

"I've been sweating a lot when I sleep."

"Probably just the hormones." She takes a handkerchief from her pocket and wipes my forehead.

The nightmares keep coming—worse since I've started reading that book. I've read the pages relentlessly, even looking on Google Translate word after word to make sense of the Old English. Things about eternal life. Circular life. However, a lot of it doesn't translate into modern speech.

There are illustrated pictures of pregnant women, magical vines, and glowing stones. It's like an anthology of fairytales.

One image won't leave my mind. A pregnant woman holding two babies, one dead and the other alive.

"I'm fine."

"*I'm fine.* I hear a lot of that but look what happened when you were 'fine' before. You ended up here. I love you like my own. You, this baby, Ben, and Emma, you all mean the world to me." She smiles, and her teeth are pearly and white. Everything about her looks new. I know she doesn't love me like she loves Ben or this child.

"And Jax," I say.

"Oh, yes, how is the boy doing?"

I sigh and lean back, handing her my teacup that she takes in her lap as she sits down next to my legs on the bed. "I don't know ... how well can a kid be doing after losing their mother?"

The sheer curtains rustle in the breeze. I don't remember opening the window. The breeze is cooler than normal.

"Well." Nadine sets the empty teacup down on the tray next to me. "I suppose that's true. I don't think they can be doing well at all right after. I know Ben didn't ... do well. He was not okay for a while. He had to take care of me ..." She stops and takes a deep breath in, searching for the words to explain the grief.

I know what it feels like to be so stricken with sorrow or fear or anger that you're frozen in time. Your child has needs, but the only thing you can do is to exist and try to keep your heart beating, when part of you wishes your body would give up.

"I wasn't always the mother Ben needed." She shakes her head. A tear falls down her cheek, and I reach out to her, laying a hand on her arm. "I really wasn't. I'm happy that he landed in your arms."

"We aren't perfect. We can't always be what they need. What's important is that we try when we can."

"Where are they, anyway? Our boys," she asks, and I suppose she's right in that statement. Jax is my boy now.

"Ben took Jax out to use his old metal detector; they're supposed to be collecting treasures on the beach."

"Oh, that's just delightful. That will be good for both of them, I'm sure." Nadine wipes the tear from beneath her eye and pulls out a compact mirror to check her make-up.

The baby kicks at my right rib, causing a sharp pain. I gasp.

"Is everything alright?"

"Oh, yeah." I groan. "Just this kid's kicks are out of control. They're much more intense than I remember at this stage."

Nadine's whole face lights up, and the few wrinkles seem to disappear into her creamy, smooth complexion. "Can I feel it?"

I want to say no, but I should be kind. My mother has disappeared on me, and Nadine is trying to help.

I nod.

"Are you sure?"

"Yeah, I'm sure." A closed smile spreads across my face. She rests her hand on my stomach, and I take my own and help her navigate it over to the place where they kicked. Her hand feels cool and bony beneath mine, which is quite swollen and sweaty. They kick, sending a jolt of pain through my lungs, but I hide it and smile harder.

"Oh!" she says, and a delightful laugh follows. "Oh, Samantha, thank you. Krysten never ... let me feel it."

"I thought you two were close?"

"I thought so, too, but when she became pregnant, she changed, or maybe she was never who I thought she was to begin with. She's not like you. I will always love her and appreciate what she gave us, but you are so much stronger and would do *anything* for your child."

It's not flattery. She really believes it. My mother never called me strong, and she certainly never demonstrated how to be a strong woman in the face of adversity. Even now, when I need her most, she ran, wrapped up in some deranged idea of a curse. It's clear that the people who live on this island view this place as some kind of Mecca. It would make sense that my grandmother wouldn't have wanted my mom to leave. Nadine moves her hand to mine, and it makes my muscles relax, and the baby stops moving.

Maybe now is the time to find out more.

"Nadine. I don't want to pry, but Ben won't really talk about it. What happened with Ben's father? What made you leave Hollywood? Why did you come back to this island?"

Nadine giggles. Her bright eyes shine like otherworldly gems. "Ben's father died from a heart attack. It was sudden, and certainly, we'd been out in Hollywood making a whole life. I never told Ben this, but his father and I were on the brink of divorce when it happened."

"Really? I'm sorry, that makes things complicated."

"I wanted to come back to the island to raise Ben. Edard didn't agree. He liked the life and the friends he had, and he was just on the brink of a big break. He got a pilot for a TV show after the other lead fell ill, but I could see that the place was changing Edard—he wasn't the man I fell in love with. He was obsessed with work and the parties and success. I had wanted all that too, before Ben came along."

"Then he was your world."

Nadine wipes her tears with a silken handkerchief. "He was. First, Hollywood had my heart, then Edard, but when Ben came along, I knew I needed to be here with my family and raise him more simply. I still loved Edard, but he wasn't going to let me take Ben. I was so scared to lose him, so that was a hard time. I called Ginny a lot. We talked about maybe I'd come for a visit with Ben, and I wouldn't leave, and that's what happened."

My stomach turns.

"Just not how I wanted it."

"Wait, he died here on the island?"

I thought Ben and Nadine had always said he died, and that's what made them return to the island so she wouldn't have to raise him alone.

"Yes," Nadine says. Her emerald eyes pierced me. I've let myself be vulnerable. "His ashes rest in the garden that Ben took you to."

Fear hits me like a ton of bricks; it must be obvious on my sweating face.

"You don't think we'd let you wander without knowing exactly where you are in your condition, do you?"

I press back the urge to yell, *How dare you! This isn't your baby!* Instead, I plaster on a face—she can't know I'm seething and scared.

She lightly rubs the top of my stomach before rising from the bed. "I wish I could stay, but I am needed at a meeting in town. Eloise is hosting it. All the residents are going."

"Everything okay?"

"I don't know if you've seen the weather report, but it appears that storm season may be starting a little early this year. It's probably nothing, but we want to be prepared just in case. Measures are in place to have supplies ready, especially with you on the island. Dr. Drear is making sure, if anything else happens, he has all the equipment he needs here."

"Storms? How bad?"

"We never really know how bad until right before." She returns to my side just to pat my hand. "Don't worry. Our buildings are made to withstand anything, even a hurricane. We chose this island for a reason, and you have nothing to worry about."

I nod, and Nadine leaves my side, closing the door behind her. She's been hiding that information. She wanted me to know that no matter what I think or feel, I'm never alone on this island, that she can read me like that little book of hers.

Puddles—Emma
August 13

The sheets are cold and damp when I wake, sweaty, with a start. I rush to silence the phone ringer before it wakes anyone else in the house. I press the green button.

"Emma, I've been trying to get ahold of you since last night. Where have you been?" Hannah's voice echoes through the phone.

"I know, I'm sorry. We lost signal yesterday. It just came back. I was..." I bite my bottom lip "... with Juniper, trying to get things ready for the big storm that's rolling in."

"You're hanging out with Juniper?" Hannah asks. I'm lying on my back with my legs against the wall. My hair drapes over the edge of the mattress. "She's a bitch."

"Hannah!"

"Hey, I can swear sometimes, and Juniper is a real bitch."

My face reddens with shame because I used to think that, too. Now, being with her is intoxicating. She's shown me things—like the garden with the same rock as Roanoke. I know that something strange is going on in Camillia: the plants, the pie, the dead people. There's a connection to that old island, Roanoke, and the disappearances. A whistle of wind comes in from the open window next to the bed. The morning light is creeping up and spilling in.

It's cooler and windier than it was yesterday. Nadine said that the storm might be worse today. I need to find out what the fuck is going on before it hits.

"Emma, are you still there?"

"Yeah. She's definitely a bitch, but she knows something about this island, about these people and all the weird plants. I have to protect my mom and Jax. She showed me something in Roanoke and in this weird secret garden. She's trying to help me, I think."

She sighs over the receiver. "Can you, like, be extra careful with her? Anyway, I found out what that inscription means."

"Tell me."

"It's not an exact translation, but it's along the lines of 'witches live forever' or 'women don't fear death.'"

"Witches. That explains the photographs." Why would Juniper show me? Does she know what her Aunt Ginny really is?

"You guys should get off the island, witches or no witches. Hurricanes are no joke."

"We can't. I can't risk taking my mom in her condition unless I know for sure that we're in danger here. Besides, all the residents always stay. They say the hurricane doesn't hit this island the same as the others or the houses are stronger. Did you go by my grandma's house?"

"I did. It looked like she was there; the lights were on. Her car was in the driveway, but I knocked and rang the bell, but no one answered."

Relief briefly allows me to stop clenching every muscle in my body. "Okay, I mean, maybe she's alright."

"Right," Hannah says, only half-heartedly. She's not convinced, either, but I can't deal with that right now. "I mean, maybe it's okay to be with them, to get through this birth thing and then get out, but it looks like a hurricane, and I'm worried for you."

If she knew what I did, then maybe she'd understand. Plus, the island is basically guarded, and they're saying we need to batten down.

"I know. Listen, I'm going to tell my mom today. I'm going to tell her what happened with Becca looking into all this stuff and about the picture I found." Now that I have enough evidence, she'll believe me this time. She needs to trust me.

"Good. I know your mom didn't believe you before. I didn't even totally believe you before, but that picture ... it doesn't make sense. All those pictures. The weird rock. Even if it's not real, the important thing is that *they* all believe it is real. These people are nuts. I couldn't get a copy of the book you sent me, but I found some pages online, leaked again by that guy who claimed to work for them. Human sacrifice, poisoned pies. I looked into it. Have you ever heard the myth of what happened when the pilgrims landed? When they went to find other colonies? He says they made a deal, and there has to be a sacrifice. A sacrifice of children ... Emma?" Static rips through the call. "... part about the dinner?"

A knock sounds on my door.

"Hold on, Hannah, I think Jax or someone is awake," I whisper into the phone and set it down. I walk over to the door and open it. The hallway is empty. I turn my head left and right, but both ends are still, quiet, and dark. The shades are still drawn throughout the house. Shadows loom all down the hall.

My stomach tightens as I step one foot into the hallway, and I can already feel it's a thousand times cooler than my bedroom. Cold, like the night of the séance. Cold, like the dead. I turn back and close the door. I grab my phone and hold it up to my ear.

"I think it's Krysten," I whisper.

"Hello? Emma?" Static. "I can't hear you!"

Knock, knock, knock.

"Did you hear that?" I whisper to Hannah. I run to the door and quickly open it, but again, the hall is quiet, cold, and empty.

Static crackles loudly. The longer I listen, the more I realize it's not static; it's the waves. Ocean waves—the whoosh of the water coming in and out over and over again. I end the call and put the phone in my pocket.

I amble through the hallway and over to the balcony loft. The reading area where there was a bookshelf, Krysten's bookshelf, is now empty, aside from a few cardboard boxes. The whooshing isn't coming from the receiver anymore. It's coming from the open sliding door downstairs. The curtains surrounding the door whip back and forth with the wind.

My feet hit the stairs, and I take shallow breaths as I descend. My hand grips the banister to steady myself. I step slowly down the stairs until I pause, my feet wet.

There's water on the floor—puddles lead from the back door. My eyes follow them; they're small and sporadic until they pool near the kitchen area, where we did the séance, where Krysten bled to death. The water doesn't stop there. I reach the end of the stairs and approach the door. It's not raining, but the dark grey skies feel like an omen. The air smells like metal and rust, like Nadine's soil. I step, grip my feet to the floor, and pull the door shut. Every little sound I produce makes my neck hairs stand straight on end, and my veins constrict.

My feet wade through the puddles on the floor until I'm standing in the big one. The puddles continue, and I follow them into the hallway, all the way over to the wall that I know is hiding that armoire until—

"Emma?" Ben calls from the other room.

I scream and nearly fall over.

"What's going on?"

"Be careful. The floor's wet!" I say.

"Alright." Ben yawns. I turn and walk out of the hallway and back into the main room. "Where's the spill?"

"Right—" The puddles are gone. The floor is dry, and the only wet things are my feet. Why wouldn't Krysten want Ben to see? "My feet are wet. I was ..."

"Don't worry about it. I'll make some coffee." Ben walks shirtless into the kitchen, right over the spot where the puddle was, where Krysten died, without so much as flinching.

"Do you feel like it's cold in here?"

"No, but the storms are getting closer. If you're chilly, you can close the windows. I don't mind," he says, letting out another loud yawn before I grab my phone from my pocket and see that once again, the signal is gone.

BEDREST—SAM

What time is it? The ice water next to my bed warmed to room temperature during my nap. The house has air conditioning, but it doesn't reach the upper level in the way I'd like it to. I get so dry all the time despite the unrelenting humidity. My lips are broken and peeling again, and the heat makes them itchy. I grab my phone; it's six p.m. That was not a nap. I've been passed out since breakfast.

I stop and listen for creaking, for any sign that someone is around. I'm immediately gratified as I hear footsteps coming up the hall.

Emma bursts through the door, and I flick on the lamp next to the bed.

"Good evening, Mother." Emma's face has a thousand more freckles than usual. Her hair is frizzy, and she's brought a serving tray to me. "Today for afternoon tea we have ... tea, and cookies that I baked with Jax. Please tell me they're delicious and worth the effort."

"Oh, lovely dear daughter, thank you."

Emma walks around the bed to the other side and sets the wooden tray down in Ben's sleeping spot. My stomach is gargantuan and constantly moving. I couldn't balance anything on it for more than a second.

"How was your nap?" she asks. She's been as bad as Ben lately, fussing over me and watching my every move.

"It was a nap. I woke up here in bed where I woke up this morning from my night sleep and where I'll take the rest of my evening and the day tomorrow."

"Very exciting lives we lead, aren't they?"

"Tell me about your life," I say, lifting my tea from the tray and to my mouth. It's scalding, but I can tolerate that these days.

"Earlier, Jax and I took a batch of cookies over to Ginny's house, and she was quite delighted with them, or she was faking. Who knows? She had a few other old ladies at the house, too. They were playing a card game and drinking gin."

"As they do."

"Always. While we were there, Ginny showed us this weird room she has."

The room with the book.

"She showed it to you?" I say, lowering my tea to my belly.

"Yeah, why?" Emma's eyes move from mine to the floor. "She showed us something that she had that was important to the island. She said she wanted me to inherit it one day. She was drunk."

"Huh ..."

"A pie dish from the sixteenth century. She said she uses it every year for the pie thing. All the women have one. Also, I heard them talking about an old colony when they thought we left. About how a sacrifice had to be made." Her cup is leaning. My chest tightens. "You know we're not far from a place called Roanoke. That's where that whole English colony disappeared."

"You're going to spill your tea."

"Sorry, but Mom, what if they all didn't disappear? Don't you think it's strange? This place? What happened to Krysten and the woman

Annabelle? You started getting sick after eating that pie."

"What are you saying?" I grab a cookie from the tray, leaving bits of crumb on the quilted blanket. The nutmeg and butter make my mouth water.

"How was your visit with Dr. Drear?"

"Fine. He moved the due date up again. He said the baby is measuring larger, which makes sense with how big I've gotten. Listen, this is good news. I should have the baby by the end of August. We'll be out of here sooner." Trying to assure her and myself at the same time.

"I think he's a witch."

I almost choke on a mouth full of cookie, laughing. Emma's face is unwavering—she's not joking. She's serious.

"Why? Because they've been a little wrong about my due date? It happens all the time. Believe me, they're just guesses."

"No ... not just because of that. I'm saying ... something isn't right, and I know it."

I chew the last crumbly bits of cookie and mull over what to say next.

Maybe these people *are* dangerous. I don't want to scare Emma, and I don't even know if I *can* leave. There's a storm coming. Not only that, but they're watching us. The whole fucking island seems to only care about one thing—making sure this child gets born. After that, we'll leave.

Emma stares, waiting for an answer.

"You're right; this place is odd. I don't believe in ghosts, but you're right that there are things here that we can't explain. I don't know why I would wake up at night in the other place, or why I had weird dreams, why ..."

"There are crows all over the roof here and fucking snakes hanging around everywhere. Why did you get so sick after that weird ass pie thing?"

Language, I'm waiting for my sister to say.

"Nadine, Ginny, and some of the other women, they probably believe in the occult or whatever weird religious thing they've got going on here, but it's not real. What's real is that we have trauma. My sister, your aunt, died. We have both been put in difficult positions and experienced horrible things that we shouldn't have."

"It's not just that, Mom." Her face grows red.

"Our time here started with a horrible tragedy. I love you, and I believe that you're scared, but I can't let you keep on thinking there's some plot against us or that I'm in danger. I'll have the baby soon, and we'll leave." My voice gets louder, desperate. "We don't have a lot of options right now. There's no such thing as witches."

I expect her to deflate, but she doesn't. She shakes, spilling the tea remaining in her cup on the bed. Emma sets the cup on the tray and storms out of the room. Each step shakes the house.

"Emma—"

Before I say anything else, she rushes back into my room and tosses a heap of papers on my stomach. The child writhes inside of me. "Look."

"What?"

"I'm going to find out what's happening here even if you won't. Becca knew something was going on. She was trying to save you!"

Save me. The words are a knife in my chest. My eyesight goes fuzzy like a missing channel on a television. My breath is nowhere to be found. I sink, then erupt back to reality in a deep pain. "This has gone far enough. You can't do this to me. You can't keep on blaming the supernatural for everything that you don't like. You need to get a grip before you turn into my mother!"

"I'm not—"

"Get out!" I shout, my throat tightening. A lump grows so large within it that it feels like it's stretching the skin around my neck, threatening to choke me.

Emma doesn't leave. Instead, she points. "Read the papers! Your sister knew something was wrong here. You tried to keep her from helping you! How did that turn out?"

"You nasty little thing! How can you say that to me?"

Emma looks like a whipped puppy.

"I'm sorry," I say, but it's too late.

"Mom. That pie, the one with the aftertaste that you kept going on about when you were sick, what color was the custard?" she asks through tears.

I search my mind. That whole night is so fuzzy, but I remember. It was strange—it was blue, not white or cream like normal custard. "It was blue."

Emma pulls a vine with Cobalt flowers from her pocket. "They say these can make you see God. Did you?"

Emma stomps out of the room. I hold my tears in, waiting—listening for her to go down the stairs and leave the house before I burst. The sobs come fast and hard.

My nose runs, causing me to sniff. I keep my eyes up—away from whatever lies in those papers as long as I possibly can. A sense of curiosity and dread fills me, so I peek at the letter on top filled with my sister's handwriting.

Dr. Drear didn't exist until 1990?

*But been practicing for more than
forty years? Blue dye?*

Sam got sick.

Sam pregnant??

*Nadine has been gone, where is she
going? Where is Ben going?*

*Sam growing at high rate. Sick all
the time.*

*Nadine is going into the oth-
er house. But she's not there. I've
followed her. She disappears and
comes home later.*

Are the houses connected?

*Sam waking up every night at 3
a.m. again.*

*No documented death for the
woman who killed herself.*

*Man from the party called. I'm
not crazy.*

Oh God.

My fingers scan over the pen on the paper in her beautiful handwriting.

My tears spill onto the page, smearing the ink left by Becca. I gasp,
panic grabbing me.

My hands grasp for something to wipe it off, my arm trembling,
searching until I find a tissue. I wipe it, but it's too late. It smears the
traces of Becca around the paper.

"No—" I cry, clinging to the wrinkled, runny paper before I pull it out of the clipped stack Emma tossed at me.

I miss her so much it kills me. When grief hits, it feels like I'm going to die. It doesn't get better. Every single moment, I miss her. I love Ben, but he doesn't know all of me. My mother doesn't know me. I won't let Emma really know me. Becca knew me.

The child moves, and I resist the urge to slap my stomach. I don't want to be reminded of this baby. It helped kill my sister. If I hadn't distracted her, she'd still be alive.

A cry of agony escapes my lips. I smash my fists into the mattress. I want to punch a wall. I want to break my hand to give me anything to focus on other than this child growing inside of me, alive, while my sister's body is nothing more than dust.

The sound gets so loud. I have to scream louder. I need something louder than the screams of my sister as she died, louder than the ocean waves and their sickening in and out to infinity. I want off this fucking island!

I push myself off the bed, spilling the papers onto the floor. My legs are like sticks trying their best to keep an elephant from falling. I take a step and then another. The pain in my stomach grows, ripping open like little hands are tearing and stretching it apart. I scream so loud it startles me, and I bend over upon myself, an instinctive movement to try to protect my body from what's harming me, but what's harming me is inside.

My face blanches, and, as I pant, I feel like I'm going to wretch, as I stare down at the floor at a copy of an old photograph. I recognize the house. I recognize a few of the people standing in front of it. It's Richard's house, so it must be his family, his grandfather. I fold in on my stomach, and the fetus protests, kicking at my ribs. The splitting pain has

passed. I stretch my arm as far as I can to pick up the photograph.
It's dated June 23, 1921.

Bracing myself with my left arm, I lower my lumbering body onto the floor—my legs stretched apart—and my eyes widen and strain.

There, in black and white, is Richard standing next to his lovely young wife. She's wearing a beaded flapper dress and has a shiny bob. They're grinning at the camera. I recognize the faces from the party. Ginny stands next to a man with dark tan skin and a bowler hat. She looks years younger, and the man looks even younger than her.

That's impossible. This can't be real. This is Photoshopped. Where did Emma find this? My eyes move from face to face, a few faces that I don't recognize emerge and then I spot one that stops me dead in my tracks.

The face of my grandmother.

What if everything my mother said was true? What if she was trying to save us all along. What about Ben?

The child rolls inside my stomach as tears stream down my face. Thorns grow on my heart with each breath I take, piercing through the bits of me that I've let become soft to him. Another man who is only out to hurt me and to use me. What do they want from us? What do they want with the baby?

I stifle my sobs so that no one can hear. I need to think. I need to get up, but as I go to stand, the hint of a contraction hits, taking my breath away. I wince at the pain, closing my eyes. Goosebumps spread like wildfire up my body; the heat has given way to an icy chill. As I peel open my eyes, I cry out, unable to hold it in any longer.

There she stands, risen from the dead. Krysten is in the corner of the room. Her dark brown hair is falling from a messy bun, her skin pale and blue, her eyes milky white. Her stomach is ripped open, and dark, nearly black blood stains her gown.

"Below," she whispers as my body prepares to scream. She's been cut wide open. I cover my mouth with my hand and grip my stomach with the other. I fall back onto the bed, and she disappears.

"Below."

I lay shaking in the sheets, waiting to make sure she doesn't come back before I lift myself off the bed, the weight of the baby pushing hard on my pelvis, and I waddle into the hall, where I cry for Emma.

A Date with an Armoire — Emma

Thunder cracks outside, and without missing a beat, lightning flashes through the room, making shadows dance across the walls. Jax grasps my hand tight; he's always been afraid of storms. We used to watch them in the garage with Grandma. He'd pretend to be brave but end up in Becca's arms every time. I wish I could stay with him, but I can't.

"Okay, tell me the plan again," Mom says, not bothering to speak low despite Ben snuggling in the bed next to her.

"You sure he's not going to wake up?" I ask.

"Not exactly, but it's better if he wakes up now and lets us know."

His snores fill the room.

"What did you give him?" Jax asks, a tremble in his voice. His arm is shaking like a leaf.

"Xanax and Ambien. Don't worry, he'll be fine."

"Do you really think Ben knew about this?" I ask.

She grabs her stomach and takes a deep breath before speaking. "I don't know. I don't think so, but how else can I explain what's happening? The pregnancies, the losses on the island, Krysten. I'm so sorry I didn't believe you sooner. She said *below,* and it can't be a coincidence. I'm not going to ignore her messages anymore."

I turn my head around the room, almost expecting to see the spectral woman that has helped lead us directly to this moment. "Okay. I took Ben's tools, and we're going to break open the wall, figure out what's in there. If it's what I suspect, if there is some weird ass witch shit going on, we grab the go bag. You have Ben's keys?"

"Yep." Jax nods. He's got a little backpack over his shoulder with all his special things from home and from Becca. Flashlight, lighter, pocketknife.

"Then we get help," I say.

"If—and I'm not saying this is what you think it is—but if you're right about the armoire and something being hidden behind the wall, come back here, grab Jax, then drive off this island, and call Hannah."

"And you," I remind her. I'm not leaving without Mom.

"No. You wait until you're somewhere safe, then tell the police, and you come back here for me then. Only then."

"Aunt Sam," Jax protests.

"I have to protect you two first. You don't have much time. Go!"

"Take my bag for now," Jax says, leaving the backpack on the floor next to the bed.

"Thanks, Jax."

Another crack of thunder hits, and when I get downstairs, Daniel is already standing where the armoire used to be. Jax is still clinging to my hand. My breath catches in my chest.

"What are you doing here?" I ask.

"Hey, so we're really doing this?" Daniel asks, completely ignoring my question.

"What do you mean?"

"The armoire, Emma. You wanted to see what was back there, remember?"

"Yeah." I turn to Jax, and he gives me a puzzled look back.

"Remember, we talked about this?" Daniel says. He leans in and kisses me on the cheek.

I can't remember telling Daniel we were going to do it right now, but maybe I did? The last couple of days have been absolutely confusing and terrifying.

"Yeah," I say, nodding toward Jax. "I— uh, yes. You sure you want to help?"

"Of course," Daniel says. "I want to know what's going on just as much as you do."

Jax pulls me hard; I turn to him. "I'm scared. I can't lose anyone else." His eyes are glossy, and another flash of lightning fills the house. Someone's in the doorway behind Daniel, a dark silhouette. *Krysten.* I keep my eye on the spot that's become lost in the darkness. I'm psyching myself out.

I grab Jax by the cheeks and stare directly into his eyes. "We will not lose anyone else. I love you, and I am going to figure out what the hell is going on, and we're going to go far away from this place. Okay? I need you to stay here with Mom to make sure she's okay. We'll be back soon."

Jax nods and makes his way to the couch in the back room. He turns on the flashlight in his hands. The plan is for him to act normal, read a comic, and distract Nadine if she shows up here. I turn back to Daniel.

"You really think they're all witches?" Daniel asks.

"I don't know," I say, taking his hand and pulling him into the hallway. No one's there. *Krysten.* "What I know is that Krysten thought they were. The book I found upstairs is all about witches and all the weird things that they do, like signs and rituals. It all fits. Nadine seems to age backward, all the stuff growing on the island, the sacrifice of children and mothers, those herbs she's growing and how sick my mom got. The women having the pie tins."

"Do you think my family is a part of it?"

"No, no, of course not, but Juniper's family, yes. I mean, Juniper is probably one of them."

"I don't know." He runs a hand through his hair.

"It could be nothing. Juniper could have no knowledge of it, like you. You've been here for how many summers and never noticed anything weird?"

"I've noticed some stuff ... I mean, people die here ... a lot. I guess I didn't want to believe it."

"I don't, either. I hope I'm crazy, but we need to find this armoire."

I rip the key from my pocket. My fingers graze the symbol, the same as the one on the stone in Roanoke, the one tying all of this together. I know it can't be wrong; it can't be a coincidence.

"Krysten made sure I found this. I trust her that there's something in that armoire that will explain everything or protect us."

"I said I'd help you, so I'll help you. I—"

I grab the sledgehammer next to Daniel and use all my strength to bring it behind my body and smash it into the wall. My arms tremble against the force.

"Holy shit," Daniel says.

I smash the walls once more before I set it on the floor and grab the crowbar, prying the drywall and wood away. I'm panting and sweaty. I stand back to see inside. Behind the wall, standing in the darkness, is the armoire.

"Hello, friend," I say.

Daniel takes the crowbar and continues to pull the wall away.

"Now what?" Daniel asks, when all the debris is gone. The armoire looms over us, tall and commanding—a lion, strong and deadly, ready to pounce.

I pull the key once again from my jeans pocket. Having pushed the brass key into the hole on the right door of the armoire, I turn it once, then twice. There's a click, and I pull the handle on the right side to open it.

A rapping begins at the back glass door. I pull Daniel close to the towering wooden beast. It feels like a living, breathing thing, warm and producing the slightest movement. Daniel knocks into me, stumbling over broken pieces of drywall on the floor.

Jax heads to the sliding door. Another crack of thunder booms, and then the creak of Jax pulling open the door.

"Jax!" Nadine says, her voice muffled.

"Uh ... hi, Nadine."

"What are you doing up so late?"

"I think they're all sleeping. It's been hard since Mom died—to sleep."

My heart is pounding. My stomach has relocated to my esophagus. Jax is lying for us, or maybe he really hasn't been sleeping, and I haven't been paying attention.

"We might need to wake them all up. We've got to get the shutters up on the house before this thing turns crazy. The storm's fittin' to come here."

"I thought you said it wasn't going to be bad and that it probably wouldn't hit the island?"

"It's coming. It might not hit us, but ... are you going to let an old woman in?"

"Uh, yeah, of course. Do you really think we need to wake up Aunt Sam and Ben?"

"Yes," she says, stepping closer toward Daniel and I. I suck in a breath.

"Their rooms are upstairs," Jax says. "So ..."

The footsteps move further away, and I let out my breath as slowly as possible so as not to make a sound. Their feet continue up the staircase onto the second floor. Another crack of thunder shakes the ground beneath me, and the lights flicker. I grab my cell phone out of my pocket.

Daniel opens the armoire's doors, revealing a set of stone stairs leading into the ground. I turn on the flashlight on my phone.

I fucking knew it.

TRAPPED—SAM

Ben's snoring is consistently getting quieter, an indication that he's still breathing. Am I lying next to someone who's been lying to me this whole time? Lightning floods the room, highlighting the dips in Ben's muscled chest. I love this man, and he loves me.

The child inside me is still, and another wave of pain begins, tearing and ripping at my cervix, traveling up and around my globulous stomach. A tiny moan escapes my lips as warm fluid leaks onto the sheets of the bed.

I am in labor.

It's too early—I think. From what the books say, the farther apart the contractions, the better, but my water has broken. I wish I had something to compare it to, but I was unconscious with Emma.

What would Becca say?

Trust your body, Sam. Trust your daughter.

The cracking of plaster shakes the walls of the house; they've begun.

The wall is coming down. I've sent my kid to rip apart the walls of Ben's home. When morning comes, and if we see that all of this was nothing, he's going to hate me. Panic grips my heart, and tears stream down my face. What if it is all true? What's the conversation going to be like then? I'll be a single mother—again, but this time without Becca.

311

The sliding door opens downstairs. The air pressure changes, making a door slam down the hall. Someone's inside. Two sets of footsteps walk around the house now. Jax better get them to leave. If we're right, we are in grave danger. I need to get the kids out.

My phone is at the bottom of the bed, just out of reach. I pull myself away from the puddle of fluid and blood just long enough to grab it.

No signal.

There are footsteps on the stairs. I wish I could talk to my mom and hear her out about everything.

They're approaching the door. I shove the phone beneath the pillow and make sure the blanket covers the wet spot on the bed.

The door opens; Nadine stands dripping on the hardwood floors. She's wearing a clear rain bonnet over her perfectly blow-dried hair. She looks like she's had a day at the spa, not been out in a storm. Jax cowers behind her, mouthing the words, *I'm sorry.*

"Sam, you're awake."

"I am. You know how it is at the end of a pregnancy. It's hard to find a comfortable position."

"Yes, believe me. I do." She removes her bonnet and steps closer to the bed, moving me the slightest bit to take a seat and rest her hand on my stomach. Please don't let her feel the moisture in the bed.

The tightening begins again, starting at the bottom and radiating up my abdomen. I won't let her see my pain. I don't want her to know what's going on.

"I came to check on you, Ben, and the children. They say there's a huge storm forming, and it might hit us."

A little gasp of breath evades my control.

"Don't panic, dear; everything is going to be just fine. I'm sure it will

312

pass," she says.

I nod as the pain grows greater than any contraction before, reaching all the way to the top of me.

"We need to put the shutters up to make the place safe. Ben, Emma, Jax, and I will take care of it. You just rest, dear."

She turns away from me, and I let the breath out. The pain subsides as quickly as it came. I breathe in and out, and a bead of sweat breaks from my brow. That one came closer to the last contraction.

Nadine walks to Ben's side of the bed, where he's lying completely unconscious. She's going to shake him, and he's not going to wake up. I stare into Jax's eyes with a look of panic and desperation. I hope he can hear the *I'm sorry* I'm repeating in my head. I'm sorry your mom died, I'm sorry I blew it for us, I'm sorry—

"Emma's not here," Jax says.

Nadine turns to him, shock painted on her face.

"She's not home. I'm so sorry, Aunt Sam. I didn't know there would be a storm or that it would be so bad, but she ..."

"Go on, Jax, spit it out," Nadine says.

"She went with Daniel somewhere, I think to see Juniper."

"Call her," she commands, stern and cold.

"The towers are out," I say.

"Then power's going to be out, too. Dammit!" Nadine slams her wrinkled hand on the post of the bed. Both Jax and I flinch. I've never heard Nadine so upset. "We need to find Emma. We need to go get her right now, boy. You're coming with me." She loops Jax by the arm. The fright that moves through his body is visible.

"No," I say.

"Ben will be here with you, and you can't move. I need Jax to help us find Emma. We can't leave her out wandering around in this storm. We'll go to Ginny's. It sounds like they were headed there."

"Jax," I say.

"Yeah?" he replies, turning back, his face pale, he swallows hard.

"Remember to take your key."

He nods, and Nadine takes him back down the staircase. I grab the pillow from behind my head, press it to my face, and scream as the next contraction rises inside of me like sheets of flame.

A Murder of Crows—Emma

"Oh God, it stinks down here," I whisper, holding my phone out like a shield. It reeks of standing water and rotting meat. It's like when we were living at Grandma's house after the flood and, a week later, discovered a whole family of rotting rats in the crawl space.

Wet, decaying, loose, pulverized flesh.

"We can go back up," Daniel says.

"Fat chance."

The walls leading down the stairs are wood beneath lined fabric stapled haphazardly to the sides of the wall. It's padded, and the fabric is squishy and soft like it's been made to help soundproof whatever goes on down here.

Something papery and cold rubs up against my ankle.

A stifled yelp escapes my lips. Daniel grabs me by the wrist, shining my light toward the ground. Snake skins line the stairway. They're draped everywhere.

"What the fuck!" I whisper.

"You northerners aren't used to any of this stuff, huh?"

I pull my arm away from him and push ahead, going deeper and lower below the ground. We finally reach a shiny black door.

"Catch up!" I hiss, but when I turn my flashlight to look back up the stairs, he's gone. I'm alone.

When I turn back to the door, I can see the damn symbol that's all over everything is also on this shiny black door. It's strange—it looks brand new, not old and decrepit like the walls around it, and as I stare at it, it appears to be breathing.

I look back up the staircase one more time.

"Daniel?" I call out, my voice cracking, but he's nowhere. It's like he disappeared into thin air. I walk up a few steps, my knees shaking beneath the weight of my body. Everything feels heavy, and my teeth chatter. I'm not cold, but I don't want to go down here alone.

"Boo!" Daniel shouts, popping out from behind some loose cloth and padding. I stumble back a few stairs, slamming into the door behind me. It pops open, and I land on the floor, causing a splash in the standing water all around me.

"Shit," Daniel says.

I pull my arms out of the water. "You think?"

"I'm sorry."

"Fuck," I say, trying to find a grip on the floor, but it's slimy, mucky, and sandy. Daniel pulls a flashlight out of his pocket. "Can I get some help here?"

"Oh, yeah," he says, making his way down the few steps, but he abruptly stops when he reaches the last one and stares, his gaze like a deer in headlights.

"Come on!" I say, my hands sliding out from beneath me, my sneakers unable to catch any tread.

"Don't move," he says.

I choke a breath in and try to stay still, half lying down and half sitting up. I clench the muscles in my abdomen hard to keep from shaking or falling and making another splash.

"There's a snake, stay calm. It's right behind you. Don't move, and it won't hurt you."

I need to make my chest stop trembling. My hands are spread out just beneath the surface of the water to try to balance my body. The slimy scales of the snake brush past my right fingertips. The cool body of the thing presses against my hip through my sopping wet shorts.

Bile rises deep inside my throat, the fear growing toxic, acid threatening to burn me from the inside out.

The snake appears at the bottom of my thigh, and the goliath serpent slithers through the space between my calves. I pull my stomach in tight. Every muscle strains, trying to hold this position, to not let it know I'm here.

My arms begin to shake, making tiny waves in the water. I stare down at the creature, enchanted by its power. Its enormous body moves in the most graceful way through my legs, through this pooling septic water. The body grows slimmer, and the tail becomes visible—it gives a little flick at the end before it disappears into the black beneath the staircase.

"Wait," I say, wanting to make sure it's gone before Daniel steps in. My knees quake.

"Holy shit. We should leave. We should get out of here. It's not safe." He reaches his arm out to me, steadying himself in the water. I grab onto him and pull myself up, nearly slipping and falling back again. "I'm serious. I shouldn't have brought you down here ..." Daniel looks back and forth.

"What are you talking about?" I ask. "I need to know what's going on here. I need to see." I snatch my phone out of the water. It's completely dead, but I stow it away in the pocket of my sopping blue jeans. I smell like death and rotting slime. "We're going to find out what's down here. Krysten wanted me to know."

"Maybe Krysten found something she shouldn't have. Did you ever think of that?" His words are harsh, but his eyes are begging me to go.

"No, I didn't," I say and pull the flashlight out of his hand, turn, and walk, dripping, toward the next stone doorway and into another room. I shine the light down at the water. Every step I take, I'm careful not to slip or step on anything that can kill me. The ground is sandy, but where it's clear, there are bricks below my feet. They are old and crumbling, making the water reddish-orange, like blood in a bath.

Water drizzles down the sides of the walls. This place will fill up soon, all the way to the top, I bet. I have to hurry. I press my hand onto the stone wall, ancient and weathered, the only thing to lean on in case I fall.

"What if we're down here when the storm hits?" I hear him calling from behind, but I keep my pace—making headway as quickly as I can without slipping.

He'll follow me. This is dangerous, so I don't turn around again. There must be something here that can help us to explain everything and to save Mom from whatever is happening to her. What did he mean about bringing me down here? This was *my* idea. He isn't telling me everything. He was in Dr. Drear's house, and he didn't tell me about it.

He lied.

His feet splash behind me. He is following me. The room we're in opens to an even larger one. I shine the light toward the walls that are made up of marbled and tarnished silver bricks. Each step closer dips me further into the water. It's bitter cold up to my knees now. The silver bricks are decorated with scenes and symbols: women around a fire, women around a pile of bones. Snakes and children.

My flashlight illuminates the room as we go. Above my head, to the left, lies a rounded doorway with script in another language. The same writing I saw in the forest with Juniper. I pass beneath the doorway. The next room is domed, the ceiling high above me covered in lush green foliage that shimmers with the slightest gold iridescence in the light. I follow them down the floor to see where they're growing from.

Piles of black, twisted, sopping-wet feathers and beaks are swathed with green, weaving vines. In and out and in and out and .... *a hand, oh God, that's a human hand.*

I gasp. It sends an echo through the chamber. The hand beckons to me, and my legs carry me toward the heap of rotting flesh and feathers. I lift the corpse of a dead raven, forcing the bile back down my throat. Beneath the hand is the bloated face of a man, his shirt covered in muck but still decidedly pink.

I freeze in terror, pulling my hand to my mouth to hide a scream or catch vomit. His face is moving, pulsing. His left eyelid opens as the head of a snake bursts through and puss drips down the side of him.

I scream before Daniel claps a hand over my mouth, stifling my cry.

He grabs me by the shoulders and turns me away from the grotesque pulsing pile.

"We shouldn't be down here. I don't want you to know what comes next."

My eyes water from fear, repulsion, and the stench. I push his hand away and take deep, gasping breaths.

"What do you mean *what comes next*? What do you know that you're not saying?"

"I don't know anything. I care about you more than you could know. I don't want this to be how it ends—and it doesn't have to be. Let's go back upstairs."

"You care about me? Then tell me what you were doing at Dr. Drear's house. Why did you lie to me about where you were that day? Tell me what the fuck I just saw!"

"What are you talking about?"

"I saw you with Eloise that day."

"What did Juniper tell you?"

"What would Juniper have to tell me? What are you hiding? Are you one of them?"

Daniel shoves past me, sloshing through the water to the opposite side of the room.

"I didn't want it to come to this. I didn't want to hurt you. I'm here to protect you—to protect the future of your family, our family."

"What are you talking about? Our family?" Chest heaving, I wade through the water toward him, push him out of the way—to my surprise, he lets me. I pass through the doorway and into the next room, dredging through vine-latticed water.

"We are supposed to be together." His splashing strides are right behind me. He tries to grab my hand, and I pull away.

"What the fuck are you talking about?"

"The ceremony wasn't supposed to go this way."

"What ceremony?"

I don't turn my back to him, but I keep pressing on, walking backwards away from Daniel and his stark blue eyes and his soft lips that are spewing nonsense. I'm shaking all over, but I keep going despite my trembling.

"I know you saw the book. I know you saw the stones. You've returned. You feel something here. I saw it in you the day we went to

Roanoke."

"Returned to what? What are you talking about?"

"To Eden. To the rightful place that the serpent took, to finally take your places, you and Sam. It's not a coincidence that you ended up here. Your grandmother tried to warn you. Maybe you should've listened."

Daniel points toward a hand floating in the flooded room and an uncontrollable scream rips through me. They fucking killed her. My body is frozen.

I swallow deeply and beg my legs to listen to me and move backwards, away from him. He's a witch, like the rest of them.

"What do you mean? What is going to happen to my mom?"

"That's up to her—her and her body, really, if she makes it through."

"Makes it through what?" I plead louder, desperate. The pink shirt's hand floats in the muck, but I keep my eyes trained on Daniel. *Focus.* I need to get back to Mom and Jax so we can get in a car and drive away from here. I take a few more steps from Daniel when my back meets something soft and squishy.

"Don't worry, everything will be over soon."

One hand reaches over my mouth as another wraps around my stomach, tearing me from the room, away from Daniel, pulling me into darkness.

THE BOY—SAM

I can't believe I let Jax go, but what choice did I have? Right now, Nadine doesn't know we suspect anything, so he should be safe with her.

A crack of thunder shakes the room, and the smell of electricity fills the air.

My hands are clammy. My chest is tight. Emma's right about everything: the book, the pictures, the garden, and the deaths. The tourniquet around my lungs is unyielding.

Mom said we are cursed. Grandma obviously did live here at some point. If only I had listened.

Thunder shakes the house beneath me. Another contraction ripples through me, my abdomen imploding on itself. I groan loudly into the empty house. As quickly as it comes, it's gone. There's still time. I don't *have* to tell anyone yet.

I wipe the spit from the corner of my mouth and swing myself over the side of the bed. My feet are cold against the hardwood floor. I waddle to the window to see if I might catch a glimpse of Nadine and Jax. They're headed back to her house, likely to get in the car and go on a wild goose chase for Emma.

The sky is green. The ocean is angry. Torqued, blackened waves smash against the shore, and lightning flashes with electric rage. A light trickle of fluid runs down my leg.

Ben's still sedated. I didn't give him that much, just enough to buy us a few hours. Maybe I should try to wake him.

The pain rips through me again, and a feral howl erupts from deep inside of me. I groan, my legs shaking like leaves in the hurricane gusts outside my window. My hands cradle my stomach, pressing into the folds of linen, protective of the child.

I'm not going to let you let yourself die. Becca's words pluck hard at my heart. She died trying to save all of us, but I was too stupid and stubborn to listen. Now *I* have to save us.

I press against Ben's arm, trying to stir him awake, but he doesn't move.

I push him again, harder this time. He moans, and I shove him onto his back. He lies there like a dead body.

I need to go downstairs to wherever Emma went and get her back here so that when Nadine and Jax return, Nadine sees she's come home.

Why the fuck did I not believe her? Why did I send my daughter into danger?

The sky lights up again followed by a howling whistle from the ever-increasing wind. I pull on a pair of stretch pants under my linen nightgown. They'll at least absorb the moisture. I put my canvas shoes over my swollen feet and glance back at Ben. He'll be okay.

Jax's backpack lies next to the bed. I lean down and kiss Ben on the forehead. Despite everything, I still love him. I grab the bag and head downstairs, stifling the urge to cry. My desire to be accepted here clouded my judgment. I should have gotten us off the island before Becca tried to drag me out.

I step out into the hallway where I can't hide the tears any longer. The restraints I've tried to put on them won't hold. They give way and I sob, teetering to the loft balcony. The lightning brightens the first floor below.

I wobble on uneasy feet, approaching the staircase. I need to be strong now for Emma, Jax, and the baby.

I lean forward, grasping the railing. Another wave of pain radiates from the bottom of me up and around my back, pulling the child down. The weight of it drags my body to the floor.

"Fuckkkk!" I howl, squeezing my eyes shut, my hands burning in an iron grip on the rails. It's gone. I gasp a breath in and open my eyes. Peering over the railing to the floor below, I see the dark shape of a woman in the middle of the room.

Krysten.

A shiver spreads over me despite the dew of sweat all over my body. I step one foot over the other and begin descending the staircase. The dark figure stands there, barely moving.

Terror grips me, but I keep pushing forward because I have to see it. I need to look at what I've been totally unwilling to see.

The figure is dripping, soaking wet.

Fear grips my heart in a vise. The door is open, and the silhouette of vines slither into the house in lyrical movement.

The flashes of lightning stop, and I'm left in darkness, an intermission. The in-between. In between contractions, in between bursts of electric energy. I reach the bottom of the staircase. I can smell the iron blood dripping down my pant leg. Holding my hands out in front of me, I approach the figure.

A crack of thunder hits. The wind shakes the house and a wave crashes into the sliding glass door. Lightning illuminates the room, and I see the woman standing in front of me, her hair wet and draped over her face. Vines chase her, slither around her; they spider up the walls and over the floor like veins and arteries, pulsing inside the home.

She turns to look at me and, in the light, I can see it's not Krysten, it's not a ghost, it's Juniper. She's drenched head to toe and has a blue vial in her hand.

"Emma's in trouble. They got her. We have to go now. We have to save her!" She moves quickly over to me, gripping my left hand and dragging me behind her. I lift my feet carefully over the wretched vines invading every crevice of the island.

"Save her from what?" I shout at Juniper as another contraction begins.

She doesn't answer, just pulls me after her into the hallway and down the stairs.

Help Me—Krysten
Sixteen Years Earlier

Ben went to the store, the pharmacy off island, to get me something for the pain, because the pharmacist *here* wouldn't sell it to him. Tylenol *is* fine for pregnant women. I know it is. Every other pharmacist I've talked to agrees, but the one on the island said no.

They all treated me like I was crazy, Dr. Drear, Nadine, and Ginny. It's not normal to grow this quickly, and to feel this bad.

I am five months pregnant, *five*, and my stomach barely fits into any of my maternity clothes. I was sick for the first three months and never got better. They say that can happen with twins, but I can't gain weight. The babies grow bigger and bigger all the time. I saw Ben's eyes the other night, looking at me naked. My bones prod at my skin. It's sick.

Since the day we moved to the island, I've never really felt like myself, and after the pie event, even worse.

Knock, knock, knock.

The sliding glass door opens with a whoosh. I wonder if Nadine has hobbled her way over here. I muster the strength to pull myself up and peek over the edge of the couch.

Juniper.

"Hello, Mrs. Krysten."

"Hello, Juniper, what are you doing here?" I ask, huffing my way back onto the couch.

"Nadine sent me over with a special tea. She heard that you weren't feeling well," the child says with a smile, holding a tray of tea and cookies. "She says you'll feel better soon."

She stands there, staring, until I motion her over. "You left the door open."

"I know. Nadine's coming, too."

"Alright then," I say, grabbing the tea.

Juniper takes a seat on the other end of the couch and pulls out a coloring book, apparently intending to stay for a while.

I pick up my book, trying to ignore the kid at the end of the couch. After thirty minutes or so reading and trying to ice this kid so she leaves, I start to feel funny. My vision begins to blur. I drop my book to the floor.

"Are you okay? Do you feel anything yet?" Juniper asks, leaning over toward me.

"What do you mean 'do I feel anything yet?' Should I be feeling something?"

"It's supposed to make the babies come out."

My chest stiffens to stone.

"What?" I say, sitting up. "Why would you say such a thing?"

"I heard Mrs. Nadine and Aunt Ginny talking. I'm sorry about your babies, Krysten. I'm sure they would have been lovely, but they said you're not strong enough. They'll have to try again. They're going to take out the babies before they start to rot inside you and bury them under the tree."

My body shakes with rage. I act quickly, slapping Juniper across the face. "You don't say things like that!"

Juniper wails.

"I'm sorry. I'm sorry," I say, grasping her arm. She turns her face up to me, and her cry turns to a laugh.

"You would have been a terrible mother anyway. You're not really one of us. You never were," she says, running back out the door she came in.

I groan and gasp for air as the pain begins to radiate down my body.

"What an awful thing to say. What an awful child, she—" I lose my breath, I can't speak.

It feels like acid is leaking from the flesh of my stomach. I try to stand, to get to the kitchen counter and pick up the cordless phone so I can call Ben.

My legs quiver as if they've fallen asleep, and my body crumples to the ground. A large crack resounds through my whole body, one that's bone-breaking. I squeal like a stuck pig.

Footsteps approach.

Someone to save me.

"She's over here!" Nadine's voice calls out as she emerges from around the couch.

Please help me, help the babies.

Richard and Eloise emerge from the hallway wearing scrubs. I gasp for breath as Eloise comes closer to me, carrying a medical kit. Maybe Juniper went to get them.

"Help me," I cry to Dr. Drear.

"Oh, dear," Dr. Drear says, kneeling on the floor toward my abdomen. "We are here to help you and your babies."

"Juniper said they're dying."

"What we saw earlier on the ultrasound was dreadful. It's not good, and we didn't want you to panic. We figured out a way that we can save them."

Dr. Drear takes a fetal doppler out of his bag and presses it to my stomach.

"We have to take them out now, though, okay? They're still alive. I know you're in pain, but we must take them out if there is to be a chance at all. Do you understand?"

I nod between gasps, hoping that he can see my response as I writhe on the ground.

I wish Ben was here. I'm doing the right thing. I have to save the babies.

"Stay still now." Dr. Drear pulls my dress up, leaving my stomach exposed. It doesn't look right; it's blue and purple. It pulses like a sack of spiders ready to be born, with millions of legs and eyes upon the world.

I must be dreaming.

"Scalpel," Dr. Drear says. Eloise hands him a blade and the burning sensation in my stomach grows more intense. Toxic waste roils inside of me. That sensation is overtaken with a new one, the very clear and unmistakable feeling of a knife slicing into my belly. My skin begins to separate, and hot blood gushes from my abdomen. My scream comes from deep inside me, a place I didn't know existed. I gasp for breath, but there is no air to be found.

Nadine crouches down by my side. Her face is bright, her eyes glowing. She lowers her body completely and lays down next to me.

"You are doing great. You are going to be a mother in a few moments," Nadine says in the kindest voice. "You have to make it through this part. You're going to be okay, and our children will be okay. You'll raise them, and it will all be okay."

She puts a cool cloth on my forehead, wiping away the sweat. My body shakes, and all the feeling is gone from my legs.

"Keep her still!" Dr. Drear yells, and my ears ring. He cuts deeper and deeper into my organs. "They're alive, Nadine."

"This might be exactly what we need," Eloise says. "This might be okay ..."

Eloise rises, jumping in glee.

Bile swells in my throat, choking my screams with acid.

"I am very sorry to tell you this, but we need to act quickly," Nadine says. "You must listen very carefully and do as I say. Do you understand?"

My eyes bulge, threatening to burst.

"Nadine!" Dr. Drear calls.

"Krysten. Dr. Drear needs you to say something. I need you to hear me, Krysten. Only one child can live through this, okay? One child, or they'll both die ... or everyone you love, and everyone you know here on the island will die. You have to say it. You have to say that we can take one child and save the other. You have to say it. You have to make the sacrifice."

I think I'm dying. This has to be a dream.

"Say it!" Dr. Drear shouts. "Hurry, or they'll both die!"

My vision is blurry, but behind Nadine, I see Juniper—watching me die.

"Help ... me," I stutter, begging the child for help. The pain from the knife starts to static out, fuzzy like an old television.

Nadine pulls my face into hers.

"If you don't say to kill your child for the other, the other will die too."

Oh God, where is Ben? Oh God, please help me. I can't lose them.

"Krysten!"

"Take it—" I cough out vomit, warm and sour. "Take the child to save the other. Take it." I cough harder, my head falling to the side. Blood and bile splatter across the floor. I suck in little breaths, breathing in my own sick.

I turn my bulging eyes toward Dr. Drear, who is holding a newborn in his arms.

"You did great, dear," Nadine says, wiping my forehead. Through my stinging eyes I see her, young Nadine, like the Hollywood photos.

Don't leave me.

"Only your God can help you now," Nadine says. Her heeled shoes click as she walks away from me down the hall.

My face is cool and tacky, and the fuzzy feeling rises through my body toward my head. Everything goes black.

THE CEREMONY—EMMA
AUGUST 13

"Let me go, you fuck!" I scream, kicking and writhing around in the arms of the masked attacker. His fingers are clawing into my arms. The asshole throws me onto the stone ground of a garden. Daniel stares down at me. He helped them—he's one of them.

Rainwater drips down between the vines that lace the top of the garden. The graying, wrinkled man spits at me, a wet, hot lump on my face. I wipe it away.

"Thank you, my lord, for your help," the man says, bowing his head to Daniel.

"Thank you," Daniel says, nodding. "Fetch the others now."

Thunder cracks. It's muffled by the stone walls, thick with moss and flowers. Their petals are luminescent, glowing around us, their pollen sick and sweet.

The skin on my legs is scraped and bloody. It's just Daniel in here, so maybe I can get away.

"You didn't have to fight it," Daniel says. "You could have listened to me back at the stairs. I would have let you run. I would have liked to let you run, but you just had to find the truth."

I kick at the stone blocks beneath me, trying to get as far from Daniel as I can. The statue of the pregnant woman looms behind him, vined and crawling with snakes. I've got to get the hell out of here.

"What the fuck is going on?" I scream. "Are you a witch? Are you all witches?"

Daniel laughs.

"I'm not a witch," he says. His blue eyes aren't warm or kind anymore. They're soulless—devoid of compassion. It was all a trick. "I'm something far more powerful than that. I am their only hope. I didn't want this for any of you. We were desperate. That girl, Annabelle, she was supposed to be the one to make the sacrifice. She was supposed to carry the children, not lose the baby and die, but she couldn't hack it. Most of them can't. They're not strong. But your mother, you ... you're strong. You've the kind of strength we need to keep this place going, and bring it to the next level, to fulfill the commitment that our people made so long ago, back in Roanoke."

He crouches next to me on the ground, and I can smell his chocolate coffee breath. He presses his lips into mine. The soft and supple lust I had for him is gone. I want to throw up. I push him away, and he furrows his brow.

"What deal in Roanoke?" I demand.

"Nadine, your great-grandmother, Ginny—they all made a deal with Lilith. They were desperate, starving to death. She came to them. She was their only hope. This place. You'd never have even been born if your grandmother hadn't made that deal."

"What are you saying? What are you going to do to my mom? What did you do to Krysten?"

Daniel sighs and paces around me, wringing out his hands. He approaches a flower, black and full, pulsing around a glowing stamen. "I wish it could have been us. I wish we could be together, but that's not how this works. They didn't do anything to Krysten. It became too much for her body to bear, so they had to take me early, and she made the ultimate sacrifice for me and for this place."

He rubs his hands along the walls, and the vines grow and move around his arm. He pets them like a living thing, and they pulse at his touch.

"What are you talking about?"

"You haven't figured it out yet? I know you read the books, Emma. You've been doing your research. You remember the part where they have to create to continue living? If they don't, they'll all die. We'll all die. That's the lifecycle and commitment they made. Eden doesn't come for free. You can't go back on a deal with the Devil. You can't go against my father."

"Ben?" I ask.

Daniel folds over, cracking up. Thunder cracks harder in the distance, and water crashes over the wall.

"No, not Ben. Krysten brought me into this world. She was only a vessel—my true sire is the most powerful being in the universe."

"You're insane!" He can't be Krysten's. "Krysten's child died! She died!"

"Yes, Krysten's child that I shared a womb with died, but I lived. That's how it was supposed to go with your mom as well. She was stronger, though. She shares the blood of the original twelve, the colonizers who came here, the ones who lived and didn't disappear. That blood courses through your veins."

Grandma tried to save us.

"Someone seriously fucked up," Daniel says. "Becca was onto something, so we had to get rid of her. Your mom wasn't supposed to be in the car. They didn't see a second passenger until it was too late."

They killed Aunt Becca.

"You fucking monster!" I cry. A snake slithers behind me, between my legs. Rage erupts through my body.

"I'm sorry, Emma, I'm sorry for all the pain—"

"I hope you all die!"

The gate behind Daniel groans, metal against stone. Someone else is in the garden.

"I'm so sorry that it has to be this way. Your mother was supposed to do the same as mine did—choose between the two inside of her, but one of the two in her womb perished in the car accident, and all that's left is my sister, and she has to be born ..."

Nadine and Ginny emerge from the stone corridor and into the garden. Jax walks between them, his head sunk between his shoulders.

"Jax!" I scream.

"Emma!" he says.

The women let him go. He runs to me, presses into me, melting but trembling in fear.

"Are you okay?" I ask, tears streaming down my face.

"I'm alright," he says, crying. "I tried to keep them away."

"You did everything you could."

"What's going to happen now?" he asks. I pull him closer into an embrace, cradling him, looking over his shoulder at Nadine. The raggedy old sack of a woman.

"Emma, you sweet little thing." Nadine's face looks distorted, droopy, like a wrinkled mask melting off her head. Her eyes are gray and covered in cloudy cataracts. "Don't worry, everything is going to be fine." One of the age spots on her face is oozing green pus. I kick at her. She snarls at me like an ancient beast. "Here," she says, throwing a rope into my lap. "Tie yourself up, or I'll kill the boy and send him to be with his mother."

My chest tightens. Water drips from the vines that make up the ceiling. The luminescent flowers grow bigger and brighter. I tie the rope around my feet.

"Tie this around my hands," I say to Jax.

"No."

"Do it!" I keep a straight face. Inside, I'm terrified.

His wet curls hang in front of my face, bouncing up and down with every heave of his chest as he cries.

I have to protect him, whatever it takes. He needs to make it out alive.

"Don't worry. It'll be okay," I whisper, my forehead pressed to his. I don't know if it's true anymore. I don't know if anything will ever be okay again. All I can hope is that somehow, Mom has gotten away to get help.

"What'd you do with Ben?" Ginny asks Nadine. Her pink lipstick smudge has grown. It hangs down to her chin, resting atop bulbous rolls of rotting fat.

"Ha! I didn't have to do a thing. Sam drugged him."

"What?" Ginny laughs. "Too perfect. You were right—she is one of us."

"Ladies!" Dr. Drear shouts, emerging from the tunnel underneath the statue. Eloise follows.

"It's really happening!" Eloise says, her blonde curls bouncing. "I can't believe it! Hail Lilith!"

"Hail Lilith," he says and takes Nadine in for a hug. "You really did it."

"I told you to have faith. I've always gotten us through."

Daniel watches with a grin from the corner.

"We all did it," Ginny interjects. "I really hoped that my girl or Juniper would be the birth mother, but this is even better than we ever could have imagined."

Thunder shakes the structure. The walls move, little bits of water making their way in.

"The other women proved to be anything but responsible mothers," Nadine says. "Samantha was so desperate for approval and love. We can guarantee her, Ben, and the children all of it. Can you imagine what her grandmother would say if she were here?"

"Oh, yes, I miss her so, but that daughter of hers had to go and mess it all up," Dr. Drear says. "I was worried we'd never get Emma and Sam back. It's such a shame about Emma."

"That's in the past now," Nadine says, spittle coming out her mouth, the glow of the green vines reflected in her milky eyes as she looks at me. My body is stiff with fear. "The night is upon us, and our faithful Juniper is bringing Samantha to us right now."

I Love You—Sam

My scream echoes off the stone and metal walls surrounding us. My feet and legs are soaked up to my knees. I can't tell if my water's completely broken or not, because the tunnels are flooded, saturating the fabric of my clothes. The whole place smells like death—suffocating and hot.

The choking rot fills my lungs as the contraction subsides, and I retch into the water. I wipe the vomit from my cheek onto my soaking-wet hand.

"Are you okay?" Juniper asks.

"I'm fine," I say, catching my breath. "We have to keep going. Where is Emma?"

"We're almost there. You trust me, don't you?" she asks, a playful smile in her eyes.

"What is this?" I ask.

"This is where the vines come from," Juniper says, disappearing into the next room. I follow her, and she points a flashlight into the corner. More hot bile pushes up my throat. The bloated face of a man stares at me from the wet, heaping pile of rot, a gaping hole where his eyes should be.

More of my vomit mixes into the putrid, standing sludge, and I trudge on after Juniper. She's prancing through the water like a sprite or a fairy of darkness and death.

Regret rips at my sides. I sob, but I can't give up now. I keep following her because there's nothing else for me to do. There's no going back. I have to save Emma and Jax.

Water spills into the tunnel from the walls, not a trickle like when we began, but gushing, flooding. It splashes past my stomach.

The slither of snakes and other creatures brush my legs. I keep thinking I'm going to see Emma's hair slithering through it, like in the dream. I can't think like that. She has to be alive. I have to be able to save her.

Dear God, I hope I can trust Juniper.

"We're here. Are you ready?" Juniper smiles, starting up a spiral staircase. Water pours from drains above our heads. Juniper hands me the glass vial, beaded in wet, and it's slippery in my hand.

"It'll make you see God," I say, guessing it's the stuff that was in the pie that night. "This is the only way to stop it, isn't it?"

Juniper nods.

I toss her Jax's backpack. "You make sure they're okay. Promise?"

She's up the winding stairs so fast, and I'm trying my best not to die or deliver this baby on the way up.

I move one foot laboriously after the other, pulling on the rails of the winding staircase for support, water beating down on me until we reach the top.

I've been here before. The cement woman towers over me, covered in snakes and glowing vines. *Where's Emma?*

"Emma!" I shout, looking around. Some fucked-up version of Nadine stands near the corner with Eloise.

"Mom?"

I turn to find Emma. She's sopping wet, and her arms are covered in scratches and blood. She's bound, and Jax sits next to her, crying. I extend my arm out to her. "We've gotta get out of here."

A rumble begins in the ground beneath my feet, not from the thunder or the titan winds, but from the stone woman, moving back into place. Snakes writhe up and down her body, covering her stomach.

I stand in front of Emma and Jax.

"Nadine, I don't know what the hell is going on here, but you need to untie my daughter and let us go."

"Mom, Nadine brought us here." Emma's face is red and swollen from tears and fighting, but it's in surrender now.

"What do you want from us?" I shout, turning to where Nadine stands. Dr. Drear, Eloise, Ginny, Daniel, and Juniper move around Nadine, filling in any space where they could possibly run.

"Oh, dear, haven't you already figured it out? I saw you snooping through my things," Nadine says, her cataract-filled eyes shining a sickly green in the light of the vines. "You snooped around Ginny's house and took my book. I'm not mad. I'm happy to see you so curious. After all, you are the granddaughter of one of the most powerful witches of our coven. It makes sense that you'd be interested."

Grandma. "This is crazy. I don't know how you all know each other or what you want, but you can't have it! Let us go!"

The crowd of them laugh, pointing at me. They coo and holler. Their faces grow more distorted, much older than the last time I'd seen them. Their eyes are hollowed dark caves with creamy rotting orbs in the center.

"It's not what we want, it's what we need," Dr. Drear says, turning to the statue in the garden. "We've been here longer than you could know, for as long as it's been called America. Your mother was born from Titia, one of the originals. Your mother was a traitor. You don't have to be like her. This is your redemption. Your opportunity to be a part of a family so big and so full of life," he says, reaching his arms out from his sides. His skin hangs off him like pieces of meat off a raggedy bone, dripping with water from the storm.

"Like you've always wanted," Nadine adds, walking from the crowd toward me. "Your family, the one your awful mother made, was never for you, not when you were being yelled at, beaten, or ignored. You never deserved any of it. You never deserved an ounce of pain," Ginny says, approaching me. Lightning illuminates the room, followed by the boom of thunder.

"You don't know what family is," I say, looking back at Emma as she trembles.

"We know what happened to you and how unfair it was," Nadine says. "Your grandmother never wanted that for you. Lilith doesn't want that for you."

"Lilith wants us to have life everlasting life. She saw how unfair god could be in smiting his children and setting up tricks for them. She wants us to live to be free of the fake morals set up by a vengeful god—"

A groan bursts from my throat, the contraction making my legs give out from beneath me. I scream.

"Mom!" Emma yells.

I pant, breathing heavily, sucking in water and hot air and sweat.

"It's time for you to take your place with us. It's time for you to finally come home and be a family with Ben and Nadine and all of us to support you," Eloise says.

"We brought Jared here to remind you what you're really leaving behind." Nadine gestures at Lilith. "Her snakes bit him, took the man who wanted to hurt you away for good."

"Bit him with her snake!" Ginny cackles and her bright pink lipstick runs down the side of her pleated face.

"Lilith knew you never wanted to be a mother, never wanted Emma, and for weeks, months, her touch made your skin crawl. It still does, doesn't it?" Nadine says, approaching me, brushing my hair out of my face. "How could you love a child born out of such hate, such violence? We don't blame you. You have the opportunity to start over and to live your life the way you always deserved to. The baby in there." She points to my stomach. "We'll raise her, and she'll grow so fast. You won't have to be a mother anymore." Her cloudy eyes stare into mine. I think of all the times Emma touched me, and I turned away, the days I spent in the dark, unmoving, while she cried for me. I did resent her—I hated her at times. "You wished, I know it, and Lilith knows it. When she was in your womb, you wished Emma would die."

Emma chokes out a cry.

"Look at me," Nadine says. Her minty, swirling green eyes catch me; they see me in a way devoid of judgment, full of acceptance and unconditional love.

Nadine's voice echoes inside my head. *You can just be you. You'll never have to belong to anyone else again.*

"You just have to say a few words, and it will all go away. It will be like none of that old life ever happened," Nadine says.

"No!" Emma shouts. "Don't listen to her, Mom!"

"The old child must die for *her* child to live and for you to live, Sam. To really, truly be alive," Nadine says.

They were right. After watching my mother screw up so monumentally by being with a man who beat her up, making us clean her wounds,

I knew I never wanted to be a mother. *I will never be her.*

"You don't have to be ashamed. We understand. Lilith understands," Nadine says, gesturing her flopping arm toward the statue.

Another contraction hits, blinding me. The pain is so intense. It's ... I can't ... a scream escapes me.

"That's it. Daniel, get her to the ground beneath the magnolia tree," Dr. Drear calls. I hold my breath, the pain ripping me apart. "This is going to be magnificent. Juniper, you bring Emma over here, too. Put her right at the other side of the tree. Her mother shouldn't have to see this when she's doing such an amazing thing for all of us and Lilith."

I gasp as the contraction subsides. "I love you. I'll always love you!" I say, reaching my arm out toward Emma as Juniper pulls her over to the other side of the tree, behind the brush. The light in Emma's eyes is out, as if she's resigned to whatever is going to happen—only the reflection of the sickly green vines remains.

"That's sweet, dear," Ginny says, helping lower me to the ground, pulling out a black silk hanky to wipe my forehead. "You'll feel so much better after she's gone. I promise you." Her grin goes wide, and her teeth are all rotten, full of holes—brown holes with bright pink lipstick on them.

I crane my head and watch as Juniper drags Emma over to the other side of the tree and out of my sight.

Jax stands there, shaking, frozen.

"Jax! You go be with her. I love you."

Jax follows orders. He might not live through this. His heart might not be able to take it.

"Samantha, are you going to be a good girl?" Dr. Drear asks. His perfect smile and enchanting eyes have turned old and sunken, and his smile is crooked. His skin is leathery and wrinkled. "You have to say it. You have to say that we can kill her. You must make the sacrifice to save yourself and the baby and everyone here who loves you. You have to say it to save your *real* family. You have to say it."

"I love you, Emma! I love you!" I scream.

Nadine gets down on the ground next to me, her face drooping so severely, exposing parts of her skull beneath her cloudy eyes that are staring directly into mine. Daniel's at my feet, ripping my pants off and spreading my legs apart.

Eloise is in the corner jumping for joy, giggling with happiness, her blonde curls framing her sunken, bony face.

"Say it, Sam! Say it!" Eloise chants.

"Not 'I love you,'" Nadine says, staring deeply into me. "Say it. Say that she has to die. We'll all die if you don't say it. How could Ben love you after killing his only living parent? How could he love you? You have to say it!"

Another contraction begins deep inside, and I release a primitive grunt.

I never wanted to be a mother. I didn't want Emma.

"Do it, Juniper!" I scream. "Take her to save the child!" My words turn into an animalistic moan from the contraction, the worst one yet, the worst pain—an ache so deep it tears me apart. I remember the pain of lying on the floor with Emma, broken, when she and Jared nearly killed me.

I scream and gasp, and then I listen. I heard Becca's voice screaming as the ground and metal ripped her apart. I hear the squishing sound of a blade into flesh, a tiny cry escaping my daughter, and then another plunge of the knife. Emma's wail grows louder. Thunder cracks, and Jax screams.

"Oh my," Ginny says, laughing. "That's a lot of blood." She looks over at the other side of the willow tree. "Oh, you're doing so great. We love you so much."

I gulp tiny breaths as water drips on my face, mixing with the tears. Jax cries, and I know this is terrible, but there's no other choice.

As Daniel's eyes widen, staring at my crotch, Dr. Drear's smile grows hideous and large. My daughter is bleeding on the other side of the magnolia tree. Eloise smiles and laughs in the corner. I know that what comes next, what can't be taken back.

I reach my free hand into my bra and grab the vial full of blue liquid.

I never wanted to be a mother.

I toss the cork to the side and watch their faces twist in horror as I swallow the entire bottle.

Do You Trust Me? —Emma

When Juniper pulls the blade from my chest and smashes it back down again, it hurts. There's the loudest, strangest squishing sound. Warm blood leaks between my breasts, down to my belly button.

So much blood.

Jax is rocking back and forth while crying. My mother shrieks in horror. The rest of them begin to celebrate. Their voices delight in my demise.

My chest is hot, warm, and sticky. She brings the knife down again, and I scream as I'm supposed to.

Ginny's seen all the blood, so that should be enough. They think I'm dying.

I'm not.

Juniper smiles at me, grabs Jax by the shoulder, and passes him the trick blade thick with fake blood. The horror on his face melts away into surprise, then the tiniest bit of hope that I thought I'd never see again.

"Wait," Juniper whispers in my ear. She presses down on my shoulder. "I'm sorry for what happens next. Do you trust me?"

Jax comes closer to me. I lie still, playing the part of a corpse. He's holding the knife hard.

"Do you have the key?" Juniper asks.

"Yeah," he whispers back.

I'm waiting for the signal so we can run, except a scream erupts from my mother that's worse than the ones before. It's a cry like she's splitting in two—and it's not fake, it's real.

"Now," Juniper says. "Run."

I turn onto my stomach as quickly as I can. Juniper helps undo the ropes. Her hands graze my arm, and her eyes meet mine one last time, making it even harder to turn and go.

"What have you done!" Nadine screams at Mom.

I look back to Juniper.

Jax is already sprinting to the other part of the garden.

Juniper pushes me. "Go!"

Something didn't go according to plan, but I have to keep going. My arms whip at the swirling and writhing vines. They grab at my ankles. I kick them away.

I run over the wet stone, over the snakes in the path.

I don't look back. My heart throbs in my ears, muffling the sounds of whatever is still going on under that Magnolia tree.

I see the vines around us begin to turn brown, moving with tremors, thick, glitching tremors. They hiss, steam coming off them as the rain pours heavier than ever. Thunder cracks so loud it shakes my lungs, and I gasp for breath.

The vines begin to turn black and shrivel. With their glow extinguished, their blooms grow fat like blood blisters and burst thick, tarry liquid over the ground.

All over the snakes.

They're all screaming behind us—everyone is screaming. It's louder than the thunder, and louder than my heart.

I stop, and Jax does, too, stopping to look behind. I need to go back to save Mom.

Jax.

I can't let him die. I have to protect him.

"Go!" I scream to Jax.

We run. Thunder claps outside the garden walls. Dragonflies and bumble bees swirl through the garden, turning black and swelling, bursting into pus in midair. The putrid, sweet scent is sticky in the humid storm. I duck, avoiding more pus.

Jax skids to a stop in front of me. A huge snake with emerald and black scales hisses, whipping its tongue out. Its jaws open wide, and its head juts back, ready to bite us. This can't be what stops us.

"We have to go!" I yell.

The snake moves, whipping its tail in the air.

Jax jumps over its enormous body, twisting to avoid its bite. Before the snake can make contact with his skin, its head explodes, shooting viscera and green venom across the ground.

"The key!" I shout.

Jax fumbles in his pocket. The screaming is growing louder. He nearly drops it before he puts it in the lock and turns it.

I leave my mom, the person I love the most, behind in the garden.

MOTHER–SAM

I scream. This is a pain like I've never imagined before. I will never see Emma again. The poison of the plant, the same one they used to impregnate me, burns my throat. The child writhes inside me.

Tears stream from my eyes, and I watch as every bit of hope in Nadine's face fades away.

"No! You can't!" Nadine screams. "You vile whore! You killed our child!"

Dr. Drear lets out an angry roar and slams his feeble hand against my leg. It lays sideways, limp. Every part of my body is ignited, hot, like there are burning coals in my veins.

Daniel's behind the doctor, kneeling on the ground, sobbing. The child's movements start to slow. I can't feel my legs. I can't hear Emma. I only hear the wretched sobs of these vile people as Ginny swells, her legs and feet becoming enormous like balloons. They leak purple blood into the creases of the stone and shells beneath her. Her skin disintegrates like sugar in tea.

The vines through the garden turn black like tar. The pain makes a little space for pulses of soothing, warm comfort as the black tunnel around my view grows thicker.

I'm dying. I will die, and so will the baby, but Emma and Jax will be okay.

Eloise cries as the skin on her legs sucks to the bone like cling wrap until she's nothing but a skeleton with papery skin and popping eyes. She collapses and shatters on the ground.

Juniper runs around the Magnolia tree and nods at me. She puts her hand on Daniel's shoulder, trying to comfort him, and he lets her.

They're the only ones left.

Nadine crawls away from me toward the stone statue that I know is Lilith, the banished woman—the killer of children. Their *savior*.

She claws at the bottom of the statue before turning lastly to me, looking through eyes that she cannot see out of. Milky cataracts have turned yellow with pus, and they swell and burst. Their liquid spatters the stones of the garden before the rain washes it away. Nadine sputters, spraying black liquid across the ground.

"You apostate! You—" She doesn't move anymore.

I scream, huffing in pain. I blink and bleat like a dying animal as contractions writhe through my body. The poison blackens the skin of my stomach, which is wrapped around my cursed womb. My back and spine contort and cramp before they relax into a warm puddle of numbness.

I never wanted to be a mother.

But I am happy that I got to be one anyway.

THANK YOU—EMMA

A squeal like a freight train whistle pierces my eardrums. The waves crashing against the island are gargantuan—thick, black, and unforgiving. Jax falls behind as we run through the rain, along Main Street and back to the house, toward the car. We pass the corner apothecary, its roof peeling in the wind like a can of tuna fish. Salty air fills my lungs that scream in pain. Plants litter the ground.

A rotting vine works its way under my sneaker, and I slip—smashing my face and my elbow against the ground. Pain shoots like a bullet through my body. A scream erupts in the distance.

Jax picks me up. I smell hot blood, and I turn back before we run again. Another scream in the distance. There isn't anyone there. Mom isn't trailing behind us. The blood is my own. I wipe the gash on my forehead, which is hot and gushing.

The whole island smells like decomposition and the sea. The wind is bending trees in half, ripping them out from their roots into the ocean.

We run onto Nadine's property. Jax has the keys. The vines here have withered like long bits of thread through the ground, waving in the wind.

Nadine's house is torn in two.

The water has taken half of it. Her conservatory is shattered glass, swirling in a cyclone. I guard my eyes, and Jax does too. Bits of glass hit my arms, bouncing off and leaving little beaded balls of blood in their wake.

The flowers and foliage around the property are gone. The vibrant greens, reds, pinks, and purples have been replaced with black, gray, unforgiving death.

"We have to go now!" Jax shouts. He tosses me the keys. I catch them in my hand and unlock Ben's driver's side door.

I stare back at Krysten's house that once looked so creepy, haunted. I was scared of it for weeks when we got here. The storm rips the siding off the back, tearing the home asunder. It reveals the upstairs bedroom where a woman stands, still pregnant, holding her stomach. She turns to look at me.

"Krysten." My heart stops. She never gets to leave the island, just like my mother never gets to leave. "Thank you!" I scream as the wave reaches over the bedroom and pulls the rest of the house into the ocean.

I hop into the car and put the key into the ignition.

I throw it in reverse and head back to Main Street.

"The bridge better be down!" I shout.

Jax grabs my hand, and I press the pedal to the floor of the car.

Where Are We Heading? —Emma

D ark waves lick the streets with fury. Lightning strikes, whiting out the black and purple sky as I speed away from Nadine's house.

"Okay, so we get over the bridge, and we're fine," I say, looking for some semblance of encouragement from Jax. He remains silent. I can barely see. All I can think of is my mother's face screaming that she loves me before I go around the Magnolia tree.

Huge shrubs and beach cruisers whip through the air.

Both our mothers are dead.

Roofs peel, and pillars fall off Greek Revival homes.

We are orphans.

The water rises on the street.

Bits of the metal gate from the Drear house torque and writhe along what once was the road. The water is flooding the island. Every way we look, down every street, every turn, everything off Main is underwater.

I turn the last corner to Main Street, praying the car doesn't stall out before we get there. I don't know if the bridge is open. The wind howls, loud, booming, all-encompassing. I can't hear anything for a few moments.

I look to Jax. He's hyperventilating.

A palm tree smashes into the building next to us, just missing the car.

"I don't know if the bridge is down!" I scream. I don't want anything else to be a surprise. I don't want to do this alone.

"What if it isn't?" Jax asks.

I don't turn to look at him. "Then we hide."

"Where?"

I squeal onto the main road, pushing the accelerator.

We can't hide in the tunnels; they're flooded.

We can't hide in the house; it's in the ocean.

We can't go to the—

"Emma! Look out!" Jax screams.

The tires squeal, and the car turns, hydroplaning until we come to a stop.

My body jerks and my head feels like it's going to break open. I gasp and try to catch my breath from the whip of the motion and the radiating pain from the seatbelt on my sternum.

Three feet in front of the car is Ben, with Mom's limp body in his arms.

"What the fuck do we do?" Jax asks.

"Language," I say. "I don't know. I don't know if we can trust him. He's one of them." Sheets of rain pour over Ben, the car, the whipping wind trying to push his body over and hers with it.

"But Aunt Sam ..." he says.

I catch my breath, mind racing.

We are probably not going to make it off this island. We might not live past this moment.

I unlock the doors, open mine, and run to Ben. Heavy buckets of rain block my vision, stinging at my arms—beating me to death.

"Is she alive?!" I shout over the storm.

"I don't know," Ben yells. "We need to get to a hospital. We have to get out of here!"

I open the back door, and Ben pushes Mom inside. I get in next to her. I grab a hoodie from the floor of the car. Ben hops in the driver's seat, closes the door, and drives.

It smells of salt and sick all over her, as well as metallic blood.

I lie next to my mother's body. I try to remember what Aunt Becca would tell me to do when I was little and scared and Mom would lie in bed for hours—I didn't know if she was alive; all those times, I didn't know.

My chest is hot and heavy.

Ben accelerates.

"Your mother did this," I say. "How could you let this happen?"

"I didn't know, Emma. I'm an idiot ... Krysten ..."

Something hits the side of the car, knocking us to the side. Jax screams in terror.

"I won't let her take anything else from me." Ben is steadfast.

I meet his gaze in the mirror. I look down at my mom, pale and blue-lipped. Her chestnut curls lay wet and sticky across the leather seat.

Don't be dead. Please don't be dead.

I press my fingers to her wrist and take a big, deep breath, trying to tune out the roar of the wind, the screams in my head, and the sound of the island dying.

I try to be still and quiet.

With tears streaming down my face, I press my ear against her chest, waiting for anything, any sign of hope. Listening for the smallest little—

Thud.

The End

Acknowledgments

Thank you so much reader for spending time with Emma, Sam, and the gang. When I wrote this book, I set out to write a gothic in the vein of *Rosemary's Baby* by Ira Levin. A woman without a secure attachment to her origin family vulnerable to the dangers of trusting too easily to people who appeared different than "the monsters she knew." What came out was a lot of my own fears, my own pain, and a universal truth that sometimes in our attempts to avoid pain we rush blindly towards our own oblivion. My mother and father were the first to introduce me to horror & specifically movies like Rosemary's Baby. I credit them for embracing my love of the macabre young and encouraging me to follow my own path with my art. My mom Wanda is my lifelong cheerleader. I would like to thank my ride or die CP and best friend Katrina Soucy. Without her expertise, feedback and encouragement this book would not exist. Thank you to my husband Nick who always lets me talk about my crazy ideas and supports my dreams. Every. Damn. Time. Thank you to my children who are always as excited or more about each little publishing accomplishment. They always give me new thoughts and perspectives when I write and are the best story tellers I know.

I would be lost without my critique partners Tobie, Zach and Rebecca on this one. You helped me see the important parts of the story and put up with my overuse of commas. My dear friend Audrey for reading the book and loving it but also being total wrong her in her opinion about the title. Thank you to all my beta readers Emily, Carmen, Heather, Lauren, Christie and Kristin who took the time to send me feedback and encouragement.

I am so thankful for my editors Alexandria Brown and Tina Beier. Alex saw my vision for this book and made me feel like she would fight for it just as hard as I would. Tina helped me sound smarter and advocated for the old English ties and the lore.

Everyone in my personal life who supports my writing, you mean so much to me! All the friends I've made on the journey to publishing my first book on social media I adore you!

I have always been curious about human nature and seen myself in the characters of horror stories since I was a child. The joy I feel getting to create characters that you can find yourself in is only second to being a mother. I hope you found something in this story I created to carry with you.

About The Author

Monique Asher is an American author who writes horror novels. She is a member of the Horror Writers Association. Monique is a trauma survivor and a therapist. Her personal experience with trauma injects reality into the stories she writes. She lives in Southeastern Michigan with her family and a small zoo that often comes along on trips to haunted hotels and dark twisty wilderness. Don't Eat the Pie is her debut novel.

Upcoming Horror from Rising Action

For fans of Stephen King and Nick Cutter, a gripping horror thriller set in Colorado's Devil's Cup State Park where survival becomes a deadly game against subterranean terrors.

March 2025